SAVAGE CITY

ALSO BY DONALD LEVIN

THE MARTIN PREUSS SERIES

In the House of Night
Cold Dark Lies
An Uncertain Accomplice
The Forgotten Child
Guilt in Hiding
The Baker's Men
Crimes of Love

POETRY

New Year's Tangerine
In Praise of Old Photographs

FICTION

The House of Grins

DYSTOPIAN FICTION

The Exile
Postcards from the Future: A Triptych on Humanity's End
(with Andrew Lark and Wendy Thomson)

SAVAGE CITY

CITY

A NOVEL

DONALD LEVIN

POISON TOE PRESS

This is a work of fiction. All of the characters, establishments, events, locales, groups, dialogs, and organizations portrayed in this novel are either products of the author's imagination or are used fictitiously and are not construed as real. Any similarity to real persons, living or dead, is coincidental and not intended by the author.

ISBN: 978-0-9972941-8-7

Cover design: Joe Montgomery

Cover photo courtesy of Walter P. Reuther Library, Archives of Labor and Urban Affairs, Wayne State University

First edition published 2021

Printed in the United States of America

This book is for Tom Galasso, who left us too soon

It's silly to go on pretending that under the skin we are all brothers. The truth is more likely that under the skin we are all cannibals, assassins, traitors, liars, hypocrites, poltroons.
—Henry Miller

FRIDAY, MARCH 4, 1932

1

CLARENCE BROWN

The tip was on the level. The snitch said Andre saw McKinney's Cotton Pickers at a midnight show at the Graystone Ballroom. Now he wants a copy of their new recording.

Sure enough, there goes Andre into Joe's Record Store. Andre Young, thief. Steals codeine-laced cough syrup from drug stores and resells it to hopheads who want a break from the pain of living.

Of which there's way too much in Detroit in 1932.

Watching from across St. Antoine Street, Clarence is sure it's him, even in the dim light at four o'clock.

Andre has a little boy with him. Small and dark-skinned, like the older man. Andre's son, maybe.

The boy stops in the doorway to Joe's and looks right at Clarence before he gets pulled by the arm inside.

Clarence crosses the street. Stops in front of the store. Whitewashed scrawls on the windows hawk the week's new recordings. Bessie Smith. Duke Ellington. Ethel Waters. Fats Waller.

A flyer in the window touts a talk given by Wallace Fard. "Are You a Prisoner of the White Man's Bible?" Sponsored by the Nation of Islam, an organization Fard made up.

Clarence peers into the store. He knows it well. Buys all his phonograph records here. He's known the proprietor, Joe, for years.

Dwarfed by bins crammed with records, the little boy's still looking at Clarence through the store's glass door. Large and grim, Clarence returns the boy's look with a scowl. The kid turns away.

Detective Clarence Brown of the Detroit Police Department opens his wool overcoat, shifts the metal plates he wears under his suitcoat. Adjusts his two pearl-handled Colt .45 pistols in holsters at his waist.

The bell over the front door tinkles. Clarence steps into the heavy cottony smell of steam heat.

Behind the counter, Joe throws him a nod from the stool where he spends the days resting his bad leg.

Clarence lifts his chin at him, eyes not leaving Andre's slim figure in a soiled raincoat.

The kid's big eyes still stare at Clarence.

The little guy tugs on Andre's coat while Andre flips through records. Andre sweeps the boy's hand away. Says, "Cut it out, now."

Clarence approaches. The wood floors creak under his weight.

Andre looks up, sees Clarence. Recognizes him, of course. Everybody knows Mr. Clarence.

"Andre," Clarence says.

Andre backs away. "Mr. Clarence." Pulls the boy with him.

"Been looking for you," Clarence says. "I hear you've been stealing cough syrup from the Rexall."

Andre comes back with, "I ain't stole nothing," already defensive and ready with his story. "My boy got a cough, Jewman over there sold me medicine for it. Nothing else to it."

"Not what he tells me. He tells me you come in and slip bottles under your coat and run out before he can catch you."

"Mr. Clarence, it's a damn lie. You know you can't believe nothing them people say. Cheat you just as soon look at you."

Clarence moves a step closer to Andre, who moves a step back. Bumps against the record bins behind him.

4

"He told me you steal something every time you come in his store," Clarence goes on. "And I know for a fact you turn around and sell that shit on the street."

The little boy peeks out behind his father's hip.

"Tell you what else," Clarence says. "Every drug store in Paradise Valley says the same thing."

"No sir," Andre protests. "I'm a honest man, Mr. Clarence."

Clarence takes another step closer. The boy cries, "You leave my daddy alone!" and rushes at Clarence's legs. Wraps his little arms around them.

Clarence is amused until Andre turns and flies through the curtain into the rear of the store.

Clarence tries to move. The boy holds tight, screams, "No!"

Clarence peels him off and sets him aside. Lumbers into the back. Pushes out the back door to the alley. Sees Andre Young two stores up, coat flapping, flying over the concrete.

Clarence doesn't have any speed any more. He'll never catch the fleeing man. He stops, pulls one of his guns, aims at Andre's back.

Reconsiders. Not going to shoot a man for stealing cough syrup.

Anyway, Andre skids around the corner of a building. He's gone.

Clarence goes back to the record store. Joe holds Andre's son up on the counter. The boy has calmed down. He squeaks out tears.

"No luck?" Joe asks.

Clarence shakes his head. "What's your name, son?"

"Andre Young, junior," the boy whispers. "Sir," he adds. "Where my daddy gone?"

"I don't know, little man. Could be halfway to Ohio by now."

Clarence sees the boy doesn't get this is a joke, or where Ohio is. "You know where you live?" he asks.

"Yessir."

"Could you show me?"

"Yessir."

"Let's go."

He lifts the boy to the ground. He's forgotten how insubstantial little kids are, how fragile their bones. Bird bones. It's been a long time since Clarence's son was that age. Too much has happened since, too much sadness to remember.

He takes Andre Junior by the hand and walks him out to the sidewalk. Big Clarence, little Junior.

The boy resists. Clarence tugs him along. "Come on, now."

Clarence walks him past the shops crowded together on the street. Busy Bee Cabs. Wolverine Barber. Neighborhood Florist's. Investment and Loan Bank. Chenault Funeral Home. B&C Social Club. Morris Loans. The occasional empty storefront, the business gone bust in the crash.

Clarence and Junior get wondering looks from the people coming in and out of the stores. *What's that young boy done, aggravate Mr. Clarence?*

People say he's too hard on the colored folks crammed into Detroit's Paradise Valley and Black Bottom. Clarence knows otherwise. First, because he's one of them. He knows what they go through every day. Goes through most of it himself. He wouldn't add to their burdens.

And second, because he's all they have. They might not like it, but they know it and have at least some respect for him. He looks out for them in ways the other police won't.

He retraces his steps back to where he left the Ford.

Junior sits beside him, hands folded in his lap. Directs Clarence around the streets of Black Bottom with more authority than Clarence would expect from a boy his age—maybe ten, he judges.

The kid guides him to a ramshackle wooden frame apartment house. Clarence stops and the boy shoots out of the car and up the front steps of the building.

Junior stomps up to the second floor and bangs on a door. Clarence follows. Gets to the landing as the door opens and the kid scoots inside.

A woman peeks out. Angry eyes. Hair awry. Dirty shift. Ground down, tired. She knows who he is. Isn't happy to see him.

"Why my boy bring the police?"

"I'm looking for Andre. He took off and left the boy at the record store."

Voices of children inside the apartment. Yelling. Crying.

"What you want Andre for?"

"I need to speak to him."

"Ain't here. Ain't seen him since this morning. He was supposed to pick up Andre Junior from school, bring him home. You see how good he did that."

The noise level inside grows. She turns her head, yells, "Hush!"

The commotion drops a notch. From further inside the house, Clarence hears coughing, wheezy and wet.

"You see him," Clarence says, "tell him I want to talk to him?"

"He don't stay here. Don't know when I'll see him, one day to the next."

"Where does he stay?"

"Boarding house over here on Hendricks."

On his way home, Clarence drives past the address she gives him.

It's an empty lot, filled with dead stalky weeds and broken bottles in dirty snow.

Clarence and his wife Bessie rent the bottom floor of a duplex on Monroe Street, not far from his precinct house. Wood frame, unpainted clapboard, like most homes in Black Bottom. Well-kept, though in 1932 the house is already old, with a sour old-wood smell in the entrance hall. One of Bessie's friends from work and her family—husband, four kids—live upstairs. It's tight for them up there—it's only a two-bedroom apartment—but with most of Detroit's Negro population crammed into the confines of Black Bottom and Paradise Valley, they make do. As everyone does.

Inside his apartment, Clarence closes and double locks the door. Hangs his overcoat in the closet. Takes off his holster belt and drapes the guns on a hook on the wall by the door where he can reach them fast if he needs them.

He smells dinner: ham hocks and greens. Hears Bessie puttering in the kitchen. "Hey baby," he calls.

"Hey yourself," she calls back. "Almost ready."

He hums his understanding, goes through the dining room to the back of the house. Shrugs his suitcoat off and hangs it in the closet. Takes the harness of his home-made bullet-proof vest over his head and leans it against the wall. Two metal plates, front and back, connected over his shoulders by leather straps. He had it built when he made detective, figuring a Negro detective made too good a target in this town.

Washes up in the kitchen sink. In the dining room, he sits and waits to be served. Man's place, at the head of his table.

Bessie places a glass in front of him and fills it with Coca-Cola. The sale of alcohol is illegal in the United States, though anyone who wants to can easily find it around the city. Most of the liquor illegally imported into the country comes through Detroit from Canada. It's no matter to Clarence. He doesn't drink anymore. He's been dry for the past two years. Instead he keeps himself going with Coca-Cola.

Bessie serves up his dinner and sits down beside him with her own plate. She says grace, including as always a prayer for their boy.

"Everything okay today?" she asks as they settle into their dinner routine.

"Usual day."

She talks. Something happened today at her job. She's a cleaner at Harper Hospital. A patient accused another cleaner of stealing his watch. They called the police. It's a terrible job, but she's lucky to have it. Seems like eight out of ten people in their neighborhood are unemployed after the layoffs from the economic crash.

Clarence listens and responds, but never talks about his days. Going through them once is hard enough without having to relive them in the retelling.

After dinner, Clarence and Bessie sit in the living room. They live a quiet life. Bessie has more friends, is part of the Missionary Society and the choir at the Second Baptist Church. Women are like that. They need sociability. Men are different.

This man, anyway.

Bessie reads the *Detroit Independent* on the couch. Neither Bessie nor Clarence went beyond the eighth grade, but she's a reader. She works hard all day and likes nothing better than relaxing with her paper or a book at the end of the day. If tonight's like every night, at some point she will fall asleep, and Clarence will gentle the newspaper from her and guide her into their bedroom.

Clarence sits in his chair. On the Victrola, "Mood Indigo," Duke Ellington and his band. If a sweeter song has been written, Clarence hasn't heard it yet.

He works on his baseball.

During the summer, Clarence sponsors a baseball league for the boys in Black Bottom through the St. Antoine Branch of the YMCA. He calls it Brown's Athletic Club. In the winter and early spring, he creates the schedules for league games. When it gets a little warmer, he'll put the word out for tryouts for the teams.

He loves the game. Loves everything about it: its gem-like precision (they don't call it a diamond for nothing), its stately pace, its rules, the way a team working together is like the engine of a car, all the parts synched, well-oiled, ticking along smoothly.

He played the game as a boy in Kentucky, and kept at it after he and Bessie moved north. He was a catcher. Sometimes when he has time, he hunkers down behind the plate to catch an inning or two in his league, squatting with the two Colts hanging at his sides.

He tried to get DeMarco interested, and the boy tried, Clarence had to allow it; the boy really tried. He just didn't have the fire in him for it. Clarence didn't want to push him.

And when DeMarco took sick in the last wave of the Spanish Flu in 1920—the disease reaching back for the sole purpose, it seemed, of carrying off Clarence and Bessie's only child—well, the sadness of the failure of Clarence's dreams of baseball glory for his son was nothing compared to the agony of DeMarco's death.

Now Clarence sits looking over a complimentary calendar from Dancy's Barber Shop. He picks dates for the games.

A knock comes at the door.

Clarence drops his notebook, rises, pulls one of the guns from its holster on the hook. Stands beside the door. Face set, mind blank, ready for anything.

"Who's there?" he demands.

"It's me." A woman's voice. "Ella."

"Oh, Ella Turner," Bessie says. "From down the street."

Holding the gun behind him, he whips open the door.

Ella is a heavy woman holding a tot. "Oh Mr. Clarence," she cries, "My baby's gone!"

"Miss Ella, you're holding your baby right here."

"My baby Darius!" Ella wails. "Something terrible happened to him, I know it did!"

"Okay, now just hold on. You come in and sit down. Let's talk about it."

She sits on the sofa and Clarence holsters his weapon. Bessie puts an arm around the distraught woman.

"Now," Clarence says, "tell me what's going on with Darius?"

"Gone!"

"Gone how?"

"He left two weeks ago and said he'd be home for supper. Ain't seen him since."

"He's been gone two weeks and you're just coming to me now?"

"His birthday today. He know we plan a special dinner for him, like we do every year. When he didn't come home, I figure he must be staying someplace. Maybe met a girl, maybe one of his friends."

"How boys are," Clarence agrees.

"When he didn't come back today, I went looking for him. But he just disappeared."

"You asked all his friends?"

"All the ones I know. Nobody seen him. Something terrible happened to him, I just know!"

"Okay," Clarence says quietly, "listen now. Maybe he'll come home tonight, you don't know he won't. If he's still gone in the morning, I'll talk to the neighbors, see what they have to say, anybody saw him."

Ella begins to sob. Bessie takes a tissue from her pocket and hands it to her.

"I can't lose my boy," Ella says. "Already lost Cleophus. Don't know how I'm going to lose my Darius, too."

"You don't know you're going to lose Darius. Maybe he just met a girl and gone off with her. Tomorrow I'll talk to the neighbors. We'll find out what happened to him. I promise you."

She sobs into the tissue. Clarence and Bessie share a glance. Ella's husband Cleophus was murdered by the police two years before. They claimed he matched the description of a serial rapist on the east side. The real rapist subsequently turned up. Cleophus died leaving Ella with Darius and pregnant with their daughter.

Clarence shakes his head, not so much at Bessie as at the unfairness that brings so much misery into their lives. Misery they can only endure, not escape from.

"Don't you worry," he says. "I'll find your boy."

Ella reaches out a grasping hand. Clarence takes it. "Thank you, Mr. Clarence. Thank you so much!"

"You go home now in case he comes back. And I'll speak to you tomorrow. Okay?"

Bessie throws her coat on and walks Ella back to her apartment.

"Don't like the sound of this," she says when she returns.

"No," Clarence agrees. "You remember the boy? He pitched in my league for four, five years. Ace pitcher."

"I remember watching him," Bessie says, "saying to myself, 'That boy could have a career in baseball.'"

Clarence nods. If things were different, Darius could have been one of the greats. He had it in him.

Unfortunately, things weren't different. And baseball for colored players is only a part-time summertime thing. Even the greats on the Detroit Stars have to work jobs. A colored man can't make a living through baseball alone.

If anybody could have made it, it would have been Darius. Tall, graceful, a natural athlete . . . he could have had his pick of teams if the Negro National League was still going.

Bessie says, "Poor Ella."

They both know the pain of a departed child. The ache of loss. The constant agony of guilt over not doing enough to stop it.

The deeper woe of powerlessness.

"I hope you can find him," she says.

"I'll do what I can."

No one else in the police force would even look. The people depend on Clarence. He comes through.

2

BEN RUBIN

The windows from Boesky's Deli throw rectangles of dim light onto 12th Street and Hazelwood, where the restaurant sits on the corner. Ben Rubin huddles against a brick wall on the Hazelwood side, out of the light.

The deli is closed. Friday night, the good people are home having their Shabbat meals. The not-so-good people—like Ben—are out, stamping their feet against the March cold, planning bad deeds.

Ben sees Eddie Millman jiving down the sidewalk.

Ben's best friend. Here he comes. Jaunty, moving with a rolling gait to a rhythm only he can hear. Owns the world, Eddie does. Or acts like it.

He comes up beside Ben. They throw quick juts of the chin to each other.

"You bring it?" Ben asks.

Eddie pats his overcoat. It's thick and woolen, warmer than Ben's high school varsity jacket. Skin-and-bones Eddie still shivers. "Right here."

"Let's beat it," Ben says. "I'm freezing my ass off out here."

They walk east to Woodward. When they pass an alley, Eddie steps in. Unbuttons his coat. Flashes it open. Ben sees the dark handle of the revolver sticking out of his waist. Smiling, Eddie strokes the pebbled grip. Buttons his coat again. Shrugs his shoulders like Cagney.

They return to the streetlights of Hazelwood and keep walking the long residential blocks toward Woodward Avenue.

Eddie said he could get his uncle's gun, but Ben thought it was more of Eddie's big talk. His uncle is Harry Millman, one of the tougher—and crazier—mugs in the Purple Gang. Harry has been breaking Eddie and Ben into the life with errands and small jobs as bagmen, then gradually larger jobs as muscle to intimidate shopkeepers.

On their own, the two friends have stolen purses, robbed candy stores, rolled colored drunks in Paradise Valley. Small-time stuff. This will be their first big-time job. An armed robbery.

The butt of the gun in Eddie's belt proves it.

They walk along in silence. Pick up the Woodward Avenue streetcar going downtown.

In the clatter of the ride, Ben remembers his conversation with his Uncle Moe before he left the house.

"Benny," Moe said, "here, take this. You should have a little money in your pocket."

Moe gave him a dollar. "Thanks," Ben said.

"Where are you going?"

"Out."

"I see that, genius. I'm asking where."

"Meeting a buddy."

"Who?"

"What's with the third degree?"

Moe followed Ben down the stairs of Ben's parents' apartment house to the front porch.

"What are you up to tonight?" Moe's breath puffed in the March cold.

"Come on, Uncle Moe. Why the hard time?"

"Save it, boychik. I know what you've been getting yourself into. It's bad, this life. Nobody comes to a good end, I'm telling you. I'm not enough to convince you?"

Moe's square face watches him, jowly, mouth drooping, almost a parody of sadness.

"Not everybody winds up like you," Ben said.

And immediately regretted it. It was hurtful. The pain shot across his uncle's face. Moe is waiting for his trial for a murder he didn't commit at what the papers called the Collingwood Manor massacre. Three other men did the killing—Irving Milberg, Harry Keywell, and Raymond Bernstein. They murdered three members of the Little Jewish Navy, rumrunners who were trying to break away from the gang and go on their own. Moe was the driver, which made him an accomplice. Milberg, Keywell, and Bernstein are behind bars in the Marquette Branch Prison in the Upper Peninsula. Moe will likely join them there.

Moe raised his hands in surrender. "Fine. Make your own mistakes." He turned and stomped back upstairs.

Now Ben sits across from Eddie, who gives him a smile like he knows exactly what's on Ben's mind.

It's the life. It draws in young men like Ben and Eddie. The money, yeah, but more. The excitement. The danger. The respect—everyone in the neighborhood knows the Purples are criminals but some admire those tough Jews.

Even the possibility of coming to a bad end was a lure, avoiding it through . . . well, whatever it takes, guts or brains or brass balls.

Which Moe's generation once had. They are old now, or dead, or tired, their best days behind them. The gang's a spent force, waiting for younger blood. Like Ben and Eddie and their pals.

And I'm not stupid enough to get caught, Ben tells himself, more in hope than certainty as the streetcar bumps him toward what tonight will bring.

They hop off at Grand Circus Park. Cars crowd the streets, Fords and Packards and Hudsons. A busy Friday night in downtown Detroit. Pedestrians hurry along the sidewalks, driven by the biting cold.

Ben and Eddie trot across Woodward to the east side of the park. Ahead of them is the Madison Theatre, on Witherell Street at the corner of Broadway. The attraction board in the steel grid framework on the roof (almost as large as the entire building itself) blazes in the hazy winter dark. *Arrowsmith.* A still of Ronald Colman and Helen

Hayes swooning in his arms hangs on a banner above the street-level entrance. To the left is the box office.

"Sure about the time?" Ben asks.

"Double-checked it."

Ben looks at his watch. 8:32.

Eddie says, "Last show starts in forty-five minutes."

They walk through Grand Circus Park until they're in the bushes across Witherell from the Madison. Out of sight of prying eyes.

They train their attention on the woman in the theatre box office.

"Fifteen minutes after the last show starts, the cashier closes for the night," Eddie says. "The ticket taker goes off on his break. The manager and cashier count up the receipts and stash the money in a bank deposit bag. After that, they go to the manager's office to fill out paperwork."

"You're sure?"

"Course I'm sure." Eddie's testy. Nervous. Bouncing on the balls of his feet. "I cased it about twenty times."

Ben starts to shiver with excitement and cold and adrenaline. He's nervous himself. This may not be their first foray into crime, but it will be their biggest take.

A harness bull strolls by in front of the theatre. Ben and Eddie melt back into the darkness of the unlit park. The uniformed copper stops at the box office. Says a few words to the cashier. Flirting, to judge by the smile on her face.

When the crowd from the previous show streams out, the copper lifts a hand of farewell and keeps walking.

Disappears around the corner.

"That's right," Eddie whispers. "Keep going."

A line forms to buy tickets for the next show.

The plan is to wait until the manager checks out the box office. Then they will run inside, flash the piece, and grab the canvas bag with the day's earnings. Friday night after a day of matinees and three evening shows, the take should be huge . . . maybe hundreds. *Arrowsmith* is still popular. Movies are a distraction from the ravages of the economy.

They would rake in even more money if they waited until tomorrow, except security is doubled on Saturdays. So tonight's their best chance to get in and get out fast.

They watch as the last stragglers run up and get their tickets. They see the manager step into the box office. The cashier closes the curtain.

Now they're in their cocoon, counting the money.

Inside the lobby, the candy counter shuts down and the girls count the evening's take. They take their money in a little cashbox to the box office.

They disappear inside the auditorium to get changed out of their uniforms into their street clothes. The ticket taker goes off on his break.

So far, so good.

Ben and Eddie wait for the light to go off behind the box office curtain. It's the signal they finished counting the money before making their way to the manager's office.

It seems to take hours.

Finally the box office goes dark.

"Now," Eddie says.

They tie kerchiefs over their faces so just their eyes show. Like movie desperados.

They trot across the street.

This is it.

They slip inside the doors to the foyer.

Past the inner doors inside the lobby. It's a small area, mostly taken up by the candy counter on the right wall.

The manager and the cashier are almost to the office, which sits under the stairway to the balcony on the right. The manager carries the money bag. The cashier carries the roll of unused tickets and the cash box from the candy counter.

When they hear Ben and Eddie, they turn.

Before they can react, Eddie runs up and sticks his piece in the manager's face. If either one of them has a gun, it's probably him so he's the one who needs to be covered.

"Give it up," Eddie growls.

The manager's a tough-looking egg, pasty-faced with a heavy five-o'clock shadow, short and built like a fire plug. He stands still for a few seconds, like he's deciding what to do.

"Let him have it, Mr. Fitrakis," the cashier says.

"Listen to her, Mr. Fitrakis," Eddie echoes. "Don't be a hero."

The manager surrenders the bag to Eddie. The two young men walk backwards, Eddie still covering the manager in case he's carrying and feels the need to defend the money.

When they get down to the front doors, the two young men turn and prepare to flee.

Except at that moment the copper comes through the outside doors into the lobby.

Oblivious to what's happening, until he sees Eddie's piece and the bandanas over their faces.

His eyes pop out of his head like in a cartoon.

He cries, "Hey!" and fumbles for his sidearm.

Eddie shoots at him.

The bullet goes wide.

The two young crooks turn and race back up the incline in the lobby. Ben sees the manager going for his own piece and crashes a shoulder into him, knocking them both down.

Ben scrambles to his feet. Bursts with Eddie through the doors into the auditorium.

"This way," Eddie yells. He goes to the left and barrels through the exit leading out to Broadway.

Ben barely feels the cold air on his face. Heart pounding.

Through the exit doors, Eddie stumbles, falls to his knees. The gun goes skittering. By now they have both lost their kerchiefs. Behind them, the copper yells, "Stop!"

Eddie takes a second to get to his feet and follows Ben down Broadway. Not so crowded at this hour. No pedestrians to dodge.

The copper chases after.

Gunfire.

Eddie falls. The money bag skids away.

Ben stops, turns. Eddie sprawls on the sidewalk. Half his head is gone.

For a split-second, Ben considers retrieving the money bag.

Before he can act, more bullets whiz by his head.

Leave it!

He turns and runs for his life.

Crosses Broadway. Runs past the Capitol Theater, down to John R Street.

Races left.

Goes right on Centre Street.

Left on Grand River.

He runs.

Only when he feels safe six blocks away does he stop.

He leans against a dumpster in a blind alley, his chest heaving with sucking breaths and sobs.

3

ELIZABETH WATERS

Elizabeth Waters stares out the window of the Maccabees Building onto Woodward Avenue below. Light snow gives the scene a hazy watercolor blur, the streetlamps and automobile headlights haloed.

She feels the headache coming on. Her nose is starting to run.

Already?

Well, it's been two days . . .

She turns from the window and looks for her handbag and the handkerchief she keeps there.

It's on her desk. She finds the handkerchief, blows her nose, sticks it back in her bag.

Beside her desk in the writers' room, flopped out on the sofa, Phil Mulcahy snores.

It's late, 9:45. Mulcahy should be working on the script for a new radio drama due to premiere at the end of the year. A detective show about a straight-arrow hero who wears a fedora and saves the country from Communists and other criminals every week. The working title is *Cody Storm on the Case!*

It's supposed to be a partner to another show the station has in development, *The Lone Ranger*. A western about a straight-arrow hero who wears a mask and saves the country from rustlers and other criminals every week.

A hot-shot New York writer's working on the scripts for that one. A smoothie with an Errol Flynn mustache and an ever-present ascot. The producers hired Phil Mulcahy to finish the beginning programs for *Cody Storm*. He's a local guy who writes industrial films for Jam Handy. He should be working on the scripts tonight so the producers can review them on Monday and start casting the show.

Instead he's sleeping one off. Again.

Elizabeth is the Assistant to the Creative staff. Really a secretary with a fancy title. Lately there isn't much to assist for this guy. Can't make much headway when he's passed out dead drunk.

And when he isn't either drinking or passed out, he's groping her. When he's around, she spends much of her time slapping his hands away. Then he gives out with a high titter like a little girl. As if they're playing a game.

One of these times she's going to pop him one. See how he laughs that off.

Except she knows she'll be fired immediately. Getting this job was hard enough. She couldn't work for a year after—

Well, rather than dredge it all up, she turns from the window. In his stupor, Mulcahy drools a thin twine of spit onto the cushion where he lays his head.

Lovely.

It's just the two of them at this hour. She could tiptoe out right now, and he wouldn't be the wiser. He'll probably sleep through the night anyway. Wake up too hungover to even remember.

She could tell him he told her to go home, he'd finish up.

In fact, she decides this is exactly what she's going to do. She has someplace to be, anyway.

Softly, so she doesn't wake him, she leaves him in the writers' room and gets her coat from the cloakroom.

Downstairs the frigid wind takes her breath away for a moment and she runs to the streetcar shelter across Woodward. In the haze from the snow, she can't see the Hotel La Salle. It's now called the Hotel Detroiter. The year before, a new owner took it over and changed the name, hoping to distance the place from its dark history.

As if you can. As if you can ever outrun your past.

Unless you're a woman with a year at Oberlin College. In which case you don't so much outrun your past as have to forget all about it when the only job you can get is assistant to a drunk.

She takes the Woodward Avenue streetcar north to Chicago Boulevard. Walks west four long blocks, through the Boston-Edison district, a neighborhood of homes ranging from sprawling mansions to regular-sized big houses, many gone up in the boom of the last ten years. Henry Ford himself, the King of the Capitalists, lived here before building his estate in Dearborn. She's headed toward one of the more modest homes, a two-story yellow brick house that is not as imposing as the manses she passes.

She pauses outside the front door. Her breath comes in white clouds. Her hip aches from the walk, a reminder of the accident she was in during college when a rich boy soused on bootleg rum flipped the car she was riding in.

She hears voices raised in argument inside the house.

She enters without knocking. The front room is warm and smoky. Men are screaming at each other. She recognizes a few she knows from meetings of the Communist Party and the Unemployed Councils, those groups supported by the Party for the purpose of organizing and providing relief for unemployed workers. She still doesn't know many people here. They're probably from the Auto, Aircraft, and Vehicle Workers of America. They're putting together Monday's march with the Unemployed Councils. The two groups get along like oil and water.

Across the dining room she spots Mary Tatum at the same time Mary sees her.

Elizabeth makes her way through the crowded room to where Mary stands. Knocks over a glass to a howl of annoyance. Steps on feet to more howls.

Mary is one of the few Negroes here tonight. She takes Elizabeth by the hand and pulls her through to the kitchen. Here are the women, working around the hot oven, where women always wind up.

Mary hugs her, kisses her on the cheek. Elizabeth is aware of the disapproving eyes on her from the other women in the kitchen.

She stares back at them. Daring them to speak.

Mary pulls away. "Drink?" she asks.

Elizabeth nods and Mary pulls a bottle from the sink full of cold water and hands it to her. "Didn't know if you were going to make it," Mary says.

"I almost didn't." Elizabeth searches for a bottle opener to pop the top. "I had to work late. And—" She shrugs rather than have to explain about Mulcahy.

"Glad to see you anyway."

"Likewise."

Mary works as a secretary for the Urban League. Dedicated to the causes of racial justice and equity for the worker. She's probably better-read than anyone here tonight, man or woman.

Elizabeth takes a long drink from the bottle. Bootleg gin, aromatic but harsh. "Funny place for a meeting of Communists."

"This stronghold of bourgeoise sensibility, you mean?'

"Exactly. Who lives here?"

"A Michigan Circuit Court judge."

"A Red?"

"No," Mary says. "Might be a fellow traveler. I know he supports the NAACP and a lot of good social programs. He's letting us use the place. I don't even know if he's here."

"Anything happening in there?" Elizabeth points the bottle at the other room.

"Ah, the Great Brains of the proletariat revolution," Mary says with a gap-toothed grin. "They started out talking about logistics for the march. It's going to be a great thing."

"Fingers crossed."

"I have high hopes. A necessary step in the development of class consciousness for everybody who'll be there. Thousands, Liz. It's going to open the eyes of thousands."

"Didn't sound like what they were talking about just now."

"No. They got off talking about the evictions," Mary says. "We have to keep trying to turn those back, for sure."

Elizabeth takes another sip from the bottle. The gin burns all the way down. It makes her stomach turn over and her head spin, and she remembers she hasn't eaten since lunch.

"People are desperate," Mary says. Elizabeth can't argue. She's seen it.

With so many out of work, evictions are spiking across the city. Everywhere you look, bailiffs have been turning people out of their homes and setting their furniture in the street outside the houses. Lately the Unemployed Councils have been sending men around to put the furniture back into the houses and chase the bailiffs away. If they had to, they were rerouting electric and gas lines to keep power to the homes.

Elizabeth goes to stand in the doorway to the living room to listen. Erroll Lembeck, the district organizer of the Young Communist League of Detroit, stands on a chair. Chides the men for not doing more to stop the bailiffs.

Critics of Mayor Frank Murphy shout him down. Despite all Murphy had tried to do to provide relief for Detroiters who were suffering such anguish and starvation—actions Elizabeth believes have been helpful—the Unemployed Councils have not forgiven him for saying they were insincere in their demands for work and relief.

"Murphy accused us of acting as a recruiting mechanism to swell Communist ranks," a man shouts. "It's unforgivable."

"So?" another voice shouts. "Isn't it what we want?"

"He denied us a permit for our demonstration last year," a third voice cries. "And you know what happened—a police riot! And Murphy sided with the police against us! He's the dupe of the bosses!"

"He's deliberately undermining our demands for bread!" another male voice says.

The clashing voices make Elizabeth's head pound. It always come down to this. Shouts, aggressive arguments, endless grievances. Pissing contests, while the real work requiring solidarity goes undone.

She listens for a while longer. Decides she has had enough of this day.

She returns to the corner of the dining room where Mary stands talking with an old man with a scraggly white beard.

"I'm going to go," Elizabeth whispers in Mary's ear.

"So soon? Thought we'd have time to chat."

She wavers—she likes Mary, hasn't had the chance to sit down with her for weeks—but she wants to get home. Elizabeth can only take so much of the blather she's hearing tonight, on top of the blather she heard all day at work.

Besides, she's craving a visit with Miss Em.

Bittersweet Miss Em.

And she has to meet a guy first.

"Sorry," she says. "No can do. Long day. I have to get some sleep. We'll figure out a time to talk later."

They hug. Elizabeth makes her way to the front door. She just gets outside when she hears her name called. She turns to see Erroll Lembeck coming through the door after her.

"Wait up," he calls.

Exactly who she doesn't want to see.

"Leaving already?" he says. "You just got here."

"Yeah, Erroll. I'm tired, okay? That all right with you?"

"I just thought we might have a few minutes together."

"What'd I just say?"

"Okay, okay." He's one of the people responsible for organizing the march on Monday. "Don't have a conniption. Still spending time with your colored friend, I see."

"My 'colored friend'? So much for racial equality in the people's republic." She turns to go. "Goodbye, Erroll."

Erroll grabs her arm.

"I'm just saying," he goes on, "you want to spend your time with a white man, I'm your guy."

"After hell freezes over? Expect my call."

She pulls her arm away and starts down the walk.

A car pulls up in front of the house. All four doors open and several men step out. A big man gets out from the back seat. Not particularly tall, but he's broad, with a large round head and a homely, frog-like face. Elizabeth recognizes him at once. Diego

Rivera. She didn't think he was due to start on his murals for the Institute of Arts until later in the year. He must have come in earlier than expected.

He turns to help a woman out of the car. She's a head shorter than Rivera, ramrod straight, pale and pretty, in her twenties with expressive dark eyes and full dark brows. Dark hair parted down the middle and held back in braids. She wears a drab cloth coat over a bright red and yellow peasant dress with large beads at her neck.

Another woman gets out of the back seat of the car and links arms with her.

The men from the car surround Rivera and walk him up to the house where the meeting is being held. The men talk excitedly to him in English. When they pass, Rivera gives Elizabeth a lascivious once-over from head to toe and keeps walking.

The woman—Frida Kahlo, Elizabeth knows; she recognizes her from her photos—follows after the men with her companion. She walks with an awkward gait, grimacing as she goes.

When she comes even with Elizabeth, Frida slows. Looks Elizabeth straight in the eye. In Frida's brief, piercing glance, Elizabeth feels as though she has become transparent, as if the young Mexican woman can look deep inside her.

Frida reaches out. Automatically, Elizabeth takes the hand she offers. "*Mi hermana*," Frida murmurs in a low voice. She gives Elizabeth's hand a gentle squeeze and walks on.

Rivera and his entourage enter the house to a great commotion. At the front door, Frida looks back at Elizabeth and gives her an almost imperceptible nod before she disappears inside.

Elizabeth feels pinned to her spot, then turns to leave. Her hip is worse as she limps down the sidewalk, as though Frida Kahlo shared some of her own pain with Elizabeth in their brief, intense encounter.

"Hey."

A figure calls from the car at the curb in front of her apartment.

Elizabeth jumps. Her mind's elsewhere, back in Boston-Edison and Frida Kahlo.

"Relax," the man inside the car says. "It's just me." He waves her over.

"Jesus," she says. "Trying to give me a heart attack?"

Vince Vitale sits in the passenger seat, arm casually out the window. She leans down. Looks across him at the driver. A young guy she's never seen him before.

"Who's that?" she asks.

"New guy. Tony Jack's nephew. Breaking him in. Here. Got a present for you."

He hands her a small rectangular package wrapped in plain brown paper.

"I've been trying to get in touch with you," she says. "I ran out two days ago."

"Then it's lucky I'm here."

"I don't have the money on me," she says. "Wait'll I go up and get it."

"I'll come with. I can take it out in trade." Gives her a frank and unsubtle leer.

"Forget it." She does not want him in her apartment. "On second thought, put it on my tab. I'll pay you next time."

"You got it, sweetie."

Inside the building, the elevator operator says, "Miss Elizabeth."

Mr. Fox. He tips his cap to her as she gets in the car. A wizened old man in a blue uniform. Whenever he works, the elevator smells of old man, sweat and an ineffable odor of male loneliness. It makes her heart ache for him.

He rides her up to the third floor. "Have a blessed evening, Miss."

She lives in the Trocadero Apartments on Manderson in Palmer Park in Detroit. Built in the last decade in the ornate Moorish style, the Trocadero is a four-story apartment building with awning-covered balconies, architectural nooks and crannies, and stunning decorative brick work. She has a large apartment, with a sprawling living room ending in a luxurious view through the wide window facing the park.

For now, though, she sits on the couch and carefully opens the unmarked package. She met Vince at a New Year's Eve party at the

Club ElSino in Paradise Valley a few years ago. He tried to put the make on her (as he does whenever she sees him), but she was more interested in what he was selling. Most especially Miss Em.

Inside the brown paper, she finds a glass container the size of a cough syrup bottle filled with clear liquid. She sets it on the coffee table in front of the couch and goes into the bedroom to get undressed and ready for bed.

She gets a teaspoon from the kitchen drawer, along with a glass of water.

Back in the living room, she pours a spoonful of the clear liquid and gulps it down. Follows it with the water to wash away the familiar bitter taste.

Feels her head start to spin.

Nice.

She goes into the bedroom and stretches out under the covers. Waits for the warmth to spread throughout her body and take away all her aches, all her discomforts, all her afflictions.

Hello, Miss Em.

Welcome back.

Mi amiga.

How I've missed you.

4

ROSCOE GRISSOM

H is wife returns to the table, frowning.

"Somebody here for you," she says. "Out front."

"Who?" Roscoe Grissom asks.

"Didn't give me his name," Melanie says.

Impatient. Snotty. He hates it when she uses that tone with him. Like she's been the one trying to find work all day instead of him.

"From the plant?" he asks.

"Maybe. Tell him we're having dinner, huh?"

His job at the Packard plant on East Grand Boulevard often had emergencies pulling him away from home at odd hours. Since he was laid off, he hasn't had any of these late-night calls. Maybe there was an accident and they need him back?

He sets down his knife and fork, tosses his napkin atop them. Naturally, as soon as he leaves the table, the three girls start acting up. He pauses at the kitchen door. "Quiet!"

They pipe down at once.

They better, if they know what's good for them. Brats.

"You doing a great job with these wild Indians," he tells Melanie. "You should be very proud."

The four females exchange a look. Damn straight. Better tread lightly.

At the front door, sure enough, it's Enoch Jones from work. Tall, stooped, thinning sandy hair. Face like a hound. "Hey," he says.

"Hey."

"Having dinner?"

"Yeah."

"Sorry."

"No problem. What's going on?"

"Well," Enoch says in his Georgia drawl, "there's a important meeting tonight, and some folks want you there."

"A meeting about what?"

"Said it was something about insurance for us guys out of work."

"Who's going to be there?"

"Harley and them."

Roscoe looks past Enoch, sees a car full of men in the driveway. Can't make out individuals.

"Who's all those guys?"

"We're all going with Harley," Enoch says. "You got to come. Hurry up. I'll wait in the car."

Back in the kitchen, the girls quiet their chatter as soon as he appears in the doorway.

"It's Enoch," Roscoe says. "He needs me to go with him."

"Now? What for?"

"Going to meet a guy about insurance. Keep my dinner warm, yeah?" Not that it's worth saving: fried potatoes and sliced hot dogs.

A huff of annoyance from her. But she says, "Okay."

"You girls finish your dinner. And listen to your mother, for once!"

Glad for the chance to leave, he gets his coat and flat cap from the closet. Out in the car, the men greet him when he climbs in the back seat. Enoch lets Roscoe sit in the middle and piles in beside him. Three guys jammed in the back, two in the front.

Strong smell of alcohol and tobacco in the cramped car, mixed with harsh male sweat. Roscoe breathes it in. The odors are perfume to him. He's used to being around hard-working men. He misses it, the company of men.

Roscoe knows them all except for one. A scared-looking guy with heavy stubble sitting next to him. Eyes big as saucers.

Don't look happy, no sir.

Roscoe sees Harley Clarke in the front seat, riding shotgun. A guy they know from the bar they frequent. Unemployed, like them and everybody they know. Big, tough brute. Nobody to fool with.

"Hey," Harley says.

"Hey," says Roscoe. "Where we going?"

"Want you to meet these people I know."

"This about insurance?"

"In a way," Harley says.

"What's that mean?"

"You'll find out."

They drive into the dark countryside north of Detroit. After a while, Harley turns again and says to Roscoe, "Ask you a question?"

"Shoot," Roscoe says.

"Are you an American?"

"Well, yeah," Roscoe says. Why wouldn't he be an American?

"I mean, are you a *good* American?" Harley presses. "A *patriotic* American? A white *Christian* American?"

Puzzled, Roscoe says, "You know I am."

"I hope so."

Roscoe don't know how to respond. Harley clams up, and nobody else speaks for the duration of the ride.

It's a long one. They go out the backroads toward Flint, northwest of Detroit.

Roscoe looks at Enoch, tries with his eyes to get him to say something about what's going on. Enoch is silent. Turns his head away.

They drive down a country road on the other side of Flint. Harley tells the driver, "Turn here."

The car bumps onto a lane toward a clearing where two other cars are parked.

Harley gets out and the others follow. Out here in the country it's even colder than it was in Detroit. Enoch sticks close behind the guy with the stubble, close enough to grab him if need be.

Three men stand around a crackling wood fire. They wear long black robes with a white skull-and-crossbones sewn over their hearts. The outfits have black capes with red linings. Black veils cover their faces with holes cut out for their eyes and mouths. On their heads are little black crosswise hats. They look like toys with a pirate's skull-and-crossbones.

Roscoe stifles a smile. It would be comical except for their eyes, visible in the dancing light from the fire. Their eyes are angry.

Harley lines up the men in front of the robed trio. The scared-looking guy stands off to the side. One of the robes has gold trim on the sleeves. The one who wears it comes closer to the fire, hobbling as if he has a false leg.

"At the present time," he says, "the two political parties are doing everything they can to undermine the liberties and privileges the founders of this country intended for the white race to enjoy. You are about to be initiated into a new and secret society. We aim to protect those liberties and privileges. You are about to become members of the Black Legion."

The guy in the trimmed robe looks straight at Roscoe. "What's your name?"

Roscoe tells him and the other man fires questions at him. How old are you? What's your religion? Can you ride a horse? Can you fire a gun? Drive a car?

Roscoe nods at all the questions.

The guy asks, "Will you take an order and go to your death if necessary to carry it out?"

"Yeah." He figures it's what's expected of him, though he's not sure if he really would.

"Will you accept for your roof, the sky; for your bed, the earth; and for your reward, death?"

"Yeah."

"You may be required to perform a duty on a higher plane than the usual night riding. This will require a blood pact. Are you willing to sign your name in your own blood?"

"I am."

The head man asks the same questions of the other men. Except for the guy with the stubble, Roscoe notices.

"Then you all must kneel," the robed man intones, "and cover your heart with your hand."

The head guy nods to one of the other robed men, who draws a pistol from beneath his robe. He points the gun at the back of Roscoe's head.

Who suddenly becomes very nervous.

He was enjoying it, up to now.

With the gun at Roscoe's head, the hobbling man says, "Repeat the Black Oath after me. In the name of God and the Devil, I pledge my life to my peers in the organization. I promise never to betray any of them, and invite my own heart to be roasted, my brain split and spread, my bowels disgorged, and my body ripped asunder should I violate this pledge. And lastly, may my soul be given to torment through all eternity. In the name of God, our Creator. Amen."

Roscoe repeats after each phrase. The other men do, too, when it's their turn with the gun at their heads.

The man in the gold striped robe gives each of them a .38-caliber bullet cartridge. Says, "A bullet like this will be used on any man who violates his oath."

One of the other men nods to Enoch and he brings the bearded man forward. Now the man looks terrified. Enoch pushes him against a tree and stands back.

"James Rogers," the head guy says, "you have been found guilty of missing meetings and shirking your duties. Now you must pay the penalty."

James Rogers begins to tremble. The robed man who had produced the gun now produces a whip. A leather cat o' nine tails with brass tips on the end of each strand.

He looks over the men who have just been initiated. "Our brother must be punished. As this is his first transgression, the penalty will not be fatal. One of you shall carry it out, to prove your worthiness. Who shall be the one to mete out the punishment?"

The new recruits stare at each other, shifting from foot to foot, until Roscoe says, "I'll do it."

The head guy coolly appraises him, hands Roscoe the whip.

"Your first assignment," the robed man says. "Will you administer the punishment to this oath-breaker?"

Roscoe takes the lash, hefts it. It weighs about a pound. Two-and-a-half feet long. Feels a thrill in the pit of his stomach. "How many lashes?"

"Twenty."

James starts to whimper. "Please," he begs Roscoe. "Please, mac. Don't do it."

Enoch turns James to face the tree and ties his hands together around the trunk with a length of rope. He pulls James's shirt over his head to expose James's bare back.

"Begin," says the robed man in charge.

Without hesitating, Roscoe draws the whip back and sends it whistling into James's back.

James's legs buckle at the first lash. By the time Roscoe finishes with the punishment, James is unconscious and slumped against the tree. His back glistens with sweat and blood in the firelight.

Roscoe is out of breath and sweating.

But what a feeling!

He vibrates with excitement and power.

And with the pleasure of acceptance. The three robed figures are looking at him through their veils and nodding under their hoods.

He has never heard of this group before. On this night, however, he knows he has been waiting for them his whole life.

SATURDAY, MARCH 5, 1932

5

CLARENCE BROWN

C larence's day off. Bessie's already at her job by the time he wakes up.

He makes a breakfast of Coca-Cola and toast and hits the streets early. Everybody knows everybody else's business in Black Bottom, and everyone knows Darius Turner. He may be his mother's sweet baby, but Darius's reputation on the street makes people hesitate to admit they've seen him. People know Darius can be tough and mean and nobody to tangle with.

The streets are full of men without work. Options for them are limited to back-breaking labor in the best of times. Now the industries where they worked have all cut back. Building has ground to a halt, hotels are closing, the auto factories are in desperate shape.

Clarence and Bessie came from Lexington, Kentucky. They grew up together, and always knew they would spend their lives with each other. Clarence worked as a tanner, and Bessie worked on a local farm. After eight-year-old DeMarco passed in 1920, Bessie said she couldn't stay there anymore so they crossed the Ohio River into

Cincinnati. Back then, the best paying jobs were porters, so Clarence got a job as a Pullman porter.

On one of his trips, he mentioned to a white passenger he was interested in moving to Detroit, where he had heard there were jobs. The passenger was a clergyman who happened to know Rev. Robert Badby, the pastor at Second Baptist Church in Detroit. The passenger said Rev. Badby had a connection with Henry Ford himself and got factory jobs for many Negro men who were part of the great wave of Negro migration north. He would put in a word for Clarence.

As it happens, the Detroit Police Department was looking to hire men like Clarence (which he took to mean big, black, and threatening). Rev. Badby's recommendation got him appointed to the department with a permanent assignment to Black Bottom and Paradise Valley. Badby's connections to Detroit's white power structure, along with Clarence's affinity for police work, got him promoted to detective.

This morning, walking the cold streets, trying to avoid the piles of slush, he talks to the people he sees. They tell him they haven't seen Darius for a few weeks. Clarence begins knocking on doors. He has no luck until he meets a man who lives on the top floor of a triple-decker.

"I seen him," the man says. He is old, hunched and filthy. A juicer. His breath reeks from bad homemade wine.

"When, exactly?"

"Can't say. Lose track of the days. Week ago, maybe. No job, no need to study the time."

"What was he doing when you saw him?"

"Watched him get in a car."

"What kind of car?"

"Long, big-ass car," the old guy says, "that's all I know. Look like one of them Jew canoes." Gives Clarence a ghastly smile with missing teeth.

"Cadillac?"

"Big-ass cream-colored thing. Pull up right beside him, Darius jump in. Car roar the hell out of here."

"Look like he got in willingly? Nobody forced him?"

"No sir, nobody force him to do nothing. Tell you what, though, had a big-ass grin on him."

"I don't suppose you saw who else was in the car?"

"Look to me like it was a lady. Couldn't tell who, though."

"Couldn't tell if was a white lady or a sister pick him up?"

The old guy shakes his head.

"Nobody else in the car?"

"No sir."

"Okay then. Thanks a whole bunch."

Clarence hands the old guy a buck. "Spend it wisely."

"Thank you, sir," the old guy says with a gap-toothed grin of yearning. "I believe I will."

Clarence tries a few more houses, gets no more precise information. Stops and asks the other Negro officers who patrol Black Bottom, but they haven't seen Darius Turner either, though they say they'll keep an eye out.

Walks down Hastings to the Rexall. Gets out of the cold, warms up with a coffee from the counter. Chats with the pharmacist, Leon Wexler, who says he hasn't seen Andre Young, the cough syrup thief.

He walks around his neighborhood for another hour. Goes past the empty lot where Andre told his wife he was staying. Clarence checks the apartment houses around the lot; nobody admits to knowing Andre Young.

He stops in at Ella Turner's to report on his progress and assure her he will keep looking for her son.

His feet wet from stepping in slush and his shoulders aching from hauling around the metal plates under his coat, Clarence goes back home. Detaches his weapons and armor. Puts on Duke Ellington's "Flaming Youth" and stretches out on the couch in his living room.

What has he learned today?

Darius might have gotten into a car, which might have been a cream-colored Cadillac. Maybe a week ago. Nobody forced him. Big smile on his face. Hasn't been seen since.

Not much to show for the day, but it's a start.

Nineteen now, Darius has been running the streets since he was fourteen. Smoking reefer and running numbers and doing who knows what all. After his father Cleophus was killed, he really went wild. The only structure he had was when he pitched for a team in Clarence's leagues. Clarence got a look at the man Darius might have grown into.

If things had been different.

Lot of things might change if things were different, Clarence reminds himself. If things were different, they wouldn't be the same.

He naps on and off until Bessie gets home.

6

BEN RUBIN

Noon. Ben wakes slowly.

Groggy. Thick-brained. Queasy stomach. And cold: frost is thick inside the living room window. Snow flurries outside.

He spent most of the previous night walking around downtown Detroit. Couldn't shake the image of Eddie Millman hitting the sidewalk. Or what was left of his head exploding in blood from the copper's bullet. There wasn't anything Ben could do for his friend.

So he keeps telling himself.

As Moe would say, it's the life we've chosen.

It didn't stop Ben from leaning against the wall of a restaurant in Germantown and sobbing when he finally stopped running. Or freezing on the walk down to the river, afraid to go home.

No, not afraid. *Ashamed* . . . because they made such a mess of the heist and because Eddie was dead and Ben wasn't.

And because he would have to confess to his parents what happened. Both his father and mother are wage-slaves, his father a lady's shoe salesman at Hudson's department store downtown, his mother a bookkeeper at a business selling popcorn and candy to the movies.

It was the life Ben was determined to escape, ten-hour days toiling away for someone else who would take advantage of you in every way possible while you frittered away your own precious time on earth. He had spent two futile years at the College of the City of Detroit before quitting after realizing it was better to grab your own life with both hands and be in control of it.

Or so he thought before last night. Now he wasn't so sure.

He and Eddie had talked about the risks. With young men's confidence, they never considered anything would happen. They certainly never thought one of them would wind up dead.

And for nothing . . . when Eddie hit the sidewalk, he dropped the bag of money. Ben didn't dare stop for it or he would be lying alongside Eddie at the morgue.

So Eddie got his brains blown out for *bubkis*.

Their first big heist.

A disaster.

Some gangsters.

When he stopped running, he circled around back to Grand Circus Park. (It was true: you always returned to the scene of the crime.) By the time he got there, the Madison Theatre was long closed and all the lights were off. The commotion that would have followed in the wake of Eddie's death was over. No more ambulance, no more uniformed coppers, no more detectives, no more ghoulish bystanders . . . and no more Eddie.

All over, like it never happened. Except for Eddie's blood on the sidewalk. Ben could see the stain even in the dark. Nobody bothered to wash it away.

He didn't want to go back to his parents'. He couldn't ask one of his other friends. They all knew what he and Eddie had planned; Eddie made sure of it. They would want to know what happened, and Ben didn't want to tell them. They would find out soon enough.

There was only one place where, if he had to go there, they would have to take him in: his sister Miriam's flat on Elmhurst. Close to Ben's parents' home on Dexter, far enough away to be a refuge. Temporarily. Three years older than Ben, Miriam virtually raised him after their parents both grew distant and depressed following his brother Allen's death in the war.

When Ben showed up at their apartment a little after four in the morning, Miriam's husband, Isaac Buchalter, was asleep. Miriam was already awake. She was getting ready for her shift as a baker at Hoptman's Bakery on 12th Street, as Ben knew she would be.

She didn't have an extra bed because Isaac was making a nursery out of the second bedroom for the baby she was carrying. She fixed up the sofa in the parlor with a pillow and blanket and gave him a cup of tea and hugged him before she left for work.

When he finally dozed off, he welcomed the relief of unconsciousness.

Until he wakes at noon and it all comes back to him.

He pads into the kitchen. Isaac's nowhere in sight. Isaac teaches third grade at Duffield Elementary School on Macomb, so Ben knows he won't be working on Saturday. He might be off looking for another job. He's told Ben his teaching job grows more insecure by the day. All the schools are cutting back as budgets fail everywhere.

He strikes a kitchen match and lights the burner with a "whoosh!" of gas. Makes himself a cup of coffee and slices challah for toast and jam. It's all his stomach can manage.

He is just finishing the toast when he hears Isaac coming in the front door.

"You're up," Isaac says. "Rough night?"

"You have no idea."

"Yeah, pretty sure I do."

"You talked to Miriam?"

"I stopped by the bakery. She said you had trouble last night. Said you didn't talk much about it."

Isaac sits at the kitchen table. "This have anything to do with what happened to Eddie Millman?"

Ben freezes. Can't reply. Can't meet Isaac's eyes.

"Thought so," Isaac says.

"How do you know about that?"

"It's all over the neighborhood. Everybody's talking about how Eddie Millman took a bullet last night trying to pull a heist at a movie theatre downtown. Word is, another guy was with him."

Ben keeps silent.

"Benny, I'm going to ask you a question and I want you to tell me the truth. Were you with Eddie?"

Ben doesn't say anything. Isaac stares him down.

"Ben?"

Ben nods.

"Oh man," Isaac says. Sorrowful, not angry.

"Ike, it wasn't supposed to happen like that."

"It never is."

"Eddie and I hit the box office at the Madison after the last show. We almost got away when this copper came in. We took off out the side door and he followed us. Started shooting at us. Eddie caught one."

"You got away."

"Yeah."

"You didn't stay to help him?"

"I took one look at him, I knew he was a goner. And I was scared. And ran. I'm not proud of it."

"If there wasn't anything you could have done, you would have been foolish to stay."

They are silent until Isaac says, "The cops came to see his mother this morning. Pretty soon it was all over the neighborhood."

"Anybody say anything about me?"

"Cops just said he had an accomplice. They don't know who."

"Won't be long before they figure it out."

Isaac shakes his head. "That life, Benny. It's not for you."

Ben can't even respond. He's not sure how he feels about it. He thought it was going to be the life he was made for. But now . . .

"You can stay here as long as you need to," Isaac says. "As long as you know you're going to have to take care of this, sooner or later."

Ben nods.

But how? What to say? And who to?

As though reading Ben's thoughts, Isaac says, "I'd start with your ma."

Miriam comes home late in the afternoon, smelling of flour and baked goods. She brings one of the pies she baked, which Hoptman allows her to do every Saturday.

"*Nu*, Benny?" she says. She sits in the kitchen over a cup of tea, her swollen feet propped on a chair.

He sits with her at the table. Says nothing.

"You sleep?"

"A bit."

She takes a sip of tea. Waits.

He tells her what he told Isaac. Figures her husband will tell her anyway. Better she should hear it from him.

She clucks her tongue in sympathy, takes his hand.

"Whose idea was it, robbing the show. Yours?"

"The idea to pull a robbery, yeah. Eddie was the one suggested the show."

"Not a very good plan."

"We thought it was a great plan. If the copper hadn't walked in just as we were leaving, we would have been aces."

"It's the life, Benny."

"Exactly what Isaac said."

"You need to face it. That could have been you last night instead of Eddie."

He sits silently. Runs his hand along a ragged tear in the floral oilcloth atop the table.

Has to admit the truth of what she says.

"Listen," she says, "me and Isaac, we're going down to the Unemployed Council. Why don't you come with?"

"No. Thanks anyway."

She takes his hand. "Come. Get your mind off everything. We'll help with the soup kitchen and listen to speeches. There's a lot of misery in this world. Take a couple hours and help relieve some of it."

Instead of wallowing in your own troubles goes unsaid.

The Unemployed Council meets in the basement of a church at Hastings and Ferry. His sister assured him none of Eddie's family or the gang would be there. It wasn't their kind of event. Ben wears a flat cap pulled low over his face anyway.

Miriam brings the pie from Hoptman's and adds it to the table of desserts in the soup kitchen. About a hundred families are already lined up for the food. Ben had read in the *Free Press* how a doctor at Receiving Hospital said at least four people die of starvation at the hospital every day. Detroit was hit worse than any other city in this depression; thousands are out of work and starving. The government can't keep up with people's needs, so private organizations like the Communist-backed Unemployed Councils are stepping in.

Miriam pulls him into the serving line behind the trestle tables and gives him an apron. "Get to work. Help out."

He stands behind a pot of what looks like stew. He ladles bowlfuls out to all the men, women, and children in the line. The men look surly, the women anguished, and the children dazed by starvation and—from the looks of the bruises on their faces and rail-thin arms—abuse.

Even standing behind the steaming table with his own belly full, Ben grows angry at what this country has done to its working people.

No, he corrects himself—not the country, the government and business. Especially businessmen like the ghoulish Henry Ford, whose beaky profile in the newsreels and newspaper photographs bore more than a passing resemblance to Nosferatu in that movie.

Ben hears a crash. A loaded tray hits the wooden floor, followed by men's raised voices.

An argument explodes in the seating area. A guy wouldn't move over at one of the tables to make room for a couple and their three children. Two men are on their feet and at it with each other.

A woman screams and tears at one of the fighter's arms. Three children scream, their trays overturned, their food scattered everywhere. The kids cover their ears.

Ben drops his ladle into the soup pot and scoots around the table to break up the fight. In the tinder-box atmosphere of the room, filled with desperate, angry men, it could spread in an instant.

He steps between them. He ducks a few punches as they jostle him, but the fight goes out of them quickly. A young woman also appears, also wearing an apron. She wraps the three crying children in her arms and draws them away from the scuffle into the serving area. All activity has stopped as everyone watches.

The two men separate. Peace returns.

What's left are loud grumblings from the men, whose pride has been trampled in the dirt already.

Ben picks the trays off the floor and gets as much of the broken crockery and food slop up as he can. A man wearing a newspaper folded into a cap limps over to take the garbage away, and returns with a wet mop and pail.

"I'll get this," he tells Ben.

Ben nods and returns to his spot in the serving line. The woman who rescued the children now brings them back through the line, which opens to make room for them.

From where he stands behind the stew, Ben hears the woman cooing words of comfort to the kids. Their faces are dirty and tear-stained. Two skinny girls, maybe ten and eight, and an even skinnier boy, the youngest. He looks on the verge of crying again.

As hard as this world is on their parents, it's tougher on kids. They don't understand what's happening or why.

They stop in front of him. He ladles stew into their bowls. The woman does not look at him, but he looks at her. She might be slightly older than Ben, maybe in her thirties, with green eyes in a narrow, freckled face and wisps of pale red hair peeking out from her bandana.

She moves with the children down the line, pauses in front of Ben's sister Miriam for a brief chat. Maybe Miriam knows her?

The woman finishes taking the children down the line and guides them to where their parents are sitting, at another table than the one occupied by the man their father fought with.

When everyone has been served and the line diminishes, Ben helps Miriam with the washing up.

"Who was the woman you were talking with?" he asks. "The one helping with the kids during the fight."

She shrugs. "Don't know her name. I've just seen her around at these meetings. Why? You interested?"

"Just wondering."

"I'm pretty sure she's one of those true-blue Reds. And a *shiksa*, to boot, Benny."

They take a seat to wait for the speeches to start.

Soon a young woman steps to the podium and begins to sing.

I'm spending my night at the flop house
I'm spending my days on the street
I'm looking for work and I find none
I wish I had something to eat.

She sings to the tune of "My Bonnie Lies Over the Ocean." Everybody joins in at the chorus:

Sooo-oup, sooo-oup, they give me a bowl of soo-oup
Sooo-oup, sooo-oup, they give me a bowl of soup.

I spent twenty years in the factory
I did everything I was told
They said I was loyal and faithful
Now, even before I get old.

Sooo-oup, sooo-oup, they give me a bowl of soo-oup
Sooo-oup, sooo-oup, they give me a bowl of soup.

I saved fifteen bucks with my banker
To buy me a car and a yacht
I went down to draw out my fortune
And this is the answer I got.

Sooo-oup, sooo-oup, they give me a bowl of soo-oup
Sooo-oup, sooo-oup, they give me a bowl of soup.

I fought in the war for my country
I went out to bleed and to die
I thought that my country would help me
But this was my country's reply.

Sooo-oup, sooo-oup, they give me a bowl of soo-oup
Sooo-oup, sooo-oup, they give me a bowl of soup.

I went on my knees to my maker
I prayed every night to the Lord
I vowed I'd be meek and submissive
And now I've received my reward.

Sooo-oup, sooo-oup, they give me a bowl of soo-oup
Sooo-oup, sooo-oup, they give me a bowl of soup.

The people in the audience clap. The young woman takes a bow and sits down. A man stands to thank her for the song, which he says was written by someone named Maurice Sugar.

Ben grows antsy from sitting among so many people. He feels like there's a sign on his back: "I'm the one who was with Eddie Millman."

He steps outside for a smoke.

And sees the woman who interceded in the fight.

7

Elizabeth Waters

Like gorillas in the zoo.

Elizabeth Waters knows what's going to happen even before the two men who are involved. She sees it forming, like storm clouds gathering. One of them, all height and ropey arms, asks the other if he'll move over so the tall man's whole family can sit at the table.

The guy who's sitting at the table, a stumpy guy in a soiled fedora, says no. The two have words—and before you know it, Fedora knocks the tray out of Tall Guy's hands and the food spills all over the floor. Tall Guy smacks Fedora over the head with his own tray and it's on.

Fedora jumps to his feet in an instant and the two of them are at it. Wild swings, body blows, clinches. Believing they're angry at each other when what they're furious at is the system that turns them this way, hungry and selfish and ashamed. As Lenin said, every society is three meals away from chaos.

Meanwhile the wife and kids are standing by. Fedora knocks Tall Guy into them, upending their trays. Stew, potatoes, cake fly everywhere.

Even though Elizabeth understands what sparked this ferocity— the hunger, the desperation, the uncertainty, the stupidity of male pride, dangerous combinations all—it's still hard to watch.

She drops the spatula she uses to dole out cake and pie and ducks around the food tables. She'll let the men take care of themselves. It'll blow over quickly as neither will have the energy to go on for long. She's worried about the kids.

She shepherds them and their mother away from the fight and leads them back around to the food table for another helping of dinner. Another man has stepped in to separate the fighters. It's a usual occurrence.

After she gets the kids and mama settled, Elizabeth takes her place back behind the food tables and resumes dishing out the desserts, which people from the movement have made and brought.

She notices the guy who stepped between the fighters looking at her down the row of tables. Where'd he come from? Never saw him here before.

Gives him a brief nod to recognize his role in keeping the peace.

It takes a while for all the hungry people to work their way through the breadline. Once everyone has been fed, they consolidate the food down to one table and leave one woman in charge. She will take care of the stragglers.

In the meantime, the speeches will begin soon. People find seats. Here is one place in the city where the races and nationalities will meet in relative peace. Except for brief squabbles like the one between Fedora and Tall Guy, most people here are in the same boat, white or black or brown, German, Italian, Polish, Jewish, Mexican, all sitting next to each other.

And the lion shall lie down with the lamb.

Though this is certainly no paradise on earth.

Harold Pratt, the director of the Communist Party of Michigan, stands. The church has no public address system so he has to shout to make himself heard. He's starting out hoarse from all the speechifying he's been making the past couple of weeks. She wonders if his voice will last until Monday's march.

Elizabeth has heard what he has to say many times before, though it still moves her to hear him catalogue the abuses the working men and women of America have to suffer. She does not come out of a working-class background. Her father—her real father, not the mook her mother married after her real father died—was the director of purchasing for Briggs Manufacturing, which supplies automobile bodies for Ford and other car companies. She grew up comfortable in ritzy Grosse Pointe Farms.

Unlike the young women in her circle, she turned against her upbringing (part of her rejection of her privileged family and all they stood for) when she was in her teens. She feels herself to be more sympathetic to the woes of the workers than of the managerial classes, even though much of that is theoretical. She has gone hungry in her life, but she has never faced the endless privations of the poor.

She listens for a while, standing at the back of the room. She scans the crowd, looking for Erroll Lembeck so she can avoid him. He's not here tonight.

The last time she saw him, she couldn't get away from him fast enough. Communist, socialist, Republican, they're all the same . . . men only want to be in charge.

And even when they're hopeless drunks like Phil Mulcahy at the radio station, they still have to believe they're in control. Earlier in the day, she got a call from her boss, creative director Sidney Ballenger, bawling her out for leaving Mulcahy the night before. Evidently Mulcahy complained when he came to in the morning and found himself alone and abandoned.

With no script.

It didn't stop Mulcahy, of course.

"He says he gave you a script to type out," Sid told her. "And you didn't do it."

"He never gave me anything," Elizabeth said. "The only thing he did last night was pass out and drool all over the couch in the writers' room."

"So you're saying you don't have the script?"

"I'm saying he never *gave* me a script."

"You're telling me there's no script for the opening show?"

"Not unless the script fairy flew in last night and wrote one while Phil was passed out."

Ballenger paused. She knew he didn't believe her. These men always stick together.

"This is not good," Ballenger said at last.

"No," Elizabeth agreed.

"No, I mean he told me he gave you a script to type out."

"And I'm telling you he never gave me anything."

"Why would he lie, Elizabeth?"

"Gee, lemme think—maybe because he never wrote it? And wants to pin the blame on me? Jesus Christ, Sid."

"Language, Elizabeth. Why would he tell me he did if he didn't?"

Elizabeth closed her eyes. You are just too stupid, she thought. She had the presence of mind not to say it.

Instead she said, "He lies. How do you not know that by now?"

"I'm going to have to talk to George about this."

George Trendle, the station manager and Boss of All Things.

"Do what you have to do."

"Be in my office first thing on Monday. We'll talk about it then," Ballenger said, and disconnected.

For her part, Elizabeth slammed down the phone. He believes that repulsive dipso over me, she thought angrily.

And now, before another man gets up to tell everybody about what he believes and why they should believe the same, she makes for the door.

Except the guy who was eyeballing her earlier, the one who broke up the fight, is standing outside, having a smoke. She has to walk past him.

He notices her and she gives him the malocchio to discourage him from saying anything. Still, when she passes he says, "Hey."

He is young, tall, slender. Thick, wavy black hair.

"Nice going back there," he says, "jumping right in the middle of it. Impressive."

She pauses. "Thanks. Likewise."

"Thought those two jamokes were going to do serious damage. I liked how you got the kids out of the way. Quick thinking. I'm Ben."

"Elizabeth."

He reaches out a hand. "Pleased to meet you."

She shakes. "Same here. Say, got another one?" Points her chin at his cigarette.

"Sure. It's a Camel, though."

"All the same to me."

He hands her his pack and she shakes one out. He lights it with his Zippo.

She takes a long drag. "I haven't seen you here before."

"Today's my first time. I came with my sister and her husband. They're regulars."

"Who are they?"

"Miriam and Isaac Buchalter."

Jews for sure.

"Don't know them," she says.

"You were chatting with her when you took the kids through the line just now. She was dishing out the vegetables."

"Oh, right. Yeah. I've seen them here. They work the soup line. Never knew their names."

"Yeah, they're members of the Party. True believers."

"Good to hear. She seems like a nice person."

"She is."

"And how about you? Are you a true believer?"

"Me?" He shrugs. "Not yet. Though what the first guy was saying? Makes a lot of sense."

"It does," she agrees. "Harold's the head guy around here."

She doesn't mention Harold Pratt is also well-known among the faithful as a pervert. He once whipped out his dick in front of her and asked her if she would watch him jerk off. She put the kibosh on it pretty quick.

"I especially liked what he said about the police," Ben says.

"The police as the agent of force protecting the capitalist state."

"Yeah. Fucking bulls. Cause more trouble than they prevent."

"Sounds like you've had a few run-ins."

"Oh yeah."

He doesn't say anything more and they smoke in silence.

"Well," Ben says. Takes a last draw of his cigarette and drops it. Smashes it under his shoe. "Just wanted to tell you I liked what you did back there. You look like you're on your way somewhere."

"No, just getting a little air. Good to meet you."

"You, too."

She lifts the cigarette. "Thanks for the smoke."

"Anytime. See you here again, maybe."

He flashes a smile. His teeth are crooked and stained, but it's a nice smile. Genuine. He has a charm about him, she has to admit.

He raises a hand in farewell and goes back inside. She stays out to finish her cigarette. Flicks the butt into the street.

Another speaker stands at the podium. Gilberto Ramirez. People call him the Mayor of Mexicantown. He owns a bodega down on Vernor and he's a leader in the Mexican community. Like everyone else in the city, the ten thousand Mexicans who live in Detroit are hurting.

Ramirez talks about other burdens on his community. The Welfare Department is pushing hard to get the Mexicans off the rolls and back south. Many are going, giving in to the government's pressures to leave and believing the lies from the Mexican government about free housing and land awaiting those who return.

Good luck with that. Every week more Mexicans are getting on trains at Michigan Central Station bound for Juarez and Laredo.

And who can blame them. Things are growing more desperate by the day around here.

Gilberto's message tonight isn't to leave. It's to stay and fight.

"Join us Monday," he exhorts the crowd. "March with us Monday and tell Mr. Ford we're not going to stand being treated like peons!"

The rest of what he says gets lost in the crowd's angry shouts of agreement. Elizabeth knows what comes next . . . the list of demands they have for Ford: jobs, medical aid, emergency relief. The Hunger March set for Monday has to be big enough to break through Ford's bubble of ignorance and unconcern.

Good luck with that, too.

Careful, you're getting too cynical, she cautions herself. You don't have the luxury of abandoning the fight.

Gilberto gets a standing ovation. Watching him, she thinks of Frida Kahlo and Diego Rivera. Were they still in town? She still feels Frida's eyes burning into her, reaching into her soul.

Mi hermana. My sister. What did she see in me, Elizabeth wonders, that made her call me that?

The next speaker stands. Another man. He starts shouting about the proletariat. She's not in the mood for this tonight. She's heard it all before.

Maybe that's her problem. She's heard everything before. She's so tired of it all.

She looks around, spots the young man, Ben, on the other side of the room. Intent on the speeches.

Maybe she needs to recapture a little of what he has . . . the gusto that comes with hearing this for the first time.

Before she makes it to the door, a man appears beside her. Says, "Hey there."

Another stranger. Tall, about half a foot taller than she is, and broad in the shoulders. Blond hair, blue eyes.

"Lizzie, isn't it?" he says.

"Elizabeth," she says frostily.

"Yeah, sorry. Elizabeth. I remember you as Lizzie. I'm Horace."

"Do we know each other?"

"You don't remember me? I'm Lulu Howcroft's little brother."

She takes a moment to place the name.

"You're Horace Howcroft?"

"I am," he says with a small sweeping bow. "Everybody called me 'Hooker.'"

"I remember. I didn't even recognize you."

"Been a long time."

"Has it ever. Hooker Howcroft. What's it been, ten years?"

"More. Since before the war."

"So long?"

He nods and she says, "I guess it has been. Wow. Hooker."

"All grown up."

"How's everybody? How's Lulu?"

"I guess you haven't heard. Lulu died a couple years back."

"Ah jeez."

"Yeah. Brain tumor. Bad way to go."

"Sorry to hear it. I'm out of touch with everybody from the old days, so . . ."

"My father died, too. My mother's the only one left."

Elizabeth shakes her head. "Sorry. So much death."

"How it goes, right?"

"Still in Grosse Pointe?"

"Still there. Were you just leaving?"

"Yeah. Been a long day for me."

"Say, I was about to go back to the house. Why don't you come with me and say hi to my mother? She'd love to see you."

Her first impulse is to say no. She's tired, she needs sleep, she wants to put this day behind her.

And she put this life behind her a long time ago.

As she stands looking at him, though, it comes rushing back to her with a momentary ache of loss for the life he represents, the life she walked away from. The obliviousness of youth; the classes and rivalries at University Liggett, their tony private school in Grosse Pointe; and the long days of summer spent with Lulu, her best friend until they lost touch after graduation and Elizabeth left for college.

And all the training. Learning to smoke, learning to kiss, learning to flirt, learning to fuck, learning how to master all the petite bourgeoise expectations of the life of idle female luxury she was destined for until she said no more and turned her back on it all.

And even the memories of Horace himself came back, and the first and only time they had sex. It was at a pool party at his house before she left for college. She was seventeen; he must have been fifteen. They were all hopping around in their bathing suits and she went upstairs to use the bathroom just as he was getting ready to rinse off. He pulled her into the shower and they did it there, standing. It wasn't the first time for either of them.

They never talked about it, except every so often she caught Horace leering at her. He would raise his eyebrows—as if to say, Wanna go again?—and she would shake her head.

"What do you say?" he asks again. "Ma would love to see you."

"Sure," she says. "Why not?"

8

ROSCOE GRISSOM

Roscoe strains to hear the radio for updates on the Lindbergh baby kidnapping. He's been following it since the first reports came in. It's been five days since the poor little guy was taken from his house, and Roscoe hasn't heard if there's been any news.

He can barely hear the announcer. The girls are upstairs screaming bloody murder. They don't want to get ready for bed because it's Saturday night, so they talk back to their mother. She just yells at them, which is useless; the little brats ignore her.

Roscoe wishes someone would fucking kidnap *them*. Take the three girls, and he'll throw in Melanie free for nothing.

When he can't take it anymore, he races up the stairs to their bedroom.

"Quiet!"

The only one who hears him is Annie, the oldest, bouncing on her bed. The other two are making so much noise they aren't even listening to him.

It enrages him.

Annie sticks her tongue out at him. He strides into the room and slaps her across the face so hard he knocks her across the bed.

The other two girls, Prudence and Harlene, quiet down instantly. Annie wails.

Melanie runs out from the bathroom where she is getting the bath ready. Roscoe swivels his head to stop her in her tracks.

"What the hell's going on up here?" he demands. "I'm trying to listen to my goddamn radio."

Melanie says, "Sorry. I'll get the girls under control."

"Chrissake, can't a man relax in his own house?!"

He turns and stomps down the stairs to the living room. Goes right to the closet and throws his hat and coat on.

He escapes from the house.

He pauses on the front stoop to savor the sudden quiet. The only thing he can hear are the pine boughs rustling overhead.

He walks down to the Dew Drop Inn on Mack Avenue. Neighborhood bars have been failing everywhere during Prohibition, when sale or purchase of alcohol is illegal. In an effort to hang on, the Dew Drop became a café once they could no longer sell alcohol, but the door to the back room leads to a not-so-secret blind pig where the owner sells beer and liquor.

Inside the joint, the smoke and the boozy reek soaked into the walls and floor make Roscoe's eyes water. His shoulders start to loosen in the familiar buzz of conversation. Here, at least, a man can feel like he belongs.

This man can, anyway.

He sits at the bar, orders a Coke, sips it slowly, smacking his lips at the sweetness. He spends most of his days here, may as well spend his nights, too, right?

He finishes his Coke, orders another one. So much better than sitting home and trying to listen to his radio while the four princesses do everything they can to sabotage his peace and quiet.

He spots Enoch Jones and Harley Clarke and a couple others around the pool table in the rear.

Harley sees him, waves him over.

Roscoe is starting to feel all right. Amazing what getting out of the house can do. He takes his Coke back to where his friends are.

Big Harley greets him. Two other men Roscoe don't know are playing pool. They nod and go back to their game.

"Recognize those guys?" Harley asks.

Roscoe looks at the pool shooters again. Ordinary looking. Bland faces, thinning hair. White shirts and dark pants. Regular guys.

Roscoe shrugs.

"We know you," one of them says. Sounds almost like a challenge. He's tall and stooped with a thin face and receding hairline. Downhome accent, maybe Carolina.

Roscoe says, "Yeah?" Prepared for anything now. "Don't believe I had the pleasure."

Roscoe feels his bad mood rising again. He hates to be at a disadvantage. Hates to be mocked. Hates it when people pretend to know something he don't. It's how he's starting to feel now.

"Let me put it this way," the guy says. "You're a good man with a cat o'nine tails."

Roscoe, not too quick on the uptake, looks to Enoch for a clue.

"Last night?" Harley prompts. "Forgot already?"

Roscoe looks at the other guy again. "Wait, you're not one of them in the robes?"

The other man holds out his hand. Heavy liquor fumes on his breath. "Laverne Penney."

Roscoe takes the hand. Bone-crushing shake.

"This here's Alden Baker. He was there, too."

Alden and Roscoe shake. A hard workingman's hand, but a softer grip than Laverne. He's shorter than Laverne, with a belly bulging over his belt.

"Wouldn't have recognized you guys in a million years," Roscoe says.

"That's sort of the idea," Laverne says with a wink. "Head man's a guy named Peg-Leg White. Michigan recruiter for the Legion. Hey, whyn't you have a seat for a while. We'll talk soon as the game's over. And here," Laverne adds with another wink, pulling a flask out of his coat on the chair. "This might put some zip in your pop."

Unscrews the top and hands it to Roscoe.

Roscoe raises the flask in appreciation and sits on a chair beside the pool table. Tips a splash into his Coke. Sips.

Mmm. Good whiskey. He tastes it even through the sugary drink. Goes to hand the flask back to Laverne. Laverne says, "Finish it."

"Much obliged."

Roscoe pours the rest into his Coke and watches Laverne and Alden resume their game.

Laverne is running the table.

After a few minutes, Laverne sinks the last ball and Alden throws his cue stick on the worn green felt in good-natured disgust.

The two sidle over to Roscoe.

"Good game," he says.

"Hard to beat this monkey at stick," Alden says. "Any plans for tonight?"

"Nothing much. What I got to do, I'm doing. Not like there's work in the morning."

"I hear you," Alden says.

"Know whose fault it is, don't you?" Laverne says. "All us white men out of a job?"

"Yes sir, I do," Roscoe says. "It's them Jews."

"Goddamn right," Laverne says. "Them kikes. You read Mr. Ford's paper?"

"I sure did." In truth, Roscoe's not a reader; he can't remember the last book he read, even in high school. He never reads the city papers. Just listens to the radio. Occasionally he read the *Dearborn Independent*, Ford's old mouthpiece, when he had the chance. So he knows what Laverne is talking about. There was a series in the *Independent* about Jews and all the trouble they caused around the world and throughout history.

"The 'International Jew,'" Laverne says. "It's all right there in Mr. Ford's paper."

"Yessir" Roscoe says. "Just like he tells it."

"Those fucking Jew Communists making it hard for every hard-working white Christian man in this country," Laverne says.

"That's a fact," Alden says.

"They own everything in the goddamn world." Laverne getting real het up now.

"That's a fact," Alden repeats.

"Like Mr. Ford said in his paper, these people been hated all down throughout history. There must be a reason. Know what we ought to do? We ought to go find ourselves a Commie kike and show him who's the true boss in this country."

Enoch guffaws.

Alden picks up on it. Says, "Best idea I've heard all day. Roscoe, what do you say?"

Roscoe drains his spiked Coke, hides a belch behind a fist. "I'm with you guys."

"I know just the one," Laverne says. "There's this Jew lawyer, works for the Reds. Even gone to jail for dodging the draft during the war."

"How's he staying a lawyer if he went to jail," Alden asks. "That should of got him kicked out."

"It did. Frank Goddamn Murphy got him his law license back."

"Fucking Murphy," Harley says. "He's a Papist, you know. Jew lover, too. And a nigger lover to boot."

Roscoe never heard of Frank Murphy, so he keeps mum.

"This lawyer I'm talking about, he defends all them union strikers when they get arrested," Laverne goes on.

"So what we going to do to him?" Alden asks.

"Why, we're going to kill him," Laverne says with a loose grin.

"Let's go find ourselves a yid," Alden hoots. The men leap up and stomp through the bar.

Except Roscoe hangs back.

"What's the matter?" Enoch asks.

"Killing a guy? I don't know . . ."

"Ah, they're not going to kill nobody. It's just Laverne talking big. They might rough him up a bit, have a little fun. Won't nobody get killed."

Feeling better, Roscoe joins the others outside. The cold air after the moist warm air of the bar hits Roscoe like a punch. First it takes his breath away, then leaves him coughing.

Roscoe follows Enoch down the sidewalk to a big Buick. Laverne slides behind the wheel. Alden rides shotgun, and Harley and Enoch and Roscoe cram into the back.

Laverne revs the Buick's engine. The other men holler and the car roars like a great monster bellowing its bloodlust.

Laverne turns onto Jefferson toward the city. "This one I'm talking about," he says over the *blat-blat-blat* of the faulty muffler, "he's got an office downtown, in the Penobscot Building. We're going to pay him a little visit."

The men in the car are silent as he drives until Laverne looks in the rear-view mirror at Roscoe sitting behind him. Says, "What do you say, Roscoe. Feel like getting your feet wet tonight?"

"I dunno," Roscoe says. "What does that mean?"

Laverne nods to Alden, who takes a paper bag out from under the front seat. He hands it over the back seat to Roscoe. Heavy and oily with a sweet metallic smell.

"What's this?" Roscoe says.

"Open it," Laverne says.

Roscoe looks inside. A .38 revolver.

Roscoe looks at Harley, then at Laverne's eyes watching him in the rear-view mirror.

"We're going to teach that Hebe a lesson," Laverne says. "You remember the oath you took about protecting Christian America?"

"Yeah," Roscoe says.

"You did good with that cat o'nine tails last night. I believe it's time for your next assignment."

Roscoe looks at Enoch sitting next to him. He's still stumped.

Finally he gets it.

"You want *me* to kill this guy?" Roscoe says.

Laverne says, "Up to the job?"

Roscoe hesitates. I dunno about this, he wants to say. Whipping's one thing. Blowing their brains out, well, that's something else altogether.

"Thought we was just going to scare him a little," Roscoe says.

"Shooting the miserable monkey should do that." Laverne still looking at him in the rear-view, waiting for his answer.

Those blue, almost transparent eyes, staring at Roscoe.

The moment stretches. The men in the car wait for his answer.

Roscoe remembers the feelings from the night before. The feelings of power, of control, of acceptance into something larger than himself.

Of having found where he belongs.

"Yessir, Mr. Penney," he says finally. "I believe I am."

It feels as if the other men in the car let out a collective breath.

"No need to be formal. Call me Laverne."

Laverne takes a right onto Griswold from Jefferson and goes down two blocks, Left onto Congress. Pulls over and turns in his seat.

"You know the Penobscot Building?" he asks Roscoe.

"Not exactly."

"End of this block. Tallest building in the city. Can't miss it. Keep your piece in the bag and hold it down by your side, like it might be your lunch. There'll be a directory on the wall when you walk in. Guy you're looking for is called Maurice Sugar."

"Maurice Sugar," Roscoe repeats.

"Take the elevator to his floor and look for his office. This time of night, he should be alone."

Alden asks, "How do you know he's even in there?"

"Oh, he'll be there. A buddy of mine told me he works here. Them Jew lawyers never let an hour go by without trying to make a buck. He's not there, it'll be his lucky night. What's the guy's name again?" Laverne says, like he's quizzing a little kid.

"Sugar," Roscoe says.

"Aces. I'll go down the side street and make a circle around the block. You ain't out when we pass by, I'll keep going around until you come out. Walk back down here, and we'll come and get you. Okay?"

"Fine."

This is it. Roscoe's chance to show them what he's made of.

Hell, it's a chance to show *himself* what he's made of.

He's never shot anybody before. Never killed anybody.

His head spins a little from all the whiskey in his Coke. And now all of a sudden his bladder feels full and starts to ache.

"Ready?" Laverne asks. "You know how to shoot a gun, don't you?"

"Sure do" Roscoe considers asking if they can find him a place to piss first. Decides he should wait until he gives this Jew the business.

Roscoe steps out of the car. Slams the door shut. The Buick peels away. Roscoe looks around. The street is empty. Quiet. The only sounds are his footsteps in the chill air.

He walks down the sidewalk past the Ford Building, its windows dark at this hour. The Penobscot Building rises next to it.

Suddenly he has to piss like a racehorse. Can't wait!

He steps into the alley between the two buildings and lets loose a furious stream behind a dumpster.

When he finishes, he goes back out to the street and looks up at the towering Penobscot. Massive, tiered at the top, with a huge arched entrance beneath the carved head of an Indian chief. Four revolving doors under transoms that gleam like gold even in the night. A few lights are on here and there. The ground floor is mostly dark except for work lights in the rear, near the elevators.

Roscoe has never been here before.

He has never been to any of the commercial buildings or hotels or restaurants in downtown Detroit. Once in a blue moon he used to come down for a movie at the Fox or the Michigan or the State, or shop with Melanie at Hudson's at Christmas. They haven't done either since he lost his job. Detroit's downtown feels like an unknown and unwelcoming foreign country to Roscoe.

He pushes through one of the revolving doors into the building. The lobby is low-ceilinged and wide, with an Indian design inlaid in the marble floor. The ornate space presses in on him. He imagines the swells who work here with their expensive suits and fancy offices and pretty secretaries. He's cowed at the thought of them. Feels himself to be small and shrinking.

He looks around for the directory. Don't see one anywhere on the marble walls.

Hears, "Help you, pal?"

Roscoe flinches at the sound. Wasn't expecting anyone.

He looks for where the voice comes from and sees an old guy in a gray uniform sitting at a desk behind a column on the left of the lobby. Guy's giving him the fisheye. Don't look happy.

When Roscoe, tongue-tied, says nothing, the geezer hauls himself to his feet and limps with a stiff leg around the counter. Comes right up to Roscoe. A short, fat, and old guy, with a round bald head fringed with white. Broad Polack face giving Roscoe the once-over.

And not liking what he's seeing.

Plus he's toting a gun in a holster on his hip.

Bigger than the one in Roscoe's paper bag.

"I asked what you want," the old guy says. Even more unfriendly.

"I'm here to meet a pal upstairs," Roscoe gets out. Hears his voice echo, lost against the marble floor and walls.

The guy keeps giving him the eye. Settles on the paper bag with the piece by Roscoe's side.

"Yeah?" The guy keeps his eyes on the bag like he can see right through it and knows what's inside. "This time of night?"

Roscoe nods.

"What's his name?"

For a moment, panic-struck, Roscoe can't remember. He wasn't expecting this. Wonders if he should invent a name. Realizes this guard would know all the people who work here. Or else he can go over to his desk and look up the name Roscoe gives and discover it's a phony.

"You can't remember your pal's name?" the old guy says when Roscoe stays mum.

"No, I'm just trying to remember if he told me he's going to be working tonight."

"You come all the way downtown to meet a guy you can't remember his name, and you dunno if he's even here?"

"He's more like a business associate."

"You remember the business name?"

Roscoe shakes his head.

"You can't remember his name or his business," the guard says. "How about the office number?"

Roscoe feels this getting away from him. He regains control, says, "If I can just look at the directory, I know I'll recognize it right away."

"How will you recognize it if you can't remember it?"

Good question. It stumps Roscoe.

Now the guard says, "What's in the bag? Or you forget that, too?"

"No," Roscoe murmurs.

"You know what, bub? It's time to go."

"Wait, it's Sugar. His name's Sugar."

"Sugar."

"Yeah. Maurice Sugar."

The old guy shakes his head. "Got nobody here by that name."

"Are you sure? Maybe check your directory?"

"I'm sure, Sonny Jim. Never heard of him. Musta got the address wrong. Now beat it."

The old guy holds out one hand to urge Roscoe toward the doors. Places his other hand on the butt of his gun on his hip for extra persuasion.

Roscoe lets himself be shepherded out the revolving door. The guard stands inside, watching Roscoe on the sidewalk. Roscoe looks up and down the street. Empty.

Laverne's car appears down at the corner and makes the fast turn onto Griswold. Screeches to a halt in front of the Penobscot.

The guard watches as Roscoe jumps into the back seat and the car peels off.

"Well?" Laverne asks.

"The old guy wouldn't let me go up."

"What old guy?"

"The guard in the lobby. Wouldn't let me in the elevator."

"Why the hell not?"

"Said our guy don't work here. Said he never heard of him."

"Goddammit," Laverne says as he speeds toward Jefferson. "Somebody gave me the wrong information."

Alden reaches a hand into the back seat. Says, "Give."

Roscoe surrenders the oily paper bag with a mixture of relief that he never got to use what's inside, and embarrassment at the spectacle he made of himself with the guard. Glad his new brothers weren't there to see it.

This can't happen again, he orders himself.

9

CLARENCE BROWN

Clarence and Bessie at home. Saturday night.

Bessie works on a quilt, painstakingly sewing worn patches of his old cotton shirts together onto a backing fabric. Her mother was a quilter, and her mother's mother. It's how she preserves their family's history and keeps herself and her husband warm in their drafty home in this Godforsaken northern climate.

After DeMarco passed, she made a quilt of his old clothes. It's gorgeous—colorful squares of his shirts and pants and pajamas with cowboys. Too good to use, so she keeps it folded in the linen closet.

Quilting also gives her something to do when her husband's mind wanders, as it often does.

Now Clarence sits and dozes. He is still worn out from his efforts earlier in the day, on top of the turkey dinner Bessie made for supper.

The telephone wakes him with a snort. "Want me to get it?" Bessie asks. He shakes his head and lumbers groggily into the dining room, where the candlestick phone rings in its alcove.

He answers, "Brown." Listens for a few moments. Sighs, says, "Okay," and hangs up.

"Who was it?" Bessie asks.

"Albert. Body on Belle Isle."

"What's it got to do with you?"

"Colored boy. Albert said he thought I should get down there."

"You in charge of every dead colored boy in the City of Detroit?"

He gives her a look.

"Is it—?" she asks.

Clarence sighs again. "I need to go see."

Belle Isle is a 900-acre island park in the Detroit River between downtown Detroit and Windsor, Ontario. Clarence takes his Ford coupe across the bridge onto the island and follows the ring road around to the far northeast side. At the edge of the woods near the zoo, a half-dozen cars are parked beside a small utility shed. Detroit coppers mill around the shed, pointing flashlights at the ground they are trampling over, obliterating tire tracks or footprints or trace evidence of any kind.

Damn fools. If there was evidence here, it's long gone by now.

What do they care? Just another dead jigaboo to them.

He pulls up and steps out of his car. Nods to Albert Holmquist, the detective who called him. His closest friend on the force, and the only white man who gives him the time of day.

"This is bad, Clarence," Albert says. "Better get yourself ready."

"What's going on?"

"Lindenauer didn't want to call you. I said it would be good to have you here."

"Tell me."

"There's a young man in there," Albert says, nodding at the shed. "He's been hung, Clarence. Colored boy."

"So you said on the phone."

Albert nods. "I thought you might be able to help."

Clarence snorts. "That'll be the day when they ask me."

The knot of police separates to let him go through to the shed. These crackers don't want him on the force. Most of them probably wish he was hanging next to the young Negro inside.

Fuck all y'all, he silently tells them. Just get out of my way.

A reporter Clarence recognizes from the *Detroit Times* stands outside the door. A round little guy with big glasses and a big brush of a mustache. He holds a notepad. A wide-shouldered uniform blocks the reporter from seeing inside.

The patrolman stands back to allow Clarence through.

"Tom Glover from the *Times*," the reporter calls after Clarence. "Are you with the police?"

Clarence ignores him.

Groundskeeping equipment fills the shed—lawn mowers, a giant pair of rusted hedge clippers, wheelbarrows, shovels, rakes, a bucket of ashes. Four detectives and two uniforms, all white, crowd the rest of the floor space. They train their flashlights on the body hanging from a rafter.

They turn to look at Clarence, who comes into the small building. The scene appalls him.

"What are you doing here?" the oldest detective of the group asks him. Ray Lindenauer, head of the precinct house detective bureau.

"Thought you could use my help."

The others turn back to Lindenauer. He takes his fedora off and runs a hand through his long silver hair. Vain sonuvabitch.

Lindenauer ignores Clarence. Gets back to describing what he sees. One of the young dicks copies it down. Danny Canavan. Skinny, unformed, rimless glasses, always looks like he's about to burst out laughing at a joke only he can hear. Usually attached at the hip to Lindenauer.

"The body of a male Negro," Lindenauer says, "suspended from a rope by a noose around his neck. Wearing only his skivvies, shirt and shorts. Age approximately nineteen to twenty years. Ligature marks on the wrists and ankles. Face shows evidence of battery with contusions. No other apparent wounds to the body."

The top of the rope has been secured over a rafter. The body sways at the end of the rope in the cold wind coming off the Detroit River through the open door. Near the body, a chair lies on its side.

"Brown," Lindenauer says, "long as you're here. You recognize this boy?"

Clarence first has a flash of anger—sure, all us shines know each other in this here city, boss—but chokes it back because in fact he does know the young man hanging there.

Clarence tries to swallow. He has no moisture in his mouth. He can only nod.

"What's his name?"

"Darius Turner," Clarence gets out.

"Make a note," Lindenauer orders Canavan. To Clarence: "Know him?"

Clarence finds his voice and croaks, "I do."

Darius can't have been here for two weeks. The body's in too good a shape. No signs of decomposition. He was put here recently.

Clarence says, "What are you waiting for? Why don't you cut him down? Why you leaving him swinging in the wind?"

"We're waiting for the coroner," Lindenauer says. "Can't do anything till he gets here and gives us the okay."

"Who found him?"

"Copper taking a ride around the park, sees the shed door open. Stops to check, finds our boy here."

"When?"

"Little over an hour ago."

"Over an hour ago and the coroner isn't here yet?"

Lindenauer shrugs. "Going to be dead whenever the coroner shows."

"Where is he now?"

"Send him on his way."

"What about it, boss," Canavan says. "Looks like we might have us a suicide."

One of the uniforms guffaws and Clarence sees red, takes a step toward him.

"Easy," Lindenauer says. "In fact, why don't you go outside. We're almost done in here."

"I bet you are."

"Excuse me?"

"Nothing." Clarence takes a look around before he leaves the shed. Ashes all over the floor, but all the footprints have made them useless for forensics. None of the tools hanging from the walls seem disturbed.

He goes close to Darius's body and examines his bare feet. No sign of ashes. Stone cold. Clarence lifts Darius's undershirt and sees a mass of bruises and what look to be recent cigarette burns.

"Suicide, my ass," he says. "Look at his face. Look at these bruises. Somebody tortured this boy before they killed him."

"Thank you for your opinion, detective," Lindenauer says. "I might tend to agree. But my interpretation's slightly different. I'd say this boy got himself in a fight, which he lost badly, by the look of him. In a fit of despair and shame, he killed himself."

Clarence can't even respond.

"You're dismissed," Lindenauer says.

Clarence leaves in a huff.

The *Times* reporter steps in front of him as soon as he gets out the door.

"What did you see in there?"

Clarence pushes him away with enough force to knock the reporter to the ground. Clarence walks away from the shed.

Albert Holmquist catches up, asks, "Do you know him?"

Clarence brushes off the question. He is in no mood for another ofay at this moment, even his only friend in the department.

He hears a siren coming on the ring road around the island. The coroner's wagon slows and stops outside the circle of prowl cars.

The coroner, Warren DeBlasio, gets out of the van and saunters into the shed. Five minutes later he comes out and motions for the attendants to start their removal of the body.

DeBlasio lights a cigar. The reporter asks what was the cause of death. DeBlasio says, "Most likely suicide."

When he sees Clarence, he throws a thumb over his shoulder. "They want you in there." Breath stinks of whiskey.

Clarence goes back in. The attendants are cutting down Darius.

"Suicide?" Clarence says. "You know this boy didn't kill himself. Where's his clothes? Where's his shoes? How'd he get here? The chair's way over there—how'd he climb up? Why were his wrists and ankles tied? Why's his body maimed? Why aren't his feet dirty?"

"How could you even tell," one of the uniformed cops mutters.

Lindenauer ignores the questions. "You know this kid, right? Know his family?"

"I know him. Only family's his mother."

"How about you do the notification. Save me time."

And a trip into niggerland.

Clarence says, "I can do it."

"Good deal."

"Sgt. Lindenauer, I want to be part of the investigation."

"Investigation? There ain't gonna be no investigation. You heard the coroner. This was a straight-up suicide."

"You know this wasn't any suicide. See the shape of him? You're telling me you're not going to look into this?"

"We don't have resources to investigate every colored death in this city," Lindenauer says.

He looks at the other detectives. "Christ, that's all we'd be doing."

The rest of them smirk.

Bessie is already in bed, ready for sleep. He sits next to her.

"It was Darius," he says.

"Oh, Clarence, no."

"They lynched him, Bessie. They hung him in a shitty little storage shack on Belle Isle."

"Oh sweet Jesus. That poor boy."

"I have to tell his mama."

She hugs him as close as she can get with the metal plates he wears under his coat and he can feel her sob. "Poor Ella," she says into his shoulder. "Poor Ella."

In a few moments, she holds him at arm's length, examines his face. He can see the wheels turning behind her eyes, figuring out what needs to be done.

She jumps into action. "I'll come with you."

She throws clothes on, puts a scarf around her head, goes out to the dining room to make phone calls. She calls half a dozen women from their church Missionary Society and tells them to meet her downstairs at Ella's building. And on the way, stop by for the women who don't have phones, and call the pastor.

While she does, Clarence sits in his chair in the living room and holds his head in his hands. He's seen plenty of death before; it's not often you know the victim.

This one hurts.

Already the what-ifs are starting. What if Clarence had looked for him sooner? What if he was a better detective? What if Ella Turner had come to him right after Darius disappeared?

What if they lived someplace else?

In another city. Another country.

On another planet.

Bessie comes into the living room. She is all business. "Ready?"

"Bessie, how many more of us gonna get killed?"

"Come on, now. You know those questions got no answer. Got to leave them in the hands of the Lord."

If that's the case, he thinks, we're fucked.

She pats his shoulder. "Come on, now," she says again. "Ella has to hear this from us first."

He trails after her down the stairs and out to the street. Down at Ella's apartment building, the Sisterhood has already begun to gather. They are crying and hugging each other. When all the women have arrived, along with a few of their men, Clarence leads them up the stairs to Ella's apartment.

He knocks on the door. Ella is still awake. She flings the door open with an expectant look. She sees Clarence standing there with his tragic face, looks behind him to see the women crying on the landing.

It takes only a moment to sink in.

"Ella," Clarence says, "can we come in?"

She screams, "Nooooo!" The raw sound tears at Clarence's heart. She slams the door on him. "No!"

Clarence sticks his foot in the doorway and Ella turns away, howling, bent double. Clarence stands aside and lets the women come in to do their work.

How it goes.

Men die violent deaths at each other's hands, and the women have to come along and pick up the pieces.

Other tenants on Ella's floor open their doors to see what the commotion's about.

10

Ben Rubin

Ben spends another hour at the Unemployed Council. He listens to speeches picking apart Henry Ford's view of the laziness of the working man, and watches children grow increasingly restless until their families leave the meeting. He looks around for Elizabeth. She must have gone. Miriam and Isaac left already. She wasn't feeling well.

As the crowd in the event hall thins, the speeches get angrier. Mayor Frank Murphy starts to come under fire from the Communist speakers for not doing enough, for being a "social fascist." "His relief programs are not only ineffective," one speaker thunders. "They undercut the more radical solutions this city needs!"

The last two speakers talk about the Hunger March planned for Monday. When one of them starts in on the Jews and their capitalist banking conspiracy, Ben decides it's time to go.

He doesn't feel like going straight back to Miriam's, so instead he walks in the general direction of his own home. The speaker's words about Jewish conspiracies still ring in his ears. It's always about the Jews . . . both Henry Ford and this guy tonight say the same thing: the Jews are conspiring to take over the world and must be stopped.

The great irony is, to Ford and his ilk the Jews are all Communists, and to the Communists the Jews are all part of a capitalist cabal.

Fucking anti-Semites.

He walks faster as he grows aggravated.

For the first time, he starts considering leaving Detroit. The anti-Semitism of Henry Ford, the anti-Semitism of Father Coughlin on his radio shows, the incidental anti-Semitism he meets everywhere outside his own neighborhood—on the street cars and buses hearing people talking about how pushy the Jews are, standing in line at newsstands talking about what the latest pamphlet said about the evils of Jews—it's infuriating.

And chilling. If Ford and the Communists are on the same side against the Jews, where can he go? Where is there refuge?

The *Detroit Jewish Chronicle* he reads at his sister's is filled with articles about the rising violence against Jews in Germany and all across Europe: Jewish students abused by the Nazis seizing power and filling schools with young followers at every level, anti-Semitic leaflets distributed in Switzerland, gangs terrorizing Jews in Bulgaria . . . no place is safe from the rising hatred of Jews across the world.

So why not get what you can? There are places we can't live, there are jobs we can't have, there are people everywhere who hate us . . . so why not rob and steal? Why wait till another person has the upper hand? Get yours now and to hell with the rest.

And yet . . . as he walks along he remembers Eddie. That's what we tried to do, get for ourselves. Instead, Eddie never came home from their bungled try.

Poor Eddie, potted by a Detroit copper. Did the copper know Eddie was Jewish? If he did, would he have felt extra good about taking out a crook and a Jew in one fell swoop?

Between the hatred unleashed by Henry Ford and Father Coughlin, this is a bad city to be Jewish.

But it's a bad city to be a lot of things right now . . . a working man, unemployed, a Negro . . .

He stops at a diner for a take-away coffee to warm him. The Greek behind the counter looks hard at him, as though trying to decide whether Ben will pay. Ben lays his dime down and the Greek grudgingly fills a paper cup.

Ben sips as he walks down the darkened streets. He needs to talk to his mother. By now she will probably have heard all the rumors about Ben being with Eddie when he was shot. He'll have to face her.

And he'll especially have to avoid Eddie's uncle, Harry Millman. Everybody knows Harry's a crazy man, a violent man to be feared. Eddie bragged about it.

Ben's parents live in an apartment building on Dexter. His uncle Moe, his mother's brother, is staying with them until his trial date. Ben's father's probably "working," the euphemism for when he's out with one of his girlfriends. He meets them when they come to shop at Hudson's where he works.

His latest is a showgirl from the Gold Dollar on Cass Avenue. Ben caught them walking out of the Book Cadillac on Michigan. She was buxom, brassy, and young, six inches taller than Ben's father—just the old man's type.

It wasn't the first time Ben spotted his father with one of his dames. Ben's mother knows all about it. When he's with them, at least he isn't home.

Ben climbs the creaking wooden stairs to the third floor of their building. Stops in front of their door. Places his ear against it and listens. Hears the radio.

Shit. His father's home after all. The old man spends his nights at home listening to the radio news on WWJ. So his mother will be asleep and Moe will be in the spare room, sleeping or reading.

Ben decides this can keep until tomorrow.

He goes downstairs and cuts across the back alley to the next street over, where Bernice lives with her parents. They own their own home; Bernice's father teaches math at Central High School.

They live in a bungalow on Buena Vista. The porch light glows. Ben goes around to the back, where the bedrooms are. He goes up to the window of Bernice's first floor room and taps on the window.

The edge of the shade opens; Bernice's little sister Laura peeks out. There's something wrong with her. She's slow. She doesn't go to school. Sweet, loving kid, though. Ben's crazy about her. He's pretty sure she feels the same about him.

Behind the closed window, Laura shakes her head.

He mouths, "Bernice," and points inside, raises his hands.

She shakes her head again. He mimes confusion and she leans down to open the window a sliver.

"She's not home," Laura hisses.

"Where is she?"

"I don't know."

Laura shuts the window and draws the shade down.

Bernice didn't say anything about going anywhere when he talked to her yesterday.

He walks back around to the front and sits on the curb. Lights a smoke. Waits.

They have been going together for over a year. They have not talked about marriage, or even mentioned love. She tells him she is "saving" herself for marriage, so sex is out. Petting is allowed, but only up to a point. She has strict rules of engagement.

Nevertheless, Ben believes they both share the common impression they will wind up together.

Three Camels later he sees her sauntering down the block. He can tell it's her because she has a characteristic sashay. She swings her shoulders and arms when she walks like she doesn't have a care in the world.

She's with someone . . . He can't tell who in the dim light of the street, just that it's a man.

They're holding hands.

Ben jumps up off the curb where he has been sitting and fades into the shadows.

He watches the guy walk her up to the front porch. They nudge each other playfully, in a way she never did with Ben.

They sit on the glider and begin to neck. Ben sees his girlfriend lay back and pull the guy on top of her. Guy's getting handsy, too, under Bernice's coat. On this cold night they're wearing too many clothes to get much done but they're sure going at it with kisses. Doing with this guy exactly what she does not do with him, Ben realizes with an ache.

Great. Just what he needs to see tonight of all nights.

His anger flares up and he steps out of the shadows. Prepares to jump in. Has a flash: no good will come out of making a scene. It will only make him sadder. And annoy her.

Instead he skulks away into the night.

He'll be spending the night back at his sister's after all.

11

ELIZABETH WATERS

"Fancy car," Elizabeth says.

She sits beside Horace as he speeds up Jefferson. It turns into Lakeshore in Grosse Pointe Farms.

"A Cord L-29 Cabriolet," Horace says.

He glances sideways at her. She shrugs.

He laughs. "Take my word for it, it's a nifty little buggy."

"So I see."

Glossy black with red trim, a soft top and white wall tires. Shiny wood interior.

"First American production car with front-wheel drive."

"Okay."

He looks at her and smiles. "Still not impressed?"

"It's hard to say how unimpressed I am."

"Not a car buff, eh."

"Nor a conspicuous consumption buff."

"Oho. You've read your Veblen, I see."

"Among others."

He drives on in companionable silence.

"What were you doing at the Unemployed Council tonight?" she asks.

"With a car like this, you mean?"

"Yeah."

"Doing a little homework."

"Meaning?"

He turns left onto Kerby, makes another quick left onto Grosse Pointe Boulevard and a right onto Vendome.

Her old street.

He pulls into the circular drive at 89 Vendome. It is a faux-chateau, with an asymmetrical plan and a complicated roofline with assorted gables.

"Let's go in," he says. "We can talk later."

Outside the car, she stands for a moment. Looks at her old home, across the street and two houses down. She expected an ache in her heart when she sees the place for the first time in years. Surprisingly, she feels nothing. It's like picking up a book she once read, one that had infuriated her when she read it but now leaves her cold, unable even to remember what had once been so distressing. People who were strangers to each other lived there then. Complete strangers could live there now, for all she knows. And all the difference it would make.

"Coming?" Horace asks.

She follows him inside his family's home.

The same cavernous spaces she remembers. She had spent more time here than in her own house. The foyer is massive, whitewashed plaster with dark wood trim. A gigantic chandelier hangs over the floor. A curving staircase with a wrought-iron railing leads to the second floor.

All just as she recalls it, as though preserved as a museum.

Or a mausoleum.

Horace leads the way through a hallway to a sitting room larger than Elizabeth's entire apartment in Palmer Park. A grand piano occupies one end. At the other end is a wall of books with hand-tooled leather bindings. They look like they have never been opened.

"Have a seat," Horace says. "I'll go find Mother."

Elizabeth's mother's house was not as grand as this one. Lulu Howcroft was her best friend all through grade school and high school. As their lives diverged, Elizabeth had heard Lulu had gotten married. She hadn't heard about her former friend's death.

But she hasn't kept in touch with anyone from those days. None of her girlfriends. None of the boys she used to know. She supposes they have paired off by now and are popping out little replicas of themselves.

Lulu and Horace's father made his money in construction. His firm supplied the materials for the Penobscot Building, the Guardian Building, and the First National Bank Building, among others downtown before the building boom went bust after '29.

Capitalism has been good to the Howcroft family, Elizabeth considers as she walks around examining the silver smoking sets on every small table, the silver candle holders, the reproductions of dancers by Degas and rococo putti, the chandeliers and shoji screens, all yoked together in this room by the force of Mrs. Howcroft's bad taste.

"Elizabeth," a woman's voice calls.

Elizabeth turns. Here comes Margaret Howcroft herself, looking like a pale, almost transparent version of the woman Elizabeth remembers from years ago. Margaret is deathly thin in a royal purple brocade dressing gown cinched tight at the waist. The deep wrinkles of a life-long smoker and drinker crisscross her white powdered face.

She totters up to Elizabeth with her cane and turns her face to receive an air kiss, which Elizabeth delivers.

"How are you, my dear," Margaret says. "How long has it been?"

"At least sixteen years, Mrs. Howcroft."

Margaret blows out her hollow cheeks. "Too long." A threadbare smile. "Come sit, by all means."

Margaret lowers herself onto an overstuffed provincial chair trimmed in gilt. Elizabeth takes the love seat beside it. Horace comes in and sits beside Elizabeth. Makes himself comfortable and smiles at her.

"Sixteen years," Margaret repeats. "I don't recall you returning to the neighborhood very often."

"I didn't," Elizabeth agrees. "I came when my mother died, but not afterwards." She doesn't mention why she refused to return when her stepfather died.

"Terrible thing, when she died." Margaret brushes invisible crumbs off her lap. "Where are you living?"

"Palmer Park. In Detroit."

"I would have thought you'd moved away by now. Do you ever see your brother? Roger, isn't it?" She turns to Horace. "I believe he's still living in their old house, isn't he, my love?"

Horace nods.

"I wouldn't know," Elizabeth says. "I've lost touch with him."

She does not mention Roger's actually her stepbrother, and she has no more desire to see him again than she did her stepfather. As someone who always represented her family as perfect, Margaret would have no sympathy for her. Elizabeth has no doubt her stepfather blackened what was left of her reputation after she moved away. The names he called her to her face were bad enough.

When she graduated high school, she went to Ohio to start at Oberlin. Her mother died during her first semester, after which her stepfather refused to further support her education (or anything else to do with her). She dropped out at the end of her second semester when she ran out of money.

Margaret makes a noncommittal sound with her throat. The subject gets put to rest.

"Horace told me about your husband and Lulu," Elizabeth says. "I was so sorry to hear."

"Thank you, dear. So hard to lose both of them so close together. At least I still have my Horace."

She reaches a shaky hand out to her son. He leans over and takes it.

"And what do you have to say about my handsome boy?" Margaret asks.

"I didn't recognize him," Elizabeth says, truthfully.

"He's moved back from Chicago, you know. He gave up a very lucrative and important job to come home. To be closer to me, you know. I just wish he'd find the right girl and settle down before I die."

Her weary, patrician tone and studied avoidance of Elizabeth's eyes make it clear that she, Elizabeth, will never be in the running to be such a girl.

"When I'm ready, Mother," he says, "it'll happen."

"So you keep saying," Margaret murmurs. "Well, my dear Elizabeth," she goes on, "what are you doing with yourself these days?"

"I'm working at WXYZ radio."

"Oh, how interesting. Doing what?"

"I'm the Assistant to the Creative staff."

"Oh, how interesting," Margaret says again. Though it clearly isn't to her.

"Well, my dear," she says, "so wonderful to see you, after all these years. I was getting ready for bed when Horace told me you were here and I wanted to make sure we said hello."

"It was good to see you, too."

"I'll say goodnight and leave you children to get reacquainted."

She rises in a pained swoop and a cloud of lavender. Horace stands with her and guides her to the door. She presents her papery cheek to him to kiss. He closes the door behind her and returns to Elizabeth's love seat. Sits closer to her.

Says, "Well."

"Well."

"Would you have recognized her?"

"Probably not. She doesn't look well."

"She's dying."

"What of?"

"It's her liver. You can't drink the way she has all her life and expect to come away unscathed."

"Such a shame."

"Speaking of drinking, I'm going to have a nightcap. Join me?"

"Sure."

She watches him go over to the bar on a cart at the side of the room. Crystal decanters filled with amber liquids and crystal tumblers. He is different from the angular young man she remembers, more filled out and fully formed.

In many respects, though, he is the same: still the confident golden boy swagger, the fair-haired good looks. The smug assurance of being the prince of his own world.

"Scotch okay?" he asks.

"Fine."

He pours them both a few inches in two whiskey glasses. Brings one to her. They tap glasses. "To old friendships renewed."

Quality hooch. None of your bootleg rotgut for Hooker Howcroft.

"Nice," she says.

"Before Prohibition went into effect, my father stocked up on enough liquor to last us for years."

"Smart man."

"Always was."

While they sip, they chat.

He asks where she went to college.

She tells him and he tells her he went to the University of Michigan. Of course. University of Michigan grads she knows always tell you within the first ten minutes of meeting them. He probably asked her where she went to school just so he could tell her about U of M.

"What did you study?" he asks.

"I wasn't there long enough to study anything. I left after a year."

"Why?"

She rubs her thumb and forefinger together in the universal gesture for money.

"I did pre-law," he tells her. "What have you been doing since?"

"Working here and there. Mostly in radio, like I told your mother. What are you doing these days? After leaving your lucrative and important job in Chicago."

He seems to miss the irony. Just like the old Horace. Born with a serious humor deficiency.

(Meantime, Horace keeps refilling their glasses from the whiskey decanter. Slyly, as if she won't notice. She lets him. She watches this unfold with amusement. She can't remember the last time she went on a bender. She's certain it won't be tonight, with him.)

He eases closer to her. Sweeps an arm around her shoulder.

"My immediate plans are focused on you," Horace says. Gives her a vulpine grin. This guy thinks he's got it all, and he's using every bit of it on her.

She wonders if this usually works with his floozies. It's not working with her.

She knows exactly what's going on. Another man on the make. She's met enough of them to be able to write a script for him.

Still, he's not bad looking. Seems fit. And it's been over a year since the last time she was with anyone . . .

It would get her thoughts away from Sid Ballenger and Phil Mulcahy and the mess at work, speaking of scripts. And the mess in the world.

And even though she feels pleasantly tipsy, sleeping with him would put her in control . . . because she's in control, even though this sap probably believes he's the one leading her along.

"What about your mother?" Elizabeth asks.

"By now she's probably already poured herself a glass of Tincture No. 23."

"Which is?"

"Laudanum. Trust me, she's already well on her way to dreamland. She won't bother us."

He stands and holds out a hand. "Besides, my room's in another wing of the house entirely. She'll never hear us."

She takes his hand and stands. The room tilts. She is drunker than she thought.

He guides her down a long corridor and up another set of stairs at the far end of the house.

She feels like she has gone back in time. His room is still set up for a prep schooler, with a University Liggett banner on the wall and newspaper photos of Charley Gehringer and Heinie Manush from the Tigers. Trophies for track and field, golf, and baseball from Liggett line the knotty pine dresser. Horace was just a boy when she knew him. She had been in many bedrooms similar to this, down to the Liggett banners and sports trophies.

She reads the inscriptions:

Horace Howcroft, Detroit High School League 1917 record holder for the 50-yard dash.

Horace Howcroft, member of the 1917 Michigan High School Athletic Association Open Class State Championship Team.

Horace "Hooker" Howcroft, Highest Batting Average and Lowest Earned Run Average, 1916 Detroit High School League.

"Weren't you just the star athlete," she says, "Hooker."

"There was a pitcher for the Tigers called Hooks Dauss. We both had a wicked curveball."

He comes up behind her, puts his hands on her shoulders, draws her close. She feels his erection against her.

"I'm ready for more grown-up games now," he murmurs into her ear. "Aren't you?"

What a smoothy. Knows exactly what's going to happen even though he hasn't seen her in almost twenty years.

He presses himself into her, starts kissing her neck. Which makes her shiver, despite herself.

She turns to face him and they kiss. He begins unbuttoning her dress. Opens it all the way and lets it fall to the ground. Reaches behind her to unfasten her bra and lets it tumble away from her breasts. Bends to kiss them and mash them with his hands.

She grunts at the discomfort, pushes his hands away. They fall to her underpants. He slips them down over her hips and she stands there naked. Get your fill, bucko, she thinks. This won't happen again.

He steps back, takes her in. Sheds his own clothes, lets her take him in. (He is starting to run to fat in the belly, she notes.) He turns the overhead light off. Guides her to the bed. Takes down the bedcovers, and, stopping only to put on a sheath, slides in beside her. A few kisses and he rolls on top of her and pushes himself inside.

"Wait," she says.

She's not ready. He doesn't care. Before she is entirely wet, he thrusts himself further in, moaning theatrically. He rocks back and forth, comes within seconds with a great groan. He stays on top until she feels him begin to shrivel. He rolls off, breathing hard.

So much for the endurance of the aging star athlete.

"That was great," he says.

He strips the sheath off and tosses it in the trash basket beside the bed. Lies there, catching his breath.

As though remembering she is still here, he reaches out and puts an arm around her. His body is warm. May as well take it where I find it, she tells herself, and lets herself be folded into his embrace.

He lies quiet for a while. He starts to snore. He has fallen asleep.

Ah, Hooker. You sure know how to treat a girl.

Rather than face getting up, throwing her clothes on, and calling a cab to take her home, which she can't afford, she settles in. Turns over and pulls the covers around her.

She's slept in worse places.

With worse men.

12

ROSCOE GRISSOM

"You done good tonight," Alden tells Roscoe. "You're a good soldier for America."

"That's a fact," Laverne agrees.

Standing beside Laverne's car in his driveway, Roscoe dips his head in acknowledgement. He's thrilled to hear them say it. Nice to get recognition for a change.

The men in the car throw him a goodbye wave and pull away.

Roscoe trudges up the front steps of his house. Goes inside.

The house is dark. Blessedly quiet. The brats must be asleep. With any luck, his wife will be, too.

Not so fast.

Before he can even get his coat off, Melanie comes into the living room in her robe. She must have been sitting in the dark in the kitchen.

"Roscoe," she hisses. "Where have you been?"

Roscoe sits in his chair in the living room. Melanie stands there, arms folded, waiting for an answer.

"I went down the bar."

"You been gone for hours. I was worried sick. I thought something awful happened to you. I almost called the police."

"Everything's fine. I saw a couple guys I know. Had a few drinks with them."

"A few drinks? Everything's fine? When I been sitting here for hours waiting for a phone call to tell me you was lying dead somewhere?"

Roscoe sulks. He never says he's sorry, and he's not about to start now. Especially after a night like this.

"Roscoe?" Melanie says. She stands over him. "Roscoe, I'm talking to you. Have you been at the bar the whole time? Roscoe, I'm asking you a question. Have you been at the bar this whole—"

Before she can finish, he is up on his feet and taking a swing at her. An uppercut connects with her jaw, which slams together with a *clack!* The punch knocks her backward and she stumbles over the coffee table behind her. She drops, out cold.

He stands over her. "Goddammit, now look what you made me do, you dumb bitch."

He hoists her up and gets her on the couch. An angry red lump is already forming where he hit her. Muttering under his breath, he goes into the kitchen and gets ice out of the ice box and wraps it in a towel.

When he gets back to the living room, she is coming around. Mumbling something. He kneels down and applies the ice pack to her jaw. The second she feels it, she begins to thrash her arms to protect her face.

Her thrashing knocks him on his ass. He stands up, throws the ice pack at her, and storms out of the house.

After a night like he's had, he don't need this shit.

The Dew Drop's closed so he walks around his neighborhood on Detroit's east side for another hour. Goes up and down the streets filled with the little box houses like his own. All dark at this hour except for the occasional light outlining a figure moving around inside. Most of the men, like him, are out of work.

He mutters to himself the things he should have said to Melanie . . . Who the hell are you to tell me what I can or can't do? I'm a grown man, I can do any damn thing I want and you can't say nothing to me. You ain't my boss. Your job is to care for those goddamn kids, and believe me you ain't doing such a hot job. You was better at your job, I might not have to leave in the first place . . .

And so on.

By the time he returns home, he has calmed down. He steels himself for another go-round with Melanie. In the living room he sees she is still stretched out on the couch, where he left her. She snores.

He decides to leave her there. He climbs the stairs, strips off his clothes in their room, and slips into bed.

Does what he hardly ever does: he reflects on his life. And how it got him to this point.

He was born and raised in Beech Bluff, Tennessee, a little burgh outside Jackson. His father was a mechanic for the railroad and a proud member of the Ku Klux Klan; Jackson was a junction for both trains and the Klan. When his father died in a railroad accident, the family—Roscoe's mother and his five brothers and sisters—fell deeper into poverty than they already were. They lost their home and went to live with his mother's parents.

Roscoe couldn't take it. So many people living under one roof, a drunkard for a grandfather who tried to beat his own frustrations onto Roscoe. He left at fifteen and went to work on a cotton farm. There he met Melanie, the daughter of another tenant farmer. He hated farming with a passion, and after he and Melanie married (over the heated objections of her family; they thought he was white trash, not that they were so fancy themselves), they decided to head north to look for work.

They settled in Detroit because they heard jobs were going begging in the automobile industry. They bought a little shitbox of a house. Melanie started pumping out kids.

It all started going to shit.

The first girl, Annie, set the tone for the others. Never could keep a decent tongue in her head. Talked back as easy as breathing. The other two, Prudence and Harlene, were no better because they had Annie as their teacher. Since the day Annie was born, Roscoe hasn't had a peaceful meal.

And they're all female so it's four against one in most arguments.

Harlene.

There's a name for you.

Melanie picked it out, of course. Named after her favorite aunt back in Tennessee. Might as well put a sign on her: *My people are hillbillies.*

Except this group he belongs to now will change all that. And they're only just beginning, too. He's getting in on the, what do you call it, ground floor of something big. Something important. For once in his life.

It's like an army. He's part of an army of like-minded men. And he's going to be one of the officers because he's in at the beginning. And they're trusting him. They're seeing what he's capable of.

They're going to win back the respect for the white race that's been lost over the years.

Roscoe tells himself they're going to do Jesus's good work on earth.

SUNDAY, MARCH 6, 1932

13

CLARENCE BROWN

C larence sits at the Second Baptist Church, even though he doesn't believe anymore. He goes every Sunday to keep his wife company. He can't believe in a God who would visit the kind of suffering on people that Clarence sees every day. A God who created people who would shake babies to death and burn their feet with cigarettes, who would shoot their husbands and wives, who would hate their fellow man with such fury, let alone have to endure the ravages of cancer.

Or have to bury their only child.

He lets his mind wander as Rev. Badby gives what are to Clarence's mind overly-simplified versions of scripture. Clarence studied scripture as a boy in Kentucky and knows there's more to Jesus than a white man sitting at the feet of a God like a benevolent old white plantation master with a long white beard. No wonder Wallace Fard is catching fire. People aren't totally stupid. Fard may be a con artist, but he's offering the people something they need . . . a way to resist a system designed to keep them inferior.

The other thing is, church lasts for hours . . . the sermonizing, the singing (with Bessie in the choir), the testifying . . .

When it's finally over, Clarence leaves his wife in the company of the Missionary Society to prepare food for the church supper later on. Afterwards, the women will take food to the shut-ins around the neighborhood, including Ella Turner. Ella couldn't get herself to church this morning, which everyone understands.

Clarence stops at home to put on his two pistols and makeshift bullet-proof plates. Bessie insists he doesn't wear them to church. Hastings Street is just coming alive at this hour of the middle afternoon. The sportin' life players are starting to stir after a long Saturday night. The righteous are headed home from church.

Dancy's Barber Shop already hops. A quartet of men sit in the shop waiting for Otis Dancy, the only barber working on Sunday. These are the men who fall between the high livers and the churchgoers; like Otis, they are regular men looking for a little earthly company to ease their burdens.

The man Clarence wants to speak with is part of the group.

The lilt of conversation and laughter in the shop stops when Clarence enters. Everything goes quiet except for the buzzing of the clippers in Otis's hand.

Clarence returns nods from the men.

"Mr. Clarence," Otis says. "How you doing this fine afternoon? Come for a haircut? Going to be a few minutes."

Clarence says, "No haircut today." He looks at one of the men sitting in the waiting area, who avoids his eye. "Ronald. Got a minute?"

It's not really a request. When Mr. Clarence summons you, you go. Ronald looks at the big policeman standing in front of him and knows he can't refuse Mr. Clarence.

To save face, he makes a joke of it. "Well, since you asking me nicely."

The men sitting around smile.

"Okay with you, we talk in the back?" Clarence asks Otis.

"Be my guest."

Clarence leads him behind a curtain to the rear of the shop, a cramped space smelling of lavender pomade and bay rum.

"What can I do for you, Mr. Clarence?"

Clarence leans in toward him. "You know who Darius Turner is?"
"I do."

"Seen him lately?"

Ronald pauses for a few seconds, like he's trying to figure all the angles in the question. Says, "Never see him no more."

"This isn't one of his stops?"

"No sir. Used to was. Another boy, he come make the pickups now."

"Who?"

"Name Joseph. Tall boy, dark skin?"

"Don't know him," Clarence says. Dancy's is a numbers shop, and Darius Turner was a runner, picking up and delivering the money pouring in from the numbers game.

"When's the last time you saw him?"

"Darius?" Ronald thinks for a few seconds. "Not for a couple weeks."

"Don't know what happened to him?"

Ronald shakes his head. "I did hear something about him setting up his own book."

"Darius going on his own?"

"It's what I heard. Don't know how true it is."

"What else you hear?"

Ronald lowers his voice. "Also heard he shorted a couple payouts."

This was serious. "Who to?"

"Dunno."

"Who'd you hear it from?"

"Just on the street. You know. You hear things."

"Who would know for sure?"

"You might try them boys down the hotel. They always on top of things."

"Okay then. Thanks."

Clarence walks out of the barber shop to the men's goodbyes. Hears them start up their conversations again with an explosion of voices.

He continues on to the Hancock Hotel further up Hastings toward Adams. It is one of the oldest establishments in the city where Negroes can stay; they are not welcome at any of the big hotels downtown. The Hancock is the hub of the numbers action in Black Bottom and Paradise Valley. All the numbers shops in Detroit feed into it, so there's constantly money going in and out.

As a result, a group of young men always lurks around the front of the hotel, providing security. They come off like a bunch of doofuses—laughing, slapping palms, flicking butts at each other all day long—but they're hard boys. Clarence has either tried to recruit them for his summer leagues when they were younger, or else nabbed them at one point or another while they were growing up. Usually it was for assault, occasionally for attempted murder or arson. These knuckleheads could be vicious, no mistake.

Two are standing, the rest sitting back against the stoop in the hotel entrance. The skunky odor of reefer is strong.

Clarence goes up to one of the young men sprawled against one side of the stoop. Lanky, hair marcelled to a shine. Cookie duster under his bottom lip. Cashmere coat, perfect creases in his slacks.

"LaMont," Clarence says, "how you doing?"

LaMont turns a placid smile on Clarence. He is a habitual reefer smoker. The weed in the city comes from the Mexicans; they bring it here when they drop their numbers off every day from Mexicantown.

"Never better," LaMont says.

His other boys stop their fooling and come up to skulk behind Clarence. He knows they wouldn't dare try him. It's just intimidation.

He opens his coat to reveal his guns anyway.

LaMont says, "How might I be of assistance, Mr. Clarence?"

"What do you know about Darius Turner?"

The name provokes a burst of throaty laughter from LaMont's boys. LaMont himself just keeps smiling up at Clarence.

"What's funny?" Clarence asks.

"Excuse my associates," LaMont says. "They got no manners."

Clarence stares them down. "Why y'all laughing?"

They glare back at him.

94

When he gets angry or annoyed, Clarence seems to puff up and get bigger and even more menacing. He's doing it now.

LaMont recognizes it. "Calm down, now, Mr. Clarence. They just playing with you."

"Did you hear what happened to Darius?"

"No. What?"

"He's dead. Found Saturday night out on Belle Isle."

LaMont frowns. His boys look at each other. "News to us for sure."

"He was lynched."

"Damn." LaMont seems genuinely saddened. He turns to his boys. "Any of y'all know anything about it?"

They shake their heads.

"Sorry to hear it," LaMont says. "I liked the young man. Ofays done it?"

"That's what I'm trying to find out. What do you know about him?"

"Only what I hear."

"You haven't seen him?"

"No, man."

"What do you hear?"

"I hear he keeping company with a hooer. Staying with her. People say so, anyway. But people say anything."

"You know her name?"

"No. People say she work for Madame Savoyard."

"Whorehouse on Second Avenue?"

"Yeah. You been there, right?"

Big shit-eating grin on his face. Titters from his audience breaks the mood about Darius. So much for their grief.

LaMont knows Negro customers aren't allowed in Madame Savoyard's, only the crème of the Detroit white power structure—politicians, policemen, business leaders. Same with the girls: all white, except for one or two Negroes for those customers with a taste for the chocolate side.

"Hear anything about a Cadillac?" Clarence asks.

"Might have did," LaMont says coyly.

If there were any prostitutes in Detroit who could afford a Cadillac, they would be the ones working for Madame Savoyard.

Still, Clarence only has the word of a juicer that there was a Cadillac or a woman in the car. Or even that Darius got in the car at all. Who knew what was the truth?

Questions for later.

"I heard something about Darius setting up his own book," Clarence says.

LaMont just looks at him. Innocent and wide-eyed, like butter wouldn't melt in his mouth.

"You hear anything?" Clarence asks.

"Darius work for Robinhood. Don't nobody set up no book without his say-so."

The city's policy king, Quincy Rowe, called "Robinhood" because of all the good deeds he's responsible for in Black Bottom and Paradise Valley . . . food relief programs, donations to churches, even cash to help pay bills. It's not enough to stem the grinding desperation of the times, but it helps.

"He in now?" Clarence points his chin toward the door to the hotel.

"No sir," LaMont says.

"Know where I can find him?"

"I truly don't."

"Nothing else you can tell me?"

"Uh-uh. Being straight with you, man."

"How about any of you?" Clarence looks to LaMont's boys. They stare stonily back at him.

"Okay," Clarence says. "I find out you lying to me, LaMont, I'll be back."

"Ain't no lie, Mr. Clarence. I tell you true."

Clarence turns to leave. After a beat, LaMont's boys step back out of his way.

LaMont says, "Hey, wait, wait, wait: I helped you, what you gonna do for me?"

Big smile back on his face.

96

"*Do* for you? I'm not gonna arrest your skinny black ass for smoking reefer. That's what I'm gonna *do* for you."

Another wave of scornful laughter from LaMont's boys.

Clarence straightens his guns at his hip and walks off.

Always leave them laughing.

Robinhood Rowe owns a half-dozen nightclubs and another dozen speakeasys and blind pigs in Paradise Valley. It might be too early for him to be up and around. Clarence checks anyway. He walks north on Hastings, across Gratiot Avenue, and looks into the Club Three Sixes, the Forest Club, Club Plantation, and a half-dozen of the storefront venues for music and illegal booze called blind pigs.

He gets lucky.

Sees Robinhood sitting at one of the tables in front of the bandstand in a nightclub. Light-skinned, with a neatly-trimmed pencil mustache under a straight nose. More than a little white in his blood, because he could pass if he wanted to, except for the conked hair.

He listens to a blind Negro guitar player with a round face. The musician sits onstage with one leg crossed over the other, picking out a syncopated ragtime tune with the tempo and energy of a stride piano while he sings in a high tenor.

Clarence sits at the next table. Robinhood notices him, nods a greeting, and lets the bluesman finish his song.

Because they got wild women in Detroit, that's all I want to see
Because they got wild women in Detroit, that's all I want to see
Wild women and bad whisky would make a fool out of me.

The musician lets the final chord ring. Robinhood claps. "Mmm," he says, "that was righteous."

"Thank you, sir," the guitar player says. Deep South accent. "Can I play you another?"

"I'd love to hear another. But look here—why don't you take five? I believe I got business with this gentleman." Looks at Clarence.

The bluesman stands. A woman comes up to guide him offstage.

"What you think, Mr. Clarence?" Robinhood asks.

"Just what you said. Righteous."

"Blind Blake. Come over from Chicago. Song called 'Detroit Bound Blues.' Voice like he knows all the suffering in the world. Music cuts right to my soul."

"Mighty fine guitar work."

"Oh, he's the best. He's opening here on Tuesday. You should come down and hear him. I'll leave a couple of ducats for you. On the house."

"I just might."

"But I believe you're not here to talk music appreciation. What can I do for you, big man?"

"I want to know about Darius Turner."

Robinhood frowns. "Poor boy. I heard he got himself killed."

"I don't guess he had much to do with it."

"Most unfortunate. What do you expect me to know about it?"

"You know most things go on in this part of town."

"My business depends on knowing things."

"Darius worked for you. Ran your numbers."

Robinhood shakes a cigarette from a pack of Lucky Strikes on the table. Fits it into an ivory cigarette holder and lights it with a complicated-looking lighter. "If you say so."

"I heard he opened his own policy shop."

Robinhood takes a drag of his smoke, blows a ring, examines the ash on the end.

"Well," he says, "I'll be straight with you. The boy used to work for me, it's true. Up and disappeared a while back. I haven't heard anything about him opening his own book. And just like you said: I would know."

"When was the last time you saw him?"

Robinhood scratches his chin in an exaggerated pantomime of cogitation. "Must be a couple weeks now. Otis Dancy, he told me Darius didn't show up for a couple days around then. I had to find another man to fill in. New young man doing a fine job, too."

"Also heard a rumor Darius was shacked up with one of the girls from Madame Savoyard's."

"Big man, the only thing I heard about Darius since he dropped out of sight was what you just now told me. I wouldn't know anything about the young man's love life."

"So you're telling me you don't know anything about what happened to one of your runners."

"Sadly, I don't."

"You didn't make any effort to find him?"

"Like I said, he just disappeared. Didn't take any of my money with him. He did, I'd be on him like white on rice. As it was, only thing I was concerned with was picking up his slack."

Takes another long drag on the cigarette.

"How'd he die?" Robinhood asks.

"Lynched. On Belle Isle."

Robinhood clucks his tongue. "This a savage city for people like us, Mr. Clarence. A savage city for sure. I'll make sure to send flowers to his mother."

"I'm sure she'll appreciate it."

"Even though he left me," Robinhood says, "I bear no ill will toward the young man. I hear anything about what happened, I'll let you know."

14

BEN RUBIN

"Well," Ruth Rubin says, her voice heavy with sarcasm, "if it isn't my wonderful, wonderful son."

She sits at her kitchen table drinking coffee in her floral housecoat. She runs her pudgy hand over the red and white check oilcloth cover, brushing away invisible crumbs.

Ben enters the kitchen and sits across from her. Already regrets having come home. "Hey, ma."

"Where have you been?"

"Miriam's."

"You couldn't let me know you're all right, your best friend was killed two nights ago? I wouldn't've appreciated knowing you were okay?"

"Sorry, ma. I was too upset about it."

"Oh, you were upset? Well, at last you're *sorry*. That's much better, I'm sure."

She gets up and lets her coffee cup drop in the sink with a crash. "Such *nakhas* I get from my surviving son. One son's a hero, and look at my other one. Practicing to be a bum like his uncle. Well, at least you're *sorry*."

She goes into the front of the house.

Ben stays put. Hates the way she makes him feel: angry, sad, humiliated, guilty . . . He should know by now. Small chance she'd welcome him home with open arms.

He goes back in the room he shared with his brother Allen before Allen volunteered for the American Expeditionary Force in the war. He died fighting in Belleau Wood. His mother tells everyone Allen died a hero. To Ben, he was sacrificed in a slaughterhouse for no apparent reason he could see.

Ben sits on the bed, tries to pierce through the miasma of emotions to decide what to do.

Finally, overcome by the need to flee this house, he pulls a valise from under the bed. Throws clothes together from the dresser drawers. He has been wearing the same clothes since Friday night. He also needs a shower; he didn't take one at Miriam's because he didn't want to use up her hot water. Maybe he can take one tonight.

He for sure doesn't want to spend any more time here than he needs to.

He didn't get a chance to ask his mother where his father or Moe was. His father is probably either working or tomcatting; Moe might be home. Ben can't stop to look for him.

He leaves without saying goodbye to his mother.

He goes to Bernice's.

Stands on the front porch with his cardboard grip like a drummer.

Knocks on the door until he hears footsteps inside her house.

Bernice opens the inner door. "Hello," she says, through the storm door. She does not make a move to open it.

"Hey."

She notices his bag. "What are you doing, moving in?"

"I just went home to get a couple of things. Thought I'd stop by, say hello."

"You're leaving?"

"For a while," he says, though he has only at this moment decided for sure.

"Where to?"

"I'm staying with Miriam for a bit. Until I find a place."

"Wait," she says.

She shuts the door so she can open the front hall closet door and opens the door again with her coat on. Steps outside to the porch.

"You don't even want me to come in?"

"My dad's sleeping on the couch in the parlor. I don't want to wake him."

"Right."

"You don't believe me?"

"I was just hoping to get warm for a couple minutes."

She hugs herself. "What's going on at home, you have to leave?"

"My mother. I can't stand it anymore."

"Did you hear about Eddie?"

Another pang of guilt pierces him. "Yeah."

"Police said there were two guys."

"I heard."

"One got away." Her gaze drills him. "The second guy wasn't you, was it?"

When he doesn't say anything, she says, "Benny, you were *there*? And you just *left* him?"

"There wasn't anything I could do. I could see he was a goner as soon as he took the bullet. The whole top of his head was gone."

"What are you going to do now? Eddie's uncle's Harry Millman. He's not going to let you get away with this."

"With what? I didn't fucking shoot him."

"He's not going to make that distinction. He's going to want to make somebody pay."

"So let him take it out on the cop who did it. Anyway, how's he going to find out it was me?"

He gives her a sharp look.

She avoids it. "Not from me."

He wants to ask what's going on, why's she so unsympathetic?

And while we're at it, who was the guy last night, and why was she letting him stick his tongue down her throat?

Her stern look makes him decide against it. The information won't do him any good. It'll just make him feel worse.

"Well, okay," he says. "I wanted to see how you were doing. Haven't seen you for a few days. You're alright?"

"Yeah, good." She gets ready to go back inside. She can't bear to spend any more time with him than she has to, he realizes.

"Take care of yourself," she says.

102

Sounds a lot like the big kiss-off of 1932.

Eddie Millman lived with his mother Rose in a two-family on Clements, north of Davison. The street around the house is parked-in with cars up and down Clements. Through the window to their flat, the lower one, he can see people moving around.

Sure you want to do this? he asks himself one more time.

And one more time, the answer is no, he would prefer not to do it. He has to. He has to pay his respects to Eddie's mother and her side of the family. Eddie was his best friend.

The front door is open. He leaves his valise in the front hall and enters the living room. The house is subdued, the low sad murmur of shiva. Men and women stand around. No one is eating much even though the dining room table groans with brisket, potatoes, kugel, rugalach and other baked goods, all brought by neighbors. Traditionally, the food is for the mourners, not the visitors. The cushions are off the furniture, sheets cover the mirrors. Sitting shiva is for thinking about the deceased, not for comfort or vanity.

Heads turn when Ben walks in. He expects accusatory glances and frowns. Instead he gets nods of acknowledgment and greeting. Maybe they don't know yet. Isn't it written all over his face? He was there with Eddie; people should be able to tell just from looking at him.

He ran away when his best friend fell dead.

He left him on the sidewalk.

He sees Eddie's cousins, uncles, and aunts. Friends from the neighborhood. Friends of his parents. All give him polite greetings.

One older man shakes his hand, says, "May his memory be a blessing."

Ben goes back into the house, looking for Eddie's mother. He finds her in Eddie's bedroom. She is sitting sobbing and rocking back and forth on Eddie's bed, as though she were davening. Her friends attend to her, the women patting her arms and rubbing her shoulders. She is a widow. Eddie's father, Harry Millman's brother, died from a stroke years before.

She looks up, sees Ben standing there.

Says, "Oy Benny," reaches out a hand. He takes it and bends down to hug her and plant a kiss on her damp cheek.

"Thank you for coming," she says. "You were such a good friend to him. My Eddie loved you."

"I loved him, Rose," Ben gets out. Tries to keep from crying in front of her. Or in front of any of them. "I'm so sorry."

"I know you are, Benny. Now he's gone. He's gone." Still in disbelief.

It starts her crying again.

Ben stands there, feeling foolish. There must be a hundred things to say, but he can't think of one.

He feels himself being pulled backwards, out of the room and down the narrow hallway. A rough hand on his arm hauls him away.

Solly Abrams, Rose's cousin, pulls him out and walks him through the living room, holding tight.

"Wait, Solly, what—"

Solly pushes him out the front door to the covered front porch.

Down the steps and around to the side of the house.

Two other men wait there. Ben knows them both. The taller of the two is Hymie Fleischman. The other one is Isadore Bernstein. All three are Purples.

Solly braces him against the side of the house.

"Solly," Ben says, "what—"

Hymie steps in and takes a swing at him with a sap. It connects on the side of his head. Ben sees stars and goes down.

Isadore kicks him in the stomach.

Solly picks him up and slams him against the brick wall of the house. He shakes his fist in front of Ben's face. Solly wears brass knuckles. "We know it was you," he says right up in Ben's face.

Ben can only manage, "What?"

"We know it was you with Eddie."

"No," Ben says, "Solly, you got it wrong."

"Yeah? Eddie told Izzie he was gonna hit the picture show with you. Tell me I got it wrong, tough guy."

Isadore stares daggers at Ben. "Why didn't you do nothing to help him?"

"No, please," Ben says, "there wasn't anything I could do."

"So you just left him there?" Isadore snarls. "He takes one in the head and you, what, saved your own ass?"

"Izzie, I couldn't do anything for him. I stopped, I did. He was already gone. I couldn't do anything."

"Well, there's something we can do for you," Solly says. He punches Ben in the stomach with the knucks. Solly holds Ben up and follows it with one to the face. It fractures his cheekbone.

Hymie pulls a revolver out of his coat and puts the barrel against Ben's temple.

"We're gonna leave you the same way you left Eddie," he growls. "With a fucking hole in your head."

From across the street comes a shout. "Hey! Hey, leave him alone," a voice yells. "Hey, somebody call the police!"

The three gangsters turn to look and Ben breaks free from Solly's grip and races into the backyard. He hears the crack of gunfire. Hymie takes a shot at him.

Ben bursts through the gate into the alley and keeps going through the backyard of the house on the next street over.

Behind him he hears one of the three men shout, "We're coming for you! You're fucking dead!"

He keeps running.

With his face killing him and his ribs aching, he runs for his life.

Again.

15

ELIZABETH WATERS

Horace sleeps late on Sunday morning.

Elizabeth was awake most of the night. She missed her nightly dose of Miss Em and didn't fall asleep till after four, and even then only got a couple hours in before she woke with a killer headache. She hates to sleep in strange beds anymore, hates to sleep with strange men, hates to wake up with a hangover.

She is too old for this.

But what did she expect? She was too tired to get up and find her way home, so she stayed.

She pushes the covers back to leave the bed when Horace reaches out and holds her with a hand on her shoulder. He wants to go again. She pats his arm and gently pulls away. Once was enough, Hooker. Once was too much.

She says, "No. My head is killing me." She dresses and pads into the bathroom. Glad to close the door and get privacy for her thoughts.

As a screw, this wasn't much. He was close to one of the worst, in fact. Over for him as soon as it began. Probably how he is in the rest of his life: out for himself, unconcerned about anybody else. A typical product of his upbringing and education.

Sex as social analysis.

So why did she go with him, she asks herself sitting on the toilet.

She can blame her two rules, she tells herself: One, never turn down sex unless the guy is totally repulsive, which Horace wasn't . . . physically, at least.

And two, never turn down an opportunity to fuck over, as it were, her background, this neighborhood, the system that gave rise to it and all the people in it. To prove to herself she is free from its spell.

He may have thought he was in charge last night, but make no mistake: she was in control.

As usual.

When she returns to his room, he is up and dressed. She feels the odd sense of distance in the wake of intimacy with a stranger, as though the physical closeness cemented the separation between them rather than bridging it.

Not for him, apparently. He enfolds her in a hug. She smells her own perfume on him. Smells his sweat. His skin.

They go downstairs. She hopes to sneak away before having to confront his mother. She's not there. Instead, a woman is going over the living room rug with a carpet sweeper.

They have a maid.

Of course they do.

And she's Negro.

Of course she is.

"Mother's already been down?" Horace asks the maid.

"Had breakfast early and went back upstairs. Wasn't feeling so good, she said."

Horace nods his thanks. "Maisie, this is my friend, Elizabeth. Elizabeth, Maisie. Maisie helps out my mother."

Maisie gives a slight curtsy, which breaks Elizabeth's heart. She wants to shout: *No! Don't curtsy to me!*

To Maisie, Elizabeth is just another white woman.

"Can I make you two breakfast?" Maisie asks.

"No, thanks," Horace says. "We have other plans."

He wants to take her to the restaurant at the Statler Hotel on Washington Boulevard downtown. She protests. She wants to go home; she is tired; she needs a bath.

He insists. Refuses to drive her home, in fact.

Over coffee at the Statler, while waiting for their food—pancakes for him, eggs benedict for her—he gazes at her with a strange smile on his face. A drunken roll in the hay has turned into a *date*.

No.

To break the mood, she says, "So. You're back from Chicago."

He nods.

"What did you do there?"

He pulls himself up straight. "I was the District Attorney's counsel for the Radical Squad. Their version of our Special Investigations Bureau."

"Your job was to keep tabs on the Communists in Chicago?"

"Actually, that was the Radical Squad's job. My job was to make sure what they did was mostly legal."

"Mostly?"

His slimy grin again. "We bent a few rules when we had to. All in the service of the greater good."

"I guess this explains why you were at the Unemployed Council last night."

"Yeah. We had them, too, in Chicago. Also organized by the Reds."

"This was the homework you were doing? See what's going on here?"

"Except it's more than curiosity. It's part of my new job."

"Which is?"

"I'm administrative director of the Detroit Police Department's Special Investigations Bureau," he says. Can't hide the smirk. "Second deputy chief in the department. I oversee the SIB. I work out of 1300 Beaubien."

Police headquarters.

She sits silently for a few moments.

"You run the Red hunters?" she says at last.

"A step up from what I was doing in Chicago. More responsibility. Plus my mother's getting older, as you could see. She's started falling, and it's been worrying me."

He takes a sip of coffee. "Now we've reconnected, we can spend more time together," he says. "If you want, of course." Like, who in their right mind would turn down such an offer.

Instead of answering, she says, "Aren't you wondering why I was at the UC meeting yesterday?"

"I assume you're connected with the Council."

"You assume or you know?"

"Last night was the first time I'd seen you in sixteen years, Liz. I haven't exactly been keeping tabs on you."

"But now you know I'm with the Unemployed Council."

"Are you a Communist?"

She tries to interpret his grin—is it patronizing? Superior? Supposed to be charming?

She decides he's calculating how in his position, it can be helpful to be sleeping with the enemy.

To test the hypothesis, she says, "Yes. In fact, I am."

He nods. "Could be useful."

"Useful," she echoes.

Her wheels turn.

"In fact," she goes on, "I bet our little reunion yesterday wasn't just a cosmic accident. You knew I'd be there. I'm in your files. You came to see me because you thought I might be 'useful.'"

He shrugs a shoulder. "How are your eggs?"

Annoyed, she leaves her food unfinished. She wants to take a cab home from the hotel after breakfast. He insists on driving.

He stops the fancy car in front of her building in Palmer Park and turns toward her. Says, "Nice place."

"Thanks."

"Good view of the park?"

She nods, suddenly groggy from lack of sleep and drinking too much last night and eating too much rich food at the Statler this morning.

And from spending too much time in the company of the Red Squad's head lawyer. It's all too much for her.

"I want to see you again," he says.

She considers the question, more in terms of how to say no than whether she wants to or not.

Gives him what she knows is a pained smile.

(Wonders if he's ever gotten one of those before.)

"I don't think so, Horace. It was nice to see you again, but . . . we don't have a future."

"Why not?"

"I think you know."

For a moment, he looks like she just slapped him. He blinks and quickly recovers. Gives her his confident smirk. "I'm going to keep asking you, you know."

She lacks the energy to dispute it with him. She gets out of the car and feels his eyes on her back as she walks to the front door of her building. She goes inside. Hears him rev the Cabriolet and take off with a squeal of tires.

Horace Howcroft, Communist hunter and rejected beau.

She lets herself into her apartment and heads directly to her shower. She was supposed to go to a meeting today for tomorrow's march. She is just too beat.

Besides, first she needs to wash Horace Howcroft off her. Scrub him out of her pores.

She showers, dries off, takes a dose of Miss Em, crawls under the covers in her bed, and sleeps.

She dozes for two hours. When she wakes, she realizes she has missed the meeting about the march anyway. No matter; she knows what they were going to say, and she knows what she is going to do.

She gets dressed and stands in front of the living room window with a cup of coffee. The apartment does have a good view of the park. She loves the view and the convenience of the apartment and the district she lives in, filled with gorgeous apartment buildings put up since the first one designed by Albert Kahn.

Warming her hands around the coffee cup, she goes to the sofa. Has the persistent feeling Horace is going to be a problem. Not just because he wants to see her again and she has no desire to continue this. No, his anti-Communist mission has the potential for causing trouble. She knows men like him, whose zeal blinds them to everything else.

Fortified by the caffeine, she gets her coat on and goes downstairs to catch the Woodward Avenue streetcar downtown. She may have missed the meeting about the march, but she can still make the Unemployed Council soup kitchen.

She makes a transfer across town and gets off at the church where the Council meets. There are three times as many men here as there were yesterday. Once the meeting about the march had broken up, most stayed on for soup kitchen.

She helps prep for the meal, getting the utensils and plates ready and lighting the cans of sterno under the pots to keep the food warm. The meal ready, she wanders around the church basement, saying hello to people she knows, inquiring after the health of children who have been sickly, finding out what she might have missed at the earlier meeting about the march.

As she suspected, there wasn't much she didn't already know about.

Just as the soup kitchen opens, she sees that Jewish couple taking their places behind the food service lines. What were their names? Buchman?

No, Buchalter.

There are just the two of them today, though. The young man who came with them yesterday—Ben—isn't here.

She looks around the room. He's not here.

She only spots him toward the end of the meal service. He has arrived late, and sticks to the sides of the big room. He looks bad. And he's moving slowly . . . Even from across the room, Elizabeth can tell he's hurt.

His sister gives out with a yelp when she sees him approaching. She drops her ladle in the pot of stew and darts around the food service tables toward Ben.

Who collapses into her arms.

Elizabeth can't help herself. When she sees someone who needs help, she needs to know what she can do.

She, too, abandons her post and trots out to where Ben and his sister are standing. As she gets closer, she sees he has been beaten. The side of his face is swollen and bruised. He has a shiner. His eye is swelling shut. Leaning on his sister, he hunches over while holding his belly. Spatters of blood—his, no doubt—dot the front of his shirt.

"What happened?" Elizabeth asks. "Can I help?"

"I got jumped," Ben says.

"By who?"

Ben just shakes his head.

"Are you okay?"

He touches the bruises on his face. "I think my acting career in Hollywood is temporarily on hold."

"Let's take him into the lavatory," Elizabeth says. "He needs to be cleaned up."

"I'm Miriam," his sister says.

"Elizabeth."

They help Ben into the ladies' and sit him down on one of the benches there. Miriam wraps toilet paper around her hand, wets it, and dabs gently at the blood on his face and head. Elizabeth wets a cloth and attacks the blood on his shirt.

"Do you know who did this?" Elizabeth asks Miriam.

"I have an idea."

"Miriam," Ben snaps. "Don't say anything."

"As soon as we get you cleaned up," Miriam says, "you're coming home with us."

"No. They're coming for me. It won't be safe at your house."

"Shah. You're coming."

But Miriam's husband says no.

He comes over to the table where they are sitting when the women have Ben cleaned up. "He'll lead them right to us," he says. "Who knows what they'll do, these animals. They'll burn the house down to get to him."

"He's right," Ben says. "I'll find a place to lie low. I'll be safe until this blows over."

"It isn't going to blow over," Miriam's husband says. "You don't know these guys."

"Maybe Moe can talk to them," Miriam says. "Persuade them Eddie wasn't Benny's fault."

"I doubt it."

"I'll stay someplace else," Ben says. "If you got hurt because of me, I couldn't live with myself."

Elizabeth brings him ice wrapped in a towel from the kitchen for his face. Miriam brings him a plate of stew. Ben picks at it without making any effort to eat it. It must hurt to open his mouth. Back at her post behind the food table, Elizabeth watches him sitting there by himself and wonders if he should go to a hospital.

When the soup kitchen hours end, she goes to sit across from him.

"How are you feeling?" she asks.

"A little better. Thanks for your help."

"Sure." She examines the bruises on his face. "Looks painful."

"Uh-huh."

On a whim, she reaches out to touch the side of his face lightly. He winces but doesn't pull back.

"Sorry," she says. "Got on somebody's bad side, did we?"

"You might say so."

"Still looking for a place to stay?"

"Yeah. Haven't had a chance to look yet. The guy I'd normally stay with died. My other buddies don't want much to do with me."

"Sorry."

He shrugs.

"Feels like there's more to the story," she says.

He gives a wan half-smile through his busted face. "A lot more."

In her mind, she's comparing his smile with Horace Howcroft's oily leer.

"Look," she says. "Stay at my place. I've got space. You'll be safe and nobody'll look for you there."

"Why would you do that? You don't know me from Adam."

"I know you need help. We help each other around here. It's what we do. It's decided. Let's go."

She can tell by the gingerly way he gets on and off the streetcar that he is getting stiff. Inside her apartment, she helps him to the sofa. "Do you want to take a bath or anything?" she asks.

"No, thanks. I'm good."

"Might help with the soreness."

He shakes his head.

"How about tea?"

"Tea sounds good."

She goes into the galley kitchen to prepare it. She sees him lying back on the sofa, one arm thrown over his face. She can hear him moaning.

In a few minutes, she brings a tray and two tea cups, the tea pot, and a creamer and sugar bowl into the living room. Before she pours the tea, she goes into her bathroom and pours a spoonful of Miss Em into a glass.

Brings it out to Ben. "Take this. It'll make you feel better."

"What is it?"

"Painkiller."

"You don't need to do this."

"You're my guest."

"Still. I could be a murderer."

"I'll take my chances."

He swallows the morphine, makes a face at its bitterness. She pours the tea and sits opposite him. "Are you comfortable?"

"I make a good living," he says with the trace of a smile.

She laughs, for the first time in what seems like weeks.

"That joke was old the first time I heard it," she says. She pours tea for them both.

"Good comedy is timeless."

"I wouldn't call that good comedy."

He grins and the pain in his face makes him wince. He blows across the cup and sips his tea. His smile is crooked, not showing any teeth. Well, she remembers he has bad teeth, so he's probably self-conscious about them.

"Who beat you up?" she asks.

"Some local guys."

"Why?"

"They think I did something they don't approve of."

"Did you?"

"Not exactly."

"Not a full-throated denial. Sounds like you got mixed up with rough customers."

"Yeah."

She watches him. Now he's watching her, too, his eyes playing all over her face, her hair. She feels looked at, *seen* in a way she hardly ever is. It reminds her of the look Frida Kahlo gave her. Most men, like Horace Howcroft, look at you to see a reflection of themselves in your face, your reaction to them. Your adoration. Not this guy.

"I bet," she says, "you got mixed up with the Purple Gang."

She can tell she's right by his look.

"How did you know?"

"I didn't. I took a guess."

"Good guess."

"I figured you're Jewish, the Jewish gangs in Detroit are the Purples, they're pretty tough guys . . ."

"Two plus two equals four."

She shrugs.

"How'd you know I was Jewish?"

"Please. Your name? Your face? It's no great mystery."

His eyes harden.

She regrets what she said at once. "Sorry. I didn't mean anything. Just an observation."

"Considering what's going on in Europe, I get nervous when a gentile talks about my being Jewish."

"How do you know I'm a gentile?"

Now it's his turn to snort and say, "Please. It's no great mystery. You have *shiksa* written all over you."

"What's that mean?"

"*Shiksa*? A gentile woman."

"*Shiksa*," she repeats.

"You never heard it before? Where did you grow up, Grosse Pointe?"

"I did, as a matter of fact."

"Grosse Pointe, yet what's all this?" He points his chin at the magazines on the table in front of the sofa. *The Progressive. Foreign Affairs. The New Force, a Monthly Proletarian Magazine of Art, Literature, and Current Events.* "You're a Red?"

"I'm a Red," she admits, for the second time today.

"Why?"

"It's complicated."

"I have all night."

She takes a sip of her tea. "I see the kind of desperation out there now." Points her cup at the view out her window. "People are unemployed. Starving. Losing their homes. Being deported. And what does Henry Ford do? He says there's plenty of work if people want to work. What planet does he live on? You especially should see through the sham of capitalism."

"Meaning what?"

"Henry Ford hates Jews, in case you haven't figured it out."

"Yeah," he says dryly, "I heard something along those lines. This city isn't a good place—or time—to be Jewish."

"The whole amoral system's collapsing in on itself. We have to create an alternative social order before it's too late."

"And Communism's the alternative?"

"It's better than capitalism as practiced by the likes of Henry Ford. Besides, I consider myself more of a socialist."

"What's the difference?"

"Socialism's an economic system. Communism's a political system. You can be a socialist and still believe in democracy."

"Which you do?"

"I don't know. The only thing I'm sure of is, the people need to stand together and take our country back. Like we're going to do tomorrow."

"At the march, you mean?"

"Yes."

"I heard them talk about it at the Unemployed Council yesterday."

"Are you going?"

"Hadn't thought about it," he says. "You?"

"Absolutely. Come with me, if you feel up to it. We're taking it right to Ford. There'll be thousands of people. We're marching to the employment office at the Rouge Plant. The leaders of the march have a set of demands they're going to present to Ford."

"Demanding what?"

"Improved working conditions at the Rouge plant and relief for all the laid-off workers."

"Will it work?"

"If not, it's an important step."

He watches her without speaking for a few moments.

"How old are you?" he asks.

"Thirty-three. How old are you?"

"Twenty-five."

Before she can respond, he stops, closes his eyes, puts his head in his hands.

"What's the matter?" she asks.

"Suddenly I'm dizzy."

"The painkiller's kicking in."

"I need to lie down."

She gets up and helps him lie back on the sofa. "I'll get you a pillow and covers, and ice for your head. You can rest for the night."

He reaches out and grabs her hand. Without thinking, she pulls it away.

"Whoa. I just wanted to thank you," he says. "That's all."

They share a long look. She takes his hand and gives it a gentle squeeze.

Gets him set on the sofa. Goes into her bedroom. Closes the door.

Pours herself a dose of Miss Em.

Lies on her bed, staring at the ceiling, waiting for it to work.

Turns the word *shiksa* over on her tongue.

She knows plenty of Jews in the movement. Yet they still seem like an alien race to her. The ones she knows are thoughtful, mannerly people. She hasn't met any of the gangsters, but even the tough labor Jews she knows have a hidden depth which people like Horace Howcroft lack. Maybe it comes from being hated for centuries, which creates the foreignness giving rise to all the anti-Semitic tropes people use to describe them . . . they're pushy, they're all about money, they killed Christ, and so on. You hear all this anywhere, at any time of day or night.

She remembers Sarah was Jewish. Sarah Kirschner.

Her Sarah.

They met at the beginning of Elizabeth's year at Oberlin. Sarah was a scholarship girl, an art student, in her first year like Elizabeth. Sarah's father was a tailor in Cleveland, an immigrant who escaped the Russian pogroms at the turn of the century. Sarah was a wild and passionate lover, Elizabeth's first love affair with a woman. There have been others since, but never with the intensity of the feelings she had for Sarah.

It was Sarah who started Elizabeth on her path to articulating her rejection of the world she came from. Sarah was eighteen and already a committed Bolshevik. In 1917, with the war raging in Europe and the czar overthrown in Russia, the world seemed poised on the brink of a change, a real leap forward. Sarah was out demonstrating for peace, and there was Elizabeth right beside her.

Elizabeth fell in love with Sarah's mind first, then her body, then her soul. They would lie in bed after making love and talk for hours about Karl Marx, Lenin, and revolution. When the fall semester ended, Sarah went home to Cleveland. She didn't return when the new semester started in January. Elizabeth wrote her and never got an answer. She tried calling Sarah's house, and never got through.

One day, she got a letter postmarked from Cleveland. She tore it open, hoping Sarah was writing to explain why she hadn't come back.

Instead, it was Sarah's mother, telling Elizabeth Sarah had taken her own life on New Year's Eve.

"We're at a loss to explain it," Mrs. Kirschner had written. "We are devastated."

So was Elizabeth. Bereft of her best friend, she began spending less time in class and more time with the wastrels who used their allowances for bootleg booze in Cleveland. One night she went out riding with a stockbroker's son from Cincinnati who, pie-eyed drunk, rolled his car off the road. He walked away unharmed, but Elizabeth came out of the accident with a severely broken leg that was never fixed properly and constant pain in her hip.

After the spring semester, she, too, left school. She ran out of money and her stepfather refused to support her education (or her injuries or anything else).

She never returned to Oberlin. She came back to Michigan and drifted to Ann Arbor. She lived with a radical student named Ralph for a few years. When they broke up, she wandered to Chicago, then out to Los Angeles, and finally back to Ann Arbor and Detroit. In between, there were men who passed through her life like ghosts, an abortion performed by an alcoholic doctor in L.A., and one or two women but none who affected her like Sarah Kirschner.

Now Elizabeth lies in bed and thinks about Sarah, one of many, many losses in a life that often feels like it's over before it's begun.

16

ROSCOE GRISSOM

At breakfast, the girls notice their mother's bruises and ask her about them. A withering glance from their father tells them not to expect an answer. Melanie wouldn't say anything, anyway. She knows better.

The girls go silent and eat their corn flakes.

Afterwards, Melanie bundles the girls up—the day is unseasonably cold—and they walk to the Bethany Baptist Church on Mack Avenue. Roscoe stays home. He has no truck with church. He had his fill of it when he was young and his own mother dragged him to the Fellowship Baptist Church in Beech Bluff. His father stayed home, as Roscoe does now.

Roscoe believes in Jesus; he believes America is and always will be a Christian country. He just don't have time for all the wailing and moaning from the women, and especially from the pastor, who everybody knows will fuck every woman with a pulse, married or single, given half the chance.

Roscoe feels Jesus in his heart. And not the pansy Jesus the preacher talks about, either. No, the warrior Jesus who chased the moneylenders from the temple. The warrior Jesus who gives his blessings in blood to what Roscoe and his brothers in the Legion are about: purifying this country of the mongrel races who aim to destroy it. The Negroes. The Jews. The Papists. The foreigners with no respect for the American way of life.

Before Melanie and the brats get home, Roscoe heads down to the Dew Drop Inn. It opens at noon on Sunday. No use leaving a note. Knows they'll figure out where he is and be just as glad he's not there when they get home.

The Dew Drop is almost empty. Just a few regulars are at the bar. The owner, Frankie Priziola, has a new stash of hooch. He gets it from his cousin Papa John Priziola. It was well-known around the Dew Drop that Papa John and his partner Nick Ditta own sugar houses and liquor-cutting factories around the city. These supply Frankie's as well as other speakeasies and blind pigs across Detroit.

So Roscoe takes a whiskey into the pool room. Frankie charges a nickel a shot. Even this is too much for Roscoe on a routine basis, but he needs a shot now. He splurges.

In a while, Enoch Jones comes in. Shortly after, Laverne and Alden join them.

They spend the afternoon drinking and playing pool. At dinnertime they order veal and peppers and kielbasa from the grill Frankie's wife runs on the weekends. She gives them credit for the food, knowing they will probably never pay.

Once they have eaten, they pile into Laverne's car.

"Where to tonight?" Roscoe asks from the back. He's feeling good, feeling no pain, loose for a change, happy to be in the warm heart of his new brothers.

"We still got unfinished business," Laverne says. "We got us a Jew to take off the board."

"We still looking for that Sugar guy?" Alden asks.

"Damn right."

"How we going to find him?" Roscoe asks.

"I know where he lives," Laverne says.

The other three men clam up.

Shit's getting real.

They sit quietly while Laverne negotiates the roads into Hamtramck, a small city entirely surrounded by Detroit.

"Hamtramck?" Alden says. "Only got Polacks here."

"Mostly Polacks," Laverne agrees. "There's a small area of kikes."

"That's where this yid lives?"

"Yup."

"How do you know?"

"I got my sources."

"You're telling me a fancy Jew lawyer lives in a shithole place like Hamtramck?" Alden asks.

"I said so," Laverne says, and leaves it there.

He negotiates the big car down the narrow lanes, with streets lined with two- and three-decker frame houses.

They cruise past one house and he says, "Here."

Laverne sails past and crawls around the block. He drives by the house one more time—one of the rare single-family homes in Hamtramck. It's dark except for a light burning in the top window.

He parks down the street. "Here's where he lives."

"What are we going to do?" Alden asks.

"We're going to knock on his front door, and when he opens it we're going to blow that dirty little kike to kingdom come."

"I bet he ain't even home," Alden grumbles. "If this is even where he lives."

"Shut up," Laverne says. He watches the house with narrowed eyes. "I know he's home. I can smell him."

"Jews got a smell?" Roscoe asks. "I knew you can tell them apart by their noses and such. Never knew you could smell them, too."

"Sure," Laverne says. "If you get up close and take a whiff, you can smell the green money oozing out of them."

"What's it smell like?"

Laverne considers the question for a few moments. "Musty. Sour. Kind of like mothballs."

"I heard if you part their hair," Enoch says, "you can see their horns. That's why they wear them little hats."

"If you sneak up on them and drop their pants," Laverne says, "you can see their tails. Got a evil little point on the ends."

"Shut up, all a yiz," Alden barks. "This is the stupidest fucking conversation I ever heard."

"What crawled up your ass today?" Laverne says.

"I'm tired of sitting around waiting."

"Then let's go."

Laverne reaches under the seat and pulls out the bag Roscoe carried the night before.

He hands it over the seat to Roscoe. Who opens it and withdraws the revolver.

"You want me to do it?" he asks.

"You missed a chance last night," Laverne says. "I don't want you to miss this time."

"How do I know what this guy looks like?"

"Don't matter. Whoever answers the door, grease them. This whole street's filled with Jews. You don't shoot Sugar, you'll get one of them regardless."

Roscoe gets out of the car holding the handgun. Laverne rolls down the window. "Hold it behind you," he hisses, "so's nobody can see it."

Roscoe holds it behind him, as ordered.

Then he stands there on the curb staring at Sugar's house like a simp.

"What's the matter?" Laverne asks.

When Roscoe says nothing, Laverne reaches out of the car through the driver's window and pulls Roscoe close.

"Listen," Laverne says, "this is what we do." Roscoe smells the cigarettes and whiskey on his breath. "We're fucking *night riders*. Get me? This is how we operate. And the new guys do the dirty work. Now get moving."

He pushes Roscoe away from the car.

Roscoe straightens. Tries to summon the spirit of his warrior Jesus in his heart. Asks Jesus to give him strength. And courage.

Feeling bolder, Roscoe starts up the street to the house with the light in the top window. If Laverne is saying anything else to him, he can't hear it. He focuses on walking in the dead silence of the street.

The evening is cold. He can see his breath in white puffs. Lights are on in every house he passes. He can feel the eyes of the residents on him from every house, though he can't see anybody in the windows or doorways.

He puts the gun in his coat pocket. If he is spotted, he won't have to worry about explaining why he's holding a .38.

Pauses in front of Sugar's house. Stands there, trying to gin up his courage. Prays to warrior Jesus.

Down the block he sees Laverne flashing his headlights.

Roscoe looks around. Nobody on the sidewalk, no cars nearby. He walks up to the front porch. Climbs the steps. Goes up to the door.

Knocks, hand clutching the gun in his pocket.

Waits.

Knocks again.

Waits.

Listens if he can hear anything inside—footsteps, a radio, conversation, anything.

Nothing.

Knocks a third time.

Decides with relief there's nobody home.

Gets down from the porch and starts back to Laverne's car.

Except another car turns the corner and approaches Roscoe from behind. Slows down. Follows him.

Comes up even with him and stops.

A Hamtramck prowl car.

A spotlight lands on Roscoe.

Who, blinded, prepares to shit a brick.

A uniformed copper gives him the eye out the passenger side window. "You. C'mere."

Roscoe walks over. Tries to be casual.

Hopes the cop can't hear his heart pounding.

"You live around here?" the copper asks.

"No sir."

"What are you doing?"

"Visiting a friend."

"What friend?"

This time Roscoe can remember the name. "Guy named Maurice Sugar." He realizes as soon as he says it that he probably shouldn't have given the right name.

"Nobody named Sugar lives in there," the cop behind the wheel says. "This part of Hamtramck's Poletown."

"Must have got the wrong street."

"Wrong city, more like."

The copper in the passenger seat keeps looking at Roscoe. "Say. What's that in your pocket?"

Roscoe realizes he's been holding onto the revolver this whole time. Squeezing it, in fact.

The cop says, "Take your hand out of your pocket. Nice and slow."

He takes his hand out, holds it to show it's empty.

"That pocket's still heavy," the copper says. "What do you have in there?"

Roscoe sees Laverne strolling toward him. Save me, he silently implores.

"There a problem?" Laverne says.

"Who are you?" the copper demands.

In reply, Laverne tips back his hat.

The copper gives him the cop stare. Tips his own hat back.

They each do this twice more. Laverne says, "Put none but Americans on guard."

The copper says, "Under the star of the guard," and raises a hand in greeting. "You two together?"

Laverne nods.

The cop takes a hard look at Roscoe. Says, "You guys better amscray. This ain't a good night to be out. Things are tense all over on account of the march tomorrow."

"Got it," Laverne says.

The copper nods to the driver and the car drives off.

Laverne grabs Roscoe by the arm. "Come on."

Walks him back to the car.

"You know him?"

"He's one of us," Laverne says. "The thing with the hats? The high sign. Best remember it."

He gets Roscoe into the back seat and says, "Pretty soon we'll be everywhere."

Laverne slides behind the wheel and starts up.

"We just got the word," Laverne says to the others in the car. "This ain't a good night for nightriding."

They drive past the house where Roscoe was knocking on the door. Standing in the open doorway now is a little girl, looking out to see who was knocking before. Small and dark, like a little Jewess.

She watches the men in the car go by.

You're one lucky little Jewgirl, Roscoe silently tells her as they pass. Five minutes earlier, and pow!

He points a finger at her, cocks his thumb like it's a gun.

Next time you won't be so lucky.

17

CLARENCE BROWN

adame Savoyard's is a pretty single-family Victorian home on Second Street with evergreens in pots around the front door. It's one of the few remaining homes left after the boom of the 1910s and 1920s saw construction of apartment buildings up and down Second.

Madame Savoyard's real name is actually Carmella Lombardo. She operates the whorehouse under the protection of Black Bill Tocco, who emerged as the head of the Sicilian gangsters who call themselves the Detroit Partnership after a gangland war during the previous decade. The Purple Gang used to control the city's vice, but now the Sicilians are moving in as the influence of the Jewish gangsters wanes. They're taking over the whorehouses, the gambling parlors, and the drug trade.

The door opens onto the glowering puss of a white man even bigger than Clarence. "Deliveries in the back," the guy snarls.

Clarence points to his buzzer pinned to his overcoat. "I'm here to see Madame Savoyard."

"She ain't got time for no spooks. Get lost."

The doorman swings the door closed. Clarence gets his big brogan in the opening and gives the door a hit with his shoulder. It knocks the brute backwards. Clarence pushes inside.

The doorman produces a sap and swings it at Clarence's head. Clarence steps back from it and comes in with a hard left to the face. Bones crunch under his fist and the guy hits the ground like a safe.

Clarence pulls one of his Colts and points it at him. "Don't you ever talk to me that way again."

On the floor, the big guy raises his hands in surrender.

Clarence straightens and sees Madame Savoyard watching him. A small woman in her forties with dark eyes heavily made up and ruby red Betty Boop lips in a disapproving frown. "What do you think you're doing?"

"Your man here disrespected me. I had to teach him manners."

"Who are you to be teaching manners?"

Points to his badge. "Detective Clarence Brown. Detroit Police."

A tiny Negro maid peeks around from behind the madame.

Clarence's badge calms the madame. "I'm sorry if he said something to upset you. You know your people are not allowed here. Many houses in your part of town would welcome you."

"I'm not here as a customer. I'm here to get some information. I'd rather talk privately."

"I don't have private conversations with Negroes, police or not."

"Fine. I'll ask my questions right here."

The doorbell rings. A customer.

What to do now? Can she be seen talking with a large colored policeman? Clarence has to smile.

The madame turns to the young maid. "Frances," Madame Savoyard says, "please take care of Angelo. Then get the door."

"Yes, ma'am," Frances says.

"You better come with me," Madame Savoyard says to Clarence.

She leads him back through the living room, where three prosties sit draped across the sofa and chairs. The room is aromatic from fresh flowers and the women's perfume. They look at Clarence as though he just dropped in from Mars.

Madame Savoyard unlocks a door and ushers him inside a small office. She sits behind a desk, leaves him to stand. "I'd rather the clientele not know you're here. Ask your questions."

"I'm investigating the death of a young colored man named Darius Turner. Do you know him?"

"How would I?"

"He was seen getting into a Cadillac a few weeks ago. It may have been driven by one of the girls here."

"My girls don't own Caddies, detective. And no disrespect, my girls wouldn't go with a colored man in any event."

"You got any colored girls here beside the staff?"

"Not at the moment. We did have one girl, who serviced clients with a certain taste. I had to let her go."

"When was this?"

"About a month ago. She turned out to be a hophead."

"What's her name?"

"She called herself Bella."

"What's her real name?"

Madame Savoyard shrugs as if this were the last thing in the world she'd care about.

"Do you know if she was seeing Darius Turner?"

"I couldn't tell you what she did in her off-hours. Except use dope. As I told you, I never heard of Darius Turner."

"Where can I find her now?"

"I have no idea. Now," she says, standing, "please leave. By the back door."

She leads him into the kitchen. Says, "Frances, see this man out." She leaves him with the maid.

Young Frances stands preparing a coffee serving. If anybody would know about Bella, it would be her.

"Frances, I'm Clarence Brown. I'm a Detroit Police detective."

She looks fourteen, maybe fifteen. He watches her in silence, tries to gauge her situation from her appearance.

"What's your last name, Frances?"

"McKenney, sir."

"Frances, anybody keeping you here against your will? Because I'll walk you right out of here, you won't have to worry about Madame Savoyard anymore."

"No sir. This my job. My family depend on me."

"Sure?"

"Yessir."

"You remember Bella?"

"Yessir. Except her real name Yolanda."

"Know her last name?"

"Montgomery, sir."

"Do you know where she went when she left here?"

Frances looks down. No reply.

"I'm not going to bring her any trouble," he says. "I just need to talk with her."

"Yolanda, she ask me not to tell nobody where she is."

"But you know?"

Frances steals a look to see if Madame Savoyard is around. Satisfied she is nowhere in sight, the maid nods.

"Can you tell me? You'd be doing her a big favor."

She doesn't answer right away.

"I know you want to help your friend," Clarence says. "So do I."

"She ask me not to tell," Frances says again.

"Somebody from here giving her trouble?"

Another nod.

"Frances, I swear to you, I won't tell anyone what you tell me. I wouldn't ask if this wasn't important."

Frances considers it. Finally she tells him the address. He writes it in his notebook.

"You were friends with her?"

"We talked. But I'm not allowed to spend time with the ladies."

"One last question. You know a colored man named Darius Turner? Thin, nineteen, light-skinned, good looking?"

"No sir." She picks up the coffee tray. "They waiting for me."

He tears off a bit of paper from his notebook. Writes his own number and sticks it in her apron pocket. "You ever need any help," he says, "you call me. And you watch yourself, Frances. This is no kind of life for a girl."

She dips her head in understanding, scuttles away with the tray.

The address is above a doctor's office on East Forest in Paradise Valley. He climbs a flight of stairs and bangs on the door. No response.

Tries the knob.

Locked.

He trudges back down the stairs and goes into the doctor's office. A pretty light-skinned Negro woman in a white nurse's uniform and cap sits behind the reception desk. Three other Negro women wait on chairs in the waiting room, hands clasped on top of their pocketbooks on their laps. In the corner, by a burbling fish tank, a little boy wields a piece of wood like a sword. He wears a toy hat.

"Help you?" the nurse says.

Clarence says, "I'm looking for Yolanda."

"Nobody named Yolanda around here."

He shows her his badge. Identifies himself.

She looks crestfallen. "What she done now?"

"I just need to ask her some questions. She's not in any trouble. She stay upstairs?"

The nurse nods. "She lives with me. She's my sister."

"Know where I can find her now?"

She gives him a suspicious side-eye. "You sure she not in any trouble?"

"No trouble. But she might be in danger. I want to help her."

"What kind of danger?"

"Please, miss. Just tell me where I can find her."

It's a restaurant at Third and Porter Streets in the city's tiny Chinatown. It harbors an opium den below a chop suey joint, Lim's Chinese. As soon as Clarence enters the front door, a Chinese waiter rushes up to him waving a finger in his face and shouting, "No no no! No allow! No allow!"

Clarence shows his badge, says, "Yolanda."

"No Yolanda!"

Clarence sighs. "Bella?"

"Bella work."

"Where?"

The waiter points down. "But no allow!"

Clarence pushes by him to a flood of angry Chinese. He continues through the dining room, empty at this hour, to the kitchen. Through the aromas of green pepper, fried fish, and sweet plum sauce. Through a door leading to the basement. The waiter still screams behind him.

On the steps down, he smells the sweet, flower-like odor of opium mixed with the stink of old laundry and dirty bodies.

The opium den is a large, wood-paneled room with pallets on the floor. It is silent except for the slow breathing of the half-dozen white men and women lying in their dreamy addictions in the dim light.

A young Negro woman tends to them. She carefully wipes the face of an opium smoker who stirs. Hands the man a glass of lemon water. She wears a kerchief around her mouth and nose.

She looks at Clarence. She seems at once frightened and amazed to see such a large Negro man here.

"Yolanda?" he asks.

A nod.

"Detective Brown, Detroit Police. Come with me for a minute?"

"I can't leave. I'm working—"

"These white folks can do without you for ten minutes."

He takes her arm and gently guides her up the stairs and into the kitchen. The Chinese cooks standing at their food preparation stations grin at them with missing teeth. They chatter in Chinese, everything sounding like an angry question.

Clarence takes her out the back door, where more Chinese men squat and smoke.

Outside, Yolanda pulls her arm away. Rips the kerchief off. She is in her twenties. Very pretty, with large, almond-shaped eyes and high cheeks. She could be Asian herself, except he sees the family resemblance to the nurse at the doctor's office.

"What do you want with me?" she asks.

"You worked at Madame Savoyard's?"

"What if I did?"

"You got fired for smoking reefer?"

"Madame Savoyard, she dunno what—"

"I don't give a shit about that. All I want to know about is Darius Turner."

This stops her. "What about him?"

"You the one he was shacked up with?"

"I wasn't shacked up with nobody. Madame Savoyard makes her girls stay in the house."

"You know him, though? You been with him?"

"So?"

"He was seen getting into a Cadillac with a woman at the wheel a few weeks ago. I assume it wasn't you?"

"I look like I can afford a Cadillac?"

"I just want to know what you know about him."

"Whyn't you ask him?"

"He's dead. Somebody killed him."

This is news to her.

"When?"

"He was found lynched on Belle Isle two nights ago."

It takes her a few moments to work through this information. "Who did it?"

"That's what I'm trying to find out. So why don't you tell me what you know about him."

"Nothing to tell. We had some fun together. And he gave me some Mary Jane."

"That's all he gave you?"

"Yeah."

She avoids his eye. He waits.

"No. He gave me other shit."

"Like what?"

She stays silent.

"I'm just trying to find who killed him, Yolanda. I want to get justice for him. I'm guessing that's what you want, too."

"He gave me what I needed to work in that shithole," she says. "Bennies for what I had to do. Reefer and H to bring me down at night."

"Where did he get it from?"

"He never told me. I never asked."

"Still using?"

"Still got shitty days to get through. In case you hadn't noticed."

"He must have liked you."

"We had something," she admits.

"Was he selling it, the drugs?"

"Not to me. But other people, yeah."

"He ever talk about having trouble with anybody?"

"No. Everybody loved him. Sweet as pie."

The back door of the restaurant flies open.

The boss Chinese bursts out screaming a mélange of Chinese and English at Yolanda. Clarence can't make out a word of it. He figures the gist is, she has to get back down mopping white folks' brows.

"One more thing before you go," Clarence says. "When was the last time you saw him?"

"A week after I left the whorehouse. Look, I got to get back downstairs."

"Go on, then."

With the boss Chinese haranguing her, she says, "Don't tell anybody where I am, okay?"

Remembering what Frances said, he asks, "Were you having trouble with somebody?"

"Man, everybody at that fucking place gave me grief."

She gives him one last pleading look before going back downstairs to the opium den.

The Chinese shouts more at Clarence and follows her. But not before slamming the back door in Clarence's face.

Darius selling drugs puts a whole new face on his death. Maybe it didn't have anything to do with the numbers after all. Maybe it was about drugs.

The Sicilians dominated the trade in bennies and horse in Detroit. The Mexicans owned the reefer trade. Neither group was good to get mixed up with. Either group could have taken him out to Belle Isle and strung him up.

If Clarence had to choose, he'd pick the Sicilians over the Mexicans for what happened. With all the noise about deporting the Mexes back home, Clarence guessed they had enough on their hands without having to deal with Darius.

But the Sicilians . . . Black Bill Tocco runs the prostitution at Madame Savoyard's, in addition to the east side heroin trade. If one of the girls—especially Yolanda—was getting her drugs from outside the whorehouse, Black Bill would have heard about it. If he found out Darius was giving it to her, Black Bill might not be pleased.

He also might not be pleased if Darius was trying to establish himself as a dealer.

Still, why would Black Bill Tocco care about what happened to a Negro whore? And if Darius was peddling heroin, he would have to get it from the Detroit Sicilians. They are the source of heroin in the city through their connections to the crime families in Sicily.

So if Darius was selling product Tocco supplied him, Tocco would make sure he got a taste of the money from Darius. Why would Tocco care who he was selling it to?

He wouldn't, not unless Darius wasn't paying him. That question still needs an answer.

Clarence knows where his next stop should be.

But not tonight. This will wait until tomorrow.

Bessie has a pot of tea waiting for him when he gets home.

"You missed the church supper," she says. Not accusatory, just stating a fact.

"Sorry, baby. This has been a day."

"Brought chicken home, you want some."

He takes off his armor and weaponry and leaves it all by the front door. Sits at the dining room table. Bessie brings him his chicken.

He tells her what he's found out about Darius.

"His mama not going to like it," Bessie says.

"No," Clarence agrees. "I won't talk to her until I know more."

"These boys, the sportin' life just too hard to resist, I guess."

"Thing they don't understand, they never come to no good end."

"That's a fact."

After he eats, Bessie takes up her quilting. He sets up the Victrola with Duke Ellington's *Jubilee Stomp* and lets the sinuous clarinet of Barney Bigard carry him away from his heavy, dirty world into one that's lighter. Cleaner. Purer.

It's only a temporary escape, but it'll do.

MONDAY, MARCH 7, 1932

18

BEN RUBIN

Elizabeth is gone by the time Ben gets up mid-morning. Fresh coffee is brewed on the counter in her kitchen and a note propped against the empty cup she left for him.

Ben—

Good morning. I had to be up early to get into work. Later on this afternoon I'm going to the march. It's going to be crazy. I'll wait for you by the entrance to the Woodmere Cemetery on Fort. It's near the starting point of the march. I'll try to find you. I'll plan to be there by one.

Elizabeth

His face killing him, he goes through to her bathroom, sees his reflection. Cheek swollen to twice its size. Dark bruise. Black eye. Even the white of his eye is red. Must be burst blood vessels there.

He opens the medicine cabinet to look for aspirin. He finds a dozen containers of women's lotions and potions, but no aspirin.

He opens a few of the jars and takes a whiff. The scents are magical and enigmatic, like a tropical garden. Women's mysteries.

He goes back to the kitchen for a cup of black coffee. It makes him feel slightly better, so he opens her fridge and discovers it's empty except for a half-filled bottle of milk and a few puckered apples.

He smells the milk: maybe a day or two from turning. He searches through her cupboards—just make yourself at home why don't you, he chides himself—and finds a box of corn flakes and a bowl. There isn't much else. She either doesn't spend a lot of time here, or else eats practically nothing.

He sits down and crunches on his breakfast. The corn flakes are stale and it hurts to chew. He gets them down anyway.

He takes a shower in her bathroom and gingerly puts on the clothes he was wearing yesterday even though his shirt is blood-spattered from the beating he took. He left the valise with his clean clothes at Eddie's mother's house when he made his hasty escape. The center section of the varsity jacket he wears, which used to be his brother's, is dark so the blood fades into the material.

He walks down to Woodward with the intention of taking a streetcar downtown. Cars and pedestrians pack the avenue. The line waiting for a streetcar stretches out. A Packard inches by filled with men and one of them calls out to him. "Going to the march?"

"Trying," Ben says.

"Hop on!"

A hand reaches out from the car and Ben grabs it and jumps on the running board. The guy inside the car holds on to Ben's sleeve and the car takes an abrupt right turn onto Six Mile Road. It accelerates down Six Mile to Hamilton, where it swings left. Ben holds on. He is freezing—it's a bitterly cold day.

They take Hamilton as far as they can, past Herman Kiefer and Henry Ford Hospitals, down to Grand River, then make a jog over to

Fort. They follow Fort west as far as they can. The traffic won't let them go further than the Hungarian cafes and acrid chemical factories of Delray. They turn off to find a parking place and Ben jumps off with a wave of thanks.

He follows the throngs of men down Fort Street toward Dearborn. A few carry hand-lettered placards:

Don't starve in the richest land on earth.

We need bigger relief checks.

In unity with the revolutionary masses we will defeat imperialist war.

Jobs for all laid-off workers.

Free medical aid for all employed and unemployed workers.

He stops at the Woodmere Cemetery, where Elizabeth said she would be waiting for him. Barricades block the entrance and a cop with a shotgun waves him away. Elizabeth would never be able to get in.

He waits around the entrance for another half-hour. By now it's one-thirty. It's impossible to find any individual in the sea of faces, each half-obscured by their hats and the vapor of their breaths. Most of the marchers are men, anyway, with only a smattering of women.

The crowd masses in the intersection of Oakwood and Fort, at the border of Dearborn. There a large contingent of Dearborn police blocks the road to the sprawling Ford Rouge plant. The march comes to a halt.

"They's trying to tell us to go home," a white man beside Ben says. He has a harsh Southern drawl. "We ain't a-leaving."

Ben hears cries of "March on! March on!" coming from the front of the crowd.

The rest of the marchers take up the cry and press forward.

Ben sees clouds of gas billowing over the front lines and the pressure forward reverses.

"Tear gas!" voices shout, and now the crowd pushes to the rear. Between the force of the front of the crowd pushing backwards and the pressure of the crowd from the rear pushing forward, Ben feels trapped in a box. Only when the mass behind him starts to thin as people escape from the tear gas can he can get moving away.

The crowd scatters where the railroad tracks converge near Woodmere. Policemen wielding clubs give chase. The cops are swinging wildly, battering any heads, arms, and legs within reach.

The cold wind disperses the tear gas. As the air clears, marchers stop and pick up stones and bricks from around the tracks and fling them at the police.

Ben joins in. It feels good to fight back.

The barrage from the marchers increases. The police turn tail and fall back on Miller Road toward the No. 1 gate of the Rouge Plant. The marchers regroup and head after them.

Two Dearborn fire trucks are waiting there. The firemen try to connect their hoses to a hydrant but the marchers overwhelm them and force them back toward the No. 3 gate.

Ben moves forward in the mass of demonstrators. Other firemen on the bridge above the No. 3 gate have attached their hoses. As the marchers approach, the firemen open up frigid jets of high-powered water. The water soaks the marchers and turns to ice on their clothes and underfoot. More tear gas bombs sail into the crowd.

Still the marchers shout: "March on! March on!"

Next, men in suits step out from behind the fire trucks and open fire on the demonstrators with handguns and rifles.

The scene: Screams. Gunfire. Chaos.

In the roar of voices, Ben hears one man shout, "Bennett's security goons!"

Two men go down right in front of Ben. Others run away, shouting, soaked from the firehoses and bleeding from gunshot wounds and billy clubs. Ben's eyes sting from the gas.

From somewhere in the rear, Ben hears a voice from a loudspeaker in a car. The words are garbled. He can't make them out.

In the meantime, the No. 3 gate opens and a car roars out. "It's Bennett!" a voice near Ben yells.

The car window goes down and Ben hears the popping of gunfire from inside the car and more workers go down. Harry Bennett, the head of Ford's private security army, holds a handgun out the car window. He shoots as the car careens through the marchers.

Ben joins the others picking up rocks and pelting Bennett's car.

The car stops and Bennett gets out, still shooting.

It looks like he takes a rock to the head and goes down. The other men with him lift him back into his car.

In the commotion, Ben hears a shout: "Retreat!" Two more men go down. Ben hears the rat-a-tat-tat of machine gun fire and the march splits apart as men flee in every direction, desperate to get away from the shooting.

A demonstrator running past with a placard on a two-by-four catches Ben on the side of his head. Ben sees stars, goes down on hands and knees, tries to keep from passing out. Passing out now will not be a good idea, he would be trampled. Stay conscious!

Stay conscious.

He struggles to his feet.

Through the haze of his blurry eyesight and the dust kicked up by the escaping marchers, Ben sees four bodies lying in the road.

Groups of two and three workers brave the gunfire and the billy clubs to lift the bodies of the fallen out of the street and hurry them away. Two bearers are having trouble lifting one of the casualties. Dizzy, nauseous, Ben gets himself together and goes to help.

Together, the three of them bear the injured man away from the guns.

From the amount of blood and limpness of the body, Ben knows the man is already dead.

Ben hears gunfire behind them as the Dearborn police continue to shoot at them.

Wounded workers are everywhere. Police swarm the street, arresting those who have been hurt and can't get away. The road in front of the Rouge plant looks like a battlefield. Discarded signs, lost hats, men helping others limp to safety. Strike pamphlets blow across the road.

When they are out of range of the shooting, Ben and the others carefully lay down the man they were carrying. A Negro woman nearby tears a strip off her underskirt and hands it to a white man to mop the brow of one of the marchers who looks dead. After a short rest, they pick up the lifeless bodies and take them away to cars.

Ben hears his name called.

He looks around, tries to isolate the sound in the confusion of screaming and crying.

"Ben!" he hears again.

He sees Elizabeth Waters twenty yards away, ministering to one of the wounded marchers. Ben leaves his own group and goes to her. She kneels beside an injured Negro man, trying to stanch the blood from his shoulder wound. "I can't get anybody to help us," she says.

"I will." He kneels beside the injured man. "What's your name, brother?"

"Booker," the man says. His face is gray.

"Booker," Ben says, "are you hit anyplace else besides your shoulder?"

Booker shakes his head.

"He's going into shock," Elizabeth says to Ben. "He needs help. We have to get him to a hospital. Do you have a car?"

"No, I hitched a ride down."

"You're bleeding!"

"It's not my blood. It belongs to him." He points to the marcher he helped carry away.

"No, there's blood on your head. You're hurt. This is terrible. It's a massacre. How can this happen in this country?"

"You said it yourself last night. It's a war. Where are the injured going?"

"We're getting as many as we can to the hospital before the police arrest them."

A Ford roars toward them and stops. Two men jump out. Ben helps them get Booker into the back seat and jumps in with Elizabeth. The car speeds away.

19

ELIZABETH WATERS

She wakes at six. Ben snores on the couch in her living room.

She stands over him, watching him sleep. His face looks worse today than it did the day before as the bruises come out. He's lucky they didn't kill him.

They'll keep trying. He should stay with her for a while longer.

He is younger, he said—twenty-five to her thirty-three. Too young for you, she tells herself as she looks down on him.

Whoa, girl, not so fast. You don't even know this guy.

And yet you invited him to spend the night.

What exactly do you have in mind for him, she asks herself. Why is he here?

You could as easily have left him at the Unemployed Council.

What's this about?

Something to do with the night she spent with Horace, no doubt. Taking in this waif is a way to show herself (if not Horace) that her roll in the hay with her former friend's brother didn't mean anything.

Ben isn't as handsome as Horace . . . or maybe just handsome in a different way, with his dark looks so different from Horace's big, blond, Protestant swagger.

And maybe Ben's being here is a microcosm of her more general rejection of the background she shared with Horace . . . opting for Ben over money, social privilege, power . . . maybe Ben reminded her of Sarah Kirschner and Elizabeth's urge to bring Sarah back in some form, even in the guise of this battered young Jew.

She tries to be as quiet as she can showering and getting dressed. She makes a pot of coffee and writes him a note. He is still asleep as she leaves the apartment.

Maybe she'll see him at the march. Probably she won't.

At this time of morning, the Woodward streetcar is almost empty. She rides it down to the Maccabees Building. She is the first one in. She peeks into the writers' room. She wouldn't be surprised to see Bill Mulcahy still asleep on the couch. The room is empty, as are the production studios, the bleak, sparse spaces where the shows are performed. The overnight engineer sits in the control booth, getting ready for the day's programming. Elizabeth lifts a hand in greeting to him, which he returns.

She goes back to her desk in the writers' room. The desktop is piled with scripts needing to be catalogued (none from Mulcahy, she notices), weekend production logs, as well as mail needing sorting.

There is also a nasty note from Sid Ballenger filled with exclamation points and underlines. It was about the same conversation she already had with him. Mulcahy claims he gave Elizabeth a script which she absolutely knows is a lie. She's going to have it out with him.

She wants to get ahead of her work so she can take time off for the march. She told Sid about it three days ago. He's probably forgotten.

She works steadily until a little after eight, when Sid comes in. He goes right to his office. She gives him a few minutes to get settled and goes to stand in his doorway.

"Morning," she says.

He's paging through a script. "Morning," he grunts without looking up at her.

"I just wanted to remind you: I put in for personal time today."

Now he looks up at her over his glasses as though this is news to him. "For what?"

"The Ford Hunger March. I told you about it a few weeks ago."

He closes the script and tosses his glasses onto it. "Sorry, kiddo. No can do. We're casting for *Cody Storm* this afternoon."

"How can you? Bill hasn't finished any scripts."

"Except for the one he says he gave you."

She sits on one of the chairs across from his desk. "Sid, I swear on my mother's life, he never gave me a script."

"Bill swears he gave you one."

"The last time I saw Bill, he was out cold on the couch in the writers' room Friday night. Maybe he dreamed he gave me a script in one of his DT hallucinations."

"This is going to be a problem, Elizabeth."

"Well, it's not going to be my problem."

"Don't be too sure. I can't very well call Bill a liar."

"Yet you have no problem implying I'm lying. And anyway, if there aren't any scripts ready, we'll have to postpone the auditions. So there's nothing in the way of my taking the time off you promised me I could have."

"I'm not cancelling the auditions. We're behind already on this. If there aren't any scripts ready, you'll have to throw something together."

"*I'll* have to throw something together? Since when am I a writer?"

"You're always saying you want to be a writer."

"Yeah, and you're always telling me I have to pay my dues."

"Here's where you start. We need it by one o'clock, when the talent comes in. Can you have it by then? Just need a couple of scenes, not a complete script."

"Phil can't do it because . . . ?"

"He's not due in till later in the afternoon."

"Sid, is this fair?"

Sid shrugs. "Fair schmair. It's the business we're in."

She storms out of his office back to the writers' room. Her desk is in the corner. They don't even give her an office.

A dilemma. She can either refuse to write the script or swallow her anger and write it.

In the first instance, Sid would fire her for sure.

In the second, she might keep her job, but she'd be late for the march.

And she would also be tacitly admitting Mulcahy was right.

Unfortunately, this is not even a choice for her. She can't afford to lose the job. Not now.

Furious at her circumstances, she rolls a sheet of paper into her old Underwood. Steals a glance at the clock: 8:12. If she can get out of here by noon, she should make it to the march.

She starts speed-typing.

```
SERIES:    Cody Storm on the Case
SHOW:      Episode #1
DATE:      March 7, 1932
```

FANFARE: Police siren and gunshots (music TBD)

ANNOUNCER: Solving crimes and saving lives on the roughest streets in the toughest city on earth, it's . . .

MUSIC: (Music background)

ANNOUNCER: Cody Storm on the Case!

MUSIC: (Music continues)

ANNOUNCER: A mysterious figure prowls the city at all hours of the day and night, on the lookout for whatever threatens the peace and good citizens of his town. Criminals, crooks, and Commies beware—Cody Storm is on the case!

MUSIC: (Cut music)

SOUND: (TYPEWRITER BACKGROUND)

ANNOUNCER: In the dark of night in the Detective Bureau of the great city's police force. Cody Storm, determined veteran of the never-ending war on crime, stays late to finish up the reports on his day's arrests.

CAP. JIM: Gee, Cody, are you still here?

CODY: Oh, hey there, Captain Jim. Yeah, just finishing up.

CAP. JIM: A detective's work is never done, is it?

CODY: As long as there's crime on the street, I'll never rest.

CAP. JIM: I can always count on you, Cody. Don't stay too late, will you? (VOICE FADES AWAY.) See you in the morning.

SOUND: (DOOR CLOSING)

SOUND: (TYPING CONTINUES)

SOUND: (URGENT RAP ON DOOR)

CODY: Now who could that be so late? (CALLS) Hello? Anybody there?

SOUND: (A DOOR OPENS)

MAISIE: (APPROACHES) Thank goodness, someone's still here.

CODY: I'm Detective Storm. What can I do for you, young lady? You look plenty worried.

MAISIE: I am, Detective, I'm ever so worried. It's my brother. He's fallen in with a bad crowd, and I'm scared something terrible's going to happen to him.

CODY: Well, just have a seat. What's your name, and who's your brother fallen in with?

MAISIE: My name's Maisie. And it's the Commies, don't you see. They've got him brainwashed into wanting to overthrow the government. And now he won't listen to a word I say. Right now, he's even at one of their meetings.

CODY: Let's go have a word with him, Maisie. (FADING BACK) And see if he'll listen to reason.

SOUND: (FOOTSTEPS FADING AWAY)

MUSIC: (Music up)

MUSIC: (Music out)

SOUND: (UNINTELLIGIBLE   VOICES   CONTINUE   IN BACKGROUND)

RED #1:   Workers of the world, unite!

RED #2:   You have nothing to lose but your Chains!

MAISIE: Detective Storm, there he is! Psst, Fred! Fred!

FRED: Sis! What are you doing here?

MAISIE: Oh, Fred, I'm ever so worried about you! These people don't mean you any good at all!

FRED: Aw, Maisie, you don't understand. These people are our friends . . . they just want what's best for every working man and woman.

CODY: I'm afraid they don't, son. They're a danger to the American way of life.

FRED: Who are you?

CODY: Detective Cody Storm, city police. Your sister here's just worried about you, young fellow.

FRED: She don't need to worry. I'm old enough to take care of myself. And you stay out of my business!

RED #1:   Fred, are you ready to go? Our comrades are waiting for us. We have planning to do.

MAISIE: Oh Fred, please don't go with them.

FRED: Just go home, Maisie. I know what I'm doing.

SOUND: (HIS FOOTSTEPS FADING AWAY.)

MAISIE: Fred! Oh, Detective Storm, whatever should I do?

CODY: Not to worry, Maisie. I have an idea.

MUSIC: (Music up)

Elizabeth tears the last page of the partial script out of her typewriter and rereads the entire thing. It's not Shakespeare, but it'll do for the auditions. And it's certainly better than Phil Mulcahy's imaginary script.

It tickles her to make the first show about the threat of the Communist conspiracy before heading off to the Hunger March organized by the local Communist Party.

She bundles the pages of the excerpt together and takes them in to Sid. He isn't in his office, so rather than look for him, she scrawls a note—"Here's the first part of the script for the audition. It should be long enough to cast the characters. –Elizabeth"—and paperclips it to the pages. Leaves it all on Sid's chair.

And she's off.

Time: 11:47.

Outside, Woodward Avenue is full of cars and streetcars and men and women walking south toward downtown in the bitter cold. Finding space on a streetcar will be impossible, so Elizabeth begins walking. She lets the crowd bear her along.

A large group turns right onto Mack Avenue, several blocks from her office. She follows. The group turns left onto Grand Boulevard, then right onto Vernor before turning left onto Livernois for the last leg to Fort Street.

As they go, they pick up more and more marchers—mostly men but a few women. Elizabeth falls into step with the women, linking arms for the solidarity and the shared body heat. The crowd laughs and shouts slogans, so Elizabeth begins singing the English version of *"The Internationale"* at the top of her lungs.

> *Arise, ye prisoners of starvation!*
> *Arise, ye wretched of the earth!*
> *For justice thunders condemnation:*
> *A better world's in birth!*

Two of the other women in her group know the lyrics and they sing along. Some of the men around them knew the song, too, and they join their voices as well.

The crowd is massing at Fort Street and Oakwood, near the Dearborn border. By the time her group nears the larger group, several thousand people are milling around. The clamor of excited voices cheers her.

The note she left for Ben Rubin said she would try to connect with him at Woodmere Cemetery. But when she passes the main entrance off Fort Street, she sees the police have blockaded the driveway. No one could have gotten in, and no one is waiting. Anyone who does stop is moved along by the police.

No Ben.

She shakes her head to get him out of her thoughts, and concentrates on the mass of humanity around her. She feels a sense of released anger and shared endeavor in the air. Men around her wave placards—

"Don't starve in the richest land on earth!"

"We need bigger relief checks!"

"Jobs for all!"

They stamp their feet against the cold and laugh and talk.

She is late arriving (thanks to goddamn alkie Mulcahy), so she winds up far from the march's central point. Amid the hubbub of the general crowd noise, she hears a murmur spreading: "Police—police—police."

More voices shout, "March on! March on!"

Instead of moving forward, the mass starts to move backward, like a living thing with a mind of its own. Clouds billow at the front of the march and she hears cries of "Tear gas!" The men around her press against the movement, and some turn and try to run but there is no place to go.

She sees the wind blowing the tear gas away from the marchers and back toward the police. "Wait," she shouts, "the wind's blowing it away! Stop! Stop!"

Her voice is lost in the tumult of the crowd trying to flee.

Policemen chase after them with billy clubs. Men running past her jostle her. She almost loses her footing but stays upright to see men stop, pick up debris along the railroad tracks, and hurl it at the police. Rocks and bottles fly.

The police retreat and the crowd reassembles and goes on the move again, this time toward the plant.

They make it as far as the No. 3 Gate. From the bridge over the road, firehoses open up and douse the marchers with ice-cold water. It freezes, glistening on their coats and hats, on contact.

Still there are shouts: "March on! March on!"

She hears the popping of gunfire.

"Retreat! Retreat!"

In the chaos, men shout, run in all directions away from the gunshots.

She hears more gunfire and sees men and women falling. They lie motionless or else writhe and scream in pain on the ground.

All around her men scramble to get away. Small groups form around the fallen to give aid. Several dozen people lie wounded on the ground or else stumble to safety with bloodied heads and limbs.

A few yards away from where she stands is a fallen Negro man. No one is helping him. She kneels by him. He's alive. Blood oozes from a shoulder wound. He looks up at her, dazed and sweaty despite being soaked with ice crystals from the firehoses.

"It's okay," she says, "I'll help you."

She unwraps the scarf from her neck and presses it to the man's wound.

"Help!" she cries. "We need help here!"

She looks up and—it's a miracle—sees Ben Rubin. He is helping to carry one of the injured. She calls to him.

He notices her, makes sure the others in his aid group can carry the man on their own. Comes over to her.

"I can't get anybody to help us," she says.

"I will." He kneels beside the injured man. "What's your name, brother?"

"Booker," the man says. His face is gray.

"Booker," Ben says, "are you hit anyplace else besides your shoulder?"

Booker shakes his head.

"He's going into shock," Elizabeth says to Ben. "He needs help. We have to get him to a hospital. Do you have a car?"

"No, I hitched a ride down."

"You're bleeding!"

"It's not my blood. It belongs to him." Ben points to the marcher he was helping to carry.

"Is he dead?"

"I'm afraid so."

"No, there's blood on your head. You're hurt. This is terrible. It's a massacre. How can this happen in this country?"

"You said it yourself last night. It's a war."

A car weaves crazily down the street toward them and Elizabeth jumps up and waves it down. It skids to a stop. Two men jump out. "Let's get him in!" one cries.

Ben helps them get Booker into the back seat, then jumps in with Elizabeth. The car speeds away.

"Where are we going?" she asks as the driver negotiates the roads filled with retreating marchers. They trudge along, battered, shell-shocked, like refugees.

It *is* a war. And we've lost this skirmish.

"Receiving Hospital," says the driver. "We'll be there in a jiff."

20

ROSCOE GRISSOM

The house is empty when Roscoe wakes up. Brats are off at school (thank you Jesus) and even the wife is elsewhere. (Ditto.)

He showers, dresses, dawdles over a cup of coffee. The quiet is like heaven. Why can't it always be like this?

His head is killing him. Whatever else Prohibition was supposed to accomplish, it didn't much interrupt his drinking habits. You need the hair of the dog, he tells himself.

Have to wait until he gets to the Dew Drop. His house is dry, thanks to Melanie. Her father was a big drinker, just like Roscoe's grandfather. Even before Michigan went dry, she wouldn't tolerate booze in the house.

After Laverne drove them back to the bar the night before, they went inside for a couple of nightcaps. Roscoe's nerves needed settling.

He reaches into his pocket and fondles the .38 caliber bullet cartridge he keeps with him. His good luck charm. His reminder that somewhere in this world is a place for him after all. It sure as hell ain't here, in this tiny house smelling like little girls.

He gulps down the coffee and leaves the cup in the sink. Let his lazy bitch of a wife do something around this house. For a change. She has a job cleaning houses under the table for the rich people in

Grosse Pointe. It brings cash in, but it don't leave her any time or energy to clean her own goddamn house.

The thought of his wife makes him jumpy. He has a sudden feeling she'll be home soon, and he wants to be somewhere else when she comes. He races around, getting his keys and his wallet, and flees the house.

Walks down to the Dew Drop. Some of the boys are already there. Like Roscoe, they don't have any place else to go. Frankie sets up an urn for free coffee and lets them put their sodas on his tab because most of them have no money. He won't allow access to his back room till after twelve noon, so the ones who can afford to buy his bootleg hooch can't get any before then.

Roscoe gets his cup of coffee and brings it up to the bar, where a half-dozen men slump. They wear their fedoras and flat caps inside because Frankie keeps it chilly. Fucking guinea don't want to make the men too comfortable. Then they'd never leave.

It's getting so there's no place left for white Americans to feel at home in this country, Roscoe thinks.

Nods all around from the regulars.

"How's it going?"

"What's new, anything?"

"Hey, boy."

Harley Clarke is there, talking about some march or other that's supposed to be going on today. "Commie demonstration," he calls it.

"Yeah," Harley says, "them dirty Jew Reds are trying to take over the unions. They're having a big demonstration today out by Ford's. Supposed to be thousands of men there."

Roscoe shrugs. "Don't know nothing about it."

"Old Henry'll let Harry Bennett loose on them. They'll be sorry."

A chuckle all around.

"I didn't have an appointment later," Harley says, "I'd go down there and show 'em what I think of them. I tell you what, there'd be blood spilled today."

Mutters of agreement.

One guy at the end of the bar pipes up. Says, "They just want what we all want. Decent pay, medical care, job security. If they can help us get those things, I'm not gonna complain."

Roscoe never saw this guy before.

Harley says, "What did you just say?"

"I said they want the same things we all want. If they can help us get any of it, what's the difference?"

Harley gives him the eye, stands, goes over to where the guy is sitting at the end of the bar. The place goes quiet.

"I'm complaining," Harley says. "I don't want no dirty Jew kike telling me how I'm supposed to do my job."

He stands glowering over the guy at the end of the bar.

The guy looks up at him, sipping his coffee as calm as anything, like he's trying to measure his chances against the big man.

They're not good, pal, Roscoe silently advises him. Don't do it.

"What do you got to say now?" Harley demands.

The guy decides not to take Harley on. He shrugs, looks down at his cup cradled in his rough hands. "Already said my piece."

But then, like he can't help himself, he adds, "Why don't you go back over there and finish your drink, eh?"

Harley starts a move on the other guy until *thwack!* Frankie slams a billy club on the bar. He keeps it under the counter in case of trouble like this. Beaten wood, black-taped handle. It's met some hard heads over the years.

"Not in here," Frankie says. "You wanna fight, take it outside." Points the club out the door.

Harley turns to the other guy. Who holds up his hands in surrender. "Got no beef with you, friend," the guy says.

Smart move. Not as dumb as he sounds.

Harley struts back to his stool. The victor in this particular pissing contest. As always.

Behind the bar, Frankie gives both of them a bottle of Faygo. "On the house," he says. "We're all friends here, yeah?"

The guy on the other end of the bar holds his bottle up as a salute to Harley.

Who just sneers and turns away.

The bar fills slowly. After a half hour, the guy at the end of the bar finishes his drink. Nods to Frankie. Slides off his stool. Strolls out.

A few moments later, Roscoe sees Harley go for the front door. In his wake trail a couple of his buddies. Enoch Jones, who has just come in, grabs Roscoe by the arm and pulls him along. "This'll be rich," Enoch says.

After the darkness of the bar, the sunlight stabs Roscoe's eyes. A sunny and cold day.

He hears Harley call, "Hey, you!"

Roscoe sees the guy from the bar up ahead on the sidewalk. Harley is closing fast.

The guy stops, turns with his hands up. Says, "Look, I don't want no trouble."

"You should have thought of that before you opened your mouth," Harley says. Sucker punches the guy with a ham-sized fist. The guy goes down and Harley kicks him in the stomach. Harley's pal picks the guy up and Harley goes to town on him. Batters his face bloody. Pulls a sap from his pocket and pummels him. Roscoe hears bones crack.

Watching the beating, Roscoe's breath quickens. He feels the same flutter in the pit of his stomach as he did the other night flogging the Black Legion guy who was missing meetings. The exercise of raw power. Exciting.

He feels for the bullet in his pocket.

I have this, he tells himself. I don't have Harley's brute gorilla strength. But I'm no less dangerous with the power of the Black Legion behind me.

Harley continues his beating even after the guy passes out. Drags him into the vacant lot near the Dew Drop. Leaves him lying in the garbage and tires and broken bottles.

Somebody goes to see if the guy's still breathing, but Harley grabs him by the arm and pushes him away. "He'll be alright," Harley says. "Bet next time around he watches his fucking mouth."

The men parade back into Frankie's. Laughing. Carrying on.

Frankie has refilled the coffee urn for them.

In a little while, it will be time to troop down to the soup kitchen for lunch . . . always a high point of the day. But it'll be hard to top this for Roscoe.

21

CLARENCE BROWN

Clarence parks in the lot on Russell Street at Eastern Market. The market still bustles with trucks and deliveries and men pushing handcarts, though the heaviest business happens earlier in the morning.

He pins his badge to his overcoat. Gets out of the car, adjusts the metal plates around his shoulders. Heads toward Market Linen Supply on Riopelle, the next street over.

He walks through the parking lot and under the sheds where farmers sell their wares. He gets a load of stink-eye from both the white workers and the Negro porters around the wholesale commercial market. *Who's that fancy shine think he is,* he can imagine them saying to themselves.

Market Linen Supply is a store-front operation on the corner. In the front is the main office. In the rear are the laundry facilities with overhead doors for their delivery trucks on Wilkins, the side street. Beside the overhead doors is a man-door which, from the outside, seems like it should lead into the loading bay.

It doesn't. It's a separate entrance to the offices of the president of the Market Linen Supply Company—who also happens to be the new leader of the Sicilian gangsters who call themselves the Detroit Partnership. Black Bill Tocco. Following the murder the previous year of Cesare LaFontaine, head of the East Side faction, the Detroit gang wars achieved a kind of peace under the leadership of West Side faction leader Black Bill.

The same Black Bill who runs Madame Savoyard's whorehouse.

Market Linen Supply is one of his legitimate businesses. Black Bill's cousin Vito runs this one. No way would Clarence get to see Black Bill just by showing up. Vito is more approachable, so he's the one Clarence is after today.

He opens the man-door next to the delivery bay. On the other side of the door sits one of Black Bill's goons having a smoke and reading the Detroit *Times* sports section. Or at least looking at the photos. Behind him a stairway leads down to a basement.

When he spots Clarence, the goon says, "Whaddaya want?"

"I want to see Vito."

"Oh, yeah?" The guinea spits on the ground, missing Clarence's shoe by an inch. "Vito ain't got time for you. Beat it."

Clarence points to his buzzer. "He'll make time."

"I doubt it. A nigger with a badge is still a nigger."

He throws the paper down, gets up, squares his shoulders to intimidate Clarence, and reaches out to push Clarence away.

Clarence loves it when these guys get tough. It means he can get tougher.

He grabs the hood's arm and twists it hard. The hood cries out in pain and Clarence mashes his face into the concrete blocks of the wall, throws him to the floor.

Clarence steps over him and goes down the stairs.

At the bottom of the steps stands another palooka. Clarence draws one of his guns and sticks it in his face before he can say a word. "Vito," Clarence says. "Now."

"Ain't here," the guy chokes out, eyes big as saucers.

"You better hope that's the truth," Clarence says. "'Cause I'm fittin' to blow your ugly white head clean off on the count of three."

"Wait, wait!"

"One."

"Wait a minute, will you? I'm telling you he's not here. You wanna go check?"

"Yeah," Clarence says, "let's check."

He holds the man in front of him like a shield, the .45 still at his head. Clarence walks him down a hallway.

A guy in a three-piece pin-striped suit sits in an easy chair in an office at the end of the hall. His cigar smells like burning tires. Hooded eyes, dead, like all the Sicilians Clarence knows. Like they passed away and nobody told them.

He looks up when Clarence comes in with his captive. "What the fuck is this?" he says.

"Who are you?" Clarence asks.

"Who am I? Who the fuck are *you*?"

"Clarence Brown, Detroit Police. I'm looking for Vito."

"He ain't here. How 'bout you let go of Carmine?"

"I told you," says Carmine to Clarence, "he ain't here."

"I'm going to ask again," Clarence says, "who are you?"

"Tony Jack Polizzi," the guy says, like Clarence should recognize the name and tremble. Clarence does the first (another of Black Bill's cousins), not the second.

"Who are you, busting into my place of business like this?"

"Detroit Police detective. What do you know about Darius Turner?"

"Who?"

"Darius Turner. Colored boy you and your goombahs hung a couple nights ago."

"Never heard of him," Tony Jack says.

"I don't believe you."

Tony Jack shrugs. Takes another puff on the cigar. Not worth a response.

Then he says, "Some mooli got himself hung. Not really news, is it?"

"He didn't get himself hung," Clarence says. "Somebody did it for him."

"What for?"

"That's what I want to find out from Black Bill."

"Now I'm confused. Who do you want, Vito or Black Bill?"

"Tell me where I can find Black Bill."

"Yeah, no, you don't find him. He wants to talk, he finds you. What's he supposed to know about this guy?"

"Darius was selling horse. I want to know if Black Bill put him out of business."

"He wouldn't be *in* business without Bill's say-so."

Tony Jack stands. Shakes the wrinkles out of his pants. "Look," he says, "this kid, he was any kind of player, I'd know about him. The fact I never heard of him means he's too penny-ante for Black Bill to care about. He don't give two shits about this guy, trust me. I wouldn't even bother him with this."

Tony Jack takes a roll of bills from his pocket, peels off two fifties. "Here, take this." Stuffs the bills in Clarence's coat pocket. "For your trouble. Forget about this guy and we'll pretend we never had this conversation. Alright?"

Clarence hears footsteps coming fast down the hall.

"Now it's time to leave," Tony Jack says. "We're going to have company."

Three more goons come into the doorway and stop when they see Clarence holding a gun to Carmine's head. One of the goons is the guy from the top of the stairs who Clarence bested, holding his arm.

Clarence swings Carmine around, Carmine still in front of him and the gun still to his head.

"Easy there, Sambo," one of the goons says. "Don't do nothing you're gonna regret."

They separate to surround him.

Clarence backs around them before they corner him and starts down the hall. He lets Carmine go and turns his gun on the other men.

Takes the money from Tony Jack out of his pocket and throws it on the floor. "Don't want your money."

"Big mistake, spook," Tony Jack says.

Clarence backs off down the hallway.

"Let him go," Tony Jack says. The goons watch without following.

Clarence reaches the stairway and takes the stairs three at a time. Trots out the side door.

Nobody follows.

Keeps going to where he left the Ford.

He was right about one thing: Darius couldn't have operated without the permission of Black Bill Tocco. The only way Tocco would have taken him out is if Darius wasn't paying his bills. Was Black Bill the one Darius was rumored to be shorting? This would be too stupid for words. The Darius Clarence knew wasn't that dumb.

That still left the problem of the manner of Darius's murder. If the Sicilians had it in for him, they would just shoot him in the head and dump his body. Darius was tortured and lynched. Something else is going on here.

22

BEN RUBIN

Pandemonium outside Detroit Receiving Hospital.

Men screaming in pain.

Bloody heads from police truncheons. Bloody clothes from gunshot wounds under the heavy waterlogged overcoats people wore against the cold.

Frostbitten hands and toes from the freezing soaking by the Dearborn firemen.

Nurses and doctors running around triaging the patients who arrive in cars every minute.

Orderlies running back and forth with gurneys to transport the injured.

The Ford pulls up in front of the hospital and Ben and Elizabeth hop out. They help Booker out of the car. He is woozy and tries to stand. His legs give way. Orderlies with gurneys and wheelchairs race past him to the whites who are hurt.

Ben stops an orderly with an empty wheelchair.

"Who's it for?" the orderly shouts. "This guy?" Points to Booker.

"Yeah," Ben says.

"Uh-uh. Negro entrance is around the corner."

"He needs help now." Ben wrests the wheelchair away. He and the other men from the car maneuver Booker into it.

Ben pushes into the Emergency Room through the Whites Only door. It's calmer inside as nurses on the check-in desk triage the arrivals. Ben pushes the wheelchair up to them.

"He was hurt in the march," he says.

"Looks more like a riot to me," the nurse says.

"That's what it turned into. A police riot."

She comes out from behind her desk and bends down beside the Negro in the chair. "Sir," she says, "can you hear me? What's your name?"

The man looks at her. He is still dazed, wincing in pain.

"What's your name, sir?" she asks again.

"Booker Harris."

She notices blood seeping from his right ear and hollers, "I need help here." She grabs a small cloth from the desk and dabs at the blood oozing down the side of his head.

"Okay, Booker, we're going to take good care of you."

In a flash, a doctor is by her side. He examines Booker's head, places a stethoscope against Booker's chest.

The doctor says. "Let's get him cleaned up and find a bed for him."

The doctor rushes off to the next patient, who seems to be in worse shape than Booker—a white man vomiting all over his chest.

The nurse pushes Booker into a room down the hall.

"So many head injuries," Ben says to Elizabeth. "I've never seen anything like this."

Elizabeth says, "From the police billy clubs. Bastards. They pretend we're the enemy, but we're not. Ben? Ben!"

Ben sways for a moment, feels a crackling inside his head.

The world goes dark.

23

ELIZABETH WATERS

Ben's eyes roll back in his head. He hits the floor.

The nurse who took care of Booker comes back. "What happened here?"

Elizabeth says, "One minute he was fine, the next he collapsed."

"Head wound," the nurse says. "Plus somebody gave him a good going-over."

"The beating isn't from today."

"What's one more crushed skull," the nurse says. She looks around, yells, "Chester!"

An orderly stops, turns in her direction.

"Bring your gurney over here."

Chester pushes the empty gurney to her. "Help me get him up," she says.

Chester lowers the gurney and the two of them lift Ben and set him on it. "Roll him into the ward," she tells Chester. "I'll be with him as soon as I can."

Elizabeth is about to follow when she hears her name called amid the clamor of the hallway.

She turns to see Maurice Sugar coming toward her. "What the hell's going on here?" he asks.

"It's all from the march."

"This is appalling."

"It was a massacre, Maurice. They started shooting—"

"Who did?" he interrupts.

"Harry Bennett and his thugs. And the Dearborn Police. They're responsible for all this."

She holds up her arms, offering the chaos around them as evidence. "This is all their work. What are you doing here?"

"I intend to represent every one of these men if they're charged with anything."

"Elizabeth!"

She turns to see Horace Howcroft striding down the corridor.

"Thank God you're all right," he says.

He notices Maurice Sugar standing there and nods coldly. Maurice doesn't return the greeting. Obviously these two know each other. They are natural enemies.

"Is this your doing?" Elizabeth demands of Horace.

Before he can answer, an orderly pushing a bleeding man on a gurney bustles between them. They move over and Elizabeth spots Ben standing, wobbly, in the doorway to the ward where he was taken.

"Ben!" she calls.

She makes her way through the chaos to get to him. "What are you doing on your feet?"

"I'm okay. Just got a little dizzy."

She puts an arm around him and walks him over to where the other two men are standing.

"Maurice," she says, "this is my friend Ben Rubin. Ben, Maurice Sugar."

"Somebody worked you over," Maurice observes.

"I'm good at making enemies," Ben says.

"So am I."

"Maurice is a labor attorney," Elizabeth explains. "And this is my friend Horace Howcroft."

Horace stands stiff-backed, does not extend his hand. He is a few inches taller than Ben. He looks down on Ben with obvious disdain.

Elizabeth gently touches the side of Ben's head, which has been washed clean of blood.

"You got that today?" Maurice asks.

"I did."

"Ben helped me rescue a Negro man who got shot by the police."

"Good man," Maurice says. He hands a card to Ben. "Call me if you ever need legal assistance." To Elizabeth, he says, "I'm going to see how people are doing. We'll talk later, all right?"

"Okay," Elizabeth says.

"And you watch yourself, young man," Maurice says. He turns and leaves without saying anything to Horace.

Who stares daggers at Ben Rubin.

"Are you going to be okay if I leave you here?" Elizabeth asks Ben. "I want to go with Maurice and see how people are."

"I'll be fine."

"Maybe you should go back and lie down?"

"I will."

"I'll speak to you later," she tells Horace.

Horace gives Ben one last dirty look and turns away.

"He seems nice," says Ben.

"Don't pay him any attention. He's an old friend. He can't do you any harm."

She catches up with Maurice Sugar and the two of them walk the corridor, chatting to the men who are waiting to be seen. There are dozens of them. Many are handcuffed to their gurneys.

Maurice is shaking the hands of the wounded if they are able. He shakes his head at the aftermath of violence from the march.

They come to the ward where they keep the Negroes separate, Booker Harris among them. "They allow them in," Maurice says, "then keep them apart." He shakes his head sadly. "What a country."

"At least they're getting care," Elizabeth says.

"At what cost to their dignity? If I were Negro, I'd want to shoot every white person I saw."

He stops to chat with a Negro man who is conscious and Elizabeth walks around the ward, touching the men on their arms and asking how they are.

She gets to one woman with a bandaged head. She stops.

It's her friend Mary Tatum.

"Mary," Elizabeth says. Mary lies unconscious. Her face is battered and swollen, and her arm is in a sling. A tube snakes an IV into her arm from a bag hung beside her, carrying clear liquid.

"You know this woman?" Maurice asks.

"We're comrades in the movement."

"Looks like she was singled out for special abuse. Most likely because of her race."

"I'm certain of it. She must have stood and tried to fight them. Too brave to run away."

Maurice pats Mary's shoulder. "Hang on, brave woman." To Elizabeth, he says, "I'll represent her. You can count on it."

He walks on and Elizabeth stands looking at what was left of Mary Tatum after the firemen and police got hold of her. The sight of her laid so low on the gurney breaks her heart.

She wants to say something. All she can come up with is, "Oh Mary. I'm so sorry."

Mary doesn't respond.

The DeSoto pulls up in front of Elizabeth's building. Elizabeth helps Ben out. Behind the wheel, Maurice Sugar leans across the front seat. Says, "You're sure you'll be okay?"

"Right as rain, thanks."

"Call me if you need anything."

"I will."

She watches Maurice pull away. Tells Ben, "I got you." His arm is around her shoulders. Her arm is around his waist.

"I'm fine," he protests. "Just a little woozy."

"You must have a hard head. It's taken a pounding over the last few days."

"I'll be all right in the morning."

"The doc told me to keep an eye on you if you fall asleep."

"Yeah, well, it's nighttime. That's what you're supposed to do."

They take the elevator to her floor. "Good night, Miss Elizabeth," the elevator operator says coldly.

"Good night, Mr. Fox."

Fox tips his cap to her, gives Ben the stink-eye. She and Ben link arms to get to her apartment.

"I think you scandalized Mr. Fox," Ben says, "bringing a gentleman to your apartment."

"No, he's seen it all. He just doesn't like Jews in his building."

"Oh," Ben says. "That's much better."

She unlocks her door and guides him to the couch.

"Down," she orders.

She shucks off her coat and goes into the kitchen. Fills a dish towel with ice cubes from the icebox and takes it to him.

"This should make you feel better."

He takes it gratefully and applies it to the side of his face. Sits back. Sighs.

She gets him a dose of Miss Em and sits next to him. "Here." She adjusts the icepack to where a nasty purple bruise has risen on his forehead.

"Thanks. How are you doing?"

She hugs herself. "So much violence. So upsetting."

"I know."

She gives a flip of her head, momentarily annoyed with him for being so patronizing. "You don't know," she spits. "You have no idea."

She feels him stiffen under the anger of her words. She regrets turning her vitriol onto him. He's not the one responsible, she reminds herself. He's a victim of violence himself.

She takes a deep, shuddering breath. "Seeing all those men at the hospital reminded me of someone else. Somebody I knew at the place where I worked before."

He is silent. He is giving her space to say what she needs to say. This is different, especially after she just bit his head off.

"This guy," she says, "was a radio commentator, and I was his assistant. I'd been working for him for a couple of years. He was an odd duck, but he was very political. I enjoyed that about him."

"What happened to him?"

"He was killed. Two years ago. You've probably heard of him. Jerry Buckley."

"Yeah, sure, I've heard of him."

"It was the night of the recall of Mayor Bowles. You remember?"

"That was how Murphy got elected."

"Jerry just finished his show at 11:30 at the LaSalle Hotel. He was waiting for me in the lobby. We were going to go out for a drink to celebrate the recall. I was in the studio wrapping up with the engineer so I didn't go downstairs with him right away. If I had, I'd probably be dead, too. Or maybe if we'd come downstairs together, we would have left the lobby and missed the gunmen. Or if we'd just stayed in the studio in the hotel . . ."

"You can't think like that. You'll drive yourself nuts."

"No," she agrees, "you're right. I try not to."

"They sure spread dirt about him afterwards."

"Said he was as crooked as Bowles and the police commissioner."

"Was he?"

"Who knows? He kept a lot from me. I knew he was close to some of the bad guys. I was young. And stupid."

She sits in silence for a few moments.

"It was a terrible shock," she goes on. "I came down in the elevator right after it happened. I saw the three guys who did it run away."

"Could you identify them?"

She shakes her head. "It was all a blur. And I was concentrating on Jerry. You see photographs of a dead body lying in a pool of blood, from these gangland killings. And it looks gruesome, sure. But still, there's something unreal about it. Something distancing about the black and white photos, I guess. But then you actually see a real dead body . . . especially someone you know . . . you're just not prepared for how awful violent death is."

She is quiet for a few moments.

"I think what was worse were the colors. Red for blood, of course. But also color you don't expect. Purples. Blue. The white of the bones. The reddish-pink of the insides of the body that are now outside the body, where they don't belong. The clods of gray that used to be brains. Have you ever seen a body killed by violence?"

"Sure. Very recently."

"Oh, your friend."

"Yeah."

"So you know what I mean."

"I do."

"After that, I quit the station. I couldn't work there anymore. I couldn't work anywhere for a long time."

"What did you do?"

"I couldn't do anything. I'd saved up some money. For a long time I couldn't even go outside. I just stayed in my apartment. Most days I cried, until one day I got up in the morning and realized my life had to go on. The problem was, I didn't know which direction it should go in. I was a bit of a dilettante."

"Is that when you got involved in the labor fight?"

"Yeah. I gravitated to the Unemployed Councils because I saw them doing the necessary work. And I'd been sympathetic to the Communists since college."

Sarah Kirschner comes to mind, and the intimacy they shared during those too-few nights at school.

Ben pulls her close.

Talking about Jerry Buckley, and remembering Sarah Kirshner, has saddened her; she remembers how much she misses them, how bereft she felt after their deaths. On top of the distress left over from the day, she feels especially alone.

"Ben? You asleep?"

He jerks his head up. Winces at the action. "No."

"No, it's fine. Let's just sit like this for a little bit. It's been a long, terrible day."

After a while, she untangles herself and goes into her bathroom. She takes her own nightly dose of Miss Em and comes out with her light cotton chemise.

Ben is asleep on the couch. She watches his face in repose for a minute.

She reaches down to take his hand. He opens his eyes.

"Come with me," she says.

Pulls him into her bedroom.

She sees the surprise on his face. And the pleasure. As if he is torn between wanting to and hesitation. Maybe he's afraid he can't perform in his current condition . . .

"Don't worry," she says. "I just need company tonight. You probably do, too."

She leads him to her bed and helps him to undress and slide under the covers in his underwear.

She gets into bed next to him. They face each other, arms entwined, lying together, looking into each other's eyes. Smiling at how comfortable and strange this feels.

"Nice," she says.

"Yeah."

In a few minutes his eyes droop shut and she hears his breathing even out.

She and Sarah used to lie like this. She remembers all the hours she spent in bed with the young woman, and the paleness of her limbs, almost like her skin glowed in the light filtered through the curtains of their dormitory room.

They talked not only about politics, but about the difficulties—the impossibility—of planning for a future neither one could imagine.

A future one of them wouldn't even live to see.

Did Sarah know then? When did she make her decision . . . how many time has Elizabeth asked this unanswerable question?

She feels the warmth of Ben's body and is comforted.

She, too, drifts off to sleep as the morphine goes to work.

She wakes during the night to find him staring at her.

Still facing her. His eyes are wide and dark and focused on her face as if he's memorizing every freckle. His breath tickles her skin.

It's unsettling.

"What are you doing?" she asks.

"I think you're so beautiful," he whispers.

She cups his face in her hands. She feels an overwhelming urge to kiss him.

So she does.

She moves closer to him and he pulls the material of the chemise up and over her hips. She slips his undershirt off and they hug, skin to skin. She has forgotten the sensation of another person's body against her own. The warmth. The comfort.

She feels him getting hard. She maneuvers his boxers down over his erection and he slips her underpants off and they are lying together naked.

He kisses her breasts and her mouth again and she grabs him with both hands. He rolls onto his back and she slides onto him—gently, mindful of all his injuries. They both groan as he enters her and she slowly lets herself down on him and puts her arms around his neck and they rock back and forth, back and forth, back and forth, moaning, moaning, until first he cries out and then she does and she collapses into his arms and her hip isn't bothering her at all.

They fall asleep and wake up at the same time in the early hours of the morning. They lie together and talk in murmurs. She asks about his family. He tells her about his father, his mother, his pregnant sister, his brother Allen who was killed in the Battle of Belleau Wood in the war. Allen was only eighteen. Ben tells her about his uncle Moe. About the Purple Gang and his own desire to be part of it once, and what he's going through now because of them. About the friends who have ditched him. About Bernice, who has also ditched him. About what happened to Eddie. About his two years in college.

He asks about her family and she tells him the bare minimum: how her real father died (a heart attack at work; he left for the office as usual one day when she was in high school and she never saw him alive again), how her mother married a jerk, how her stepbrother is a rat.

How he tried to rape her once until she kneed him in the balls.

How her mother died after she left for college. How her alcoholic stepfather (previously her father's best friend at Briggs Manufacturing) manipulated his way into the estate and cut her off.

She tells him about her job, about "Cody Storm on the Case," about "The Lone Ranger." About Sarah Kirschner and how much Sarah meant to her (though not about the depths of their relationship; no need to scare him off). She tells him about a few of the men she's slept with, turning often unpleasant encounters into funny stories.

She does not tell him about Horace Howcroft.

He listens to her talk and strokes her hair. It feels to her as if her world—or all the world that matters at this moment—has contracted to the size of this room in the milky morning light of Palmer Park.

24

Roscoe Grissom

This is a big day. The Ford Rouge plant is mostly shut down, but when the tiny afternoon shift straggles into the Dew Drop, they bring stories of the big ruckus there. Heads broken, Harry Bennett shooting at protesters, Commies killed . . .

The regulars are boisterous even though none of them took part in the battle. They love it the lefties got their asses kicked.

Roscoe leaves with all the others when Frankie kicks them out. A couple of the men offer him a ride, but he decides to walk home. He'll go the long way. The scenic route, his father used to call it in his rare sober moments.

Tonight a long walk will do him good. Give him a chance to clear his head and brace himself for what awaits him at his house.

He walks past the vacant lot where the guy got dumped earlier. The guy's gone. Roscoe don't know if he left under his own steam or somebody called an ambulance or the meat wagon and it hauled him away. Nobody mentioned it inside the Dew Drop.

Served him right. Commie rat bastard.

He strolls up to the corner and turns down the side street. His is a quiet neighborhood of bungalows. Half are empty, abandoned by the residents who couldn't pay their rents or their mortgages and moved out. Or else were thrown out by the banks. Usually they left at night so no one would see them go in their shame.

A lot of the homes have their furnishings tossed out on the street. Piles of sofas and mattresses and chairs and stoves and lamps and all the junk folks accumulate—pots and pans, old clothes, framed photographs, here and there books. The older things are soggy from being out in the snow all winter. Most of the tables and chairs and other pieces of wood were long gone because people broke them up for firewood to keep warm.

Roscoe came up from the south. He hated the winters here but he wasn't planning on going back any time soon. With his relief checks and the little bit Melanie makes from cleaning rich people's houses, they were scraping by. It isn't easy.

They don't make it easy for the working man, those kikes who run this world. They just don't care about us. All they care about is counting their money.

And getting more.

Well, they'll be sorry. Roscoe and his new friends will do for them soon enough.

And his new friends are another reason why he won't be moving south anytime soon. These guys are what he's been waiting for his whole life. They like him and already trust him. Look at all they've asked him to do already.

He's walking down the street when Laverne Penney pulls up in his Packard. Rolls down the window.

"Just the man I'm looking for," Laverne says.

"Hey," Roscoe says. "How'd you find me?"

"Frankie said you just left. Up for an errand?"

"Sure thing. Long as it ain't a one-way ride," he says with a grin.

Laverne gives a hoot. "Hop in."

Roscoe jumps in the back seat. Two strangers are already in the car, one in the passenger seat and the other in the back.

Laverne pulls away. "This is Roscoe Grissom," he tells the other two. "Guy I was telling you about. He's one of us. He's a good'un."

Roscoe glows inside at the praise.

He sees Laverne's eyes peering at him in the rear-view mirror. "These two boys're part of our regiment," Laverne says. "When the weather's better we'll have a gathering and you'll meet the rest of them. We're getting stronger by the day."

The two guys look Roscoe over, staring hard at him. Laverne says, "Roscoe's the man I was telling you about."

He drives down Mack and pulls into a parking lot beside an empty building. It used to be a meat market before the crash.

The two others turn toward Roscoe. "Damn shame about that Jew the other night," Laverne says.

"It is," Roscoe agrees.

"We'll get him sooner or later, don't you worry. Tonight we got a different target."

He looks to the man in the passenger seat.

"Roscoe, this is Derrick Musgrove."

They shake hands. Derrick's grip is a bone-crusher.

"Hollis Pistole," the one next to Roscoe says. Southern accent, maybe North Carolina. Don't extend a hand.

"We got a problem Laverne says you can help us with," Derrick says.

"Sure," Roscoe says.

"Aces. Ever hear of an egg named Tom Glover?"

Roscoe shakes his head.

"Reporter for the *Detroit Times*."

"Okay."

Roscoe never reads any of the papers, so the name means nothing to him.

"It's a rag," Derrick says. "This joe's been giving the mayor of Highland Park a lot of grief. Keeps running him down, telling lies about him, how corrupt he is, and this and that. Trying to gin up opposition to the mayor in the next election."

"Okay," Roscoe says. Highland Park is a small city completely surrounded by Detroit. The politics don't mean anything to him.

"Problem is," Laverne says, "the mayor, he's one of us."

Roscoe understands this to mean the mayor of Highland Park is a member of the Legion. "Okay."

"This reporter, he needs to be shut up," Derrick says. "For good."

"Got to happen tonight," Hollis says.

For a few moments, Roscoe can't speak. His mouth goes completely dry with the thrill of the assignment.

"Can you do it for us?" Laverne asks.

"I surely can," Roscoe gets out. "What about the police?"

Derrick and Hollis share a look. Both reach into their pockets. They each pull out a bright gold police buzzer and flash it at Roscoe.

"You two guys are coppers?" Roscoe says.

"Highland Park dicks," Derrick says.

"Why don't you take care of him yourself?"

"Roscoe," Laverne says, "you're still new, so you don't know what's what. In this organization, the dirty work gets done by the new recruits. Which would be you. It's like part of the initiation."

Roscoe says nothing.

"So you in or what?" Hollis asks.

"Hunnert percent."

Laverne drives them up Woodward into Highland Park. They tell him Tom Glover lives in a bungalow on Farrand Park between John R and Brush Street. Laverne cruises by once and sees a Ford in the driveway. "His car," says Derrick.

"He's home," Laverne says. "Good."

"We going to take him here?" Roscoe asks.

"No," Derrick says. "He's got a wife and two little kids. They don't need to see their daddy shot to pieces."

"We already talked to him once," Hollis says. "Asked him to lay off the mayor. He didn't, so . . ."

"There's a city council meeting tonight," Derrick goes on. "He has to go out and cover it. I say we take him afterwards, on his way home. When he's by himself."

Laverne drives around the block and parks on Farrand down the street from Glover's house. "We'll stay here," Laverne says, "and follow him once he goes on the move."

The two coppers grunt in agreement.

"Okay with you?" Laverne asks Roscoe.

"Sure."

"Need to call the little woman, tell her you won't be home for dinner?"

"Nah. She ain't my boss."

"Good man," says Hollis.

The reporter doesn't leave the house for another two hours. Laverne, Derrick, and Hollis smoke constantly. The car is a fog of tobacco smoke. Roscoe opens the side window but it doesn't help much.

At quarter to seven, a man comes out onto the broad front porch of Glover's bungalow. Short and stocky. Wears a wool coat and a flat cap. Big mustache and round glasses.

"That's him," Hollis says.

"Here we go," Derrick says.

Laverne starts up the car, keeping the lights off. The four men watch Glover get into his car and back down the driveway. He heads off in the other direction from where Laverne is parked, toward John R. Takes a right on John R and Laverne follows.

"City Hall ain't but five blocks away," Hollis says. He takes a revolver out of his coat pocket and hands it to Roscoe.

"Remember this?" Laverne says. "You didn't get to use it last night."

"You will tonight," Derrick promises.

"You fired one of these before, ain't you?" Hollis asks.

"Sure," Roscoe says. "These meetings, how long they last?"

"Couple hours," Derrick says. "They usually start at seven and finish up by nine."

John R goes south one way, downtown, so Glover will have to exit the City Hall parking lot onto Woodward when he's done. Laverne parks on Woodward, south of the lot, so he only has to pull out after Glover's Ford.

"Where you want to take him?" Laverne asks Derrick.

"We shouldn't do it on Woodward. Too busy. Let's wait till he turns the corner down his street. We'll cut him off and take him there."

The other three nod agreement. Again they wait in silence and cigarette smoke.

After a while, Roscoe says to Derrick, "Where you from? You sound like a Southern boy."

"Raleigh, North Carolina. You?"

"Little place called Beech Bluff, Tennessee."

"Never heard of it."

"Halfway between Memphis and nowhere."

Derrick nods. Smokes in silence. "What brought you north?"

"Jobs," Roscoe says. "Back when there was jobs."

"Same here. I heard the police forces was hiring Southern boys to keep the niggers in line. So I joined up. Guess my job's more stable than yours."

"Guess so," Roscoe agrees. "Spades always going to be criminals."

"That's a fact."

The men lapse into silence again.

At quarter after nine, the City Hall doors open and people file out.

"Don't see Glover," Roscoe murmurs.

"No," Derrick says, "he stays until the end, jawing with the politicos."

"Why'd you decide to do this tonight?"

"He's been pushing real hard to recall the mayor. His article last week was the last straw. Especially after we told him to back off."

"So this is his order, the mayor's?" Roscoe asks.

"Nope," says Laverne. "Joint decision by the leaders of the regiment."

No more questions, his impatient tone says. Roscoe clams up and concentrates on what he has to do.

He knows he's going to have to kill this Glover guy. His insides begin to tremble, from nerves or excitement he can't tell. Tonight he's going to make his first blood. All the business with the Jew lawyer was just a warm-up. Tonight's the real thing.

Finally Glover and another man appear at the top of the stairs leading from City Hall. The other man reaches in and turns off a set of lights and pulls the big wooden door shut.

"Who's the other guy?" Roscoe asks.

"City Councilman. The mayor's opponent," Derrick says. "Papist, like Glover." He sucks his teeth in disdain.

"Whyn't we just kill them both?" Roscoe suggests.

The three others snicker. Derrick says. "Let's just do one at a time, tiger."

"Besides," Hollis says, "we kill them both, they'll know the murders are linked. The reporter's more dangerous to us. We punch his ticket, the councilman'll figure out what's what and drop right out."

Glover and the other man walk to the parking lot.

"Don't get in the same car," Derrick whispers.

In the parking lot, Glover and the other man shake hands and go to different cars.

"Good," Derrick says.

"Okay," Laverne says, "here we go. Look sharp." Starts his car up.

The councilman pulls out first and goes left on Woodward. Glover's car pulls out and turns right, toward his home. Laverne swings out behind him.

"Easy," says Hollis, "don't crowd him."

Laverne eases off the gas, lets Glover get a block ahead.

Glover turns onto Farrand Park and Laverne follows. Speeds up. There are no streetlights here, just a glow of light from behind them on Woodward.

"Now!" Derrick says.

The street is wide. Laverne swings out to pass Glover on the right to cut him off. But Glover's too quick. He speeds up at once and roars ahead of Laverne. Races down the street. Passes his house. Makes a screeching right turn onto John R.

Laverne is after him now. John R is well-lit and empty. Glover can certainly see what is happening in his rear-view mirror. His car leaps away on John R.

Glover takes another screaming right onto Colorado Street. Punches it again up to Woodward.

"Don't lose him!" Derrick yells.

"I won't," Laverne says.

At the intersection, Glover barely slows and roars out onto Woodward. Heads left, in the direction of downtown Detroit.

"Go!" Derrick hollers.

Laverne wrestles the big Packard onto Woodward after Glover. Glover has the newer, faster car. Laverne tries to keep up, but Glover increases the distance between them.

The reporter blows through a red light and Laverne has to stop to avoid hitting a car coming crosswise. He loses more time.

Glover's car is already five or six blocks ahead of Laverne's and increasing his lead.

"Don't lose him, goddammit!" Derrick shouts.

Laverne can't make up the distance. Derrick is yelling about catching Glover and pounding the dashboard.

It's not going to happen. The other man's Ford Roadster is easily outrunning Laverne's heavy Packard.

Glover's taillights disappear to the right up ahead near the Masonic Temple. Laverne tries to follow. He gets caught at a light and can't break through crosswise traffic. By the time he can make a right turn, Glover's car is nowhere in sight.

Laverne slows at every intersection—Park, Cass, Second.

Glover has disappeared.

"Godammit!" Derrick cries, and smashes a fist on the dashboard in front of him. "You lost him!"

"Wait," Laverne says. Keeps going up and down the streets. Still no sign of Glover's roadster.

He's gone.

Roscoe is deflated, again—for yet another time, he has been denied the chance to make his first blood.

"Shit!" Hollis yells. "You stupid fuck!"

Laverne keeps zigzagging around the city streets. There is other traffic on the road, but not the roadster.

It's no use. Glover is gone.

"You lost him," Derrick says again.

"Keep your shirt on," Laverne says. "We'll go back to his house and wait for him. He has to go home sooner or later."

"He knows we're looking for him. Think he'll go back there?"

"Then we'll hold his family hostage until he does," Laverne says.

"That's against our code," Hollis shouts.

"Pull over," Derrick orders. "You stupid son of a bitch." He's sputtering in rage.

Laverne pulls over to the curb on Henry Street, behind the dark hulk of the factory-like Cass Technical High School.

Hollis grabs the .38 from Roscoe and shoots Laverne in the back of the head.

Roscoe stifles a scream.

Blood and brains and teeth splatter the driver's window and windshield. In the front seat, Derrick produces a handkerchief and starts wiping down the dashboard, his side of the car, the passenger door hardware. Hollis grabs Roscoe by the wrist and pulls him out of the car.

Roscoe and Hollis stand in the darkness behind the massive high school. Roscoe is shivering.

When Derrick finishes wiping the car of their traces, he joins Hollis and Roscoe. "We'll leave it there," Derrick says.

They walk up to Cass Avenue and head north in the direction of the looming Masonic Temple.

Next to the Temple is the Hotel Fort Wayne. Inside smells like disinfectant. Hollis leaves Roscoe in a deep chair in the lobby while Derrick makes a phone call.

"You did swell back there," Hollis says.

"I didn't do nothing," Roscoe says.

"No, you were stand-up. You were ready to do your job. You showed me something. This guy?" He lifts a thumb toward the street, indicating where they left Laverne in the car. "Shows you what happens when you fuck up an assignment for the Black Legion. You paying attention?"

Roscoe nods.

"Good. This is no joke. We're on a mission to save white Christian America. We can't afford no mistakes. Now here, take this." He hands Roscoe a handkerchief. "You got some blood on your face. Right there."

Roscoe takes the handkerchief, rubs where Hollis points. He could go into the bathroom to wet it except he doesn't think he could stand looking at his own face in the mirror right now.

Derrick comes back and says, "We're set."

In another fifteen minutes they hear a car horn outside, and Derrick and Hollis guide Roscoe out of the lobby and into a Highland Park Police sled.

Roscoe don't recognize the copper behind the wheel. As soon as they jump in the car, it pulls away. Derrick in the front again, Roscoe and Hollis in the back.

Derrick turns to Roscoe. "Doing okay?"

"Yeah," Roscoe says. Hides his shaking hands by folding his arms. "Except I need me a drink in the worst way."

"That can be arranged," Derrick says with a wink at Hollis.

TUESDAY, MARCH 8, 1932

25

CLARENCE BROWN

When Clarence walks into the muster room at the Hunt Street Station, the chatting stops like somebody flipped a switch. There's already one colored uniform officer, Ernest Cummings, sitting off by himself. Clarence joins him. One colored policeman can be ignored. Two is too many.

Clarence is used to it. He has been a member of the Detroit Police Department since 1924, assigned to Hunt Street the whole time. The other coppers made it clear they wanted nothing to do with him, and he was just as happy to steer clear of them.

The only white cop who was different was Albert Norquist. Albert was another Southerner, as a lot of the other cops were, though he didn't share the others' race hatred. Albert respected Clarence and had since the day they met. Albert was driving the paddy wagon the day Clarence rescued a group of Negroes from the Paradise Theatre in Paradise Valley after an angry white mob stormed the theatre. The petrified manager called the police and they sent Clarence.

Who scoped out the situation and commandeered Albert's passing paddy wagon. Clarence told Albert to back it up to the theatre doors so those trapped inside could escape safely. Since then, Clarence and Albert had been close—or as close as a Negro man and a white man could be in Detroit in 1932.

Albert sits in the muster room, too, with the other white cops. He and Clarence share a look—as close as they can get to a greeting in this department.

Now Clarence half-listens as the sergeant rattles off the daily crimes and assignments at the front of the muster room. Whatever else the others would be doing, Clarence knows he and Ernest will be going back to Black Bottom and Paradise Valley.

Niggertown, the white cops call it.

The Jungle.

Where the jungle bunnies live, filled with shine boxes (the Negro nightclubs). The white cops have said as much to his face.

The sergeant starts talking about the Hunger March yesterday and Clarence listens more closely.

"The Commies got their ass whipped yesterday out at Ford's," the sergeant says. "Dearborn's finest showed them what we do to Reds in this country."

An approving murmur comes from those assembled.

"On orders from the mayor," the sarge says, "we were told just to accompany the marchers to the Detroit-Dearborn border. Which we did. Once they got into Dearborn, their coppers did what I'm sure our boys had been itching to do the whole time. Four Reds dead, another couple dozen in the hospital."

Cops clap. Others shout approval. Clarence and Ernest stay silent.

"Commies ain't taking over *our* city," one cop yells.

This causes a general raucous outbreak until the sergeant shouts them down.

"Shut up! As a direct result of what happened yesterday, the Special Investigation Bureau's doing a major crackdown on Reds. They'll be raiding the headquarters of the Communist Party, the Auto Workers Union, and private homes harboring Reds or Red sympathizers. The following of you people are assisting."

He reads a list of names and Clarence stops listening. He knows he won't be tasked to the Red squad today, or anyplace else besides his usual assignment.

Which is just the way he likes it.

Out on the street. His beat.

As cold as it was the day before. Crimes he needs to investigate today: a purse snatching, a botched drugstore robbery, a fight over a girl between two young bloods that put both of them in the hospital, a couple of store thefts . . . chickenshit stuff. He knows this level of crime is part of the daily life of the people who live here, and they depend on him to police their streets. Still . . . the others are Red-hunting and he's dicking around with this shit . . .

He takes care of his list before noon. The knuckleheads who pull off this kind of shit aren't mental giants or criminal masterminds. The purse snatcher is a friend of the cousin of the woman who got it snatched; easy to track down and bring in.

He visits the apartment of the two morons who botched the robbery of the drugstore. They resist and he beats them senseless—not that they had much sense to begin with—before taking them to the station.

(He remembers he still needs to find his other drugstore thief, Andre Young. Neither of the idiots he collars knows where Andre is.)

The girl who the two young men fought over is making time with a third young man, so Clarence gives her a come-to-Jesus talk and lets nature take its course.

The thefts from the stores will be harder to solve, so Clarence puts those off until after lunch.

Which he decides he will eat at Tipton's Luncheonette up on Hastings in Paradise Valley. He sits on a stool at the counter and orders the daily special, barbeque chicken and mashed potatoes, and washes it down with a Coca-Cola.

He spots a copy of the *Free Press* on the counter. While he eats, he idly reads the main story on the front page.

4 DIE IN RIOT AT FORD PLANT

MURDER CHARGES ASKED AFTER RED MOB FIGHTS POLICE

Inflamed Communists Hurl Stones and Clubs in Pre-Arranged Outbreak

Harry Bennet and Others in Hospital Following Battle Started When Agitator Fires Six Shots

Six shots fired by a Communist hidden behind a parked car were cited by police Monday night as the match which touched off a riot at the Ford Motor Co. plant, Miller Road, early in the afternoon in which four men were killed and 29 seriously injured.

Scores of others among some 2,500 rioters were beaten and bruised before they were dispersed by Dearborn and Detroit police, State troopers and deputy sheriffs with pistols, shotguns and tear gas.

Harry Bennett, head of the Ford Service Department, was wounded and is in Henry Ford Hospital, not in danger. Stories conflict as to how he was injured.

Three May Face Murder Charges

Three reported ringleaders of the mob, who may be charged with murder, are among 29 prisoners, five of whom are women, held at the County Jail and Dearborn police headquarters.

Sounds like a mess. Of course, there's no guarantee this is what actually happened. Anybody who's been part of a news event and read about it in the papers afterwards knows they always get it wrong.

He's lingering over a cigarette and the last of his drink when a girl slides onto the stool beside him.

Dorcas Coleman.

Skinny, teenaged, looking like she hasn't slept or changed her clothes in a week. He knows her. He's pinched her father. Her mother does domestic work to keep the family together.

"Hey, Mr. Clarence," she says.

"Dorcas. How you doing?"

"Fine."

She draws out the word, swinging around on the stool. The waitress comes over to take her order. Dorcas shakes her head, says, "Nothing for me. Ain't staying."

"How you getting on, Dorcas?" Clarence asks.

"Fine," she says again.

"What are you doing here, girl? Why aren't you in school, this time of day?"

"This my lunch hour."

"Lunch? You don't look like you been eating lunch to me. You even been to school today?"

"Yeah. I been in school all morning."

"Don't be telling me stories. Look of you, I bet you haven't been to school in a week."

"Oh, Mr. Clarence."

"So what do you want?"

"Got a message for you."

"From who?"

"Junior."

"Why can't Junior give me his message himself?"

"Because he axe me to. He say he don't wanna be seen talking with you."

She slouches across the counter, tugging on a piece of straightened hair.

"Well, what is it?" Clarence asks. "Tell me and you can get on with your busy day at school."

"He say he know something about that boy you asking about."

"What boy?"

190

"That boy Darius."

Now she has his attention.

"What's the message?"

"He say he need to meet with you."

"Junior does?"

She nods.

"Why?"

"It's all he told me to tell you, Mr. Clarence. I don't know nothing else. He just say it's important."

"Okay, then. Where?"

"He say he meet you in the back of Mr. Fred's."

"Girl, I know five hundred people in this town named Fred."

"Mr. Fred who own the billiard parlor."

"The one on Beaubien?"

"Yessir."

"When?"

"Junior say he there now."

"You coming right from seeing him?"

"Uh-huh."

"I thought you said you were in school all morning?"

She flashes him a broad smile, caught in the lie. "Oh, Mr. Clarence. You so funny."

She pulls herself together and leaves.

He watches her go and the waitress comes over with a new Coca-Cola.

"Mr. Clarence," she says, "can I refill you?"

"No, Miss Etta, thank you. I believe I'm finished."

"You enjoy your lunch today?"

"Every day, Miss Etta. It's why I come so often. Can I get my bill, please?"

"Oh no, Mr. Clarence, Mr. Tipton, he don't never charge you for your food."

Clarence knows this, asks anyway. It is a routine they go through whenever Clarence eats here. Tipton the owner likes to have Clarence be seen in his restaurant. The sight of the large police detective discourages anybody who might be wanting to cause trouble.

Clarence leaves a fifty-cent tip for Miss Etta and follows Dorcas out the door.

A smoky room. Dim pools of light above each table, cutting through the gloom.

Clarence gets nods from the pool shooters as he walks through. The ones he's nabbed before avoid his eyes.

Fred sits behind the counter. He's in a wheelchair from injuries he suffered during the Great War. His right leg below the knee was blown away.

He nods to Clarence. Says, "Waiting on you in the back." Raspy voice. Fred was gassed, too. Sitting in a fog of cigarette smoke day after day in the pool parlor can't be good for him. He throws a thumb over his shoulder in the direction of a door.

Inside is a cavernous space with boxes of Cross & Peters Chips and cases of Faygo pop. A circular stairway leads up to the second floor.

There Clarence finds a smaller pool room. Fred's VIP area. Only one of the tables is in use. Junior Robinson, playing by himself.

"Junior," Clarence says.

Junior is taller and more filled-in than the time Clarence met him—must be three years now. Junior loved to tinker with cars, so the neighborhood people with cars brought them to Junior for tune-ups and mechanical fixes. In one of the vehicles, Junior found an envelope containing $5,000 in cash in the glove compartment. Rather than leave it there, Junior took the money.

Which turned out to belong to Robinhood Rowe, who wanted it back in the worst way. Clarence negotiated the return of the money along with a promise from Robinhood not to hurt Junior beyond a beating from one of LaMont's boys for the inconvenience. Ever since, Junior helps out Clarence with a word or name when he can. It was Junior who tipped him off about Andre Young last week.

Junior lines up his shot carefully and scratches. Grimaces in annoyance. "Damn. You made me miss my shot, man."

"Dorcas said you got something for me."

192

"I do."

Junior walks around the table, retrieving the balls from the pockets and rolling them onto the felt.

"Well?" Clarence says.

"I heard you looking for the guy who iced Darius Turner."

"How you know that?"

"Little birdie told me."

"Little birdie have a name?"

"Let's just say I can help you out."

"How?"

"I know who did it."

Clarence waits a few moments. "Are you going to tell me?"

Junior racks the balls up on the table. "Well, see, the thing is, I don't know his *name*, exactly."

"Uh-huh."

"I know the next best thing."

Clarence waits.

Sighs. "Junior . . ."

"I know where you can find him."

"How do you come by this information?"

"I hear things, man. You did me a favor back in the day, I do you a favor today. How it works, right?"

"How it works."

Junior chalks up his cue. "Play a little game?"

Big Clarence takes a step closer, looms over his snitch. "Just say what you have to tell me."

26

BEN RUBIN

He wakes to an unfamiliar lavender scent. The soft feel of tousled bedding. The strange sight of a half-empty bed beside him. It takes him a minute to remember where he is and how he got here.

He sits up. He is naked. The middle of the night comes back to him.

His head throbs and his shoulders and legs are stiff. He swings his legs out and stands. Takes a few moments to make sure he has his balance. Fights down nausea. He pulls his clothes on. Pads barefoot into the living room of Elizabeth's apartment.

She stands in a gray satin robe at the counter in the kitchen. Fragrant coffee is percolating.

She turns when she sees him. "Morning."

"Good morning," he croaks. His mouth is totally dry.

"Here." She pours him a glass of water, which he drinks greedily. "Better?"

"Better."

"How are you feeling?"

"I'm not my all-time best."

"I don't expect you would be."

"May I?" he asks, points to the coffee percolator.

"Help yourself. How do you take it?"

"Black is fine."

He pours it out and takes a sip. Feels the effects immediately.

"Are you hungry?" she asks.

"I don't know yet."

"Sit down. I'll bring you something."

They sit at the table in the dining room. Like all the other rooms, it is large and sparsely furnished.

She sets the box of corn flakes and a bowl on the table and returns for a pitcher of milk and a spoon.

"You're not having anything?" he asks.

"I don't usually eat in the morning."

He pours out the cereal. Takes a surreptitious sniff of the milk—still good—and pours it over the cereal. Lifts a spoonful. Chewing is painful with his fractured cheek, so he holds each spoonful in his mouth and sucks on it until it's soft enough to go down easily.

"How are you?" he asks.

"Fine. For the most part."

He feels shyer with her than she seems with him. He's not sure how to broach their sex.

She beats him to it. "I guess you were ready after all last night," she says with a wry grin.

"I guess so."

"How's your head?"

"Hurts."

She nods. "Tough day. I still can't believe the Dearborn police fired into the crowd."

"And Ford's security goons, too."

He gobbles up more corn flakes. He is hungrier than he thought.

"We have to make sure the truth gets out about what happened," she says.

"How?"

"We're having a meeting about it tonight."

"The Party?"

"Along with the union people. The thing they don't understand, this is just the beginning of what's going to turn into a long war. More coffee?"

"No thanks."

She goes into the kitchen to refill her cup. "What are you going to do," she asks, back at the table.

Again that question.

"First thing, I'm going to talk to my uncle. See what he has to say about my situation."

"You're welcome to stay here as long as you need to."

"Thanks."

He takes a sip of the coffee. They sit looking at each other, like they're both wondering what happened during the night, or if they dreamed it. And if not, whether it will happen again.

Or maybe just Ben is.

She stands, and the moment passes. "I have to get ready for work."

"Sure."

Before she takes her cup into the kitchen, she leans down and kisses him on the lips. Hers are soft, pillowy. It lingers. It answers a few of his questions.

This time of the morning, he knows his Uncle Moe will be at the schvitz on Oakland and Melbourne Street. It's a risk to go there. The Bernsteins and their boys relax there, but Ben is ready to chance it to see his uncle.

He takes the Woodward Avenue streetcar downtown to Euclid and walks the five short blocks to the massive gray Oakland Health Club.

Inside, he climbs the stairs through the muggy fug permeating the building from the baths. The effort makes his cheek throb. He goes to the lounge beside the check-in desk. Already a handful of men are on the leather sofas, old guys relaxing after their steam baths and dip in the cold pool. They chat in Yiddish.

An old man with white grizzled stubble and a yarmulke stands behind the counter. He says, "Something you want?"

"I'm looking for Moe Feigenbaum."

"Still downstairs." The old guy throws a look at the clock behind him. "He'll be up soon."

"I'll just wait up here, if you don't mind."

"Around the corner, *you* don't mind. Leave these *alter kakers* to their stories." With a flick of his wrist, he dismisses the men in the leather chairs.

This brings a flurry of Yiddish from one of the men, followed by laughter all around. Except for Ben, who misses the joke because he doesn't speak the language beyond a few all-purpose words (*momzer, mazel tov*, and *plotz*, primarily).

He goes around the corner to an alcove with square tables. A quartet of men sit at one of the tables playing Pinochle. Rosy from their steams, they stop to give Ben the once-over before getting back to their game.

In a few minutes Ben hears the old man behind the counter say something else in Yiddish, and his Uncle Moe peeks around the corner.

"You," he says.

"Hey, Uncle Moe."

Moe goes to grab him in a bearhug but Ben says, "Easy!" Everything hurts.

Moe backs off. He is fragrant from the exotic herbs in the *plaitza*, the rubdown of oak leaves from a bucket of soapy water, part of the schvitz. "Let's get out of here," he says. "We'll have tea down the street."

He hustles Ben out of the bathhouse and out to a luncheonette on Oakland.

There they order two teas. Moe takes a long look at Ben's face.

"They worked you over but good, boychik," Moe says. "Lucky you still got your teeth. You took a risk, coming there. You could have run into the very mugs who did this to you."

"I thought if you were there, nothing would happen."

Moe shakes his head. His jowls jiggle. "Now I'm waiting for my trial, I don't have the influence I used to have."

An old woman smelling of mothballs shuffles over with their tea in glasses on a tray. Moe says something to her in Yiddish and she nods and goes away.

"What did you say?" Ben asks.

"I said, 'Thank you, my old friend.' What did you think was I going to say? 'Call the hoodlums, Ben's here'?"

"You'd never."

"Goddamn right. So. What's so urgent you have to meet me in the belly of the beast?"

"I'm in trouble, Moe."

"I heard. Here's where I say I told you this would happen."

"You were right."

"I heard about Eddie. I also heard the boys got hold of you and kicked the shit out of you."

"This isn't all from them." Ben puts his hand up to the side of his head. "I had an accident at the march yesterday."

"Now you're a labor agitator? You're living dangerously, Benny."

Ben sips his tea. It is scalding hot. Pain flares up in his cheek in protest.

"So, *nu*? What is it?" Moe asks.

"Uncle Moe, they said they're going to kill me. Even though what happened to Eddie wasn't my fault."

"They don't see it that way."

"You talked to them?"

Moe shrugs. "People talk. I hear things."

"Can you do anything?"

"Call them off, you mean?"

"Yeah."

Moe puts a cube of sugar in his mouth, takes a sip of tea in the old Russian style. "Eddie was Harry Millman's nephew."

"I know. Eddie bragged about it all the time. Izzie Bernstein said Harry wants to leave me the same way he says I left Eddie. With a bullet in my head. They're talking like I killed him."

"Look. I can try and talk to them. I can't promise nothing. When these guys get an idea in their heads, it usually stays there. And it doesn't end well."

"If you can't talk them out of it, I'm going to have to leave town."

"If I can't talk them out of it, they'll try to get you before you go. And if they can't get to you, they'll get to your mother. Or your sister."

Ben puts his head in his hands and rests his elbows on the table. "Isn't there anything you can do?"

"I can try."

"Uncle Moe, thank—"

Moe raises his hands. "Not so fast. I'll try to talk Harry out of it. Like I said, I don't have the juice I used to. They don't trust me the way they once did."

"Why not?"

"They know I'm awaiting trial. They're afraid I'm going to cooperate to get a lighter sentence."

"Don't they know you wouldn't?"

Moe shakes his head sadly. "These are dangerous men, these *meshuggenehs*. Believe me, I know. I used to be one of them."

"Whatever they want me to do, I'll do, if it gets me out from under them."

"Where are you staying? With your sister?"

"Isaac doesn't want me there. Says it isn't safe."

"He's right. How can I reach you?"

Ben writes Elizabeth's phone number on a scrap of paper from his pocket and gives it to Moe.

Moe folds the paper. "I'll be in touch. In the meantime, stay out of sight, all right? And *don't* come back to the schvitz."

27

Elizabeth Waters

The ringing phone drags her out of her bathtub, dripping wet. Erroll Lembeck. District organizer of the Young Communist League of Detroit. "Elizabeth, thank God you're still there."

"What's the matter?"

"You haven't heard?"

"No."

"They're sweeping us up."

"Who's sweeping who up?"

"The coppers. Run by the fucking Special Investigations Bureau."

Horace Howcroft's department.

"Who's getting swept up?"

"Everybody. They raided the Party headquarters and arrested everybody in sight. Also the Auto Workers Union, the ethnic halls, private citizens . . . they're grabbing people off the streets, Elizabeth."

"Because of the march?"

"They're rounding up everybody connected with it. I'm calling from a phone box in the street. I was on my way in to work when they raided headquarters. Stop asking questions and get yourself someplace safe!"

Elizabeth hangs up and throws her clothes on. She runs a brush through her hair when a banging comes on her apartment door.

She goes into the front hall, but before she gets to the door they burst in. They knock her down and tramp into her living room.

Four men. Two in cop uniforms, two in double-breasted suits.

With shotguns.

The two uniforms flip her on her stomach and handcuff her behind her back. The suits ransack her apartment. They drag her to her feet and out to where a paddy wagon idles on Manderson. Neighbors on the street stop and watch Elizabeth getting thrown into the back.

She is alone in the wagon except for the cops, who don't speak to her. The paddy wagon makes a few more stops in Hamtramck and fills up with Mexican women. Like Elizabeth, they are dragged out of their homes and sit, too frightened to speak.

They go to Police Headquarters at 1300 Beaubien downtown.

The women are manhandled off the wagon and shoved inside the sally port where they are made to line up. Women are already in line. A few are white; some are Mexican.

They're using this as an opportunity to collect the Mexicans and prepare them for deportation, Elizabeth realizes. This is exactly what Gilberto Ramirez was talking about at the Unemployed Council meeting last weekend.

But they are not booked. Instead the women are taken inside and searched by a pair of bull dyke matrons with rough hands that wander all over Elizabeth's body and under her clothes. The matrons are under the direction of a hard-looking woman with a pasty face and a solid body beneath her gray tunic. Women who talk back are strip-searched right then and there.

They are taken down to the women's holding cells. The Mexican women who dare to put up any complaints get even rougher treatment from the matrons.

"Wetbacks," the head matron spits. "Shut your filthy mouths. Go back to Mexico where you belong."

As the morning passes, more women are brought down to the cells as paddy wagons unload them. On the other side of a partition, they can hear men driven into their holding pens. From the slaps and groans and thuds Elizabeth hears, they sound like they are being treated worse than the women.

All in all, thirty women are crammed into one holding pen. They are not all from the march; beside the Mexican women in their peasant dresses, Elizabeth recognizes a handful of members of the Communist Party. Others seem to be prostitutes—or at least they're dressed like it, with blowsy hair and low-cut dresses and hems up to their thighs. They are more blasé about their situation than the other women. Elizabeth supposes this is nothing out of the ordinary; jail is a revolving door for them while their johns see no interruption to their lives whatsoever.

There is a single flush toilet in the corner of the cell for all of them. Soon they run out of toilet tissue and the toilet begins to overflow. The smells of urine and shit are strong and disgusting. The women clamor for attention from the matrons, who ignore them.

"Speak English!" is all the matrons say. When the women speak their heavily-accented English, the matrons sneer at them and call them spics.

The Party members congregate in one corner of the pen. Like Elizabeth, they were dragged without explanation from their homes and from Party offices around the city. Elizabeth sits with them. They share what little information they have. They've all been treated the same way.

In a few hours, the Mexican women are taken one-by-one from the cell. Each returns in twenty minutes, shaken and disheveled. Elizabeth can't figure out what went on with them because they speak in break-neck Spanish to each other. When she tries to find out what they are saying, they scream at her in more Spanish.

After one woman is taken away and never returned, Elizabeth finds a spot on the floor to sink down into away from the toilet. Even so, the spot is filthy, sickening with the reek of urine and vomit.

She lets her head fall into her knees.

Someone must know I'm here, she hopes.

Except the only people who will know will themselves be in custody.

28

ROSCOE GRISSOM

"Have you heard from Laverne?" Enoch asks.

Roscoe tries to keep a poker face. Bleary-eyed, hungover from the night before. "No. Why?"

"Nobody can figure out where he is."

Roscoe sits at the bar at the Dew Drop. Sips his coffee in silence. Says, "Ain't heard nothing from him. I expect he'll turn up sooner or later."

"You were with him last night," Enoch points out.

"What am I, his fucking nursemaid?"

"All right, all right. Don't bite my head off."

Roscoe didn't leave the bar last night with Derrick Musgrove and Hollis Pistole until after midnight, way after closing time. Roscoe was in his cups from the bootleg hooch. The two Highland Park coppers seemed sober enough to drive Roscoe home.

Now he's back in the Dew Drop.

Another long day stretches out ahead of him.

Another long, boring day of shooting the shit with Enoch and the rest of the morons, while the only thing he can see when he shuts his eyes is the pattern of Laverne's brains and blood on the windshield.

"So," Enoch says, "how was he?"

Roscoe rubs his forehead. Wishing he could rub out the pain. And the nausea. Or at least drink them away. Sadly, it's not time for Frankie to open up the back room yet.

"He was fine when I saw him."

(Which is true, Roscoe reminds himself, mostly.)

(Except for the part about Laverne getting his brains blown out.)

"We went out on a mission," Roscoe says, "and afterwards he dropped me home and left."

"He didn't say where he was going?"

Roscoe shakes his head.

(Hurts!)

"Crazy," Enoch says.

Roscoe shrugs.

"What was the mission?"

Roscoe makes a quick calculation. Wants to impress Enoch, but don't want to bring the Highland Park dicks into it. "There's a reporter out there making trouble for us."

Loves saying *us*.

"We were going to punch his ticket," he continues.

"You do it?"

"Nah. He got away. So Laverne took me home and I never seen him after that."

He wants to make sure Enoch gets it through his thick skull: Roscoe has nothing to do with Laverne's disappearance. Especially since Laverne—or what's left of him—will probably be found today.

Might already have been found, in fact, moldering his car.

Unless Derrick and Hollis had a trick up their sleeves and got the car moved before it could be found. Which they probably did. Cops knew all the ins and outs.

The thought cheers him. It even settles his upset stomach.

At twelve sharp, Frankie opens the back room and the regulars gas up on his hooch. Roscoe borrows some coins from Enoch so he can get a drink, too.

Then more bullshitting.

Lunch at the soup kitchen.

Back to Frankie's for the rest of the afternoon.

Roscoe sits with Enoch and the others. He can't get rid of the image of Laverne's brains and blood painting the inside of the front windshield. Thick clots, white and gray and red and black, even in the darkness.

He remembers Derrick and Hollis praising his nerve.

Nerves. It reminds Roscoe of the strings of red and white dripping from the glass. From the car's headliner. From the steering wheel.

Roscoe finishes his drink and stands.

"Hey," Enoch says, "where you going?"

Without answering, Roscoe takes off.

He tramps around the neighborhood streets, struggling with the memory of Hollis killing Laverne. The visual images, but also the loud "Bang!" The smell of the gunpowder in the enclosed space. The metallic stench of blood and the sickening odor of shit when Laverne's bowels let loose.

Walks up to Van Dyke. Goes north until he comes to Harper, where he sees the marquee for the Eastown Theatre. The theatre is showing "20,000 Years in Sing Sing." Exactly the kind of movie Roscoe would never get to see because his wife hated prison movies. She said they reminded her of her own father, who did time in the West Tennessee State Penitentiary after killing a man when he was young. This was before he abandoned the family when Melanie was ten.

As luck would have it, the next show starts in fifteen minutes. And Roscoe has a dime in his pocket left over from the money he got from Enoch. He buys his ticket. The smell of popcorn makes him crave a box. Not enough money for a box, and anyway he just ate lunch at the soup kitchen.

At this time of day, in the middle of the week, the theatre is mostly empty, just a handful of men spread around the auditorium. Out of work and out of luck, like Roscoe, with nothing except time to kill.

He finds a seat in the middle of a middle row, and settles back when the lights go down.

Before the main feature comes on, he watches coming attractions for movies he isn't interested in.

When they end, a newsreel starts. Brassy trumpets announce a Universal Newspaper Newsreel. The first story:

GRIM PACIFIC ARMADA SAILS TO PARTICIPATE IN HAWAII "MIMIC" WAR

It's about an armada of American warships sailing to Hawaii to take part in large-scale war games. The Great War ended just thirteen years ago. Roscoe was too young to fight. He should be just the right age for the next war, which seems right around the corner, to judge from these newsreels.

He has no idea whether the United States will join the coming war or not. Depends if the Jews push the country into it, he knows. Either way, it'll be nothing to do with him. Let the foreigners kill each other. The fewer of them in the world, the better.

Next comes a story about a dirigible in New Jersey going aground before it can rise with its passengers.

SUDDEN GALE INJURES AKRON AS COMMITTEE AWAITS TRIAL FLIGHT

Why would anyone in their right minds get on a gas-filled balloon, Roscoe wonders as he watches the clumsy airship the Akron try to rise. Then like a wounded animal it crashes in slow motion to the ground.

The third newsreel catches his attention.

MOSCOW MENACE PROVOKES MELEE OUTSIDE FORD PLANT

It's about the march on Monday.

How did they get it ready so fast? It must have been made overnight and released today.

The brass-balls-voice of the narrator screams about the "Moscow Menace" and the heroism of Harry Bennett and his troops as the screen flashes black and white images of men charging the police and fire brigades. Thanks to tear gas and water cannons, the hordes were driven away from the Ford River Rouge plant and back into Detroit.

"Outside Communist agitators took advantage of beaten-down Detroiters to whip up a riot," the narrator cries. "The forces of law and order did what they had to do."

Next on screen is a clip of a man Roscoe don't recognize.

"The Honorable Frank Murphy, the mayor of Detroit," the narrator says, "promises an investigation into how the day descended into chaos."

The mayor says, "There's no excuse for this level of violence at a march that started out peacefully. I'm going to direct my police commissioner, James Watkins, to launch an investigation into what happened and why."

The feature starts, Roscoe has trouble concentrating. Spencer Tracy plays a man sentenced to thirty years in Sing Sing. Watching the problems Tracy has to deal with, all Roscoe can picture is his own future in prison if one of his Black Legion missions actually does succeed—as one will, sooner or later—and he's caught.

Especially if he's the one to pull the trigger, which poor Laverne was determined to make happen. Because even if somebody is an enemy of the Legion, there will still be someone else to say they shouldn't be killed.

He looks at it from every point of view and decides no, he'll never wind up in prison.

Even if he's caught (which is doubtful, since so many of the police are in the Legion), the DAs and mayors will all be in the Legion, too, and probably most of the jury. He believes he's at the beginning of a movement that will spread further and further across the American landscape until the enemies of white America are defeated.

It's a crusade. And Roscoe is a crusader.

So even if Laverne's body is found, Derrick and Hollis will keep themselves out of it. And they will also keep Roscoe out of it, Roscoe hopes.

Besides, he tells himself, he didn't do nothing. He was just an innocent bystander when Laverne Penny got his brains blown out. He's completely innocent.

So he tells himself.

Roscoe starts to rest easy in the darkness, knowing the fix will be in for him if the worst should happen.

He rests so easy, in fact, he falls asleep.

When the scattered men in the auditorium begin shushing him, he pops awake. He has been snoring.

"You wanna sleep, get a room," one man across the theatre growls. His voice echoes in the nearly-empty auditorium. "I'm trying to watch the picture here."

Roscoe shakes his head to clear it, raises a hand of apology, and watches the rest of the movie in perfect confidence Spencer Tracy's fate will never be his own.

29

CLARENCE BROWN

The building is a four-story brick apartment house on a cul-de-sac off St. Aubin. Clarence parks down the street. Nobody goes in or out during the half-hour he watches and waits.

Junior told him the man he needs to see stays in an apartment on the third floor in the rear. Junior acts coy about how he got this information, so Clarence trusts it even less than he usually would from somebody as shady as Junior.

Still, it's worth a look. There isn't much else to rely on at the moment.

He gets out of the car and adjusts his guns and metal plates. Walks slowly down the street of quiet apartment buildings. Nobody else is around. He can hear traffic sounds from East Grand Boulevard nearby—engines, horns, the occasional angry yell.

He stands outside the building, wraps his overcoat around him in the chill wind. Inside the foyer, the inner door is unlocked, so he enters. The lobby is tiny and dark with heavy wooden panels on the walls. Gray mailboxes line one wall. Clarence is looking for apartment 3C. There are no names on the mailboxes.

The building is a walkup. He climbs, pausing on the landing of the third floor to catch his breath. The hallway up here is narrow and smells of ammonia. Two doors on either side, one in the middle.

Clarence stands outside 3C for a minute, trying to listen. He might hear the murmur of voices. He can't be sure.

Stands beside the door considering his options. His instinct? Break the door down, crash into the room, and see what happens. He judges the door won't be any problem for him. The lock and the hinges are old, like the rest of the building. Count to three, take a running leap at the door.

He reconsiders. Maybe not the best approach for going into a situation where he doesn't know what's waiting for him on the other side of the door. Especially if Junior was right, and whoever lives here is responsible for Darius Turner's death.

He opens his coat and draws both Colt .45s. Moves aside from the direct line of the door. Taps on it with the barrel of a gun.

When there is no response, he taps again, says, "Detroit Police."

A voice inside calls, "It's open."

Standing at the side of the door, Clarence turns the knob, pushes the door open. Takes a peek inside.

A living room. Unfurnished.

In front of a fireplace are three white men. For a moment, he wonders if they are part of the Purple Gang—they are in their forties; the one in the middle holds a tommy gun; the others stand with their hands in their overcoat pockets, like movie gangsters. All are in fedoras.

They look like they were sent over from Central Casting.

They are staring at him and sneering.

He enters the doorway. "Who are you guys?"

"Don't you recognize us, Sambo?" says the one on the left.

Clarence swallows his anger. Decides to try something.

Says, "You must work a different precinct than me. Don't recognize you."

The guy with the tommy gun loses his smile. Must have hit too close to home. "Come in and close the door."

Clarence stays put.

The guy on the left says, "Suit yourself. Hey, you been asking a lot of questions, Sambo."

The guy in the middle says, "And yeah, Black Bill Tocco says hello."

The guy on the left takes his hand out of his pocket and raises a police-issue .38 and fires point-blank at the center of Clarence's chest. The bullet hits the metal plate. The force drives Clarence backwards.

The third man takes a gun out of his pocket and also shoots Clarence in the chest. This one drives Clarence back against the wall behind him, out in the hall.

The guy with the tommy gun raises it. Clarence takes him out with one shot to the head. Bullets from the tommy slam into the wall inside the apartment as the gunner falls.

The other two get off two more shots each, but only hit the metal plates Clarence wears, as the first shots did. They pound his chest and don't do damage.

Clarence steps into the apartment blasting away. Finishes them both off.

The gunfight is over in seconds. The plaster on the walls still rings with echoes of the blasts. Clarence holds his ground in case others are in the apartment. When nobody comes around the corner, Clarence rushes toward the back of the apartment, guns up and ready.

Empty.

He holsters his weapons and quickly searches through the pockets of the dead men. Two of them are police. The one on the left is a detective from the Twelfth Precinct. The one on the right is from the Eighth. The guy in the middle with the tommy gun isn't a copper. Clarence recognizes his name as one of Black Bill Tocco's thugs.

So Tony Jack told Black Bill Tocco after all about Clarence's visit to the linen supply company.

The Sicilians working with the coppers . . . no, the Sicilians don't *work* with the coppers, they *own* the coppers. If the coppers are involved, it's because the Sicilians want them there.

And now both sides want Clarence dead.

He can't linger. There will be sirens in the air soon. It won't be long before both the coppers and the mugs know their ambush failed. They'll be after him all the harder.

First thing he has to do, though, is pay Junior a return visit.

He runs out of the apartment and down the stairs. As if he isn't in enough trouble, on the second floor a couple of lookie-loos have come out of their apartments to see what all the commotion is about.

They'll get a good eyeful of a large colored man running like hell down the stairs with his coat flapping around two pearl-handled cannons at his waist.

They'll surely remember the sight and describe it in great detail for the cops who show up.

As always, groups loiter around the doors to Harper Hospital on John R. One-legged vets leaning against the walls on their crutches. Juicers sitting by the side of the entrance pavilion. Hopheads of every kind trying to sleep off a nod or else get into one in the fastest way possible.

Clarence bypasses the volunteer at the main desk inside. She directs patients and visitors to every corner of the hospital, but Clarence knows exactly where he wants to go. He takes the stairs up to level three, where the Maternity Ward is. Bessie's working here this week. It's one of her favorite assignments.

She loves babies. After their DeMarco was born, she found out she couldn't have any more children. It turned out she had what the doctors called cysts on her ovaries. DeMarco's birth was even a fluke.

There are women who might have stayed away from babies after that. Not Bessie. She loved to be around them. She always asks for this assignment.

On the third floor, he follows the signs to Maternity and goes through the double doors at the end of the long corridor. This hospital only serves white folks. Everybody he passes gives him a look of surprise followed quickly by anger.

He stops at the nurse's station. "Excuse me," he says, "where can I find Bessie Brown?"

The charge nurse—an old warhorse of a white nurse, built like a fireplug with a face like a fist—looks up in, guess what, surprise and then anger.

"She's not a patient here. You people have your own hospital."

212

"Yes ma'am," he says, slowly. "She's not a patient. I'm looking for my wife. Bessie Brown. She cleans the rooms here."

Slightly mollified, the nurse seems to deflate and says, "The cleaning staff isn't supposed to have any guests. They're *working*, you know."

Rather than engage her any more, he walks away and decides to search for her himself.

"Hey!" the nurse cries from behind the desk.

Clarence ignores her and peeks into the rooms on one side of the hall.

From behind him, he hears, "Call Security!"

Clarence walks down the hallway, away from the hubbub at the desk. Looking into rooms.

He finds Bessie swabbing the floor in the last room at the end of the hall.

She looks up with a start. "Clarence!"

"Hey, baby. I just want to make sure you're all right."

"Of course. Why wouldn't I be?"

He doesn't want to tell her the whole story, so he gives her a quick version: an ambush, people might be after him, it would be best if she didn't go home tonight. Maybe she should stay with her sister.

"Why they after you?"

"I believe it has to do with Darius Turner."

"Why?"

"I've been asking around about him. Seems certain people don't like it. I'm not staying at the house tonight, either, in case they come looking for me."

"Where you going to stay?"

"Don't know yet."

"Baby, it's our *home*!"

"Which is why you have to stay someplace else. Maybe Edna's. Just for a day or so."

"I don't like this one bit."

Before he can respond, Clarence sees a fat white security guard trotting double time down the corridor towards him. Jowls shaking, belly jiggling over his belt.

"Hey," the guard says when he's closer. Stops out of breath. "You. Can't. Be. Here," he huffs and puffs. "Niggers ain't allowed. I'm only telling you. Once. You get outta here. Right. Now!"

"I'll get out when I'm good and ready. I'm talking to my wife."

"I don't care what you're doing. Colored folks ain't allowed up here who don't work here."

He makes to grab Clarence's coat lapel—presumably to try and drag the big man out the door. Clarence says, "Don't be touching me." He pushes the guard away.

The guard turns and yells down to the nursing station. "Call the cops!"

"Get out of here, baby," Bessie says. "Please. You gone get me fired."

"Nobody touch me. Nobody."

"Just go, okay? And keep yourself safe!"

She gathers up her mop and pail and scoots into another room.

Clarence reaches into his pocket for his buzzer and pins it to his coat. Glares at the guard.

Clarence adjusts his coat and walks down the hallway like he has all the time in the world. The nurses and orderlies in the hall part for him as he strolls past.

"Cops are on their way," the head nurse at the station says.

Clarence ignores her.

30

BEN RUBIN

O utside the luncheonette where Moe took him stands a
payphone. Ben stops to call Elizabeth. No answer at her
apartment.

He calls her radio station.

The woman who answers the phone asks him to hold while she
transfers him to the Creative Department.

"What?" a harsh voice on the line demands.

Ben says, "I'm calling for Elizabeth Waters."

"You are, eh?"

"Yes."

"Miss Waters hasn't deigned to come to work since she put in an
appearance on Monday."

Ben knew she was going to be off the day before because of the
march—though it didn't sound as if this guy on the other end of the
line knew.

"Okay," Ben says, "thanks."

"If you should see her, you might let her know Sid says she's
fired."

Sid hangs up.

Now Ben is worried. He doesn't know much about her—knows
almost nothing, in fact. Not even who he might call to find out about
her.

He makes his way to Woodward and walks north to the Palmer Park apartment district. As soon as he steps out from the elevator on her floor in the Trocadero, he knows something is wrong. Her door is broken open, splintered at the doorframe. It looks like there was a struggle in the living room. The wooden coffee table is smashed. Books and magazines are scattered around the floor. A chair is overturned.

He takes a walk through the rest of the rooms. Nothing else seems out of order. Nothing seems stolen, though the only thing he remembers is a radio and Victrola in a cabinet, and both are still there. The typewriter on a table in her bedroom is still there, though the ink spool is missing.

Elizabeth herself is gone.

One working lock is left on the front door, so he gets the door shut and locked.

He begins restacking the books and magazines from the floor. He sits on the sofa. *The New Force* catches his eye. He picks it up and thumbs through it. Articles on the significance of May Day, a piece by lawyer Maurice Sugar, an article on the social heroic film, and several cartoons by someone called Ben Yomen.

He hears a tapping at the door. He opens it to see a woman in her fifties. Dressed to the nines in a long purple Chinese number. Bottle-blonde hair, tightly permed. Mules on her feet clashed with the rest of her outfit.

She peeks past him.

"Help you?" he asks.

She nods. Her motions are quick, birdlike. "Is Elizabeth in?" Raspy smoker's voice.

"She's not here," Ben says.

"I was just wondering if she was okay."

"I'm not sure. Do you know what happened here?"

The woman looks uncertainly at him. "Are you okay? Who are you?"

Ben thinks fast. Judging from the look the elevator operator gives him, he's thinking the truth would not be a good idea. "Her brother," he says. "I'm staying with her for a few days. Name's Ben."

"I'm Gladys Hart."

They shake. Gladys gives him the side eye. "Her brother, eh?"

Ben says nothing.

"Honey," Gladys says, "you're no more her brother than I am. Don't try to shit a shitter."

He stands back out of the doorway. "Maybe you better come in."

"Just for a minute," Gladys says. "I've got company across the hall."

She pads in. Looks around, her attention lighting up the areas of Elizabeth's apartment. Turns her gaze on Ben. "Lizzie and I are pals, Ben. I know you're not her brother, okay?"

"Okay. I'm a friend."

"Whoever you are, buddy, it's no skin off my nose. You don't have to answer to me. And neither does Lizzie. Do you know where she is?"

He shakes his head. "Do you? What happened here?"

"They hauled her off earlier today. I was hoping she'd be home by now."

"Who did?"

"Four men. Two had on police uniforms. I heard all the commotion. Sounded like they just burst in. And they were carrying guns, too. Big long guns." She held her arms out to demonstrate, cradling an imaginary rifle.

"When was this?"

"This morning."

"I don't suppose they said where they were taking her? Or why?"

"They didn't say anything to me."

"Did they take anyone else away?"

"Not that I saw."

She looks around the apartment. "They left a mess, didn't they?"

"They sure did."

"Can I help you clean up?"

"Thanks, but I got it."

"Aces. Look, let me know if there's anything I can do for Elizabeth. Or for you. Let me know if you hear anything. I like the gal."

Ben says he will. He thanks her again and closes the door.

Those thugs.

He straightens up a bit more. If the police did this, the police would know what happened to her. And where she is.

When he gets the apartment as neat as he can, he leaves and walks the mile up Woodward Avenue to Seven Mile Road. A few hundred yards off the corner of Seven and Woodward is the Twelfth Precinct house for the city cops.

He stops outside the entrance. Do you seriously want to go inside? he asks himself. They might be looking for you. This is a risk. Do you want to take this kind of a risk for a woman you barely know?

Yeah (he continues the argument with himself), except they won't know I'm the one they're looking for in the Madison robbery. How could they have my name?

On the other hand:

One of the Purples could have told them. They're looking for you, too. Maybe they have an informant with the police who gave them your name.

Maybe they have an informant in the police?

It's a sure thing.

But right now, finding Elizabeth is more important than anything the cops might do to him.

A big harness bull lumbers out the front door. He lights up a smoke, sees Ben standing there. "What do you want?" he says.

"I'm just wondering about a friend who's gone missing."

The copper jerks a thumb in the direction of the door. "Talk to them."

Ben has one final argument with himself, decides he will go inside after all. Nods to the copper and goes inside and steps up to the bull behind the welcome grate.

"Yeah?" the man says. He's as massive as the guy outside. Sour face, tight-fitting blue uniform with sergeant's stripes. I'm already sick of your shit, his expression says.

He looks Ben over. "The hell happened to you?"

Ben ignores the questions. "I'm looking for somebody who got arrested earlier today."

"What's the name?"

"Elizabeth Waters."

"What's your relationship?"

"A friend."

"Aint much I can tell you, then," the sergeant says. "You ain't a relative, you're shit out of luck, bud."

"Can't you even confirm she was arrested?"

"Was she apprehended in the Red roundup?"

"She was."

"Well now, that's a shame, ain't it? I wouldn't tell you where she was if I knew. I suppose you're a Red, too?"

With a sneer, the copper turns away to answer a ringing telephone.

When he's finished, he turns back to the open grate. Acts surprised Ben is still there.

"So," Ben says, "you're telling me all those people are being held incommunicado?"

"That's a big word. What are you, her shyster lawyer?"

"No, I told you, I'm a friend."

"Get lost, bud. You're not getting any more dope out of me."

The copper turns away from the grate and goes behind a door inside the station, out of sight.

Ben walks back to the corner of Seven Mile and Woodward. He spots a phone booth on the corner. The mention of a lawyer gives him an idea.

He searches through his pockets for change and for the business card Maurice Sugar gave him at the hospital. Dials the number and gets the attorney's secretary.

"Maurice Sugar," Ben says.

"Who's calling?"

Ben gives her his name and she says, "I'll see if he's in." He waits as she puts him on hold.

In five more minutes, he hears a man's voice. "Sugar."

Ben identifies himself, says, "We met yesterday at the hospital."

Was it just yesterday?

"Sure," Maurice says. "I remember you. You were with Elizabeth Waters. How are you feeling?"

"I'm okay. In fact, it's Elizabeth I'm calling about."

"Is she all right?"

"I'm not sure. Apparently, she was arrested today."

"Exactly what I was afraid of. The police are rounding-up everybody they can find who's connected with the Communist Party. They must have grabbed her."

"Why?"

"Because the Communists were organizers of the march yesterday. And it wasn't enough to kill them, now the police have to punish them, too."

"Do you know where she's being held?"

"Unfortunately, I don't have any idea."

"How do we get her out?"

"Look, first we have to find her. Let me call around and see what I can dig up."

"In the meantime, can you think of anybody else I should call for her?"

"Actually, there's a way you can be very helpful."

"I'm all ears."

"I don't know if you've seen the newspapers today?"

"Never read them."

"They've already started on the coverup of what happened at the march."

Ben hears rustling in the background of Maurice's call.

"Here's the headline from the *Free Press*," Maurice says. "'Communists Inflamed by Pratt Hurl Stones and Clubs in Prearranged Outbreak.'"

"That wasn't what happened at all."

"Exactly. The papers are already starting to shape the narrative. Or misshape it, I should say. The papers are owned by the same business interests the workers are fighting against."

"What can I do?"

"You were there. The best thing you can do is talk with a reporter who's friendly to the movement and try to get the truth across. And hope they print it."

The thought of contacting a reporter—and possibly getting his name in the paper—terrifies him.

"I dunno," he says. "Talking to a reporter . . . Not crazy about the idea."

"The thing is, Ben, people were killed yesterday. Shot and beaten in cold blood. Just for trying to make the world a better place for everybody. Now other people are being arrested, fired, punished for trying to do the right thing. If you were there, you have a responsibility to help get the truth out."

"Except this isn't a good time to get my name in the paper. Or my face."

After a silence, Maurice says, "Are you in trouble with the cops?"

"You might say."

After another moment, Maurice says, "Look. It's your decision. But from where I'm sitting, whatever you're afraid of, you need to set it aside. I'll help you in any way I can, if you need representation and so forth. But Ben, this is your moment to step up."

More rustling and shuffling of papers on Maurice's end of the phone.

"I have a name for you," Maurice says. "Tom Glover. Works for the *Detroit Times*. He'll give you an honest hearing. And he'll know to keep your name out of it, if you ask him to. What do you say?"

Ben considers it.

"I know you're not comfortable doing this," Maurice says. "Trust me, it's going to be the most important thing you can do."

"If you say so."

"Good man. Got a pencil? I'll give you his number."

"I don't," he says. "I'm standing at a phone box on Woodward."

"Where can I get hold of you?"

"I'm staying at Elizabeth's for a few days. You have her number?"

"I do. I'll call Tom and have him get in touch with you there."

"Okay," Ben says. He's not sure it is.

"Meantime. I'll work on getting our friend out of the devil's clutches. Fight on, young man."

31

ELIZABETH WATERS

"Waters."

A matron in the cell hallway calls her name.

Elizabeth looks up from the corner of the cell where she sits, knees up, back against the wall. During the day, the occupants of the cell have changed. Some have been taken away and not returned, New women were brought in. She can still hear the sounds of the men being beaten in another section of the jail.

Elizabeth stirs, raises a hand.

A male guard appears and unlocks the door for Elizabeth to step into the hallway.

The matron takes her by the arm in an iron grip and pulls her down the hall. Flings her inside an interview room. "Sit there." Closes the door and disappears.

It is a small, cold room. Cinder block walls and hard stone floor. A table in the middle, a chair on either side. Elizabeth's legs ache from stiffness and her back aches from hunching over in the cell.

She walks around, letting the blood circulate to her body. In another few minutes, the door opens and the matron reappears with a tray. She sets it on the table. "I was you, I'd eat this. Don't know when you'll have another meal."

She leaves again.

A sandwich on a paper plate and a paper cup of milk. The sandwich is stale white bread; she lifts the top piece of bread; a thin slab of mystery meat. She sniffs. Maybe baloney, once upon a time.

She hasn't eaten all day—she was about to sit down to coffee and a piece of toast when the coppers swarmed in and hauled her away. She is starving, so she takes a bite of the sandwich. She still can't tell what kind of meat it is.

It's putrid. She looks around for a wastepaper basket to spit it into, sees nothing. She can't imagine swallowing, so she spits it into the thin napkin on the tray.

She takes a sip of milk to get the taste of the sandwich out of her mouth. The milk is warm and sour.

She forces down a mouthful and sets it down beside the inedible sandwich. As hungry as she is, she can't bear to eat or drink this.

She sits and waits. Hugs herself from the cold.

After a while, a bored-looking white man enters the interview room. He has a bald head and a droopy face, like a basset hound's, with loose hanging jowls. His belly overwhelms his waist. His body odor fills the room. He carries a green folder.

"Sit down," he says. Avoids her eye as he sits at the table. She sits across from him.

He opens the folder, makes a show of reading what's there. Her booking sheet is on top but there are several sheets underneath it. He takes forever looking it all over.

"Why am I being held here?" she asks.

"Shut up."

"I demand to know why I'm being held."

He reaches across the table and slaps her hard with an open hand across the face.

Her ears ring. Her eyes water.

"Got any more demands?"

She is too shocked to reply.

"Didn't think so. You Elizabeth Waters?"

She nods.

He holds up a sheath of papers. "Know what this is? We keep summary sheets of suspected seditionists. These are yours."

He lays black and white photos in front of her. They are images of her at the Unemployed Council, as well as at labor demonstrations and Party meetings.

"How did you get these?" she asks. "Am I being followed?"

"How long have you been a member of the Communist Party?"

"I refuse to answer on the grounds—"

He wallops her again, harder this time. The blow knocks her off the chair. He comes around the table and picks her up roughly by one arm. Slams her back in the chair.

She wipes her mouth with the back of her hand. It comes away bloody.

He reaches into his pants pocket, comes up with a studded sap. Slams it on the table.

"Next time I use this," he says. "I ask a question, you answer it. That's how this works. Get me?"

She stares daggers at him. Trembling, she says, "I demand a lawyer."

Prepares herself for another smack, this time with the blackjack.

He looks at her like he's picking his spot.

Instead, he says, "You don't want to do this, toots. Take my word for it. This'll go a lot smoother if you just answer my questions."

Playing the nice guy now.

Asks, "Where were you yesterday morning?"

"I have a right to a lawyer, and I demand to exercise my right."

He gives her a sneer, but no more smacks. Slams the folder closed. Pockets the sap. Gets up and leaves the room.

But not before throwing, "Lotsa luck," at her over his shoulder.

Five minutes later, the matron comes back. "Let's go, honey."

Instead of taking Elizabeth back to the holding pen, the matron guides her down a flight of stairs to the sally port leading outside.

"Wait," Elizabeth says, "you're taking me outside? I need a coat—it's cold out." She wasn't allowed to take a coat when the coppers took her away in the morning and she froze in the paddy wagon.

"Shut up, doll face," the matron says. She grabs Elizabeth by the arm and takes her over to a paddy wagon idling by the door.

Four other women wait inside. Elizabeth recognizes them. They were taken away from the holding pen and never brought back.

The women huddle together for warmth and the copper at the wheel starts up.

"Where are we going?" Elizabeth asks him.

The driver ignores her.

"Does anyone know where we're going?" she asks the other women. They shake their heads. They accept her into their huddle so she can try to keep warm with them.

The driver takes them on a long drive through Detroit streets. They wind up at the back of another precinct house. It is dark by now, so Elizabeth can't tell what part of town they're in. Her head hurts and the side of her face where the detective hit her stings.

The wagon pulls inside the sally port and another copper opens the vehicle's back door. He herds the women out. Off to the side, in the shadows, two cops work over a man with brass knuckles. She hears his grunts, sees blood and teeth flying.

This time there is no matron. Instead, a man—uniformed, tall—is waiting to take them to another holding cell. If possible, this one is dirtier than the last. The smell of vomit and excrement makes her gag.

She is here so long, she loses track of time. It feels like hours. Then the same copper comes to take the women away again. They pile into the same paddy wagon with the same driver and again drive around with no apparent purpose. They come to another police station.

"What is happening?" one of the women asks her with a strong Spanish accent. "What are they doing?"

"They're trying to outfox the lawyers," Elizabeth says.

The woman shrugs in a lack of understanding, Elizabeth says, "They take us for short stays from one station to another. It's so the lawyers can't find us to get us out. They're probably going to be doing this all night. We won't get fed and we won't get any sleep."

"Why they do this?"

"Because they can."

The women spend the rest of the night shuttled from one station to another. She and the rest of the women learn to catch short naps in the paddy wagons between stations because they are not given the time or peace to sleep at any one place.

They are not offered food again for the duration of the long night.

32

Roscoe Grissom

After dinner, everyone is awake at Roscoe Grissom's.

His madhouse, more like.

Two of the girls are raising hell in the bathtub. He hears the splashing. The floor is probably soaked. The third girl is jumping around the living room, bouncing from chair to sofa to chair.

Standing in the middle of the living room with all the chaos around him, Roscoe feels like he's going to lose it, go down to the basement and pull a hammer out from where it's hanging on a board by his tool bench and go from room to room, beating the living shit out of each of the girls and then, only then, after the girls are bloody messes, going after his wife.

And punish her for trapping him in this life.

He knows he can't do it. Whatever else he's up to for the Black Legion, nobody—the neighbors, the rest of the family, his friends, the police—will look the other way if he takes out his fantasy of punishment on his wife and daughters.

Like Hollis said, it's against the Black Legion code. Protect the family.

Fortunately, he has an out tonight. Harley Clarke called him earlier. "Pick you up at eight," he said.

Now Roscoe waits in the front hall, looking out the door, trying to ignore the commotion behind him.

At eight on the dot, Harley pulls in front of the house.

Roscoe is out of the house like a shot.

"How you feeling?" Harley asks when Roscoe jumps in the sled.

"Never better. What's going on?"

"It's big. And you, my friend, are in the center of it."

"That's swell."

Harley takes a sidelong glance at Roscoe. "Feeling okay?" he asks.

"Yeah. Why?"

"Smell like you been hitting Frankie's back room pretty hard."

"Yeah, maybe. This afternoon, though."

Harley pulls over outside a diner on Mack.

"What's the matter?" Roscoe asks.

"You got to be on your toes tonight."

"So?"

"So sit tight. I'm getting you a cup of joe."

Harley jumps out and comes back with a paper cup. Hands it to Roscoe. "Drink."

Roscoe sips the bitter drink.

"I'm fine, I tell you," Roscoe says.

"Just drink it."

"What's so big, I got to drink this horse piss?"

Harley pulls out into traffic again. "You'll find out soon enough."

Roscoe expects Harley to drive him to the Dew Drop Inn. Instead they head toward downtown Detroit.

"Where we going?"

"Just sit there and drink your fucking coffee and don't worry about it," Harley says.

They wind up on Woodward Avenue heading north. In a few miles, they take a right on Arden Park Boulevard, across from the ritzy Boston-Edison District. Roscoe has never been down this street. He has never seen homes this big. Mansions line the block. They make him gape in wonder.

They're like castles. Turrets and battlements and concrete porches. You could fit eight of my house in one of these monsters, he marvels.

As if that wasn't enough, huge expensive cars such as Roscoe has only seen in the movies line the streets.

Harley parks in front of one of the mansions and they walk to number 74. Fancy cars line the driveway all the way back to the carriage house in the rear.

The house is three levels, wide as a football field (or so it seems to Roscoe). A sprawling front yard with stone statuary on pedestals on either side of the front porch.

"Jesus," he says.

"Jesus ain't coming tonight," Harley says, "but other big-shots are. Watch your step, okay? And don't say nothing stupid."

They walk up to the front porch between a row of hedges.

"Who lives here?" Roscoe asks.

"Some big swell in the auto industry."

"What's he want with us?"

"Shut up."

The heavy leaded glass front door leads to an entry foyer. It is larger than Roscoe's entire living room. A uniformed Detroit cop stands there cradling a tommy gun.

"This the guy?" the copper asks.

"Yeah," Harley says.

The copper makes a notation in his notebook. Knocks twice on the inner door and it opens. He steps aside and Harley goes in, followed by Roscoe.

They step into a vast hall. To the left is a huge sitting room with heavy plush sofas and dark wooden tables holding photographs and crystal vases. At the end of the room a fire snaps and burns inside a massive fireplace with a tile surround. To the right of the entrance hall, another copper with a tommy gun stands in front of closed dark wooden sliding doors.

"They ain't ready yet," the copper says. "Go sit down." He points the barrel of his gun at the room with the fireplace.

Roscoe hears heated men's voices behind the doors. They're arguing about something. The only thing he can make out is a loud nasal voice saying, "He must be stopped before anything else happens."

"Go on," the copper says, "get in there." He pushes Roscoe out of the hall. He and Harley go in and sit by the fireplace. They can still hear the men arguing in the other room.

After a while the door slides open a foot. The cop goes up next to it. Someone whispers something to him. He nods, turns, beckons Harley and Roscoe. "Come on in."

The door slides all the way open and Harley and Roscoe enter a sprawling dining room. Seated around a table are men Roscoe don't recognize. Two women bustle through a swinging door at the left, carrying away plates with what look like the remains of the men's dinners. Steak and potatoes and salad. Roscoe can't remember the last time he had such a meal.

At the head of the table is a gaunt, craggy man in a suit. The more Roscoe looks at him, the more this guy looks kind of familiar. Roscoe can't remember where he knows him from.

The man sitting across from him at the other end of the table has a round Irish ruddy face with apple dumpling cheeks over a clerical collar. Beside him sits a compact man in a double-breasted suit with a bow tie. He has a bandage on the side of his head. He turns a pair of hooded eyes toward Roscoe.

A fourth man is younger than the others, sandy-haired and handsome. Two more men are sitting on the other side of the table.

Everybody greets Harley. The clergyman says, "This your guy?"

"This is him," Harley says. "Roscoe Grissom."

Smiling broadly, the priest stands and steps forward. Shakes Roscoe's hand. "Father Charles Coughlin," the priest says, as though he expects Roscoe to recognize the name. Which of course Roscoe don't.

Roscoe never shook hands with a priest before. The guy's hand is warm and soft as a girl's. Probably never did a day's work in his life.

The mug in the bow tie stands and steps toward Roscoe. "Harry Bennett," he says. They shake. Roscoe never heard of him, either.

"This is Mr. Ford," Bennett says with reverence. Points to the gaunt man at the head of the table. Henry Ford, *the* Henry Ford, does not stand or extend his hand. He looks at Roscoe like Roscoe's something that needs to be scraped off the bottom of his shoe. He makes no effort to hide his disdain.

The handsome, sandy-haired man steps up with his hand outstretched. "Horace Howcroft," he says. His handshake is painful. "Legal advisor to the Detroit Police Special Investigations Bureau."

Roscoe don't know what that is, and don't want to ask.

The other men around the table now stand. One is tall and stooped. "Leon Hupp," he says. "Welcome to my home."

Another man has pouty lips and slick hair combed all the way back. "Mayor Charles Bowles," the man says.

"*Former* mayor," a voice says. A man comes forward. He is tall and thin, with a head of silver hair combed straight back. The man offers a hand. "Ray Lindenauer," he says. "Detroit Police."

"Now the introductions are out of the way," Harry Bennett says, looking at the watch on a fob on his vest, "shall we get down to business?"

They take their seats at the table and invite Harley and Roscoe to sit, too.

The men pour amber liquid from a decanter into crystal glasses. From its smell, Roscoe can tell it's the good stuff, probably smuggled in from Canada. Henry Ford fills his glass from a carafe with what looks like water. Neither Roscoe nor Harley are invited to have a drink.

The men break out cigars and cigarettes. The air in the room quickly turns blue with smoke.

The man named Howcroft stands up and walks to the end of the table where the man named Lindenauer sits. Howcroft leans down to whisper into Lindenauer's ear. Howcroft slips a stuffed envelope out of his suitcoat pocket and into Lindenauer's waiting hand.

Equally as smoothly, the envelope disappears into Lindenauer's jacket.

Howcroft pats Lindenauer's shoulder and returns to his chair.

"Roscoe," the priest intones through cigar smoke across the table, calling Roscoe's attention back, "has Harley here told you anything about what we're here for?"

"No," Roscoe says. He can't bring himself to say "Father." He hates Papists even more than Jews.

"Let's get down to brass tacks," Henry Ford says sourly. "I don't have all night."

He looks at Harry Bennett.

Who says, "Gentlemen, with one exception"—he nods to the priest—"we came to a joint decision over dinner. Has anyone had second thoughts? Are we still agreed on our course of action?"

He looks at each man around the table in turn, except for Roscoe and Harley.

"This is not a decision to come to lightly," the priest cautions. "While I believe the current situation warrants drastic action, I can't be seen publicly to support this plan."

Every man nods his head.

"This . . . menace . . . has been doing terrible things to this city," Henry Ford says. "And by extension, to the country. He needs to be stopped by whatever means necessary."

Roscoe wonders what terrible things who has done. He hopes Ford isn't talking about him.

Howcroft steps into the silence left after Ford's pronouncement. "He's allowed the seditious Communist element to infiltrate and take over the labor union movement."

"He's encouraging the entire radical element, including the workers as well as the dark races," says Harry Bennett.

"Especially the Jews," Henry Ford puts in.

"Goes without saying," the priest adds.

"The debacle on Monday was entirely his doing," Ford continues. "He might not have pulled the trigger. The deaths of those men are on his hands. And he's one of yours," Ford adds, looking at the priest.

"While it's true he's a devout Catholic," the priest says, "he's entirely too lenient on the ethnics of Detroit. The Jews, the coloreds, the Poles, and so on. Whenever I say anything against the Jewish bankers, for example, he tells me to go easy."

The priest shakes his head, raises a finger in the air. "I will not 'go easy' on those foreign traitors. Any more than I will for the traitor who's on his way to the White House in the fall. The shadow Jew, Franklin D. Rosenfeld."

"I thought you liked him," Henry Ford says.

"What I say for public consumption and what I say in this setting are two different things."

Ford nods once, as if this validates everything he ever thought about priests in general and this one in particular.

Harry Bennett says, "Gentlemen, we don't need to lay out all the arguments for our guests. What's important is the decision we've come to."

He gives Roscoe an ice-cold smile.

Takes a photo out of the inner pocket of his suit and lays it in front of Roscoe. "Recognize this man?"

Roscoe looks at a formal photograph of a man in a light-colored suit. Irish good looks. High forehead. Short curly hair worn all back. Furry eyebrows. Determined eyes looking away from the camera. Lips curved, as though trying to stifle a smile about a private joke.

He seems familiar. Roscoe can't place him. He shakes his head.

"As you've just heard, we've been discussing this for a while," Bennett says. "Monday's events put an urgency on our determination to remove the man in this photograph for the good of all."

"And quickly," the priest puts in. "There's a funeral procession for the dead marchers in the works. He's letting it go forward. It can't be allowed to take place. It would be a catastrophe."

"You're right, Father," Bennett says. "My spies tell me the funeral march is scheduled for Saturday. Thousands of people might be there. The worst kinds."

"If that happens," Henry Ford says, "we might never put the kibosh on the Jewish-Communist union movement. Our nation and all we've worked for will be destroyed."

"We advised him to stop it," the man named Lindenauer says. "He as good as told us to go to hell."

"He'll get there first," Henry Ford says. "We're sure Couzens will be our man once he takes over?"

"He's a wild card," the man named Bowles admits. "He's got a holier-than-thou nose in the air. Comes from being brought up in money. Still, my allies on the City Council will keep him in check if he goes in the wrong direction."

"The Klan sympathizers, you mean?" the priest asks.

Bowles glares at him. "Thought we were all on the same side here," he says.

The priest shakes his head. "Politics makes strange bedfellows."

The men around the table are silent until Horace Howcroft says, "Roscoe, we've broached the subject with Harley, and he says you're the man for the job. Do you understand what we're asking you to do?"

In truth, no. In part because the man in the photograph is a stranger to him. But he picks up on their purpose from the way the discussion is going.

He looks at Harley sitting beside him. Harley gives him a tiny nod.

Roscoe decides to risk it.

Points to the photograph.

"I believe y'all are asking me to ice this man."

The men in the room are quiet, as if hearing it said out loud in such vulgar terms by an outsider makes it more of a possibility than it has been. Nobody wants to confirm it.

Finally, Harry Bennett breaks the silence. "Are you the man for the job, Roscoe?"

"Yes, sir. I believe I am."

He takes the man's photo and examines it. As he looks, he realizes he has seen this man before. He can't remember where.

"We'll tell you how to find him, and get you whatever you'll need," Harry Bennett says. "Harley, you and the rest of your group will support Roscoe in any way he needs. Clear?"

"Clear," Harley says. "He'll have the Legion's full support."

"And needless to say, Roscoe," Harry Bennett says, "you can't tell anybody about this. Not your wife, not your family, not anybody. This must be held to absolute secrecy."

"I get it," Roscoe says.

"Nobody must ever know of this meeting tonight," Horace Howcroft says.

"Yessir."

"If this gets out," Harry Bennett tells Roscoe, "we'll know it came from you. And the result for you will be severe."

"Yessir."

"By the same token," the priest says, "with such a public individual, there will be an outcry. Calls for an investigation. We will do everything in our considerable power to protect you and keep your involvement hidden."

"I understand," Roscoe says.

Harry Bennett says, "We'll take care of everything, including the weapon you'll use. When and where are up to you."

"Okay."

"As long as it's soon."

Henry Ford, who has been watching this entire conversation with tart-faced disdain, says, "Do you have any questions, young man?"

Roscoe looks at the photo again. "Just one. Who is this guy?"

The men around the table share a look. Like, *uh-oh.*

"You don't know?" Ford says.

"No sir."

"That man," Bennett says, "is the mayor of the City of Detroit."

"The *current* mayor," Charles Bowles puts in.

Harry Bennett says, "His name's Frank Murphy."

Roscoe nods. This is the mug he saw in the newsreel.

These guys want Roscoe to get rid of the fucking mayor of Detroit!

The consequence of this meeting hits him hard.

Henry Ford must be picking up on Roscoe's misgivings, because he turns to Harley Clarke. "Are you sure this . . . man . . . is the right one for the job?"

"Yes, Mr. Ford, I believe he is. Roscoe's one of our most dedicated soldiers. I know he'll do the job for us."

As Ford looks at Roscoe, the deep lines of his face etch into a sneer. "I hope you're right."

"We'll make sure of it, Mr. Ford," Bennett says.

Ford turns to Bennett. "I thought the Sicilians were going to handle this. This kind of thing is right up their street."

"I approached them, Mr. Ford. They didn't want to get involved with the removal of a public figure."

"No, the guineas only kill greaseballs like themselves, I suppose."
To the others, Ford says, "Anything else?"

The men agree nothing's left to discuss.

To Harry Bennett, Henry Ford says, "Let's get out of here. I don't
have all night."

Harley Clarke is quiet all the way back to the east side and the Dew
Drop Inn. Roscoe is, too. His respect for Harley went up over the past
hour. Harley knows Henry Ford and all those other muckety-mucks
back there. He's evidently been in meetings with them before to talk
about this mission.

They are still silent when they get to the back room of the Dew
Drop and Harley pours them each a drink from Frankie's stash.
Frankie is trying to shoo the regulars out so he can close up, but he
lets Harley and Roscoe stay.

They clink glasses. Roscoe gulps the hooch. It burns going down.
Like guzzling gasoline.

Harley fills the glasses up again. They down the hooch in one gulp.

No, not even gasoline. Turpentine, more like. If not bear piss.

"Another?" Harley asks.

"Why not?"

Roscoe is feeling good. The nervousness that had overtaken him
at the meeting is gone, dissolved in the burn of the hooch. These were
important men—the most important men in the city, if not the
world—Henry fucking Ford!—and they were putting their trust in
him. In Roscoe Grissom from Beech Bluff, Tennessee, for an
important job.

Probably the most important job he will ever have.

A soldier, Harley called him. One of their most dedicated.

How swell that sounded!

If he did this right, he would be on easy street from now on. He
might go all the way to the top of the Black Legion.

Harley fills their glasses again. The two men down their drinks.

"So," Harley says. "What's all this sound like to you?"

"Sounds pretty fucking aces."

Harley lowers his voice. "There was talk about if you was up for the job. Tell you the truth, I ain't worried a bit."

"No?"

"Hell, no. First minute I seen you, I says to myself, 'This boy's gonna bring honor to this organization. And to himself.' And now you are. I just didn't know it would be so soon."

"Thank you, Harley."

"Hey, no need to thank me. I know a good soldier when I see one."

Good soldier.

Roscoe beams in the light of the compliment.

As though reading his mind, Harley says, "You're in the big leagues now, boy." He slaps Roscoe on the back.

"Now," Harley goes on, "remember what they said. This has to happen by the weekend. In the morning, I'll find out where this jamoke lives, and I'll get you a clean piece to use."

"Okay."

"Meantime, I'll drop you home so you can get a good night's sleep while I put everything together."

Inside his house, all is dark and silent. The girls are in bed. His wife is in their bedroom with the door closed.

They couldn't even leave the goddamn lights on for him. No consideration for him at all.

Without even bothering to go into his room, Roscoe goes down into the cellar.

Tired and happy, he takes his clothes off. Stretches out on the cot.

Tries to relive what happened tonight at the mansion and with Harley. It's no good. His head spins. He has drunk too much of Frankie's bad whiskey to put two thoughts together.

Instead, he covers himself with a quilt and falls asleep imagining himself in an apocalypse of blood, gunfire, and flames leading to the renewal of these United States as a white Christian nation.

Just like the Founders intended.

And the man who will lead the way there?

Roscoe Grissom.

33

CLARENCE BROWN

Clarence stands across the street from his house. Waits for a half hour to make sure nobody's following him.

He goes inside to throw clothes into an overnight bag—underpants, a clean shirt, a change of socks. Bessie wasn't happy about the message he delivered to her. She understood, though. He knows she will do the right thing.

He heads off to the poolroom. Jammed tonight. Voices raised in shouts and laughter. The chunk of pool balls into pockets.

Players stop with their cues poised as they see Clarence Brown enter. From the doorway, he scans the crowd through the smoky haze. No Junior.

He weaves through the tables until he gets to the counter. Nods to Mr. Fred as he barges into the back room and up the stairs.

A different group is at the table Junior used earlier in the day.

"Anybody know Junior Sykes?" Clarence asks them.

Blank stares.

He picks out one of the players, the biggest man in the room, with a huge gut and completely bald head.

"How about you?" Clarence asks. "You know Junior Sykes?"

"No, man," the big guy says. "Never heard of him."

"He's a little guy, skinny as a rail, looks like a drowned rat. No bells?"

"I said I never heard of him," the big guy says. "Going to axe me again?" He holds the pool cue diagonally in front of him like a rifle at port arms. As if getting ready to use it on Clarence.

Clarence moves his coat flaps back to reveal his pistols.

The big guy's friends silently take their feet and move behind him. They all reach slowly into their pants pockets for their own guns. The air grows thick with menace until somebody says, "Hey now, Mr. Clarence. Let's all take it easy."

A voice from the back of the group. Heads turn to look at him, except for the big guy, who keeps giving Clarence the stink eye.

Clarence recognizes the guy who spoke. One of Robinhood Rowe's runners. Name's Lester. Clarence has nabbed the guy a few times for assault.

"You know him?" Clarence asks.

"I do."

"Know where I can find him?"

"No, man," Lester in the back says. "I just know the dude."

"Anybody else know where I can find him?"

Dead silence.

Lester gives Clarence a high sign. Nobody else catches it. He knows something.

Clarence goes back downstairs and waits around the entrance.

Fifteen minutes later the guy comes outside. Lights up an Old Gold and strolls over to where Clarence waits. "What's up, Mr. Clarence?"

"Staying out of trouble, Lester?"

"Trying."

"Trying or doing?"

The question earns a broad grin from Lester.

"You know Junior?" Clarence asks.

"Like I said."

The guy takes another lungful of smoke. Holds it in, lets it out. "Yeah, this time of night, Junior, he usually on Belle Isle. By the fountain."

Clarence reaches out a hand. "Thanks." They shake.

"Sure thing," Lester says. "Maybe you remember me the next time I need a favor."

The Scott Fountain on Belle Isle was built a few years before to honor one of Detroit's most famous misanthropes. James Scott was a lazy, morally-dubious gambler who nevertheless bequeathed the city money from his fortune to build a monument to himself. It is a massive structure on the southern tip of the island in the middle of the Detroit River. At night, the police presence on the island is mostly on the island's northeast side, looking for rum runners from Canada on the opposite shore.

As he drives over the bridge onto the island, Clarence remembers the previous week when he saw Darius Turner's body. If this was Junior Sykes's nighttime hangout, Clarence now wonders if Junior had anything to do with it, or knows something about it.

The lights and the water are off around and inside the fountain to save money for the penniless city. Clarence makes out silhouettes on the far side of the fountain from the entrance drive. He turns his headlamps off and coasts over in the darkness.

As he draws near, he hears men's voices echoing in the night air. He stops on the other side of the fountain from them and makes out Junior's small frame. Clarence sees the glowing tips of cigarettes. With the window down, he smells the skunky perfume of marijuana.

He eases around to where they are standing. Soon as Junior sees who it is, the little rat takes off running.

Clarence pops his lights back on and drives after him. Junior runs across the parking area and out to the lawn toward the bridge. Clarence tears after him, bumping up curbs and keeping just behind him. No way Junior can outrun a car. And the knucklehead runs parallel to the roadway, so Clarence has no trouble staying close.

Say what you will about Junior, he's no criminal genius.

As though reading his thoughts, Junior veers toward the grass in the center of the island. In the dark, he runs right into a wooden bench and flips over.

Clarence skids to a stop and jumps out. Trots to where Junior lies sprawled on the grass, moaning. Junior's nose is bloody and his face is stippled with pebbles and dots of ice from the header he took on the frozen ground.

"Junior," Clarence says, "you and me gonna talk."

He lifts Junior up by the back of his jacket and pulls him around to the bench. Pushes him down on the seat and leans right into his face. Smells the marijuana on his breath and his clothes.

"Oh man," Junior says, "Mr. Clarence, I done told you everything I know about Darius."

"Uh-uh. You sent me on a wild goose chase this afternoon."

"I was just passing along a message."

Junior can't look at him. Clarence wraps a big hand around Junior's neck and makes him look Clarence in the eye.

"Know what was waiting for me at the dump you sent me to?"

Junior tries to shake his head. Clarence holds his face too tightly. Junior squeezes his eyes shut.

"Three motherfuckers with guns," Clarence shouts into Junior's screwed-up face. "Why did you do that?!"

Junior starts whimpering. He mumbles words Clarence can't understand. Clarence lets go of his neck.

"I'm sorry, Mr. Clarence. I'm really sorry."

"Who told you to do it?"

Junior starts to cry real tears now. "He made me!"

"Who?"

"The police man," he blubbers.

"Goddammit, Junior, what you talking about?!"

Grabs Junior by the lapels and shakes him.

"That dick. I don't remember his name."

"What he look like?"

"White man. Young, maybe just a little older than me. Only he starting to lose his hair."

A young, white balding police detective with a grudge against him. "He wear glasses?"

"Yeah. Them skinny glasses. Little circles." He makes circles out of both thumbs and forefingers.

241

Got to be Danny Canavan.

"He told you to send me to that address?"

"Yessir. I didn't know what was gonna happen, I swear it."

"I almost got my fucking head blown off," Clarence roars.

"I didn't know, Mr. Clarence, I swear I didn't know."

"Why'd he say he wanted me there?"

"I don't know, Mr. Clarence. For real, man. He told me he was going to say he found some horse on me and send me away forever, I didn't do what he asked."

"You didn't have any on you?"

"No, sir. I just smoke my jive, that's all. I swear. I didn't know they was tryna kill you!"

"When'd he tell you this?"

"Last night. He come to my house late."

Clarence sits heavily beside him on the bench.

"I didn't know they was gonna kill you, Mr. Clarence. I wouldn't have told him nothing if I did. I swear."

"What did you think they were going to do, you dumb shit?"

Junior starts crying again. "What you gonna do to me, Mr. Clarence?"

Minutes earlier, Clarence was ready to pound Junior into the ground. Now, however, he says, "C'mon, fool. Not going to do anything. Tell you this: once they figure out I'm still alive, they're not going to be happy with either of us. I was you, I'd lie low for a while."

"They going to come after me?"

"I wouldn't be surprised."

Because they're damn sure going to be coming after Clarence again.

The doorbell sounds inside Albert Norquist's home on Outer Drive in Detroit. After a minute, the light overhead goes on and the round face of Clarence's sole white friend in the Detroit PD looms behind the window in the door.

The door swings open and Clarence steps inside quickly.

"Shut it," he orders Albert.

"What's the matter?"

"Just shut the door!"

Clarence goes into Albert's living room, where Albert has been listening to the radio and, by the look of the newspapers all over the floor, snoozing. A dead bottle of bootleg hootch lies on its side. The funk of cigar smoke hangs in the air.

Clarence pulls the curtain closed on the front windows.

"Clarence, what the fuck?"

"Can I stay with you tonight?"

"Bessie throw you out?" Albert asks with the beginning of a smirk.

"Nothing to do with Bessie." He walks around Albert's house, turning out the lights.

"What's going on?"

Clarence goes into the kitchen and shuts the light off. He sits at the kitchen table in the dark. A rectangle of light comes from the streetlight a few doors down.

He rests his head in his hands.

"What's the matter?" Albert says. "What happened?"

"I got a lead Darius Turner's killer was at an apartment in Black Bottom. Turns out I was walking into an ambush."

"Who?"

"Two of them were Detroit PD. The other was one of Black Bill Tocco's gunmen. Would have got me, too. They didn't know about my protection." Clarence raps his knuckles on the metal under his coat. "I got them first. By now the coppers and Black Bill all know they didn't finish the job."

"You want a drink, settle your nerves?"

Clarence is tempted for a fraction of a second. But he says, "No." He's come too far. "Wouldn't mind a Coca-Cola, though."

Albert busies himself preparing the soft drink and opening a new bottle of bootleg whiskey for himself. He gets his supply from the Purple Gang. A present for looking the other way when a shipment comes across from Windsor.

When he finishes, they sit and sip their drinks in the dark quiet of Albert's house. Albert's wife died five years before, and he's tried to keep it exactly the way it was when she went into the hospital and never came out. In spots, the dirt is at least five years old.

Clarence tells him what he's done to find Darius's killer already. He's not only giving Albert the background, he's making himself go over the details of the case to try and put them in some order.

"Way I see it," Clarence says, "this may be about Darius getting mixed up with selling drugs. When I braced my stoolie about what happened, he told me Canavan blackmailed him to set me up."

"Canavan did?"

"Yeah. A girl Darius was keeping company with told me he was selling mootah, maybe hop, too."

"Yeah, everybody knows the cops in that precinct are on the take."

"They get a piece of the madame's prostitution and also Black Bill's drug business. Goes from the precinct commander all the way down the line to the patrol bulls. Maybe Black Bill killed Darius for stepping in on his territory. And he had cops try to kill me because I was getting too close to the truth."

Albert looks away when Clarence mentions being on the take. Clarence knows Albert has been on the arm from the Purples for a long time. When he worked the Seventh Precinct down by the Detroit River and Belle Isle, the Purples used him as a lookout for their deliveries of bootleg whiskey from Windsor. His reward was money.

One time, the Purple—Abie Goldstein—gave Albert a brooch for his wife. When Albert gave it to her, she asked him where it came from; Albert didn't want to tell her. So she said she would never wear it and Albert told Abie he just wanted cash or hooch after that.

Clarence knows Albert has been feeling guilty about what he did since his wife died. He's trying to detach himself from the Purples. Their time is coming to an end anyway, as the Sicilians and smaller gangs are taking over. Detaching is not so easy, as he's finding out.

"And when you come nosing around," Albert says, "you're getting too close for comfort and Canavan orders the rub-out?"

"Canavan isn't in charge of anything. This must have come from higher up the chain."

"Lindenauer."

"Be my guess."

"What are you going to do?"

"First me and Detective Canavan need to have a little talk."

"Not tonight, buddy," Albert says. "It's too late. Rest up. Talk to him tomorrow. C'mon. I'll make up the sofa for you and you can pack it in. You're not looking your all-time best."

Clarence takes a moment to consider. Takes inventory of his body, which is exhausted and beginning to stiffen up from his acrobatics earlier in the day when the gunmen were shooting at him.

He agrees.

And when he does, a wave of weariness passes over him, as though he has just given his own body permission to shut down for a few hours.

Still, he lies awake on Albert's sofa, worrying about Bessie.

Imagining what he will do to anyone who harms her.

34

BEN RUBIN

The telephone pulls him out of a dead sleep.

Ben dives for it, hoping it's Elizabeth telling him she's out of jail.

Instead it's a man's voice asking for Ben Rubin.

"Who's this?"

"Tom Glover. I'm a reporter with the *Detroit Times*. Maurice Sugar suggested I call. Is this Ben?"

"Yeah."

"Maurice said you had information about the Hunger March?"

"I do. He told me—"

"Wait," Tom breaks in, "don't say anything else. Where are you?"

Suddenly suspicious, Ben says, "What do you want to know for?"

"Tell me what part of town you're in and I'll come and meet you. We shouldn't talk like this over the phone."

Not wanting to give his location away—especially if somebody is listening in—Ben says, "Near Woodward and Six Mile."

"Swell. There's a Chinese joint on Six Mile in Palmer Park. Kow Kow Inn. Can you get there in thirty minutes?"

The restaurant is in a brick building with dark windows and a brightly-lit red and yellow sign over the front door. A red neon OPEN sign flashes in the window.

Inside smells of chow mein and bleach. Though it is late in the middle of the week, the restaurant is packed. To the right of the entrance, a bar runs the length of the wall. Nobody seems to notice Ben coming in, so he sits at the bar and orders a coffee.

Soon the door from the kitchen opens and a heavy-set, disheveled young man walks in. He comes over to where Ben sits. "Ben?"

Ben nods.

The reporter shakes his hand. "Tom Glover." He sits on the stool beside Ben. "Thanks for meeting me. Ever been here?"

Ben shakes his head. "I don't live around here."

"Nice little place. Good to know where you can get a decent Chinese meal for under fifty cents."

The reporter has sad eyes behind wire-framed glasses. He has a bushy mustache that looks pasted on.

A Chinese woman comes over from behind the bar.

"The mysterious Madame Chen," Tom says with a grin.

"Barney Google," the woman says. She laughs, a surprisingly raucous sound that she covers with her hand over her mouth.

"This is my friend Ben," Tom says.

"Mr. Ben," she says. "What you need?"

"Just a tea for me."

"Make it my usual," the reporter says.

"You got it, Barney Google."

She serves Ben a pot of tea and a tiny cup. For Tom, she pours a cup of coffee, which she holds under the counter and splashes in liquid from a flask. Tom winks at Ben. She gives him his drink and goes to the other end of the bar so they can speak in private.

"She says I look like Barney Google, from the comics," Tom says. "Not sure what she means." He lifts his cup in a silent toast to Ben.

"Maybe it's the mustache,"

"Maybe. Maybe it's my big honker. I dunno."

Tom takes a drink from his cup. Smacks his lips.

"I come here a lot," he says. "Decent food, nice people. Madame Chen gives me a little extra in my coffee. Have you known Maurice Sugar long?"

"I just met him yesterday."

247

"At the march?"

"No. Afterwards, at the hospital."

Tom pulls a notebook from his pocket. "Mind if I take notes?"

"Be my guest."

The reporter starts writing, fast lines scrawled across the pages, the curves and squiggles of shorthand.

"The stories in the papers are pretty much all from Ford's point of view," Tom says. "Commie menace and so on. You were there. What's your angle? That where you got those bruises?"

Ben brings a hand to the cut on his head. "Just this one. Got clobbered by a sign in all the confusion."

"Where are the other ones from?"

"Couple guys who don't like me."

"Trust me, I know how it goes. What did you see at the march?"

Ben goes into it all . . . the tear gas, police beatings, freezing hoses on the fire trucks, shootings, goons from Ford, the chaos.

Tom takes it all down in his notebook. "You know what this sounds like?" he says. "A police riot. It jibes with other things I've heard. As I say, it's not the story the papers are telling. I can change it with this." He holds up his notebook.

"It was peaceful until the Dearborn cops came after us," Ben says.

"I heard the Detroit cops were there, too."

"They accompanied us until we got to Dearborn. I didn't see what they were doing after that. Once it kicked off, all I could see were blue suits running everywhere, breaking heads and shooting people."

"The Detroit coppers pulled off the sweeps today."

"You know about those?"

"Sure. It's been happening all day."

"What can you tell me about them?"

"The coppers swept through the city, picking up known Communists wherever they could find them."

"How would I go about getting someone out of jail who was picked up?"

"You have to ask Maurice Sugar, not me, pal," Tom says. "Somebody you know got swept up?"

"Yeah."

"Sorry. Maurice will know, if anybody does. You said you were also at the hospital afterwards? Tell me what you saw there."

Ben tells him about the broken and bloody bodies he saw at Detroit Receiving. About the beaten bodies handcuffed to their beds.

Tom takes more notes. "Got it. Anything else you can think of?"

Ben shakes his head.

Tom closes his notebook with a snap. "I'll file the story tonight. It'll be in tomorrow night's paper."

"You're sure it'll run?"

"Positive. The newspaper business is all about selling copies. And nothing sells copies better than conflict. And you're telling me about a beaut of a conflict. They won't turn it down. It also has the additional if slightly irrelevant virtue of being true."

"Can you keep my name out of it?"

"I'll make sure nobody knows who you are."

Tom leaves a buck on the bar and tosses a wave at Madame Chen. He slides off the stool and heads for the door to the kitchen. "I'll call you if I need anything more, okay?"

"How come you're going through the kitchen?"

"I'm leaving out the back door. Come with, I'll explain."

Tom leads him into the kitchen and through the food prep areas. Chinese men and women are standing at chopping boards filling up bins with green peppers, chicken parts, mung beans, and other exotic foods. They are yelling in the particular way Chinese people talk, as if they were mad at each other.

When they get to the back door, Tom says, "Long as you're here, do me a favor? Look out there and see if anybody's around?"

Ben pushes the door open and steps out. No one in the alley. The shadows of the apartment buildings behind the restaurant are empty.

He sticks his head back in. "Coast is clear."

"Where'd you park?"

"I walked over. I'm staying nearby."

"I'm parked around the corner. Walk with me."

They walk in silence down the alley. Turn the corner onto Second Avenue.

"I have to be careful," Tom says.

"Reporters make a lot of enemies?"

"This one does. My enemies are dangerous. Ever hear of the Black Legion?"

Ben shakes his head.

Tom stops in front of an Essex coupe. He slides behind the wheel and Ben gets in the passenger side.

"I've been writing stories about these guys. They're violent men. They hate anybody who's not white, male, and Protestant. They especially hate Jews, Catholics, and Negroes."

One more group who hates us, Ben thinks. Just what the world needs.

"They're just starting to be active," Tom goes on, "spreading into Michigan from Ohio and Indiana. So I'm not surprised you don't know about them yet. They're seeding themselves everywhere around here . . . in police departments, in political positions at every level, including city councils and mayors' offices. They're even in the auto factories. They keep an eye on the so-called 'radical element' and report to management."

"And they're after you?"

"They started following me. I had to outrun them the other night. They chased me all the way downtown. Fortunately, I lost them. They ever catch me, I'm a goner. People they don't like tend to disappear without a trace. I had to send my wife and kids up north. I've been sleeping at the paper."

"Do the coppers know about them?"

"*Know* about them? The coppers are *part* of them."

"Still you write about them?"

"Hell, yeah. They can scare me, but they're not going to stop me. People need to know about them. They're a menace. And it's only going to get worse in the years to come."

Tom starts up the coupe. "Sure I can't drop you someplace?"

"No thanks. I can walk from here." He already has enough people after him. He can do without getting caught in crossfire from the ones after Tom Glover.

He hops out of the car and gives a wave as Tom speeds off.

He is only a few blocks from Elizabeth's building. He spends most of the walk looking over his shoulder. One more danger to worry about.

When he gets to Elizabeth's apartment, she is still not back.

WEDNESDAY, MARCH 9, 1932

35

ELIZABETH WATERS

Another bull dyke matron shakes her awake.

Elizabeth had just fallen asleep sitting on the floor with her back against the cinder block wall. She's in a cell in the fourth cop station since she was arrested.

"Waters," the matron says, "you got a visitor."

Elizabeth runs her fingers through her hair and adjusts her clothes. She and the women who have been looped with her have not been allowed to use any bathroom facilities except the toilets in their cells, which soon overflow and run out of toilet paper. They have not been given food or water. Their watches have been taken away so no one knows what time it is.

"Let's go, gorgeous," the matron says. "I ain't got all day."

The women in her cell reach out for Elizabeth to touch her hand for luck as she is taken away. They know she may not return. No one knows what happens to the women who are taken and don't come back. In the horror of their night, they have bonded as a group. The differences in class, race, and language have dissolved in their common predicament.

"Can we stop at a lavatory so I can throw water on my face?" Elizabeth asks.

"No."

The matron grabs her arm and pulls her down a hallway and into an interview room. "Sit," she orders.

A table and two chairs in the room. Elizabeth sits in one of the chairs and rests her head on her arms on the table. She is hungry, dehydrated, and exhausted. She's nervous about what to expect from this interrogation and jittery from being away from Miss Em.

She closes her eyes and dozes off. She pops awake when the door swings open.

In walks Horace Howcroft.

Looking so clean and well-shaven he fairly squeaks. He's in a double-breasted pinstripe suit and carrying a cup of coffee in one hand and a file folder in the other. He wears his bug-spray cologne.

"What are you doing here?" she asks.

"I might ask the same of you."

He sits across from her and sets the coffee in front of her.

"Here," he says. "You look like you need this."

She pushes it away. "No thanks."

"What's the matter? Aren't you thirsty?"

"I'm dying of thirst."

"Well, drink up." He pushes the cup back toward her.

She glares at him. "I don't want it, Horace. Seriously, why am I being detained? And why are you here?"

"As I explained the other day, it's my job to keep tabs on radical elements. I was going over the roster of detainees this morning and saw your name."

"So you thought you'd pop in and wish me good morning with a coffee for an eye-opener?"

"Testy this morning."

"You're goddamn right. What time is it?"

He glances at his watch. "Eight-fifteen."

She buries her face in her hands.

"Sure you don't want the coffee?"

"Not unless the rest of the women in my cell can have some, too. Nobody's given us any food or water while we've been frog-marched around the city all night."

"Sorry. No can do. This is a personal favor for you. A perk of knowing the boss."

"Then I don't want any."

"Aren't you the noble one."

She's in no mood. She sweeps a hand out and knocks the cup on the floor. Liquid goes flying.

Horace jumps up so the coffee misses his suit. "Hey!"

"How much longer is this going to go on?" she demands.

"What do you mean?"

"This treatment. This torture."

"I'd hardly call it torture."

"Maybe not from where you're sitting. From this side of the table, it's cruel and unusual."

He watches her for a few moments. "You want to get out of here?"

"Of course."

"I can get you out. Today. Right now."

"What's the catch?"

Horace leans forward and lowers his voice.

"I have it on good authority," he says, "there's going to be an attempt made on the life of a prominent local politician within the next few days."

"Who?"

"I can't tell you until we shake on the deal."

"What's the deal?"

"Patience. The attempt is going to be made by a friend of yours."

"*Who?*"

"I can't tell you, not just yet."

"So what's the fucking deal already?"

"I know you know this person. You tell me where I can find him—or better yet, promise me you'll arrange to meet him at a location we control—and I'll let you walk out of here right now. No questions asked. Your record disappears. Otherwise, if we have to find him ourselves, he's going to be a dead man. And who knows how long you'll have to stay here then?"

"How would I even know where all my friends are?"

"Oh, I bet you know where this one is. I've seen you two together. I happen to know you're close."

Elizabeth stares at him. She hasn't seen him in sixteen years, until three nights ago. Who has he seen her with?

She was at the Unemployed Council meeting on Sunday. Who could he have seen her with?

The next time she saw him was at the hospital. Who was at the hospital with her? Maurice Sugar? Maurice Sugar couldn't possibly be planning on killing someone. That's just not how he works.

No, she was also with someone else at the hospital . . . someone Horace saw her with.

Ben Rubin.

She laughs out loud at the thought of Ben as an assassin.

"Man," she says, "are you nuts. You're talking about Ben Rubin?"

Horace inclines his head. "What do you know about this guy? Other than he's a yid, of course."

"I'm pretty sure he's not capable of killing anybody in cold blood."

"Really?" Horace opens the folder in front of him. "Did you know Ben Rubin is a member of the Purple Gang?"

"Can't be right."

He takes two black and white photos out of the folder and lays it in front of her. The first shows Ben standing on the porch of a house filled with people inside. In the second, Ben stands in the driveway at the side of the house, talking with three rough-looking men.

"This is a photo of Ben Rubin entering a house owned by Harry Millman, a high-ranking member of the Purple Gang. This," he says, tapping the other photo, "shows him conversing with Solly Abrams, Hymie Fleischman, and Isadore Bernstein. Known members of the Purple Gang. Think they're talking about the weather?"

"That doesn't prove a thing."

He places another photo in front of her. It's a mugshot of an older man sneering into the camera.

"Ben Rubin is the nephew of yet another Purple Gangster, Moe Feigenbaum. This guy. Moe lives in the same house with Ben and his mother and father. Feigenbaum's awaiting trial for his role in the Collingwood Manor massacre. I assume you've heard of that?"

When she does not reply, Horace lays another photo in front of her. "Here he is with his uncle outside the Oakland Health Club, a known gathering spot for the Purple Gang. Again, from the looks on their faces, they're not talking about whether it's going to rain."

Elizabeth looks at him open-mouthed. "How do you have these? Have you been following him?"

"No. We have surveillance on other members of the gang, including known hangouts like the health club."

"If you knew he was there, why didn't you pick him up?"

"I've only just seen these myself. Additionally, Ben was one of two men who attempted an armed robbery at the Madison Theatre last week. The other man was shot to death. Ben escaped. He's been in hiding ever since."

Which explains why he's needed to stay with her.

"How do you know this?"

"I can't show you this because it's confidential," Horace says, holding up a yellow sheet. "It's the record of Ben's brushes with the law. He's been nabbed for rolling drunks in Paradise Valley, breaking and entering, and public fighting, among other anti-social activities."

"How do you know this?" she asks again.

He collects the photos and puts them back in the folder. "We have an informant inside the Purple Gang. Now you want to try and make me believe the next step in this pattern of illegal activity *isn't* the murder of the mayor of the City of Detroit to cement his reputation with the gang?"

"The *mayor*? Frank Murphy?"

"I have it on good authority Ben Rubin will make an attempt on the life of Frank Murphy within the next two days. Unless you help me stop him."

"I can't possibly believe that's true."

"How long have you known him?"

"What does that matter?"

"I'm just saying, you might not know everything about him."

She stares at him. He stares back.

"Well?" he asks. "Do we have a deal? You tell me where I can find Ben Rubin and I'll walk you out to freedom myself right now."

"We have a deal, all right. Here's our deal: I tell you fuck all. And you can go straight to hell."

36

ROSCOE GRISSOM

R oscoe is up early. The brats in school, his wife gone. He can get used to this. It's almost as good as living alone.

After breakfast, he hears a horn in front of his house.

Harley Clarke.

Who beckons him out to his car, and hands him a heavy package wrapped in butcher's paper.

Roscoe takes it. Knows immediately what it is. "How'd you get it so fast?"

"Don't worry about it. Listen," Harley says, "this needs to happen quick. The funeral march? It's supposed to be on the weekend. This has to be done by then. Best by tomorrow."

"Tomorrow?"

"Can you do it? I'll find out his schedule for the day and get it to you."

"Look, it don't matter what his schedule is during the day. I can't walk right up to him and shoot him. He'll have bodyguards, people around him. We got to do this at night, when he's by himself. He married, this guy?"

"No. Matter of fact, there's a rumor he likes boys. I'll try to find out his schedule at the end of today. When he gets home, and so forth. That might be best, after all. Fewer people around and such."

Harley nods at the package in Roscoe's hands. "Meantime, there's what you'll need. Guaranteed clean. Got a box of shells there, too."

"Good deal. I'll protect it with my life."

"We'll talk more about this later. Going to be at the Dew Drop?"

"Where else?"

Harley takes off and Roscoe brings the package into the house. Unwraps it on the kitchen table.

It's a Colt .45 automatic. Bigger than the other guns they've given him. Looks like it's seen a lot of use. A simple machine, brutal on his kitchen table. Long blue barrel. Pebbled hard rubber grip. A prancing horse inside an oval etched on it.

He picks it up. Frowns at its unfamiliar heft.

This is no good. He needs to practice. He can't just shoot it once and hope it works.

He wraps it back up and walks down to Mack. Takes the streetcar downtown to the river. Jumps on the Jefferson line to Belle Isle. Walks across the bridge to the island. On this cold day in March, hardly anyone is out. He tramps into the woods and, making sure he's alone, loads the weapon and practices shooting into the trunk of a tree. To get the feel of it, he stands close and fires into a knot in the bark. The tree splinters and the kickback almost takes his arm off.

He figures out how to manage the kickback. Takes a few steps away and repeats the process until he is about twenty feet away.

Still can't hit the knot consistently. After a while of this, he realizes there is no way he's going to be able to shoot Frank Murphy accurately from a distance. He isn't a very good shot, never mind how many times he can plug a tree.

He is going to have to walk right up to him and blow his brains out from close range.

The thought gives him a thrill from his groin to his chest.

He'll have to look the mick right in the eye and pull the trigger.

Bam!

Who's a shitkicker hillbilly now?

Once he has that insight, he practices sneaking up to a tree from behind and putting a bullet into it and slipping away afterwards.

He's not going to be an ace killer, maybe, but it gives him practice getting comfortable with the gun.

When he feels he's made his entry and exit as quiet and smooth as possible, he takes the streetcars back to his house. Melanie is still gone, so he hides the weapon in a suitcase under the cot in the basement and walks up to the Dew Drop. Harley will get in touch with him there.

Roscoe gets back to the bar too late for lunch at the soup kitchen. But is Harley waiting for him at their usual table in the rear.

Roscoe drops into the chair beside him. "Hey."

"Hey," Harley says. "You know the thing? The location?"

"Yeah?"

"Yeah, I got it."

Harley grins, makes a gun of his right hand, points it at Roscoe. His thumb cocks like the hammer. Makes a small "pop" with his mouth like a gunshot.

"Great," Roscoe says. "Great."

"What do you say we take a run over there now, while it's still light, and get the lay of the land?"

Harley drives them down to Jefferson Avenue, and heads west. They take a right onto Parker Street and go up a long block and a half. A sign says, "West Village."

Roscoe completely loses his sense of direction as they enter another area of the city that is as foreign to him as a kingdom in a fairy tale, with their broad lawns and huge brick houses. The people who live here don't go hungry or want for anything, of this he is certain.

They stop down the block from a two-story brick Colonial. It seems huge and solid.

"This where he lives?" Roscoe asks.

"Yup."

"Fucking fortress. How the hell we going to get in and out?"

"'We'? That's your problem, pal."

Roscoe keeps staring at the house. "Drive by it, yeah?"

Harley puts the sled in gear and they cruise slowly by the house. A large entrance door in the front, with a walk of five steps leading up to it. No garage. The front lawn is not as wide as some of the others on the block. No hedges or trees to hide behind. Houses on this street are close together, with no driveways.

"Have to hit him when he first gets home, before he goes inside," Roscoe says. "Or wait till the morning and hit him when he comes out. Otherwise, there ain't no goddamn way I can see to get inside. I'm no fucking cat burglar."

Neither man speaks. Harley continues down to Agnes Street. Makes a left onto Van Dyke and a big swing around the block to come back in front of Frank Murphy's house. "Getting a feel for the neighborhood," Harley explains.

They take another slow swing around. "Okay," Harley says, "let's come back tonight and see what happens."

"What time's he get home?"

"I dunno. But I know how to find out."

Back at the Dew Drop, Harley uses Frankie's phone behind the bar and returns to the table where Roscoe sits.

"We're set," Harley says. "We got a guy inside the mayor's office. He says the mayor's last meeting's at six."

"So he should be home by what, seven, seven-thirty?"

"Give or take. We'll leave from here at six, just to be sure."

They stop by Roscoe's house to collect the gun from where Roscoe hid it. Back to the Dew Drop. They work through a bottle of Frankie's bootleg rye to pass the hours and, for Roscoe, to stiffen his courage.

When the time comes to leave, Roscoe is surprised to discover he has had a few too many stiffeners.

He stumbles over the threshold on the way out, catches himself quickly.

This is it, boy, he tells himself. This is it.

Pull your sorry-ass self together.

37

CLARENCE BROWN

In the morning, Clarence calls the Hunt Street Station, tells the desk sergeant he's sick and can't come in. The desk sergeant grunts his understanding and hangs up on him.

"Goodbye to you, too," Clarence says to the dead line. Just another of the thousand daily indignities he has to swallow.

He paces around Albert Norquist's home all morning. He's alone. Albert has gone into the station. The silence and the purposelessness drive him crazy. He has to hit the streets.

He wears his metal plates under his coat but instead of his usual fedora he wears a flat cap pulled low over his eyes. He borrows the cap from Albert. He can't do anything about his size.

He drives over to Hastings. Parks and strolls his patch. Sees the other Negro policeman, Ernest Cummings, but doesn't stop to chat. On foot Clarence crosses Lafayette. Crosses Congress. On Jefferson he takes the streetcar up to Belle Isle. Walks across the bridge. Follows the roadway around to the utility shed where Darius Turner was found.

The lock on the shed is still broken. Cold inside. The only remaining traces of the murder are the footprints in the ashes from the coppers who milled around beneath Darius's body, mocking and laughing, and the coroner's team.

He stares up at the rafter Darius was hung from. Suicide, they're calling it. Not even worth the time it would take to do an autopsy.

Just another dead nigger.

Looking over the scene, he feels not anger but a great sadness at the inevitability of it. This will never change. If Clarence is alive in ten years, or fifty—or a hundred years, for that matter—he is certain Negroes' lives will still not be worth much. Other people will be standing where he stands today, gazing as sadly at the aftermath of racial violence as Clarence is today.

Maybe not in this exact shack. But on this island, in this city. In this country.

How not to fall into despair? It might get better, sure. But however much it changes, decent Negroes will always be second class citizens in this country. That's a fact. Scratch a white person, you're going to find a racist just below the skin.

His thoughts go back to the night Darius was found. He repopulates the shed from memory. Along with all the other policemen, including Lindenauer in charge of the pretend investigation, Canavan was here, too, laughing at the corpse of Ella Turner's son. Calling it suicide, despite every bit of evidence to the contrary.

Canavan also got Junior Sykes to lure Clarence into the ambush that almost left him the latest Negro corpse in Detroit.

Clarence leaves the shed and traipses down to the Scott Fountain. A cold wind sweeps up off the river and makes his eyes water.

He blinks, rubs them with the rough sleeves of his bulky overcoat, pulls it closer around him and his hat down lower.

Nobody is at the fountain today. The wind is too sharp. Anyway, the sporting life players are probably still in bed; they won't come out until later in the day. He wonders if Junior will come back like always, or if he is going to lie low, as Clarence told him to. Considering the level of Junior's smarts, Clarence would bet his snitch will be out and about for all to see.

Clarence eases himself down on the cold stone of the fountain's outer edge. Looks out over the river. Ice floes pass lazily in the current and bob near the shore. It hasn't been warm enough to melt them yet.

He considers what he knows about Darius's murder.

Or maybe a better way to say it is: what *doesn't* he know?

One question he never got answered was, whose Cadillac did Darius get into? If it actually was Darius who was seen getting into a Cadillac. If it actually was a Cadillac. He only has the word of the old juicer he talked with the day after Darius's mother came to see him.

Nobody else mentioned seeing Darius getting into a Caddy. Though LaMont, Robinhood Rowe's muscle, mentioned Darius was shacking up with a girl from Madame Savoyard's whorehouse.

It wasn't Yolanda. She told Clarence they weren't shacking up. Why would she lie to him? And if it wasn't her, who would it be?

If it was *anybody*. Could LaMont even be believed? Clarence's mother used to say a lie flies and truth comes limping after. Everything he's seen as a policeman has proven the truth of it.

And anyway, as Yolanda said, she wouldn't be able to afford a Caddy no matter what. And wouldn't have any opportunity to get her hands on one.

So who would?

There was only one woman at Madame Savoyard's who could afford a Caddy: the Madame herself.

Why would she have any contact with a low-level crook like Darius? She had access to the movers and shakers of Detroit's white political and social elite . . . why would she spend time with a man like Darius Turner?

Angelo opens the door to the house on Second. The look on the bouncer's broad face lets Clarence know he recognizes Clarence at once. He gives Clarence the stink eye.

Says, "Get lost."

"I need to talk to Madame Savoyard," Clarence says.

"Ain't here."

Slams the door in his face.

Clarence goes around the back, to the rear entrance. Sees someone inside through the window. Taps on the door. Little Frances opens it.

When she sees who it is, her eyes grow wide. She looks behind her to make sure nobody is looking.

Clarence says, "Remember me?"

"I do. Madame, she ain't here right now," she whispers.

"You're the one I want."

She steps out on the back porch and closes the door behind her. Hugs herself against the cold.

"You remember I asked about Yolanda?"

"Yessir. Did you find her?"

"I did. I got another question for you."

"Yessir."

"Remember I asked you about Darius Turner?"

She nods.

"Did you ever see the madame keeping company with a young Negro man? That would have been Darius."

"No, sir. She don't have nothing to do with no Negro men at all."

Clarence remembers the madame saying as much. She didn't even want to be seen with Clarence.

She steals a look into the kitchen. The coast is still clear.

"Madame Savoyard, does she drive a Cadillac?" Clarence asks.

"Yessir. Big cream-color thing."

"You're sure it's a Cadillac?"

"Yessir. I've seen her in it."

"Does she keep company with any particular white man?"

"Not that I seen."

She throws a nervous look back into the kitchen. "Please, sir. Can I get back inside? I'm getting cold. And I got my work to do."

"Go on, now. Thank you for your help."

She goes back inside and he walks out to Second Street.

So Madame Savoyard owns a cream-colored Cadillac. There must be a thousand in the City of Detroit. One more bit of information, maybe useful, maybe.

According to the little maid, the Madame wouldn't keep company with a Negro. So if it was Darius getting into her cream-colored Cadillac, who was driving?

From the brothel he walks up Second to Grand Boulevard, and from there to Woodward. Jumps on the Woodward streetcar and takes it across Mack. Exits at Ledyard and walks into Paradise Valley. Makes sure nobody's following him, or even observing him as he walks down to Hastings, where he left his Ford.

He passes the familiar stores . . . luncheonettes, tailor shops, hand laundries, mom-and-pop markets, bars. In every window are posters for Wallace Fard's meetings to talk about the Caucasian devils and rediscovering the lost tribe of Shabazz . . .

Clarence stops dead.

Coming out of the Rexall Drug Store up ahead is Andre Young.

The cough syrup thief.

Moving fast.

Clarence goes after him.

Andre's pockets are bulging and he's fast-walking down the sidewalk. He turns off on a side street and Clarence is about to follow until he hears his name called.

"Mr. Clarence!"

So much for following Andre, who has also heard Clarence's name called out and is now tearing down the alley, coat tails flying. In seconds he's out of sight.

Clarence turns, sees Junior Sykes standing in front of the C&C Bar across the street.

Waving at him.

Trotting across the street to him.

"God*dammit*, Junior," Clarence says, "this your idea of staying out of sight?"

"Mr. Clarence," Junior says, "glad I saw you."

"Come on, let's get you out of the middle of the street. You dumb shit."

He takes Junior by the arm and walks him down the alley where Andre disappeared.

Damn fool. Might as well walk around with a sign: *Kill me.*

"Now what is it?"

"I been asking around, Mr. Clarence."

"About what?"

"About what we talked about yesterday. The policeman who made me give you that message?"

"What about him?"

"I felt so bad about it, Mr. Clarence, I been asking around about him. And I found something you might be interested in."

38

Ben Rubin

B en goes out to buy a paper at the newsstand on Six Mile and Woodward to see if Tom Glover's story made the early edition of the *Detroit Times*.

It was there. The reporter was right, the editor couldn't pass it up.

POLICE BLUNDERS LED TO RIOT

VIOLENT RESPONSE TURNED PEACEFUL MARCH DEADLY

EARLY REPORTS MISLEADING

Initial descriptions of the cause of Monday's deadly march were incorrect, according to new reporting.

Sources say it was the police, and not the Communists as first thought, who were responsible for the chaos that resulted when 3,000 unemployed workers converged on the Ford Motor Co. plant in Dearborn demanding basic rights.

The Dearborn police changed an orderly demonstration into a riot, with death and bloodshed as its toll.

Plans by the marchers to present their petitions to Ford for jobs, medical aid, and emergency food relief were derailed by the harsh overreaction of Dearborn police and fire units, and of the Ford Service Department.

Initial reports that the riot began with six shots fired by marchers were not corroborated by sources.

The *Free Press*, on the other hand, still has the same hard line: the riot was caused by the Reds. He's curious to see what the city's other major paper, the *News*, has to say.

Ben hurries back. He feels like he's a target, with every eye on him between the police and the Purples.

In Elizabeth's apartment, he calls Maurice Sugar. His secretary says Mr. Sugar isn't in. Ben hopes he is out trying to free Elizabeth, the way he said he would.

Before noon, he gets a phone call from his Uncle Moe.

"Hey, boychik, they want to meet you, see if we can iron out all the misunderstanding."

"Who?"

"The three you had a run-in with. Solly Abrams, Hymie Fleischman, and Izzie Bernstein."

When Ben doesn't respond, Moe says, "What's the matter?"

"I dunno if I want to meet those guys again."

"Here's your chance to put things right. Want me to come with you?"

"Would you?"

"If it makes you feel safer, sure," Moe says. "Look, Benny, they want to settle this as much as you do. Nobody likes bad blood."

"If you say so. When and where?"

The meeting is set for Sol's, a delicatessen on Oakland near the schvitz. Ben's apprehension grows as the day wears on and there's no word from either Elizabeth or Maurice Sugar. Unable to sit still, he leaves the apartment and takes a Woodward Avenue streetcar down to Melbourne. From there, he walks the four blocks to the deli.

He gets there early. Still not entirely trusting this situation, he walks around the block, hugging the shadows of the buildings. As the meeting time draws near, he starts to relax. Moe wouldn't betray him. (*Would he?*) This must be on the level.

And Moe will be there, too. They won't do anything with Moe present.

(Would they?)

Except he knows it's a foolish hope. These mobsters have a long and bloody tradition of killing their own.

He wants to wait for Moe to come before he goes inside the deli. He loiters down the street beneath a flower shop sign.

A Cadillac pulls up outside Sol's. Three men get out. The three Purples he's supposed to meet. He recognizes them. They seem relaxed as they go inside.

A few minutes later, a car pulls up beside him.

Moe sits in the passenger seat. Behind the wheel is a man Ben has never seen before.

Moe rolls down the window. "Benny. Get in."

"What's going on?"

"Get in and I'll tell you."

Ben climbs into the back seat. Moe says, "Get down."

Ben does as he says and they speed off down Oakland.

"What the hell's going on?" Ben asks.

"Stay down," Moe says as the driver careens down the street and screeches around a corner.

They come to a stop and Ben sits up.

The guy at the wheel turns around to Ben. "You okay?"

"I'm fine. Who are you?"

"Irv Kaminsky." The driver extends his hand.

"Irv's a pal of mine," Moe says. "We've done business from time to time. You can't go to this meeting, Ben."

"Why not?"

"It's a trap. They're going to ambush you."

"How do you know?"

"From Irv."

"How do *you* know?" Ben asks him.

"Let's just say I'm privy to information from certain people."

"And said information told you . . .?"

"You were going on a ride you weren't coming back from."

Ben sits back. Tries to take this in.

"They didn't know I was coming with you," Moe says. "They would have punched both our tickets."

Irv drives them to a luncheonette in Warren northeast of Detroit. The three men sit in a booth at the back of the restaurant.

"What are we going to do now?" Ben asks his uncle.

Moe takes a sip of coffee and a bite of his hamburger. Ben's face is too sore to let him eat anything. "You're not going to do anything," Moe says. "I'll take care of it."

"How? They were ready to slaughter us."

"Everything can be negotiated."

Ben looks at his uncle in a different way than he has before. All his life, Ben looked up to Moe—more, even, than he looked up to his own father—as a man with guts and smarts. Now as he watches his uncle chewing his hamburger slowly, cow-like, he begins to wonder if maybe Moe isn't past his prime after all.

If maybe he can't fully grasp the circumstances they're in.

"Seriously, Moe," Ben says, "how?"

"These guys can always be bought off. It's either money or something else. That's all they're interested in. They don't give a shit about honor or decency or even loyalty. It's always an eye for an eye with them. They're like Old Testament Jews, these guys."

The savagery of his disdain for his friends in the gang surprises Ben.

"I still don't understand how you're going to negotiate with them."

"Don't worry about it. I won't let anything happen to you. My word on it."

If they don't believe in honor and loyalty, how does Moe? Ben decides not to bring this up to his uncle.

"I don't understand. What are you going to give them?"

"I'll talk to them. I'll get you out of this."

Ben looks from Moe to Irv, sitting there nursing a coffee.

"Are you going to help him?" Ben asks Irv.

"Moe don't need my help," Irv says.

"Why are you doing this for him?"

Irv says, "Moe and me, we started out at the same time, just on opposite sides. I used to drive a hack. Once these three Purples flagged me down. They were going to hijack my taxi to use in a bank robbery. I heard them talking about it. They were talking about what to do with me. Two of them wanted to shoot me right then and there. I'd already seen their faces. I figured I was a goner right then and there. The third man was your uncle here. He got them to back off and let me go. Ever since, I do him favors when I can. He does me favors, too. I owe him my life."

Ben looks at Moe, who shrugs. "Way of the world, Benny. Way of the world."

"I still don't see how you're going to get them off my back," Ben says to his uncle.

Moe gets a look in his eye Ben has never seen before—a kind of sadness, or resignation.

Ben looks at Irv, who has the same look.

"What are you going to do, Uncle Moe?"

"I get you out of this, you have to promise me one thing."

"Anything."

"After this, you're done with the life. And these mugs."

"You get me out of this," Ben says, raising his coffee cup, "I'll make that promise."

They clink cups. Irv Kaminsky joins them.

"Irv," Ben says, "you still drive a cab?"

Irv and Moe share a small smile between them.

Irv shakes his head no. "Let's just say I'm in sales," he says with a wink.

"Everybody buys and sells something," Moe says. "Irv's commodity is information. Not much happens around this town he doesn't know about."

They finish their meals and get ready to leave. Irv Kaminsky taps Ben on the wrist. "One more thing. Another bit of information for you. Stay out of downtown tomorrow."

"Why?"

"I heard there's going to be a shooting around City Hall."

39

ELIZABETH WATERS

By Wednesday afternoon—at least it seems like it's the afternoon; they took her watch so she doesn't know what time it is—Elizabeth has been to five precinct houses since she was picked up. Only two of the women she started this nightmare with are left. The rest have disappeared throughout the previous night and this day.

Early in the day, they were given a stale muffin and cup of watery coffee each. They have not had any other food or drink since the day before.

This precinct house (wherever it is; she has no idea) contains no matrons. The male cell guards are responsible for managing the women who are kept here. One male guard now comes to her holding cell.

He calls: "Waters!"

He unlocks her cell and walks her down the jail hallway. His hands are all over her. She is exhausted from lack of sleep, weak from lack of food and water, and past caring from lack of Miss Em. She knocks his hands away from pawing at her breasts and her ass.

He pulls her past the interview room and continues down the hall to the release desk.

One more pat on the ass to show her who's boss.

Maurice Sugar waits for her at the release desk.

She was never so glad to see anyone in her life.

"Hey, kid," he says.

His face darkens when he sees the shape she's in.

She wants to run to him. The guard has her by the arm.

"Let her go," Maurice tells him.

The guard makes a show of weighing the pros and cons, releases his grip. She pulls away from him and Maurice draws her into an embrace.

"Did you post bail?" she asks. Her voice is scratchy, her throat dry.

"No," he says, his voice still barely controlling his fury. "You were never processed."

She can't take it in for a moment.

"You mean they've been holding me all this time—"

"Without charging you, yes."

"I never knew they could do that in the United States of America."

"They can do whatever we can't stop them from doing. Did you have a purse?"

"No. They rushed me out of my apartment so fast I didn't have time to grab it. I did have a watch, though."

Maurice glares at the duty officer. "Well?"

The cop shrugs. "Ain't here."

"Where is it?" he demands.

"You can fill out a lost items requisition," the policeman says.

"Never mind," she says.

"No coat, either?" Maurice says.

"They didn't give me time to get one when they took me."

"Bastards," he mutters.

She is slow, light-headed. Maurice helps her out the door.

"Thank you," she says.

He shakes his head; he is too furious to say anything.

She sniffs herself. "I stink."

"Not as much as this whole business. What do you want to do first, get a meal or go home and shower?"

"I'm starving."

He takes her back to his office in the Barlum Tower in Cadillac Square. His secretary runs to the door when he comes in with Elizabeth. She helps guide Elizabeth to the sofa in the outer office.

"What would you like?" Maurice asks Elizabeth.

"Anything."

"Inez, call down to the restaurant, please. Have them send up a hot hamburger sandwich dinner. And a big cup of coffee."

While she makes the order, Maurice says, "I'll be back in a minute."

He goes into his office and Elizabeth can hear his thunderous voice on the telephone. He is yelling about her treatment, threatening to sue the city, the police force, every policeman who was in contact with her.

Elizabeth leans back and closes her eyes.

The next time she opens them, the meal has arrived. Inez has it on the coffee table in front of her. A slab of meat between two pieces of white bread soaked in brown gravy, a dollop of mashed potatoes, and mushy peas.

"This is all they had left from lunch," Inez says.

"Smells like heaven. Thank you."

"Dig in."

Maurice comes out of his office and watches her eat for a few moments. She is wolfing the food. She can't remember being this hungry.

"You look better already," he says.

She swallows a mouthful. "Have I said thank you?"

"You have. You should also thank Ben Rubin. He's the one who told me you were in custody."

"How did you find me?"

"Wasn't easy. They do this so you can't be found. It's happened so often I've developed a network of contacts in the police department. I'm sorry it took this long."

She shakes her head. "Nothing to apologize for. I'm grateful beyond words."

Maurice goes back into his office to make phone calls. She finishes the meal.

"Is there a place I can go to freshen up?" Elizabeth asks Inez.

Inez walks her down the building corridor to the Ladies. Elizabeth goes in and sits on the toilet for a few minutes after she's finished, gathering her strength. She finishes up and washes her face.

She leans on the sink, gazing into her own face in the mirror.

Beyond the effect of the past two days, she sees the signs she is getting old. She is haggard, with dark circles under her eyes and a fine network of wrinkles angling from the corners of her mouth and eyes.

She returns to Maurice's office. "Better?" Inez asks.

"Much. I won't feel like myself until I go home and have a bath and a fresh change of clothes. But I'm on the way back."

She knocks on the door of Maurice's office.

He beckons her inside. She sits in the visitor's chair across the desk from him. "Maurice, I spoke with Horace Howcroft this morning."

"What did the rat bastard want?"

"He told me there's going to be an attempt made on Frank Murphy's life."

"Mayor Murphy?"

"Yes."

"He knows this how?"

"He wouldn't tell me."

"Of course not. Did he say when? Or by whom?"

"In the next couple of days. And he said one of my friends is going to do it."

"Who?"

"Ben Rubin."

She can see Maurice is momentarily confused. "The guy you met at the hospital on Monday," she says.

"I know who he is. I just find it hard to believe. I talked to him on the phone yesterday. He didn't strike me as a killer."

"Why did you talk to him?"

"He called me to see if I could help find you."

Elizabeth is touched at this information.

"Did Howcroft say why he's going to do this? Has Ben ever said anything against the mayor?"

"Never. I never even thought he was particularly political. Horace says Ben's going to do it as an initiation to the Purple Gang."

"Baloney. The Purples are a lot of things, but they aren't a political hit squad. With other gangs, yes, they're ruthless. Even among themselves. They stay away from political assassinations, except if a politician is dirty. And nobody's cleaner than Frank Murphy."

"It didn't sound right to me, either."

"Why did he tell you?"

"He was giving me a deal: I could tell him where he could find Ben Rubin and I could walk right out of custody. Needless to say, I told him to go fuck himself."

"Good for you. Are you sure he's on the level?"

"We have to get to Ben and find out."

"We also have to let the mayor's office know. In case some part of this is real."

"Let's go."

"First thing you need to do is go home and change your clothes," Maurice says.

The Detroit City Hall stands west of Campus Martius, at the intersection of Woodward and Michigan Avenues downtown. Not far from Maurice's office, it is a four-story sandstone structure with a mansard roof and a cupola with a clock facing four ways on top. A rag-tag line of unemployed men, whites and Negroes, snakes out of the entrance, down the steps, and around the building.

A police guard stands on duty in the doorway.

"We need to see Mayor Murphy," Maurice says. "This is an emergency."

The policeman looks Maurice up and down, lets his eyes linger over Elizabeth. Maurice drove her home so she could take a quick shower and change into fresh clothes. The cop is frankly ogling her standing there in a pair of tan slacks and white jersey under her open coat.

"What about?" the copper says.

"It's a matter of urgency. I need to speak with the mayor."

"Ain't gonna happen. He ain't even in the building."

"Then I need to speak with someone on his staff."

"Look, I don't know what you're trying to pull. You ain't getting in to see nobody. They're all busy. Can't you see all them deadbeats signing up for relief? Get lost."

The policeman towers over Maurice, wide as the doorway in his double-breasted uniform.

"This is ridiculous," Maurice says. "I insist on seeing someone in the mayor's office."

He goes to walk around the copper.

Who places a beefy hand on Maurice's chest. Three other coppers appear out of nowhere to back him up.

"You're not getting in," the policeman says. "Forget it."

The four coppers form a wall between Maurice and Elizabeth and the door. The coppers' blank faces dare them to try it.

"Let's go," Maurice tells her.

They find the same reception at 1300 Beaubien.

The duty sergeant there won't let them talk to anyone, either. He takes their information grudgingly. Elizabeth is sure he's going to throw it away as soon as they turn their backs.

"What are we going to do now?" she asks.

"I'm going back to the office. I should drop you back at your apartment. You need rest."

"Maybe Ben's there. Or if not, maybe I can get hold of him."

"And say what?"

"The number one thing I'll ask him is, are you going to kill the mayor of Detroit?"

40

ROSCOE GRISSOM

Harley Clarke collects Roscoe at the Dew Drop Inn. It's late afternoon. Purple clouds in the sky look like they might carry snow.

Roscoe is feeling no pain.

After drinking all day, his nerves are calm at last. He has never killed anyone before, and every time he would imagine the job that lay ahead of him, his hands would start shaking. This is different from the last few times he has gone out with his fellow soldiers. This time feels real. They have a target and a timeline.

And these are serious men.

With half a bottle of Frankie's bootleg rye in him, he's cool and calm. I can do this, he tells himself (though he has never actually done anything like this before).

They get into Harley's sled and Roscoe opens the window to blow cold air into his face. I'm not drunk, he tells himself. I'm relaxed. I'm ready.

By the time they get to Frank Murphy's house, Roscoe's calm has been replaced by an alcohol-fueled rage. It's directed not against Frank Murphy (who Roscoe knows nothing about), but against the people who live in the houses in West Village. Large, perfect castles with their perfect lawns, families safe and sound inside, no worries, no problems, tummies filled, no screaming children, no nagging wives, nobody having to worry about where the next meal will come from, or the next paycheck.

Matter of fact, these people get the paychecks that by rights belong to people like Roscoe. They steal from him.

So he has persuaded himself.

He seethes in drunken fury.

Harley parks down the street from Murphy's house. And they settle in to wait.

Harley is silent. Tense. Tapping his fingers along the steering wheel. Smoking nonstop.

In the silence and the smoky confines of the car, Roscoe shuts his eyes.

Drifts off.

At some point, Harley nudges him. "He's here."

Roscoe pops awake. For a few moments his vision remains clouded. His brain cottony. It takes him several seconds before he remembers where he is.

When he does remember, he sees two cars turning down the street. The one in front is a police unit, lights flashing. The other is a dark, late model sedan.

"First sled's his security detail," Harley says. "There'll be another copper driving the one Murphy's in."

"You know these guys?"

Harley strains to see into the first car. "Dunno. I know a couple of the security guys. Can't tell who's there now."

"How'm I supposed to shoot him right in front of his bodyguards?"

"It'll happen so fast, they won't know what's going on. One to the head. *Bang!* Now go! I'll pick you up after and we'll get the hell out of here. Go!"

He pushes Roscoe out of the car.

Roscoe is not happy. Pushed out on the sidewalk, he feels exposed, like he's wearing a sign saying, "Killer."

"Remember: one to the head," Harley says in a harsh whisper.

Remembering Laverne Penny's brains all over the windshield— one to the head—for failing to do what he was supposed to do, Roscoe begins the long walk down the sidewalk. Insides trembling. A great rumbling in his ears. Go slow, he urges himself. For all anyone knows, you're just out for a stroll after dark.

As if you belong to this neighborhood.

Yeah, right. Fat chance.

Walks on.

One to the head.

The police cruiser stops up in front of Murphy's house. The car Roscoe assumes contains Frank Murphy pulls up behind it.

He tries to time it so he passes Murphy's car at the exact moment Murphy steps out.

For the last time.

Welcome to the last breath of fresh air you're ever going to take, he silently tells Murphy.

He sees a silhouette in the back seat. Assumes it's Murphy.

Roscoe holds the pistol in his coat pocket. He flicks off the safety.

Rehearses in his mind how it's going to go one last time:

Murphy steps out of the car. Roscoe rushes up behind him (just like the trees in the Belle Isle woods he was practicing on).

Plugs him.

While the cops stand flatfooted, Roscoe runs. Jumps into Harley's car.

And they are gone.

Mission accomplished.

Now Murphy's rear passenger door opens. This is it.

The copper behind the wheel of the front car gets out.

Two coppers from Murphy's car get out.

All three security men surround Murphy and walk him up to his front door.

Roscoe stops walking.

The copper left in the front sled gives him The Look. Roscoe gets his legs moving again.

The moment is gone.

He can't turn around and go back to Harley, so he keeps walking. Feels the coppers' eyes boring into his back.

Behind him, he hears the heavy roar of Harley's car pulling away.

It's not coming toward Roscoe. It's going in the opposite direction.

Roscoe continues down the block, his mind abuzz with betrayal.

Turns left at the corner.

To his great relief, he sees Harley rounding the next corner. He pulls over and Roscoe jumps in.

They tear off down the narrow road.

"Shit," Harley says.

"He goes straight into the house like tonight, this ain't gonna work," Roscoe says. He is still trembling, but now in relief.

"No shit."

Back at the Dew Drop Inn, they each have a whiskey and talk about their options.

"We need another plan," Harley says. "And fast."

He knocks his drink back. Goes off to call his friend inside the mayor's office.

Returns after a few minutes. "It's set for tomorrow morning."

He raises a glass to Roscoe.

Roscoe clinks his glass. Only postponed, not canceled.

They have to go through this all again tomorrow.

41

CLARENCE BROWN

Apartment buildings rise on Vernor Highway between Brush and Hastings Streets in Paradise Valley. Most of them house the working men and women who scrape out a living in a city that tries its hardest to keep them from it.

Clarence knows a few of the apartments along Vernor are home to women (and men) who cater to those whose taste in sexual adventure runs toward the bizarre. In one of these apartments lives Mistress Anita. She is a favorite of men (all of them white) who crave punishment from a strong Negro woman. Most of her clients know she is really a man. It gives the experience an added tang.

Tonight one of her clients is Detective Sergeant Daniel Canavan of the Detroit Police Department.

Or at least he is according to Clarence's snitch Junior.

Who got the word directly from Mistress Anita herself.

Again, according to Junior.

Junior put the word out among the demimonde he inhabits . . . he wanted to know if anybody had any contact with Detective Canavan. Mistress Anita (real name: Max Johnson) told Junior about Canavan visiting her tonight for one of their regular sessions. Junior passed the word on to Clarence as a way of making up for almost getting him killed.

Clarence parks across the street and goes up to the front door. Buzzes Mistress Anita's apartment.

A gruff male voice answers. "Yeah?"

"Demetrius?" Clarence asks.

A pause. "Who's this?"

"Clarence Brown. Can you come down here for a minute? Got a question for you."

"What about?"

"Come down, I'll tell you."

Another pause—Clarence can almost hear Demetrius's thoughts in his head.

He comes back. "Wait there."

Another five minutes and the door opens. Demetrius Taylor comes out. With dark skin and marcelled hair, he is a handsome man despite the scar down one side of his face. Wears a tailored suit, surprisingly slender for a man who keeps order for a dominatrix. Demetrius's appearance is deceptive. He is a hard man.

"What about it, Mr. Clarence," Demetrius says.

"How you doing, brother."

"Awright."

"Busy night?"

"They all busy. What you need, man?"

"You got a john up there with Anita, skinny young white man with little round circles for glasses?"

Demetrius nods.

"He come in with anybody?"

"No. Alone. Like always."

Clarence takes a $5 bill from his wallet and stuffs it in Demetrius's coat pocket. "I need a favor."

"Uh-huh."

"I need a few minutes alone with him."

"He with Anita."

"I know. Just be a small interruption."

Demetrius shrugs. Clarence follows him up three flights of stairs to Mistress Anita's apartment. It could belong to anybody's grandmother. It is furnished with an overstuffed sofa and chairs with antimacassars on the backs. The only thing out of place is the desk in the entrance foyer where Demetrius sits.

"In the back bedroom," Demetrius says. "Only thing I ask is, no blood."

Clarence listens at Anita's door for a few moments, hearing murmurs and groans.

He barges in.

Canavan is on his hands and knees beside a bed. He is naked except for a leather strap around his genitals and a studded leather collar around his neck with a leash attached to it. A gag blocks his mouth in the form of a black ball attached by a black leather strap tied around his head.

His hands are cuffed together.

Anita holds the leash. She is dressed head-to-toe in a black gown with a skull and crossbones embroidered at her left breast. She wears a black veil with holes cut out for her eyes and mouth. On her head is what looks like a toy pirate hat with the same skull and crossbones. In her right hand is a whip.

Her high-heeled shoe is on Canavan's back. She wears fishnet stockings.

Canavan tries to scream when he sees Clarence. It comes out as a high-pitched squeal. He struggles to rise. Anita keeps him down with a jab of her high heel.

Clarence stands there, taking in the scene.

Says, "Out."

Mistress Anita hands him the leash. Slow-walks out of the room.

Clarence closes the door behind her. Looks down at Canavan, who is glaring at him. His blue eyes burn with hatred.

Clarence kneels. Unties the strap around Canavan's head.

Canavan spits out the ball.

"Well, well, well," Clarence says. "What have we here?"

"I'm going to kill you!" In his circumstance, Canavan does not have quite the authority he would like.

Clarence looms large over him.

"You tell Junior Sykes to give me a message today?"

"I don't know nobody—"

Clarence leans down, grabs a fistful of hair with one big hand and slaps Canavan's face with the other.

Canavan droops. Blood from his nose spatters on the floor. Clarence has already gone back on his word to Demetrius.

A sink is in the corner of the room. Clarence gets a towel. Dabs at the blood on Canavan's face and the floor. Rests the towel under Canavan's head.

"Ask you one more time. You tell Junior to give me a message?"

"Listen, you fucking nigger, you can't do this to me."

Another handful of hair. This time a punch.

More blood, with teeth.

Clarence stands. Opens the window as wide as it will go. He grabs Canavan by the arms and pulls him up and leans his bare torso face-first out the window.

Canavan shrieks like a little girl.

"Tell me why," Clarence says. "Or you going out."

"Lemme go!" Canavan squeals. He squirms but can't escape Clarence's iron grip.

"Tell me why," Clarence repeats.

"It was Lindenauer!"

The DPD chief of detectives.

Clarence's commanding officer.

"What about him?"

"He told me to do it."

"He told you to set up the ambush?"

"Yes! I swear! I swear to God I did it because he told me to."

"Why?"

"I don't know!"

Clarence boosts him over the sill and dangles him out the window by his naked ankles.

"Talk! Why did he do it?"

"I don't know. I swear to God, Brown. He just told me to arrange to get you taken out."

"He never said why?"

"No! Pull me up! Please!"

"So you just went ahead and did it? You knew you were sending me to my death, and you never thought to ask why? Who were the cops you sent?"

"Just a couple of Legion guys. I don't even know who they were." Canavan starts to sob. "Please!"

"What do you mean, Legion guys?"

"The Black Legion. You don't know about them?"

"Educate me."

"It's a secret society a lot of us belong to. It's new. At meetings, people wear the robes the Mistress had on."

"That dumb-ass pirate outfit?"

"Yeah."

"What's the purpose?"

Canavan yells: "To rid this country of niggers like you!"

Clarence lets go of one ankle. Canavan shrieks.

Clarence looks at him, handcuffed, hanging naked by an ankle, upside-down outside the window. Remembers the three men who tried to kill him, evidently on Lindenauer's say-so. Imagines their smug faces, their casual hatred.

Remembers how Canavan set up the ambush.

Remembers Canavan's mocking laughter in the work shed with Darius Turner's body twisting in the breeze off the river.

Summons up all the casual white hatred he has run into his entire life. Every day. All the rage he swallows. All the indignities. All the names. The looks.

Considers how easy it would be to imbue it all in this skinny rat bastard and just let go. Watch him fall three stories to the sidewalk.

One less member of the Black Legion.

One less racist cop.

He is tempted.

So tempted.

All he has to do is relax his grip. Let the little shit slip away.

Boom.

So easy.

Splat. There goes Canavan.

The moment stretches. He can see Canavan sobbing.

He can't bring himself to do it.

He pulls Canavan up and lets him flop on the hardwood floor. Canavan is quivering from the cold and the fright.

Clarence takes his chin in his big hand, slaps him with the other hand. "One word about this to anybody," he says, "and I'll finish the job on you. Plus everybody on the force will know about these weekly visits to a colored he-she whore. You understand me?"

Canavan is too shaken to answer. Clarence says, "Get me?"

Canavan nods his head and collapses into sobs.

In the living room, Mistress Anita has taken off her Black Legion costume and sits cross-legged on the sofa, languidly smoking a cigarette. She wears a black leather bra and black leather panties and her fishnets attached to a garter belt. Except for her Adam's apple, you wouldn't know she was a man.

"Done with him?" she asks.

"He's all yours."

He stops at the phone booth on Vernor down the block from Anita's. Dials the number for Bessie's sister Edna.

The number rings twice.

"Hullo?"

"Hey, Edna."

"Hey, big man. How you doing?"

"Hanging in. Can I talk to Bessie?"

"Naw, baby, She gone to bed already."

"She doing okay?"

"Worried about you, Clarence. Not happy having to stay here."

"I know. Not going to be for much longer. Look, tell her I called?"

"I sure will. You take care of yourself."

They disconnect and he climbs into his Ford. Turns the engine on, sits back. But before he puts the car in gear, he turns the motor off.

He was going to head back to Albert's, but a sudden thought stops him.

Flooded with guilt for displacing his wife, in the aftermath of all the bile that rose in his throat following his encounter with Canavan, he asks himself if going back to Albert's is wise. If the police under Lindenauer are gunning for him, how far could he trust Albert?

Clarence knows if it came down to Albert siding with Clarence or with the other white coppers, Albert would come down on their side, not his. Not that he'd want to; it's just the way it is.

Don't forget, he tells himself, when all is said and done, Albert Norquist is still a white cop. And white is right in this world, no matter what.

So maybe it's not such a good idea to go back there tonight.

No, he needs to go someplace where nobody will think to look for him. Where whoever he stays with will not betray him.

It's a small list of people.

He drives to one of the colored whorehouses on Adams Street in Paradise Valley. A six-floor walk-up, red brick, sandwiched between the Club 666 and Morris's Loans.

From heaven to hell. And everything in between.

Clarence knows the place. Knows the madame, Rosita. Knows the security man. Knows most of the girls. He spent a lot of time here, back in the day. They're just like everyone else, trying to get by in a world that does everything to keep them from it.

The security man recognizes Clarence. "Hey, Mr. Clarence. Been a while. Welcome back."

They shake hands.

Three Negro men are sitting in the parlor, having drinks. Clarence recognizes them. High rollers in Paradise Valley: the head of an insurance company, the owner of the Gotham Hotel, and a boxing promoter. They give him a quick nod—everybody knows Mr. Clarence—and go back to their conversation.

Rosita comes out through a beaded curtain in her standard business attire, a black evening gown cut low in the front. Light-skinned, still trim, looking as fine as she did the last time Clarence saw her. Her beauty is structural, built in the bones and planes of her face, not accessible to age.

They stand looking at each other without speaking for a few moments.

She says, "Look what the cat dragged in."

She steps forward, offers him her cheek to kiss. He inhales the odor of her face powder, the sweet smell of gardenia he will always remember and associate with her.

"To what do I owe this surprise?"

"Rosie, I need a place to stay for the night."

"Do you, now. And I'm, what, running a hotel for homeless cops?"

"I just need a place for one night. Where nobody will look for me. Nobody ask questions. I need your help. Last time we talked, you said if I ever needed you, just ask. I'm asking."

"And Bessie? She know you're here?"

"Nobody knows I'm here."

She says nothing.

"I'm on the run, Rosie. But you don't want me here, I'll go."

"You must be in some big trouble, you want to stay here."

Now he says nothing. She examines his face. He knows it will tell her everything she needs to know.

Like always.

"Relax, big man," she says. "Like I said. You'll always have a place with me. Come on—let's find you a room."

He follows her elegant back down the hall. Black, rustling material.

It reminds him of something.

Canavan's pirate outfit on Anita.

But what does *that* remind him of?

42

BEN RUBIN

"Remember what I told you," Moe says.

"I will."

Ben jumps out of Irv Kaminski's car on Six Mile and Woodward and walks down to Elizabeth's apartment.

He is almost there when a door opens in a car parked at the curb in front of her building. A goon steps out, grabs Ben by his coat before Ben knows what's happening, and throws him into the back seat.

The car peels away and races around the winding streets of Palmer Park back to Woodward. Two guys in the front seat, a driver and the ape who grabbed Ben. It looks like a police cruiser, with a siren mounted on the front dash.

"What's going on?" Ben asks. "Who are you guys?"

'Shut up and sit back," the driver says.

They got him. Either these guys are police or they're working for Bernstein and the Purples. Or both. One way or the other, he's going to have to answer for the Madison Theatre job.

He wonders if Maurice Sugar takes on criminal cases. Or if he'll even have a chance to ask him. This might be the one-way ride everybody talks about.

At least he won't have any trouble keeping his promise to his uncle Moe.

Easy to leave this life if he's behind bars or at the bottom of the Detroit River.

And he told himself he was too smart to get caught.

Stupid schmuck.

They drive south on Woodward all the way to the river. They take a left on Jefferson and another left onto Brush. Ben hopes they will continue on to police headquarters, which will mean they're cops and he at least has a theoretical chance of surviving the night.

Instead, they pull over in front of Jacoby's Tavern two blocks down on Brush Street. The ape gets out and pulls Ben from the car. Manhandles him into the tavern.

In the back of the restaurant, a man sits having dinner. The goon throws Ben into a chair at his table.

The man is working through a schnitzel atop a fragrant mound of sauerkraut. Ben tries to place his familiar slick, golden boy good looks, sitting there in his shirtsleeves with a cloth napkin tucked into his collar.

"Ben," he says. "Remember me?"

"Remind me."

The man finishes chewing a mouthful, brushes his lips with the linen napkin. Holds out a hand. "Horace Howcroft."

They shake. The bones of Ben's hand crack.

"We met on Monday. At the hospital, after the riot? You were with Elizabeth Waters."

"Okay," Ben says.

"Remember now?"

"I do."

Ben looks around. The goon and the driver who brought him sit glaring from a nearby table.

"Something to eat?" Howcroft asks. "A drink? They got everything here. On me."

"No, thanks. I'm good."

"Best German food in town."

"No doubt."

"Oh, but wait, you people don't care much for things German nowadays, do you?"

You people.

"Not hungry."

"Suit yourself."

Howcroft takes another forkful of his dinner. "Mmm. Good."

Ben says, "So what am I doing here?"

"I thought we should have a talk. I heard you're looking for Elizabeth."

"How do you know?"

Howcroft gives a crooked grin. It's meant to be endearing. "It's my job to know things."

Ben waits.

Howcroft takes another forkful of schnitzel.

Washes it down with what smells like a fragrant glass of gin. Smacks his lips. "Sure you don't want anything?"

Ben shakes his head.

"Elizabeth, she's in a lot of trouble, you know that, right?" Howcroft says.

"How so?"

"She got caught up in the Red sweep yesterday. But I'm not telling you anything you don't know. You've been looking for her."

"Do you know where she is?"

"As it turns out, I do. As it further turns out, I can get her out."

Ben waits.

"Elizabeth and I go way back," Howcroft says. "She tell you? We're old friends. Close, *personal* friends. Grew up together. I want to do her a favor. I want to do you a favor."

"Why?"

"Goodness of my heart?" Howcroft looks around the tavern, like he's not sure. "I could tell how it was with you two when I saw you at the hospital. She likes you. You like her."

"So why don't you just let her out? What do you need me for?"

Howcroft smiles again, this time a lizard's lazy grin. "You know who I am?"

"You just told me."

"No, I mean you know what I do?"

"No idea."

"I'm the Second Deputy Chief of the Detroit Police Department. Special Assistant for the City of Detroit Special Investigation Bureau."

"You run the Red squad."

"In so many words," Howcroft admits.

"Elizabeth's a Red. You hunt Reds. She's locked up. Case closed, no? What do you want from me?"

"I want you to work for me."

Ben can't stifle a shout of laughter.

"You find that humorous?"

"I find it fucking hilarious."

"We gather and disseminate intelligence on the subversive activities of individuals and organizations in this city," Howcroft says. "We've been placing people in wide sectors of the working class to counter the Communist presence in the labor unions. I want you to use your association with Elizabeth to keep us abreast of what's happening with her and the others in her circle."

"You want me to spy for you? On Elizabeth and her friends?"

"'Spy' is such a harsh word."

"The activity's even worse. Forget it."

Ben starts to stand.

The two coppers at the next table half-rise.

Howcroft holds him down with a hand on his arm. The bonhomie is gone. Ben sees the steel in him.

"I can make it worth your while."

"No, you can't."

"I understand you have a disagreement with some Jewish gangsters."

"It's none of your business."

"I heard Harry Millman wants you dead."

Ben knows this, but to hear the other man state it so plainly and casually . . . it rocks him.

"I can make it go away," Howcroft says. "The department has people in the Purple Gang, too. Highly placed. High enough to change the minds of the men who want you dead."

This has Ben's attention. If Howcroft can get his death sentence lifted, maybe it would be worth appearing to play along.

"Only thing I'd want," Howcroft says, "is to know what the plans are for the funeral march on the weekend."

"I would have thought you had your own spies in the movement."

"Oh, we do. Your information would be fresher. Closer to the source. Look. To prove my goodwill, I'll release Elizabeth. But only to you, nobody else. It'll take a day to make the arrangements. It's too late to do anything tonight. There's a meeting at the home of Frank Murphy tomorrow night. I'll be there. You be there, too, and I'll bring Elizabeth. I'll release her to you. Word of honor. After that, she's free . . . no court date, no follow-up whatsoever. You don't show, she's back in the pokey."

Ben considers it. If this guy can deal with the Purples and get Elizabeth out of jail, it might be worth playing along.

Only *playing* . . .

"Deal?" Howcroft asks.

"I need to give it thought."

"Of course. All I can ask." Howcroft reaches out for another bone-crushing handshake.

He takes a slip of paper out of his pocket and writes an address on it. "Eight o'clock tomorrow night. Elizabeth will be freed. But only to you."

"Why are you doing this?"

"Like I said. A gesture of good will. Now go on. Enjoy your evening. My boys'll drop you wherever you want to go."

The apes appear and frog-march Ben back to the car.

He can't abide the thought of another enclosed space with these two. Ben says he doesn't want a ride; he'll manage himself.

The apes shrug. They drive away.

Ben starts walking north on Brush. Crosses through downtown to pick up the Grand River streetcar heading west.

He mulls over the meeting with Howcroft. Ben has no intention of spying on Elizabeth and her friends. The thing is, this may be his only chance to get Elizabeth out of jail.

And if Ben agrees, then goes back on his word? Howcroft isn't the type to let it slide; there would be hell to pay, Ben is sure.

At least Elizabeth would be out. And the Purples would be off his back.

For a brief time, anyway. It might even buy Moe enough time to sort things out.

He taps on the door to the flat on Elmhurst. He sees a light on inside.

His brother-in-law Isaac brushes the curtain aside to see who it is. His face lights up to see Ben.

Opens up. Gives Ben a hug. Pulls him inside.

"*Benyamin*," Isaac says, giving his name the Hebrew pronunciation.

"*Yitzhak.*"

"We've been worried about you. Come in."

"I didn't wake you, did I?"

"I'm up grading tests. Miriam's asleep. God knows where Moe is. Say, I have tea made."

"Tea would be great."

Isaac takes him into the kitchen, pours a cup. Gathers up the tests in a pile on the table so Ben has room to sit.

"Hope I'm not interrupting," Ben says.

"I don't expect I'll be doing this for much longer. Cutbacks are coming at school, the budgets are so bad. I'll be one of the first to go."

"Sorry."

"Everybody's desperate these days. Have you been safe?"

"Yes," Ben answers, realizes the bruises on his face say otherwise. "For the most part," he adds.

"Moe said he saw you at the schvitz yesterday."

"Yeah, we had a talk."

"You get it straightened out?"

"Not entirely."

Ben tells him about the deal proposed by Horace Howcroft.

"You're not going to do it, are you?" Isaac says, horrified.

"No, no, of course not."

"But you're thinking about it. I can tell."

"Thinking about it because it means I can get my friend out of jail."

"Won't there be consequences if you go back on the deal?"

"I can handle them."

"I don't know, Ben. You haven't been in touch with her, your friend?"

"No. Don't know where she's being held."

"You look beat."

"Nothing compared to how I feel."

"Where are you staying?"

"At her place."

"Look, it's late. Don't go out now. Stay here for the night."

"I don't want to bring you any trouble."

"You won't. Not for one night, if nobody knows where you are."

"Thanks, Ike."

Issac waves it away.

They drink their tea in silence.

Isaac says, "Benny, Miriam and I, we're worried about you. You can't go on like this."

"I know. I appreciate it. But seriously. I have a plan."

"Hope you know what you're doing."

"So do I."

43

Elizabeth Waters

In her exhaustion, Elizabeth stumbles crossing the threshold into her apartment in the Trocadero.

Maurice Sugar tried to make her see she wasn't safe there. Elizabeth insisted he take her home. For one thing, she wants to know if Ben is there. She needs to talk with him.

For another, she has to spend the night in her own bed, in her own place, with all her own things around her.

So she told Maurice while she appreciated the thought, she has to come back here.

Now she sits on the sofa in her living room. No Ben.

She still sees traces of him—empty dishes in the sink, the apartment straightened up after the whirlwind of her arrest the day before, the bed in her room roughly made, not the precise way she likes to keep it . . . he must have spent the last night here.

Where is he now? And how can she possibly get hold of him?

She realizes she knows almost nothing about him. She knows he has a sister, but not where to find her. And beyond that? She has an inkling of what his politics are, but not if he has a propensity toward violence.

Alone in the apartment, she wonders if he could really be planning to assassinate Frank Murphy. On its face, it sounds ridiculous.

Yet a small part of her does believe Horace Howcroft. Ben told her he wanted to be part of the Purple Gang. He knew how violent they could be. Is this what attracted him to them?

He also told her he was in some trouble with them. Could this be a way of paying off whatever debt he owed them?

She has to admit it sounds plausible.

A knock comes at her door. She jumps in fright.

There is no peephole, so she stands behind the door and says, "Who is it?"

Hoping it's Ben.

It isn't.

Gladys Hart, from across the hall.

Elizabeth opens the door. "Gladys, is everything all right?"

"That's what I'm trying to find out," Gladys says. A raspy, cigarette-roughened voice. "Is everything okay here?"

"Fine."

"I was so worried when they took you away the other day."

"Thanks, honey. So was I."

"And your young man was, too."

"Who?"

"You know, the young man who's staying with you."

Ben.

"He tried to tell me he was your brother, but I wasn't buying it."

"When did you see him?" Elizabeth asks.

"Last night. I tiptoed over to find out if you were okay and he answered the door."

"Was he okay?"

"Looked like somebody took him out behind the barn and gave him a good whipping. He was asking about you. Didn't know what happened to you."

"He didn't say where he was going to be today, by any chance?"

"No." Gladys shakes her head with regret. "I thought he was still staying here. You're sure you're okay, honey?"

Elizabeth nods. "Just very tired."

"Feel like a nightcap?"

"Mighty tempting, Gladys. But no. Have to pass. I'm exhausted."

"Sure. Let me know if you need anything, okay?"

A man's voice bellows from the hallway. "Gladys! Get your ass back here."

"Sorry," Gladys says. "Gotta go. Just wanted to make sure you're okay."

Elizabeth thanks her and closes the door.

If she needs anything?

Where to start?

Elizabeth *needs* to know how the women she left behind in custody were. She got out and they didn't because of who she was and who she knew.

She *needs* to know how her friend Mary Tatum is doing. She will have to call the hospital in the morning. If she's even still there. They may have released her, or sent her over to one of the Negro hospitals.

Mary was targeted for special abuse because she's a Negro. And she almost did not get the care she needed for the same reason.

Elizabeth *needs* to get more involved in this battle for basic human rights for Negroes, for the working man, for poor women . . . it's not enough to renounce her background while still relying on its advantages.

She *needs* to start taking the fight to the Horace Howcrofts who assume the world belongs to them. She's been doing what she can with the Unemployed Council and the soup kitchen. It's not going to be enough.

And right now, she *needs* her Miss Em.

It's gone from the bathroom medicine cabinet.

No!

She tears through the bathroom, looking to see if it fell behind the sink.

Not there.

She searches in her bedroom, in the living room, in the kitchen. Her bottle of morphine is nowhere.

The police must have taken it when they arrested her . . . it's the only thing she can think of. So they can use it. Or sell it.

Bastards.

The perfect ending to this day.

As though triggered by the realization Miss Em is gone, an ache begins to grow behind her eyes and in her stomach.

Fortunately, she is simply too tired to do anything about it.

She goes into her bedroom and gets undressed. Crawls into bed. She can smell Ben in the bedclothes . . . a smokey scent like scorched coffee.

She closes her eyes and tries to sleep. All she sees are the faces of the women in the cells with her. Frightened, angry, resigned to their lots.

The ache in her head gnaws behind her eyes.

She sits up. She can't do it. Phones her supplier Vince Vitale for a delivery.

As she suspects, she can't get through. There is nobody to even leave a message with. He's careful that way. The personal touch, he calls it. Really it's just him being careful about who might be answering the phone when his customers call.

She considers getting dressed and going back out to see if she can find him. Immediately dismisses the idea. Instead she goes back into the bathroom and swallows three aspirins. Washes it down with a glass of water. It will have to do.

Hopes the aspirin can trick her body into believing she's going to be all right. At least for one more night.

THURSDAY, MARCH 10, 1932

44

ROSCOE GRISSOM

Roscoe looks out the picture window. Harley Clarke leans on the horn of the Buick in the driveway.

Harley backs out and roars off as soon as Roscoe gets in.

"Say," Roscoe says, "can we stop for coffee? I didn't have no breakfast yet." He spent the night on the cot in the cellar again, so he and Melanie have not faced each other yet this morning.

"No time," Harley says. He's in a foul mood. "You got your ass out here when you were supposed to, we might've had time. Now we don't. Be a miracle if we're not late as it is."

Roscoe does not respond. Last night was a hard night for him. After getting home drunk from the Dew Drop, he didn't sleep well. He woke up several times to run up to the kitchen to puke into the sink.

"Where are we going?" he asks.

"There's a big thing downtown this morning with the mayor. He set up this program, you know, for disabled vets to sell apples in the street?"

Roscoe shrugs.

"He's going to be talking about it with reporters out on Michigan Avenue in front of City Hall. Get his picture taken with the crips. And that's when you're going to blow him away."

"In front of all the reporters? Are you fucking crazy?"

"Think of the publicity."

"Think of all the witnesses."

"They'll be too shocked to remember anything. I'll get you out of there before anybody figures out what's what."

At the mention of remembering, Roscoe remembers something he forgot. "Uh-oh."

"What?"

"I left the package back at the house."

Harley looks over at him in the passenger seat. "What?"

"I forgot the gun."

Harley pounds the steering wheel. "What the hell kind of a gunman are you?"

"Sorry. I forgot we were going to do it this morning."

"Even though I told you last night?"

"I was kinda pie-eyed last night."

Harley sighs, mutters, "You're kinda pie-eyed every night." Slows the Buick and pulls over.

Stops and turns to Roscoe. "This ain't no lark, you know," he says. "You're a Christian soldier for America. There's no excuse to get potted every fucking night. We're in a war for the soul of our country."

"I know. I'm sorry. I'll be more on top of things. I swear."

Harley sighs again. Makes a u-turn.

When they get back to Roscoe's house, Roscoe jumps out of the car and runs inside and down the cellar. He hid the gun in the suitcase under the cot down there.

He's running with it up the stairs and through the living room just as his wife comes down from the second floor.

He stops short.

She sees him holding the gun. "What you got there?"

"None of your fucking business. You didn't see nothing."

He's out the door again before she can respond.

Curses himself for not putting the gun in a bag. When he got home soused the night before, he took out the gun to admire it and wipe it down with a cloth. He remembered to put it back in the suitcase, just forgot to put it back in the oily paper bag it came in. Now in his haste he just grabbed it up and ran out with it.

Melanie looks out the front door just as he is jumping back in the Buick with Harley. She takes a good look at both of them.

"Who's she?" Harley says, staring back at her.

"My old lady."

"She saw you with the gun?"

"She won't say nothing. She don't know what's going on."

"Better not."

"Don't worry about it. She's one of us," Roscoe says. (Knowing she isn't.)

Harley heads out again for downtown. "Sure you remembered the bullets?" he mutters.

When they get to Campus Martius downtown, nothing is happening in front of City Hall except for the usual traffic. No reporters, no crowd, no mayor.

"I don't get it," Harley says.

"Sure you got the right place?" Roscoe says, happy now to give it back to Harley for what Harley said to him about the gun.

"This is what my guy in the mayor's office told me."

Harley drives around the block, sees only a lone apple seller in the square in front of City Hall. Behind the building loom the spires of the Penobscot Building. Roscoe remembers the disaster of that night with an ache of embarrassment.

Harley stops in front of the apple seller and gets out. The guy has purple scars on his face and one trouser leg pinned at the knee. He leans on a crutch behind a wooden bin with a hand-lettered sign:

War vet
Unemployed
Buy Apples
5¢ each

"Hey, bud," Harley says.

"Hey," the guy says. "Nickel apiece. Three for a dime."

"You hear anything about the mayor supposed to be out this morning getting his picture taken with you apple guys?"

"Nah. I ain't heard nothing. But I'd be the last to know."

"Okay, thanks."

"You don't want no apples?"

Harley jumps back in his sled and roars off. "I'm sure my guy told me there was going be a thing out here this morning."

"Maybe he got the time wrong. Maybe we're too early. Or too late. Or it got cancelled."

"Let's drive around a little, see if maybe he gave me the wrong location."

Harley drives all around downtown Detroit and sees only isolated apple salesmen on a few corners. No sign of the mayor, or anything out of the ordinary.

After a while he gives up and they go to the Dew Drop Inn.

"I got to get to the bottom of this," Harley says, fuming. He uses Frankie's telephone. After a few minutes, he comes back to the table where Roscoe sits.

Drops into the chair. "We got snookered."

"What do you mean?"

"The low-down I got last night was all wet. The mayor changed his schedule this morning at the last minute. Turns out there wasn't going to be no apple seller photographs today after all."

"Well, shit."

"Not so fast. My guy told me we'll have a better chance later on tonight."

45

CLARENCE BROWN

The roar of a vacuum cleaner wakes him.

From the hallway outside his room. He pads over to the door and cracks it. A woman runs the noisy contraption over the carpet runner.

"Oh," she says when she sees him, "did I wake you, sir?"

"No, no. I had to get up."

"I'm sorry, Mr. Clarence."

How does she know his name? He looks at her more carefully and it occurs to him he knows her, too. Sophia. Rosita's maid.

"I'll be done here in a second. You go back to sleep and I won't bother you no more," she says.

"Do what you have to. I'm up."

Pulls his head back into the room. Sits on the bed. Leans over with his head in his hands. He dreamed about pirate costumes.

The dream disappears quickly in the morning light, but what remains is the familiar thing about the costume the dominatrix had on the day before.

He tugs his clothes on and goes out to the breakfast room. Rosita is already up. She is now in her dressing robe, a luxurious purple silk gown she has artfully arranged to display her bare legs. Her hair is wrapped in a turban; damp tendrils escape. She eats a roll with jam very daintily. Rings on every one of her slender fingers.

"Morning, sunshine," she says to him. "Start with a Coca-Cola?"

"You remembered."

"Of course. Or would you rather have some coffee?"

"Wouldn't mind."

She rises and pours him a cup from the percolator on the portable stove. Sets it in front of him and resumes her seat. "You take it black as night, as I recall."

He nods. Takes a sip.

The coffee is hot and bitter. "Still your special blend," he says. The taste brings back all the moments he spent with Rosita.

As if reading his mind, she purrs, "Just like old times. We made some good memories together."

They did, he has to admit. They saw each other every week from the time he first made detective in '28 until two years ago. He and Bessie were having a hard time of it and he needed a refuge. Finally he couldn't live with himself, running around on Bessie; he wasn't built for it. He quit Rosita and quit booze at the same time.

She said she understood. But he wasn't sure she ever forgave him. They hadn't been in contact since.

Still, when he needed a place to spend the night last night, she came through for him. Maybe she's starting to forgive after all.

Or she's starting to forget.

"Thank you, Rosie."

"I told you. No questions asked."

They lock eyes. As he watches, the sparkle of sly amusement in her eyes turns to sadness.

He downs his coffee. "Better go."

"Clarence." She reaches out, takes his hand. "It's been too long."

He says nothing.

"Will I see you again?" she asks.

Her face is older now but still beautiful. Amber eyes. Soft sculpted cheeks. Silken skin.

He remembers her skin. Silken all over. Perfumed, light, lemony. "No."

"In that case." She rises and bends over to kiss him full on the lips. Her dressing gown falls open around her breasts.

She stands, wraps her gown around her. "We never had a chance for a proper goodbye when we weren't screaming at each other."

He gives her a nod and leaves before he puts his arms around her and feels her body against his own one last time.

He drives to the doctor's office on East Forest in Paradise Valley. The building where Yolanda Montgomery stays with her sister.

As he had hoped, the same young woman sits at the reception desk in her nurse's uniform.

"Yes?" she says when he walks in. Cold. Suspicious. Remembers him.

"I was here a couple days ago asking about your sister."

"Uh-huh."

"When I came by, there was a little boy playing in the corner, over there by the fish tank. Playing with a toy sword."

"Yeah."

"You don't know who it was, by any chance?"

"My son, Gabriel. Why? There a problem?"

"No, no problem at all. He's not around right this second, is he?"

"No."

"When I was here, he was wearing a little black hat. Skull and crossbones on it. Looked like a toy pirate hat. You remember where he got it?"

"His auntie gave it to him."

"Your sister? Yolanda?"

"What you want to know for?"

"You don't know where she got it, by any chance?"

"She brought it home for him one day," she said. "Said she found it at the house she used to work."

"Madame Savoyard's?"

"Yeah. Why you asking?"

He is already on his way out the door. "Thanks," he calls over his shoulder.

Young Frances opens the front door for him. Steps away so he can come in. "You got my message," she says.

"What message?"

"I left a message for you at the number on the card you gave me."

"No. That's the precinct house. I haven't been in for a few days. I came to see the madame."

"Not up yet. Too early."

"Would you go and get her, please?"

"Madame, she don't like me to wake—"

"You tell me where I can find her and I'll wake her up."

Frances gives a huff of annoyance. "Wait here."

She guides him to the parlor and glides away. Too annoyed to sit, he walks around, examines the paintings on the walls—erotic scenes of naked white men in different sexual positions with naked women. Mostly white women with the occasional dark-skinned exotic.

In twenty minutes, Frances returns trailing behind Madame Savoyard.

The brothelkeeper wears a modest jersey and long pants. Her hair is clipped short. She has doused herself with lavender perfume. "I told you the last time, I have nothing more to say to you."

"You lied to me."

She turns to her maid. "Frances, get Mr. Thatcher on the phone." To Clarence: "My lawyer. I won't speak to you until he gets here."

"Where'd you take him?"

"I have no idea what you're talking about. And once my attorney does get here, I'll ask him to file a complaint of harassment against you."

"This isn't harassment. I just don't like it when people lie to me."

"I'm afraid I couldn't care less what you like or don't like."

Frances returns.

"Well?" the madame asks.

"Mr. Thatcher, he not in today."

The madame sighs.

"I just want to know why you picked up Darius Turner," Clarence says. "And where you took him."

She gives him a sneer. "I have very highly placed clients. Judges. Attorneys. The highest-ranking policemen—your bosses. Are they going to let you intimidate me over the death of some random Negro?"

"I'm just trying to find out why a young man who had his whole life ahead of him was killed. And I believe you know. And I believe your highly placed friends—and especially their wives—are not going to like it when I release their names in connection with a whorehouse."

"Oh, please. As if they'd care. Or their *wives* would care? You'd be surprised how many of their wives I service in here."

"Do you have any children?"

"None of your business."

"Because Darius Turner wasn't just 'some random Negro.' He was somebody's son. And his mother loved him, just as much as your mother loved you. He deserved to have a life, but it was stolen from him. And I would like to know what your part was in it. Now, I know you picked him up. And I know about the Black Legion."

This gets her attention.

"You allow meetings of the Black Legion here," he says. He only suspects it based on the pirate hat Yolanda found and gave to her nephew.

"You don't know what you're dealing with," she says. "Or who. Now I'll ask you to leave. Frances, show him out before I get Angelo to throw him the hell out of here. And this time, don't come back."

She turns and stalks off in a cloud of lavender.

Little Frances stands there looking at him.

She is silent until she hears a door slam in the rear of the house. Then she beckons Clarence to follow her.

"You know what I'm talking about, don't you?" he asks.

She nods. "Why I called you."

She leads him to a door at the side of the entrance foyer. With a set of keys from her apron pocket, she unlocks the door, which opens to a stairway going up. He follows her to another story of the house. They go down a hall to an unnumbered door.

Frances unlocks the door. "She gave me these keys," she says, "because she wants me to clean in here."

The door opens into a large room set up as another parlor. There is a large bed in it and a bare spot beside it where a large oval rug appears to have been.

"Something terrible happened here," Frances says. "I knew if I cleaned it up I would hide what happened. So I haven't yet. I wanted you to see it first."

He takes a quick look around the room, spotlighting with his attention the bed, the dresser, the sofa, two deep arm chairs. He kneels down beside the bed and sees what looks like blood spatter on the walls and around the outline of where the rug used to be.

Against the wall beside the bed is a sink. He stands and peers into it.

Blood caked on the porcelain. An ashtray filled with butts in the wastepaper basket under the sink. Underneath the butts, bloody towels.

Frances watches him from the doorway, afraid to enter.

"Something very bad happened in this room," Clarence agrees. "I believe this is where Darius was killed."

"Yes sir. I believe so, too. I heard the madame talking about it night before last."

"What did she say?"

"The man she was talking with, he say, 'That boy was asking for it. He need to be taught a lesson.' I just knew in my heart they were talking about Darius."

"You told me you didn't know Darius."

"Yessir. But I did."

"Do you know who the madame was talking to?"

"Yessir. Man come here a lot. Used to, anyway. Always ask for Yolanda. Only go with her, before she left."

"Know his name?"

"No sir. But I made sure I got a good look at him. He was a white man. Very tall and skinny. And his hair was all white. Didn't seem he was old enough to have so much white hair."

"How did he wear his hair?"

"All the way back. Like this." She sweeps her hands back, indicating a pompadour.

Clarence knows just who she is talking about.

46

BEN RUBIN

In the morning, Isaac and Miriam are both gone when Ben gets up. Isaac must be at school, Miriam at the bakery.

He lies on the sofa for a while, getting his bearings. Feeling the way he did when he was a child sleeping on the sofa of his *bubbe* and *zayde's* apartment, protected and at the same time vulnerable in a strange place.

Except I'm not a child anymore, he tells himself. Though you wouldn't know it from the decisions I've been making lately.

This is not what he had in mind for himself . . . sleeping on the sofa at his sister's apartment because he has no home of his own to go to. Caught between mobsters and the police, hunted by one, squeezed by the other.

He pads into the kitchen. Cuts two slices off a loaf of challah and toasts them. Makes coffee. Sits at the kitchen table while he eats the toast with jam.

He cleans up and because there is no phone in the apartment, he goes down to the phone booth beside the drug store on the corner to call Maurice Sugar. He is not happy about being out in public, but there isn't anything to do about it. He needs to make the call.

"He's not in," Maurice's secretary tells Ben. "Want to leave a message?

"Could you let him know I have a way to get Elizabeth Waters out of jail?"

A pause. She says, "Elizabeth's already out."

"What do you mean?"

"Maurice got her out yesterday. He brought her back to the office. I brought her food. Poor thing hadn't eaten in two days."

"Where is she now?"

"She wanted to go home. Maurice took her."

"Her apartment?"

"I presume so."

"Okay. Thanks."

"Still want to talk to Maurice?"

"I do. He can call me at Elizabeth's."

As soon as they hang up, he fishes another dime out of his pocket and calls Elizabeth's number.

"Ben!"

"You're free."

"Maurice got me out. How are you? *Where* are you?"

"I stayed at my sister's last night. Now I'm using a phone near their flat. How are you?"

"It's been an ordeal. In general, I'm none the worse for wear. But Ben, we have to talk."

"I know. I can be there in a half hour."

"I have to be somewhere. Can you come over later?"

"I'll be there when I can."

When he leaves the phone booth, he sees his sister coming down the sidewalk. She is dusty with flour from the bakery, moving as fast as she can move with her bulky pregnant body.

Not looking happy. This is not good.

"Miriam," he says. They hug. She is crying. "What's the matter? The baby okay?"

"Mama called me at the bakery. It's Moe."

A chill grips him.

"He's dead, Benny. Uncle Moe is dead."

She goes up to her apartment to change out of her bakery clothes and together they go to their parents' house. Even from outside, Ben can hear their mother wailing.

They climb the front steps. Ben has a feeling: hang back. Don't go in.

Decides to act on it. "No," he tells Miriam, "I'll wait out here."

"Why? It's Mama's brother, Benny."

"I know. I just don't want to go in. I have a bad feeling about what'll happen if they see me. You go and come back out and tell me what's going on."

"What's the matter with you?"

"Go on," he says. "They're not going to want to see me."

He turns away. Goes down the steps to the sidewalk.

Miriam gives him one final withering look and goes inside. He hears their mother wail even louder.

Ben crosses the street. His bad feeling remains.

In a few minutes, it isn't Miriam who comes out. It's Isaac.

Spots Ben and crosses over to him.

"They called you out of school?" Ben asks.

Isaac nods. "It's not good, Benny."

Isaac takes him by the arm and walks him down the block, away from the house.

"What's going on?" Ben asks.

"They found Moe's body this morning in the street outside Boesky's."

"What happened?"

"He was shot to death. Abie Bernstein says it was the Purples."

"Abie's inside?"

"Yeah."

Abie Bernstein. Leader of the gang.

"Why would they do that?" Ben asks.

"Abie says they killed him because Moe was a rat."

"I don't understand."

"Moe turned State's witness. He got Milberg, Keywell, and Ray Bernstein convicted."

"I don't believe it."

"Why do you think he hasn't been tried yet? He was still giving them information. Abie took me aside and told me what happened. This was a rub-out."

For a moment, Ben can't speak.

At last he says, "Do they know in there? Do they know what happened?"

"Not yet. They'll all find out sooner or later. Won't take long to get around."

Through his sorrow, fury cuts.

Ben steps around Isaac. Heads toward the house.

Isaac reaches out to hold him back. "Where are you going?"

"To see Abie."

"You're going to confront Abie Bernstein about Purple Gang business? Not a good idea."

Isaac is right, Ben knows. What would he say to Abie? Hope you're satisfied with your pound of flesh?

Ben turns away so Isaac won't see his tears.

The one thing Ben knows is, he has to get away from here.

With no place else to go, he starts out toward Elizabeth's apartment in Palmer Park.

47

ELIZABETH WATERS

F eels like a month since Elizabeth was last at work. It's only been since Monday.

Three days.

Time flies whether you're having fun or not.

She drops her coat and purse at her desk in the creative department bullpen. Strangely, there's nothing on her desk. When she takes a day off, she always returns to stacks of mail, scripts, production schedules needing to be filed. Now there's only the desk blotter she uses as a calendar. Someone has even straightened up her office supplies. Pencil cup, wheel eraser with a little brush, bottle of rubber cement stand all in a row at the back of her desk.

She goes in to see Sidney Ballenger.

Stands in his doorway. He ignores her until she taps on the frame.

"Well," he says, "if it isn't . . . what was your name again?"

"Very funny. Can I talk to you?"

He beckons her into his office. "Shut the door."

"I need to explain what's been happening," she begins.

He stops her with a raised hand. "Before you go any further—did your friend ever give you my message?"

She shakes her head. "I don't know what you're talking about."

"I told him to let you know I was terminating your employment here."

"Sid—"

"No, don't 'Sid' me. Christ almighty, you disappear for three days with no notice? What did you expect?"

"If you'd let me explain?"

"It's too late. Because you weren't here, we're behind schedule, we had to cancel the talent auditions for the new show, rehearsals for 'The Lone Ranger' are all screwed up, you lost the script for the first episode of 'Cody' . . ."

"I didn't lose the script! Phil never gave it to me. How many times do I have to explain it?"

"Don't raise your voice to me."

A hesitant tapping comes at Sid's door.

"What?" he shouts.

The door opens and an older woman peeks in.

"Mavis," Sid says, "come in."

"Sorry to interrupt," Mavis says. Sickly-sweet voice. "Here are those letters you wanted."

Sid takes a stack of papers from her and she tiptoes out. Eases the door closed behind her.

"Who's she?" Elizabeth asks.

"Your replacement."

"Seriously? You replaced me already?"

"Look, kid," he says, "I appreciate your politics. And I respect you for it. I do. I might even share some of your ideas. But we're in a schedule-driven business. I need an assistant I can count on. And these last few days showed me it's not you. I'm sorry, Liz. We'll give you a week's severance. Best I can do. Orders from the top."

The last thing he says makes her know it's all bullshit. When a coward wants to avoid responsibility, he blames orders from the top.

"From Mr. Trendle? Can I talk to him?"

"Sorry, Liz. It's done."

She takes the Woodward streetcar home in a daze.

First things first: she calls Vince Vitale again. Miss Em isn't going to visit her by herself.

Again doesn't get through.

She stands at the big picture window in her apartment, looking out over the park. She read someplace that Palmer Park had a greater variety of trees than on the entire continent of Europe. She didn't know if it was true or not. She was never a nature girl. The only thing she could tell from looking out over the skeletal branches was, many of them were already starting to fill out with buds.

March.

Spring.

Renewal.

Yeah, no. Not this year.

The world around her is sinking into chaos, and now she has no job. She spent most of her savings while she was out of work the year before. Now there's nothing left. She faces the same prospects of prolonged unemployment without any resources that so many others in the city feel. The economic catastrophe has sucked her in.

She looks out over the park and starts to make a plan of action. Because this is what she does. Others talk. She acts.

Thanks to the Unemployed Councils, her situation isn't as dire as it might otherwise be. She might be able to get some relief money. Some meals. She'll join the line of men she saw the other day in front of City Hall.

Still, she might lose her apartment if she can't pay the rent.

Where would she go? She's turned into a hermit over the past few years. Lost touch with her friends. Cut ties with what's left of her family. Who would she even ask to spend a night with if she loses her home?

As she stands there, she sees a figure drifting among the park's bare trees and flat brown lawns.

Looks like Ben.

It is.

She raps hard on the window, as if he could hear her across the street and all the way into the park.

Of course, he can't. As she watches, he seems to be searching the area before crossing the street to her building. She loses sight of him as he disappears under the portico.

She waits for him to use the key she let him have.

Happy to see him. Plays it cool. Stands back and lets him come in. He looks tired. She can smell his scorched coffee odor.

"Hey," he says.

"Hey."

"You're a sight for sore eyes."

"Yeah," she says, "I may have had worse days, but I can't remember when. You don't look so hot yourself. You look like you need coffee."

She leads him into the dining room.

She busies herself making coffee. It gives her brain something to focus on besides the fact of her unemployment. Grinding the beans in the hand grinder, tossing two spoonsful into the basket from her silver percolator, filling the belly of the device with water, inserting the basket and the top, plugging it in. Hearing the satisfying start-up hiss.

Ben comes into the kitchen and stands beside her. She feels his presence oddly, as if he were vibrating. Or maybe it's her. They're both vibrating, but at two different frequencies.

She looks closely at him. The bruises on his face are turning yellow. The swelling has gone down.

"How are you healing?" she asks.

He shrugs.

"Gladys across the hall said you looked like somebody took you out behind the barn and gave you a licking."

"I talked to her the other night. She came over asking about you."

"We've gotten friendly, two single women. She's a rich widow. Fascinating woman. Certainly knows how to live the high life. Keeps a whole string of gentlemen on the line. I see them up here every so often. She's a bit of a floozy, to be honest."

He seems distracted.

"What's the matter?"

"My uncle was killed last night."

"Oh no," she says, and folds him in her arms. "I'm so sorry."

He hugs her back and she can feel his shoulders judder as he tries to contain sobs.

They stand for a few moments, until she breaks away. Cups his unhurt cheek in a palm. "Tell me what happened."

They sit in the dining room while the coffee perks.

She lets him talk about what he learned this morning.

"Your uncle was in the Purple Gang," she says when he is finished. As if this explains it all. Which it really does. "Are you really so surprised?"

"He kept warning me. I knew it was a risky life. It was part of the attraction, right? And I thought my uncle was too smart to wind up dead."

She reaches out and takes his hand. She tries to reconcile what she knows about him with what Horace said he plans to do.

"I'm so sorry," she says again.

"I feel like this is my fault."

"Why? You didn't kill him."

"I'm responsible for the situation that got him killed."

"How do you figure? You had nothing to do with the Collingwood job."

The Collingwood Manor massacre, where Moe was the wheelman.

"No," Ben says, "but it feels like I added to the pressure on him."

She is about to remind him that his uncle made his own decisions about his own life, and they led to this ending. She decides not to mention it. Not right now.

Instead she goes to get the coffee. Pours them two cups.

He tells her about the night before, when Howcroft's goons picked him up on his way back here. What Horace told him. About his deal to release her.

"If I agreed to rat on you and your friends, he said he'd let you go."

"You didn't say you would, I hope?"

"Of course not."

"Horace talked to me, too, yesterday."

"When?"

"Before Maurice got me out. At one of the police stations they kept switching me to."

"Here I'm talking all about myself and you had your own ordeal," he says. "Tell me about it."

She tells him . . . how she was hauled away from her apartment, interrogated, beaten, denied food and water, shuffled from one station to another, finally released by Maurice Sugar.

"Which reminds me," she says, "Maurice said it was you who told him I was locked up."

"I called him. I didn't know if he'd find out or not."

"Thank you. I'd still be in jail. Horace told me one more thing. About you. He said there was a plot to assassinate Frank Murphy. And you were going to do it."

"*Me?*"

"Yeah."

"How does he know?"

"I have no idea."

"Did he say why I'm supposed to do this?"

"Some kind of initiation into the Purple Gang."

"That's nuts, you know that, right?"

"It is." She looks at him intently. "Isn't it?"

"Of course."

"He gave me a deal, too. If I told him where to find you, he'd let me go."

"He picked me up last night. Why didn't he hold me?"

"Because he knows you're not going to try to kill Murphy at all. If there is a plot to assassinate the mayor, Horace is laying the groundwork for pinning it on you."

"We have to tell somebody about this."

"I told Maurice. The mayor's office wouldn't talk to us. We couldn't get to anyone in the police department, either."

"I know somebody who can help. I need to make a call."

She points out the phone and he takes a slip of paper from his wallet.

Dials. Waits.

"Who are you calling?" she asks.

"This guy I know. A reporter for the *Times*. I trust him."

After a moment, he says, "Tom Glover? It's Ben Rubin. I've got some information you're going to want to hear. Can we meet?"

Before they leave to meet Tom Glover, Elizabeth calls Vince Vitale one more time.

This time he picks up.

"Looking for Barney Google?"

Madame Chen gives them a broad smile. She points to a booth in the back corner of the Kow Kow Inn. "Waiting for you!"

Tom Glover waves a pair of chopsticks at them. Ben and Elizabeth walk through the nearly empty restaurant and slide in across the table from him. He is eating his way through a plate piled high with beef chow mein.

"Want any? I'll get more plates over here."

Ben and Elizabeth both decline. "Thanks for meeting us," Ben says. Introduces Elizabeth.

"Sure. What's up?"

Ben tells him what he knows about the rumored assassination, and what Elizabeth has told him.

Tom listens, rests his chopsticks on his plate. Makes some scratchings in his notebook. "And you know this how?"

"I'd rather not go into it," Elizabeth says.

"I can't help you if I don't know the source of the information."

"It's solid," Ben tells him.

"Unfortunately, I have to be the judge of that," Tom says.

"You may as well tell him," Ben says to Elizabeth.

She hesitates. "I got my information from the same source Ben got his."

"Howcroft?"

She nods.

"Any chance he's blowing smoke up your asses?"

"Can we take the chance?" Elizabeth says.

Tom works on his chow mein again. Chews thoughtfully. "Let me make a call."

He goes off to use the restaurant phone behind the bar.

"I called my contact at City Hall," Tom says when he comes back. "He told me Murphy's in meetings at City Hall all day today. But there's something scheduled for tonight at his house."

"That's where I'm supposed to go collect Elizabeth," Ben says.

"Tonight's the night of the assassination attempt," Elizabeth says. "Now do you believe us?"

"I never disbelieved it," Tom says. "I just needed to be sure the information was solid."

"So what should we do?" Ben asks.

"Nobody in the police can be trusted with this," Tom says. "If I had to bet, I'd bet the police are in on it. My contact is close to the mayor. I'll try to get the word out through him. Meantime, don't do anything until you hear from me."

They agree. The door to the restaurant opens and a bulldog of a guy comes in. Young, handsome, wavy black hair. Looks around.

Elizabeth is up on her feet as soon as she sees him. Makes her way to the front. Takes him by the arm outside.

Vince gives her his oiliest smile, says, "Ain't you gonna invite me to stay for dinner?"

"I'm with people. Just give me what you have for me, okay?"

"You went through the last one pretty quick."

"The cops stole it when they took me away. They've probably already sold it on."

"Hope you didn't tell them where you got it. I already pay enough protection to those mugs."

He gives her a small package wrapped in brown paper, like the one he gave her before. She throws him a handful of bills. "Here's for this time and the last time."

He slips away into the darkness.

She goes back into the restaurant. Ben watches her pass by their table and go into the lavatories.

She unwraps the bottle and takes a short swig.

She shudders at the bitterness. Feels the effects at once. Rewraps the package and goes back to the table.

Tom Glover is gone.

"He had to leave," Ben says. "He said he'll get back in touch as soon as he finds anything out."

"Good."

She downs half a glass of water.

"What was that all about?" Ben asks.

"What?"

"The guy you went outside with."

She shakes her head. "Nobody important."

He sits looking at her. "What did you take?"

"When?"

"Come on, Elizabeth. Your whole face is changed. What did he give you?"

Madame Chen comes over, asks if they want anything. Elizabeth uses the opportunity to order an egg roll before answering.

"I was in an automobile accident when I was in college and it left me with constant pain in my hip," she says. "What that guy brought me I need for pain."

"The same thing you slipped me?"

"Yeah."

"What was it?"

"Morphine."

"You just took a hit of *morphine*? *Now*?"

"I'm fine. I just needed to take the edge off the pain."

"You're not fine. You look like you're going to fucking go to sleep."

"I'm fine. Trust me. I've been taking this long enough to know how much to take so I can still function."

He sits looking at her for a few more moments.

"I hope you're right," he says.

48

ROSCOE GRISSOM

Another fight at the soup kitchen.

A daily occurrence. Two guys out of work and desperate will take any little thing as a slight. Most of the scuffles, like this one, are quickly broken up. The two fighters get thrown out.

When the distraction of the fight ends, Roscoe finishes his lunch. Mystery-meat stew and a slice of bread with watery coffee and a piece of apple pie. He trudges back to the Dew Drop, where Harley dropped him after the trip downtown. Along with the other men from the soup kitchen who spend their days at Frankie's, Roscoe is logy from the meal. No problem. There's no place else to be.

What a life. If he didn't have the Legion to look forward to, what would he do?

He settles in his chair at the table in the back of the Dew Drop. Gets ready to pass the long afternoon while waiting for Harley to come back for him. He has no money for Frankie's hooch. None of the cheapskate regulars will float him any. He's forced to stay sober.

After so many false alarms and failed missions, Roscoe's starting to lose faith in Harley. Every operation he's been involved in seems to come to nothing. Pretty soon, people will start blaming him, Roscoe, for what Roscoe sees as Clarke's fuckups.

And he has seen what the Legion does to people who fail . . . Laverne Penney's brains all over the windshield of his car was proof enough of it. Roscoe don't need any more convincing.

He might ask to be partnered with someone else.

He has to be careful, though. Clarke's higher than Roscoe up the Legion ladder. Have to wait and see how tonight goes.

If tonight even goes . . .

Roscoe starts to doze in his midafternoon slump when two Detroit coppers enter the Dew Drop.

Big mugs. Standing in the doorway and looking around like they own the goddamn place.

One of them goes up to Frankie behind the bar. Leans over, murmurs something. Frankie looks to the back of the bar in Roscoe's direction. Points right at Roscoe. The copper zeroes in on him.

For an instant Roscoe wants to race out the back way. Before he can get going they're standing in front of him. Big. Broad shouldered. In puttees with high boots, like the motorcycle boys.

"Roscoe Grissom?" one of them says.

"Who wants to know?" Roscoe says.

Stupid thing to say, but the first thing he can come up with.

The ape grabs him by his shirt and hauls him to his feet. "Listen, shitbird, are you Roscoe Grissom or not?"

"I am, I am."

The big copper throws Roscoe against the wall face-first and pats him down. "Where's it at?"

"Where's what at?"

"Your wife said you're carrying. Where's the gat?"

"My wife?"

"She called the station and said she seen you run out of the house with a weapon in your hand."

"Stupid bitch. I'm going to kick her ass when I get home," Roscoe says through gritted teeth.

"Yeah," the first copper says, "beating women, you're a regular hero. Where is it?"

"I don't got it. I'm telling the truth!"

He is, too. Harley Clarke took the gun with him when he dropped Roscoe at the Dew Drop.

"Get your coat on," the first copper says. "We're leaving."

They're a foot taller than Roscoe. The bigger one grabs a fistful of Roscoe's belt at his waist and walks him out of the bar.

All eyes are on him, Frankie's and the rest of the habitues, watching him get hauled away.

"Wait a minute, fellas," Roscoe says when they get outside. "Can't we talk about this?"

"Shut up," the copper holding him says.

They march him to their patrol car.

A Ford, unmarked except for the spotlights sticking out the side wings, pulls up beside them.

Two guys in suits get out.

Roscoe recognizes Derrick Musgrove and Hollis Pistole, the two Highland Park dicks. They go through the whole hat-tipping high sign with the two big Detroit coppers.

"Thanks, boys," Derrick says. "We got him from here."

"With pleasure," one of the Detroit cops says. Derrick and Hollis take custody of Roscoe.

They throw him in the back seat of their car. Roar off down Mack. Go left on Gratiot.

"Man, I'm glad to see you guys," Roscoe says.

"Shut up," Hollis Pistole says from the passenger seat up front.

They don't seem to be headed either to Roscoe's house or the police station.

"Hey," Roscoe says, "where are we going?"

Hollis turns around. "What part of 'shut up' don't you get?"

They drive north for a half hour and turn into the empty lot of a shuttered dry-cleaning plant in Roseville. The car rumbles over broken concrete and pulls around behind the building. Deserted loading docks. Tires and other trash dumped everywhere.

They stop. Hollis Pistole turns around again. "We know what happened this morning."

"With the apple sellers?"

"Yeah. Clarke fucked up the time. You're going to get another chance to do the deed tonight. The guy you're after? There's going to be a big get-together at his house later. You'll do it there."

"We already tried at his house. It's impossible to get to him there."

"It won't be tonight. We'll make sure of it. Soon as his driver lets him off, *pow!*"

"What about his bodyguards?" Roscoe asks.

"Out of the picture. They called in sick today. You won't have any interruptions."

"You guys think of everything. Harley's taking me again?"

"No," says Derrick Musgrove behind the wheel. "We are. We'll pick you up at 5:30. Soon as the guy you're after gets home, you'll jump out of the car, do it, double tap, *bam! bam!* and jump back in and we'll go like hell. It'll be over before they even know it."

"But Clarke still has the gun," Roscoe says.

"Not anymore," Hollis Pistole says. He hands Roscoe a heavy paper bag. "It's a different one. Don't forget to hang on to it after you do the thing."

Roscoe takes it out of the bag. Sure enough, it's not the gun he was going to use this morning, the one Clarke gave him for the job. He won't have practiced shooting it.

Hollis asks, "Do you want to go home until later, or back to the Dew Drop?"

"The Dew Drop."

He'll deal with Melanie and her betrayal later.

Right now, his comrades-in-arms need him and he wants to be ready for them.

"Say," he says, "I'm a little short in the cash department. Can you float me fifty cents?"

He spends the rest of the day avoiding company at the Dew Drop. Hunched over his usual table at the back of the joint, he keeps his courage up with a few bottles of Frankie's special brew courtesy of the money he cadged from Derrick and Hollis.

Problem is, he has too much time between the time the two cops dropped him off and when they're going to come get him again, at 5:30. He's not used to reflecting on a subject for any length of time, though what lies ahead of him sits heavy on his mind.

He loves being part of the Black Legion. Loved it from the first moment when he held the cat o'nine tails and handed out punishment on his first night. Loves it they're already tapping him for important jobs. Loves the camaraderie, loves what they stand for, loves he's helping to make this country great again.

Loves they trust him enough to give him these jobs, though he ain't happy so many of them are winding up going bust. Ain't happy about the prospect of killing the mayor of the City of Detroit, either.

He has nothing against the guy—don't know much about him at all, truth to tell. Wouldn't know him from Adam. Or from the Jew they were tracking the other night.

No, the thing bothering him is, this guy's a big shot. One less politician in the world won't bother Roscoe. All the hullaballoo that's going to happen after he rubs this guy out, that's something else again . . . something Roscoe ain't looking forward to. If he kills the mayor, they're going to be on him like flies on shit.

If he kills the mayor?

No. *When* he does it.

They said they would protect him. Do everything in their power, the priest said. Except how can he trust the word of a priest? They lie as soon as look at you, Roscoe knows.

And what kind of priest goes in on the murder of a fellow Papist? Roscoe guesses they're all alike.

Except those men around the table, they have to help him, don't they? He's doing it for them.

Yeah, but they're working through the Black Legion. They're the ones Roscoe is truly working for.

The thought of the Black Legion makes him start to relax. This is for them, after all. Not for the priest, or any of the other big shots in the house. Not even for Henry Goddamn Ford himself. No, the Legion has assigned him this job, and he has to do it for them. That's where his loyalty lies. He's a soldier. A soldier for Christ and country, just like they told him on the first night when they initiated him.

By the time Derrick and Hollis return to pick him up, Roscoe has convinced himself this is exactly what he was put on earth to do.

49

CLARENCE BROWN

Mack Park, on the east side of Detroit. The baseball diamond. Clarence Brown sits in what's left of the grandstand and remembers.

The Detroit Stars, Detroit's Negro League baseball team, used to play here until they moved to the new Hamtramck Stadium. Now their old field wasn't used any more except for when Clarence could schedule his summer leagues here. The grandstand was partially destroyed by fire a few years back. After a soaking rain, the grounds crew tried to dry the field by spreading gasoline everywhere, which ignited when some dope dropped a lit cigarette in it.

Clarence remembers the games he saw here when the Stars hosted teams from all over the Negro National League. The legends he saw: Turkey Stearnes. Satchel Paige. Spoony Palm. Pepper Daniels. Crush Holloway. Andy Cooper. Jimmy Lyons. The names of the great players are like poetry to Clarence, their grace out in the field the definition of poetry in motion.

Now it was gone. The Negro National League dissolved the year before, after founder Rube Foster went nuts and died. The East-West League was going to start up in the summer as a replacement for the Negro National League. Clarence didn't have much hope for them, or for the Detroit Wolves, which formed to join the league. This was not a good time to start new ventures.

The great plays he saw here remind him of all the boys he was privileged to bring to the game in his youth leagues.

And the best of them was Darius Turner.

He was a natural. There wasn't anything Clarence could teach him. Clarence was a catcher, not a pitcher, though he could always tell those boys something . . . how to hit, how to catch, how to slide, how to throw a change-up. Darius knew it all. It was like he was born knowing how to throw a wicked curve, or a fastball nobody could hit. How to fool a batter. How to work a 3-2 count.

Darius knew it all.

And those fucking ofays killed him.

And it was Ray Lindenauer who did it, the man Frances described as tall and skinny with a big white pompadour. He did it in the hidden room in Madame Savoyard's whorehouse. They tortured him and killed him to teach him a lesson—as little Frances said Lindenauer told the madame.

And what was the lesson?

Taking money out of Lindenauer's pocket by selling drugs on his own was a mistake? Because it reduced the cut Lindenauer gets from the Sicilians for protecting their business and sends up the line in the department?

Or maybe just being a Negro and trying to make it in the Black Legion's city was the real mistake. In the 1920s it was the Klan terrorizing them. They collapsed, and now the Black Legion seems to have taken their place.

After they tortured Darius to death, they took him out to Belle Isle and did a piss-poor job of making it look like suicide because they knew nobody would break a sweat figuring out if anybody killed him.

They stood there later and laughed as that beautiful, graceful boy swung in the cold river wind. When Lindenauer himself took on the case, he would make sure it went nowhere.

Except Clarence was not going to let the murderer of Darius Turner go unpunished. Or if not unpunished, at the least he wasn't going to let him go unrecognized.

Clarence bundles his coat around him and gets up and leaves the stadium.

Heads toward the precinct house at Hunt and Dubois.

Careless, in his fury, of what will happen to him there, with the coppers all out looking for him.

Just knows he wants Lindenauer to pay for what he did.

He walks down St. Aubin through Hamtramck. Past Warren. Past Mack. The closer he gets to the station, the more squad cars he sees, the more coppers lounging outside having a smoke. Their eyes narrow as they see the huge Negro going down the sidewalk. Some know him, some don't. All are aware of him because of his size and his determination.

And of course his color.

Inside the building. Up the stairs to the Detective Bureau on the second floor.

"Hey, Brown," he hears, "I thought you're on personal leave?"

Clarence ignores it as he enters the Detective Bureau bullpen. Most of the detectives are out. A few are in—including Albert Norquist.

Who jumps to his feet as soon as he sees Clarence.

Shouts his name. "Clarence! Wait!"

Clarence ignores him as he heads toward Lindenauer's office.

Albert intercepts him. Stands in his way so the big man has to stop in his tracks.

"Clarence," Albert whispers, "Jesus fuck, man, what are you doing here?"

"I came to see Lindenauer."

"He ain't in," Albert says. "Pal, you can't be here. Come on. You can't be here!"

He puts his hands on Clarence and for a moment Clarence sees red. He pushes Albert out of the way. Albert falls back against a desk.

Albert jumps back to his feet and says, "If they find you here, they'll kill you. Listen. Listen."

He stands in Clarence's way again.

"Do you hear me? Lindenauer ain't here. If one of his humps sees you, you're a dead man. Clarence? Clarence!"

Albert grabs Clarence by the arms and shakes him. "Listen to me!"

As if breaking the spell Clarence has been in since freezing in the ball park, this at last gets his attention.

"It's not safe for you to be here."

"I want to know where Lindenauer is," Clarence says.

"He's out."

"Where? When's he going to be back?"

Albert looks around to see if anybody's close enough to hear them talk.

He leans in and lowers his voice. "I'll check with Carmen, okay?"

Carmen Brierly, the Detective Bureau secretary.

"Meantime, look, you can't be here. Let's talk someplace else. Please."

"Meet me at the cemetery," Clarence says. "Mt. Elliot entrance."

Clarence turns and barrels down the stairs and out of the station.

Up to Vernor Highway and right on Mt. Elliot. Down to the Elmwood Cemetery.

Shows his badge to the gatekeeper on Mt. Elliot and finds a bench on the main drive inside. It's an old graveyard. The famous of Detroit are buried here, dating all the way back to the Indian wars. Some people said they saw ghosts here, or blood when it rained. It was peaceful, though, and far enough from the station house and private enough to talk amid the quiet of the graves.

In another twenty minutes, Albert comes along. Sits beside him.

"I didn't want to tell you this back there," Albert says. "They found Canavan's body."

"What?"

"No shit. They found him on the sidewalk outside a building where a hooer he visits lives."

"When was this?"

"This morning."

"They know what happened?"

"I heard it looks like he fell out a window. Or was pushed. They're looking for the hooer's pimp."

"Guy named Demetrius?"

"Yeah. You know him?"

Clarence nods. "Why are they looking for him?"

"Canavan was a police detective," Albert says. "Somebody got to pay for it. And this Demetrius mug was there. He's got a record. He's the natural suspect."

"And the most convenient Negro."

"They questioned all the girls at the house this morning. Everybody said the cop was fine when he left."

"If everybody says he was fine, why are they looking for Demetrius?"

"Like you said. The most convenient Negro. The boys are out looking for him now."

Clarence decides not to mention his visit there last night.

"They're already bragging about what they're going to do to him when they find him."

Clarence knows what they will do. On the way to the station, it's standard practice to stop in an alley and work over whoever they nabbed. Clarence imagines Demetrius's handsome face battered and swollen. They would do it just for the hell of it, and if they thought he killed a copper they would be even more brutal. He might not survive the trip to the pokey.

"Where's Lindenauer now?"

"He's in meetings all day with the State Police. Here." Hands Clarence a sheet of paper.

"What's this?"

"Where he's going to be tonight."

The address is in Detroit. Clarence recognizes it as a street in the West Village.

"Who lives here?" Clarence asks.

"The mayor."

"He's meeting with the mayor tonight?"

"Yeah. It's what Carmen told me. I don't know if he's going to be in the meeting, or he's going to provide security for it."

"Why would the mayor need him for security? He has his own detail."

"His regular security men called in sick today. Carmen told me Lindenauer volunteered for the duty."

"What's the meeting about?"

"They don't tell the likes of me," Albert says. "If you want to talk to Lindenauer, he'll be there."

"I'm going to do more than talk to him."

"Clarence, please—*please*—be careful."

There's nothing left of Canavan except a stain on the sidewalk where his body was found. Clarence rings the buzzer for Mistress Anita's apartment.

He hears her tinny voice over the intercom. "We're closed."

"Anita?"

A pause.

"Yeah?" Her voice artificially light, breathy.

"It's me, Clarence. Let me up."

She buzzes him in. Stands at the open door of her apartment. She wears her civilian clothes, a rose-colored blouse and wool slacks. Without her dominatrix makeup and costume, she could be any young wife. Except her eye is bruised.

She steps aside so he can enter.

"How you doing?" he asks.

"Not so good."

She locks the door behind him and leads him into the living room. "They had me down the station all morning. They're looking for Demetrius. They say he threw the cop out the window."

"I heard. Do you know what happened?"

"After you left, I went back in there and picked up where we left off. Only Danny, he was done for the night. He was yelling and screaming and crying about what would happen if they found out about him at the station."

"I told him I wouldn't tell anybody."

"He must not have believed you. He was all, 'What's my boss going to say when he finds out about this?' I tried to calm him down but he went apeshit and started punching me."

She raises a hand to her eye.

"I screamed, and Demetrius, he run in to see what the problem is. He and Danny start to tousle, and Demetrius got him calmed down and under control. Danny got dressed and left. And that's it, Mr. Clarence, I swear. Demetrius stayed up here with me."

"Canavan was fine when he walked out of here?"

"Right as rain. He sure didn't go out any damn window."

Clarence nods, chews it over. Puts together a possible scenario: afraid Clarence is going to spill what he saw at the dominatrix's, Canavan gets to Lindenauer first. Tells Lindenauer about Mistress Anita, and also gets it in his head to tell Lindenauer what he told Clarence about the attempt to murder him.

Or maybe Lindenauer just wormed it out of him.

In a fit of rage—or to keep Canavan quiet—Lindenauer kills him and takes the body back to this building and lays him out in the street as if he'd been thrown out a window. Then he would make sure the story of Canavan going out the window got currency when his body was found.

"Demetrius didn't do nothing wrong," Anita says. "You got to help him."

"Where is he?"

"When he heard the police was looking for him, he ran off. He was talking about going to his sister's in Ohio."

"Good. Let's hope he stays there for a while. At least until I can sort this out."

"You got to, Mr. Clarence. You just got to."

50

BEN RUBIN

Ben and Elizabeth wait for a few hours. They don't hear from Tom Glover.

Despite her protests about staying sharp, Elizabeth is drowsy. She takes a nap for an hour and wakes up looking and sounding better.

"We can't wait any longer," he says. "We have to go to Murphy's."

"They're going to be watching for you," Elizabeth warns him.

"Let them watch. We can't let this happen. Do you have a car?"

"No. I know who does."

They tap on a door down the hall.

Gladys Hart opens it. When she sees the two young people together again, she beams. "That's what I like to see."

"Gladys," Elizabeth says. "I have a big favor to ask."

Light is still in the sky when Ben and Elizabeth cruise by Frank Murphy's home on the quiet street of the West Village neighborhood. Elizabeth drives Gladys's Ford coupe; Ben does not have a driver's license. She seems to be alert enough to drive.

The street is empty in front of the mayor's home.

"I don't see anybody," Ben says.

"It's still early."

They drive down Jefferson past the Belle Isle bridge. They stop at a phone booth outside a tavern near the Mount Elliot Cemetery. Elizabeth stays with the car while Ben calls Maurice.

Maurice is in.

"I just got back to the office," he says. "I got your message about tonight. I've been working on this all day. I'm trying to get in touch with the police commissioner. He's not returning my calls."

"Well," Ben says, "we're not going to let it happen."

"Watch yourself. These are dangerous men."

They park down the street from Murphy's home. Several cars have arrived since they passed the house earlier and are now parked in front of and around the mayor's house. In the fading light, Ben can't see if anyone sits in the cars.

They wait. Nothing happens.

Seven. Seven-thirty. Eight. Eight-thirty.

"I don't understand," Elizabeth says.

"Maybe there was a last-minute change of plans."

"I don't get it."

Ben opens the door and steps out.

"What are you doing?" she hisses.

"I want to see what's going on."

"Stay here!"

"I'll be fine."

"Famous last words. At least walk on the other side of the street."

Ben raises a hand in acknowledgement and begins the walk down Parker toward Frank Murphy's home.

51

ELIZABETH WATERS

E lizabeth rolls down the window, leans out to watch Ben go. The air is cold and the street is quiet. A few cars are parked up and down the street. Nobody's gotten out of them.

Her head is clear; the morphine let her take a step back from the pain while still keeping her wits about her. After her earlier nap, she's fresh and alert.

Lights are on in Murphy's house. From where she sits behind the wheel, she can't detect any movement inside.

Ben draws even with Murphy's front walk. He slows. Tries to look inside the house.

As she watches, a man steps out from a car in front of Murphy's house. He is tall and lean in an overcoat and fedora. He stands a few yards from Ben. In the silhouette from the street lamp, Elizabeth sees him come around the front of his car and extend an arm toward Ben.

She sees the flame of a gunshot spurt from a weapon at the end of the arm. She hears the report a second later.

Ben stands frozen. She can't tell if he's hit.

Elizabeth lays on her horn and pops on her headlamps. The street explodes in light.

The light momentarily distracts the shooter. This gives Ben time to recover and duck behind one of the other cars.

Before the shooter can fire again, another shape—another man, bigger and broader, hatless—steps out from the shadows further up the street. Comes into the cone of light cast by Elizabeth's headlamps. She hears him call out.

The man who shot at Ben turns. He and the big man exchange words. She hears voices but can't make out what they say.

More gunfire.

The hatless man falls backwards. He's shot but remains upright. Comes back firing two guns, one in each hand, at the man who shot at Ben.

Bam bam bam bam bam!

The man who shot at Ben falls.

Elizabeth sees the front door of Murphy's house jerk open. A figure she recognizes as Frank Murphy himself steps out onto the porch and stands in the light from the fixture over his head, peering into the street to see what's happening.

He has been in there the entire time, she realizes.

Out of the darkness, one more figure appears. Another man. Short, thin, hatless. Coming from around a house up the block.

Running toward the front porch where Frank Murphy stands.

Arm extended.

She hears popping.

He is shooting wildly at Murphy.

And missing.

This is it. The assassination attempt.

It's happening right in front of her.

Ben appears from where he took cover. Races across the street.

Leaps forward to tackle the short guy shooting at Murphy. Elizabeth's stomach lurches.

Both men go down.

They struggle. The assassin clubs Ben with his gun, over and over. Ben lies motionless.

Without considering the danger, Elizabeth jumps out of the car and hobbles toward him as fast as her bad hip lets her.

Yells: "Ben!"

The big man with two guns rushes toward Ben, too.

Meantime another man appears from inside the house and steps onto the front porch. Pushes the mayor back into the house. Draws a gun and fires at the big man in the street.

Why shoot at *him*? Elizabeth wonders.

Bullets from his gun hit the big guy—she hears the sound of metal on metal, sees sparks explode from his chest. The big guy gets rocked backward but keeps his feet.

The man on the porch now aims in Elizabeth's direction and shoots at her as she comes into the scene.

Shooting at me?

She sees the flash from the gun.

An instant later, she feels like somebody punched her hard. Her left arm goes numb.

She stumbles. She goes down.

52

ROSCOE GRISSOM

From the evergreen bushes where he crouches up the street, Roscoe hears the crack of gunshots.

Two men exchange gunfire in the street in front of the mayor's house.

The front door of the house opens. A man steps out onto the porch. In the porch light, Roscoe sees this is his target.

A voice in his head screams: *Now! Now! GO!*

All the shooting around him fades as Roscoe bursts from the bushes and runs toward the front porch.

Gun out, aiming while running, shooting shooting shooting shooting . . . can't tell if he's connecting or not, the unfamiliar big gun kicking wildly.

From out of nowhere, someone tackles him.

Roscoe goes down.

His brain screams *NO! NO! NO!*

Whoever tackled him holds tight. Roscoe flails, gets his gun hand loose and tries to shoot his attacker. The gun just clicks. Out of ammo.

Roscoe beats the guy with the gun butt, smashing his arms, his shoulders, his head until something connects and Roscoe feels the guy let loose and lie still.

Roscoe hears a voice down the street—a woman's shout. Sounds like, "Ben!"

Who's Ben?

Now somebody else approaches him, a big man. A Negro. Roscoe tries to get himself untangled from the arms and legs of the guy who tackled him. He is badly, terribly frightened. This was supposed to happen smoothly but it's all gone to hell.

Roscoe hears gunfire coming from the front porch.

Too many things going on at once!

What's happening?!

He ducks down and steals a look—a guy's on the target's porch, shooting in Roscoe's direction.

And the target is gone . . .

Roscoe expects to feel bullets slamming into him. Instead he sees the bullets strike the big Negro—who keeps coming toward him.

The big Negro is hit square in the chest. Roscoe can see the holes the bullets make in his overcoat. Yet he keeps coming.

And he's shooting now.

Roscoe scrambles on hands and knees out of the line of fire, plunges back into the darkness where he was waiting. Adrenaline makes him shake uncontrollably. He stumbles to his feet and races across the lawns of the neighboring houses.

He runs and runs. Hears the shooting continuing behind him. Expects at any second to be either shot or tackled again.

Miraculously, he stays on his feet.

He makes it down to the spot where Derrick and Hollis left him off, on the cross street, Lafayette. In his adrenaline rush, he has even less sense of direction than before. He's totally lost. Cars are parked on both sides of the street. None of them the one he's looking for.

Where are they?

He runs up to Jefferson. Turns right, because—why not? Still don't see them.

Did they ditch him?

Did those fuckers leave him here?

Did they expect he'd get killed and they wouldn't have to worry about picking him up?

They just left me here?

He keeps running down Jefferson. The roadway is empty. He sees the hazy lights of the Belle Isle bridge up ahead.

Slows down. Gradually gets his breath back, the adrenaline rush easing.

As it eases, he realizes his left side is wet.

And sticky.

He still holds the gun. He stumbles to a stop, sits down at the edge of a vast lawn. Stows the gun in the bushes next to the sidewalk and feels his side. He has been shot.

He didn't escape unharmed after all.

A bullet caught him. He can't remember feeling it. Everything happened so fast.

He's light-headed. Going to pass out.

He collapses backwards. Suddenly he has no energy, nothing left to draw on, nothing he can use to get himself out of this jam. He's empty. Weak. Powerless.

He looks up at the sky. In the purple night, the stars seem to sparkle, like they're winking at him. Mocking him because they're so carefree. He remembers Derrick Musgrove giving him a quick little wink as Roscoe stepped out of the car.

The sky winks at him now. Twinkling.

Twinkle, twinkle.

Little stars twinkling. He used to read it to his oldest daughter from a book of nursery rhymes when she was little. And now it's like they are laughing at him.

He finds this extremely funny.

He is lying there on the grass, chuckling to himself, when a dog walker finds him.

53

CLARENCE BROWN

G unfire.

Clarence jumps out of the car parked down the block from the address Albert gave him. Sees car headlamps further up the street suddenly illuminate the scene.

Sees a man in silhouette in front of the Murphy house.

Sees Ray Lindenauer standing there, too, shooting at the guy.

Clarence calls: "Lindenauer!"

Lindenauer turns to face Clarence. His face is twisted in rage.

"Darius Turner," Clarence shouts. "Why did you kill him?"

"I knew you'd figure it out. That's why we had to pop you."

"Why?"

"He ruined her."

"Who?"

"My Yolanda. He ruined her with his drugs."

This stops Clarence. "You and Yolanda?"

"Sweetest little piece of nigger ass I ever had. And your boy ruined her. Fed her so much junk she got shitcanned and now nobody will tell me where she went."

"You killed him for that?"

"You bet I did. He wouldn't tell me where she went. I had to punish him."

"And Canavan, too?"

"He came to see me the night you talked to him. I couldn't take a chance on him blabbing to anybody else."

"Ray Lindenauer, you're under arrest—"

Lindenauer shoots Clarence point-blank.

The bullets slam into Clarence's metal shields, knocking him backwards. Clarence straightens and gives Lindenauer both .45s.

Lindenauer goes down.

The shooting stops. In the sudden silence, the front door of Murphy's house opens. Frank Murphy appears on the front stoop.

A small, rat-like man bursts out of the darkness and races toward Murphy. He fires wildly. He shoots out the big picture window in Murphy's house. The mayor is untouched.

A guy comes out on the mayor's porch and steps in front of Murphy.

At the same time, a figure darts across the front yard and tackles the skinny rat-like guy.

Now shooting comes from the front porch.

The little guy scampers back into the darkness and disappears.

The shooter on the porch directs his fire at Clarence. He feels bullets whiz by him.

Who's shooting?

He feels pounding into his chest plate. He falls backwards. He can't return fire because he might hit the mayor inside.

The guy stops shooting at Clarence and directs his fire toward a woman who is running down the street in their direction.

She is hit. Stumbles. Falls.

Both men on the stoop withdraw into the house.

The street is suddenly silent. Gunsmoke hangs in the air, ghostly in the lights from the streetlight and the car's headlamps.

Clarence holsters his weapons and sees to Lindenauer. He's beyond help. Clarence runs to where the woman has fallen. She is breathing. Her left shoulder is a mass of blood.

Clarence makes a quick calculation: don't waste time going up to the mayor's house and asking for help, or calling for an ambulance. After all, the man who shot her—and at Clarence—is in the house with the mayor. In minutes, the street will be filled with police.

There's only one thing to do: take her to the hospital himself.

Clarence wraps the woman in his coat. Carries her to his car and lays her on the back seat.

He roars down Parker Street to Jefferson, goes west. Twenty-one minutes later he pulls up in front of Detroit Receiving.

They ask him who she is, and he says he does not know. Of course, they call the police because they assume Clarence is the one who shot her even though he shows them his badge and tells them he's police.

Unfortunately, he is also the most convenient Negro. Like Demetrius.

The patrolman who responds promptly puts Clarence under arrest, even though Clarence pins his badge to his coat. The patrolman calls his sergeant, who calls his lieutenant, who calls the chief of detectives, who calls the police commissioner, James K. Watkins.

Who, as it turns out, is on his way to the scene of the shootout at the mayor's home.

Watkins knows Clarence, however, and the word goes back down the line: release Clarence.

The nurse notices Clarence himself has been shot in the arm. The head nurse on duty tells him the hospital has a strict no-Negroes policy, so he would have to drive himself to Dunbar Hospital in Paradise Valley, the nearest hospital for Negroes.

Clarence knows this is a lie. Rather than argue, and satisfied the woman he brought is being attended to, he opts to skip the trip to Dunbar.

Police squad cars, ambulances, and the coroner's van clog Parker Street by the time Clarence returns. The coppers on the periphery won't let Clarence pass. He flashes his badge and bulls his way through.

Lindenauer's already in the meat wagon. An ambulance attendant sees to the guy who tackled the attempted assassin.

"You okay?" Clarence asks him.

"Yeah." The guy is tall and slight, with a bandage around his head. Looks like he's been in a few other brawls recently.

Clarence reaches out a big hand. "Detective Brown," he says.

The guy returns the shake. "Ben Rubin."

"Pretty gutsy move, taking down that guy."

Ben shrugs. "Pretty clear what he had in mind."

"You know the woman who was shot?"

"A woman was shot?"

"She came running down the street and one of the men in the mayor's house potted her."

Ben tries to get up. The ambulance driver keeps him down. "Is she okay?" Ben asks. "Is she alive?"

"She's okay," Clarence says. "I took her to Receiving. She's being looked after. She had no ID on her—you know her?"

"I do. Her name is Elizabeth Waters. Her handbag should be still in her car up the street. I'll get it."

He tries to get up again. No, he wavers, falls back. He is too woozy.

"Stay there," Clarence says. "I'll get it. Which car is it?"

"The one with the headlamps on."

"Before you go anywhere," the ambulance attendant says to Clarence, "I need to look at your arm."

Clarence protests—"It's fine, it's a through-and-through."

The attendant insists.

With his wound cleaned and bandaged, Clarence walks back to retrieve the handbag. He shuts off the headlamps and pockets the key. Goes up to the porch of the Murphy home. Ben leaves the ambulance to join him.

Another policeman at the door stops them. James K. Watkins, the police commissioner, fills the doorway. He is a big man, as big as Clarence, a former football player at the University of Michigan. He knows Clarence is the only Negro detective on the force. Watkins was not a career policeman; Frank Murphy appointed him to put a man with integrity and decency at the head of the department.

Watkins shakes Clarence's hand. "Detective."

"Sir," Clarence says.

"I hear you were involved in this business."

"Yes sir."

"Mr. Howcroft here"—he turns to the man standing behind him, whom Clarence recognizes as the one who shot at him and Elizabeth Waters—"says you killed Detective Lindenauer."

"I did, sir."

"Murdering a police officer is serious business."

"He was shooting at me, sir. I had to return fire."

"Why was he shooting at you?"

Clarence glances at Howcroft, now beside the commissioner. Clarence doesn't know this guy, doesn't trust him. Doesn't know why Howcroft shot Elizabeth, or why he was shooting at Clarence.

"Can I see you outside, sir?" Clarence asks.

Watkins steps out onto the porch.

"I didn't want to speak in front of them in there," Clarence says. "I attempted to place Detective Lindenauer under arrest."

"What for?"

"The murders of Darius Turner and Detective Daniel Canavan."

"Turner . . . the young Negro who was lynched on Belle Isle?"

"Yes sir. I also believe Lindenauer was on the take from racketeers."

"You know this how?"

"My investigation into Darius Turner's murder uncovered Lindenauer's connections with brothels and the drug trade. Just now, he confessed to killing Darius and Detective Canavan."

"These are serious allegations."

"Yes sir. I also have reason to believe he's a member of an organization called the Black Legion."

"The what?"

"The Black Legion. It's a secret society," Ben Rubin pipes up, behind Clarence. "A vigilante group. Like the Ku Klux Klan, only worse."

"And who are you?" Watkins asks, eyes narrowed.

Ben tells him his name. Clarence says, "This young man foiled the assassination attempt on Mayor Murphy tonight."

"Rubin, you said?" Watkins considers for a moment. He turns and barks, "Horace."

352

Horace Howcroft comes up to the door. "Sir?"

"This the man you were telling me about? Rubin?"

Horace glares at Ben, says, "That's him."

Watkins grunts. "Detective Brown," he says, "place this man under arrest."

"For what?" Clarence and Ben both say.

"Attempted murder of the mayor of Detroit," the commissioner says.

"Sir, there's been a misunderstanding," Clarence says.

"*Now*, Brown."

"But he—"

"*Do it!*"

Well, he'll sort it out later. Clarence reaches under his suit coat for his handcuffs.

Ben jumps off the porch and races away down the street.

"After him!" Watkins shouts.

"Sir," Clarence says, "there's been a miscommunication here. He—"

Watkins pushes Clarence off the stoop. "For the love of God, boy, go after him! Or I'll have *you* arrested."

Clarence rolls his Ford slowly down the darkened streets of the West Village and neighboring Indian Village. Shines his car's searchlight into the bushes and around cars parked in the driveways.

He's not entirely sure what he will do with Ben Rubin once he finds him.

At the foot of Burns is a large wooded area between Jefferson and the Detroit River. Clarence makes out two figures among the trees.

He parks. Takes his flashlight from the glove box. Gets out, walks into the darkness.

Makes out two men.

"Ben?" he calls.

No response.

"Ben Rubin. Come on, man. Let's talk."

Ben emerges from behind a tree, followed by a heavyset white man.

"Who are you?" Clarence asks.

"Tom Glover. Reporter for the *Times*."

Clarence glances at Ben, who looks ready to keel over.

"What are you doing here?" Clarence asks Glover.

"I called him," Ben says.

"No, what are you doing *here*."

"I was waiting at the police barricade on Parker. When I saw Ben take off running, I cut down one of the other streets and followed him."

"You tell him what's going on?" Clarence asks Ben.

"Yeah."

"He told me you're going to arrest him," Tom says. "That's not right."

"No," Clarence agrees, "it isn't."

"Then why are you doing it?"

Before Clarence can answer, Ben starts to sway.

Clarence grabs him by the arm to steady him. "Before we do anything," he says, "we get you checked out at a hospital."

"I want to see Elizabeth," Ben manages to say.

54

BEN RUBIN

It's a weeknight, but the emergency room at Detroit Receiving is hopping with gunshot wounds, stab wounds, heart attacks . . . all the collateral damage of living in the middle of the worst times in the nation's history.

People can't take their anger and desperation out on the system, so they take it out on each other in blood.

Ben himself has blood everywhere from a wound to his scalp from the battering he took from the would-be assassin, so a nurse gives him a cold compress for his face until there's room for him inside the ward. He waits among others who have taken sick or been damaged by their loved ones, their friends, or, rarely, complete strangers.

Clarence gets inside the ward to check on Elizabeth on the say-so of the head nurse, who remembers him with embarrassment from earlier in the evening. He comes out after ten minutes to sit beside Ben.

"Did you see her?" Ben asks. "How is she?"

"Doing better. She's conscious. Got a sling on her left arm. The bullet went right through the meat of her shoulder, so they patched her up. They're going to keep her overnight because she took a nasty hit on the head when she fell."

"I want to see her."

Clarence nods. Gets up and walks over to the nurse's desk. Points to Ben. "When are you going to take him in?"

"I'll find out." She disappears in the back.

Returns in a minute. "He can come in now."

Clarence helps Ben through the double doors into the ward. It's small, with six beds for men on one side of a curtain.

"Stay put," the nurse says.

A doctor comes over, examines his head, checks his nose, determines range of motion on his limbs.

"Looks like you made a few enemies," the doc says to Ben.

"Everywhere I go."

"Well, you got a busted sniffer," the doc says, "and cuts and bruises. Looks like your cheekbone's fractured, too. Not much to do with it right now. Be careful with it. May need surgery to repair it. Try to stay out of fights for a while."

"Okay."

"We'll set your nose and get you cleaned up and out of here as soon as we can."

He breezes away to the man moaning on the next bed.

"Where's Elizabeth?" Ben asks.

"Over this way."

He leads Ben through a curtain to the women's section. She is the only one there. She's awake and perks up as soon as she sees Ben.

He rushes to her. She grabs his arm with her free hand. He leans down to wrap her in a hug, taking care not to jostle her sling.

"Is the mayor all right?" she asks.

"He's fine," Ben says. "Not a scratch on him. Thanks to our friend here."

Clarence waves it away. "You were the one who stopped him. Good thing he was such a lousy shot."

"We haven't met," Elizabeth says. "I'm Elizabeth Waters."

"Detective Clarence Brown."

"Clarence brought you here," Ben says.

"You were out of it," Clarence says.

"Thank you so much," she says.

"Don't mention it."

"Who were those people? Who was the guy who tried to shoot the mayor?"

"We don't know yet," Clarence says. "We'll find him."

"And who shot me?"

Clarence says, "We'll find him, too."

"They're going to keep you overnight," Ben tells her. "For observation."

"And what about you?"

"Beating up on me is the new national sport," Ben says. "I'll be fine. They're just going to set my nose and I'll be free to go."

She puts a hand to her head. "So much violence . . ."

The nurse comes over. "I thought I told you to stay put," she says to Ben.

"I just wanted to see how my friend was doing."

"You two were in the wars tonight?"

"The three of us," Ben says. And notices the ragged bullet holes in Clarence's bulky suitcoat.

The nurse packs Ben's nose with cotton and tells him he can go.

"I want to stay with Elizabeth," he says.

"Sorry, man," Clarence says, "I got to take you in."

"For what? I didn't do anything."

"The commissioner ordered me to. I'm not going to hold you, but I have to take you down. We'll get this straightened out at the station. Then you can be on your way."

55

Elizabeth Waters

She watches Ben leave with the big detective. She is surprised at how bereft she feels to see Ben go.

She lies back in the smell of ether and urine hanging in the air. The nurse said they would get her up to a regular bed as soon as they could.

Earlier, the nurse asked if she could get in touch with anyone for her. There's no one, Elizabeth said. The nurse gave her such a sad look. Is that what I am, she now asks herself as she waits for transport in the women's section of the Emergency ward. Am I so pitiable?

She is unsure if any of her family is left. Her mother, father, and stepfather are gone for sure. Her stepfather finagled her mother into putting his name on the deed and then changed her will without her knowledge so when he died the entire estate went to his son Roger. Her stepfather left Elizabeth out of his will entirely.

Roger. Roger Dodger. Usurper of her life, her house, and whatever her father intended to leave her.

He probably still lives in her family's old house. She doesn't care. It's not her house anymore. She wouldn't live there if she could, even though there's a real chance she might lose her apartment.

The last time she talked to him, she couldn't wait to get away from him. She bumped into him at a fundraising party for the Detroit Institute of Arts she attended with Jerry Buckley, the radio announcer. There was Roger putting the moves on some imitation flapper. This was before the crash of 1929 when there was still enough money floating around Detroit to donate to the arts.

Roger spotted her first, so she couldn't slip away. "Well, well, well," he said. "Look who's here. Still whoring around?"

"Still trying to rape teenagers?"

It was the extent of their conversation. He laughed in her face—brayed, really—and she turned around and left the party. She didn't even tell Buckley she was leaving. Roger was probably too drunk to notice the slight.

Now she stirs in the hospital bed. Her shoulder starts to ache.

The morphine they gave her must be wearing off. The nurse said they don't administer very much of it since so many soldiers came back from the war addicted to it. Elizabeth said she understood perfectly.

She tells herself she is not addicted to it, but knows, in her heart, that she has made it a habit. A serious habit.

What some might call an addiction.

She tries to puzzle through how she got here. What was the last thing she remembers?

It was Ben getting shot at. He was walking down the road and stopped in front of Mayor Murphy's house. And a guy appeared out of nowhere and started shooting at him.

She turned on the car's headlamps—which, in retrospect, was probably not a good idea since it shone a clear light on Ben and made him a better target.

Then she was running down the street.

She can't remember anything else until waking up here.

Ben told her the big man, Clarence, brought her here.

She has no memory of that, either.

Her shoulder is really starting to hurt.

She calls: "Nurse!"

By the time the nurse arrives, she is in considerable pain. "Please," she says, "can't I have more morphine?"

The nurse checks Elizabeth's chart. "You've already gotten the limit."

"I'm in terrible pain."

"Let me check with the doctor."

"Thank you."

"You must have a high tolerance for morphine."

"Yes, I suppose I do," Elizabeth replies.

56

ROSCOE GRISSOM

When the dog walker who found Roscoe gets home, he calls the police and tells them about the drunk he saw passed out at the side of Jefferson.

Before the police get there, Derrick Musgrove and Hollis Pistole cruise around looking for him. They spot him on the grass, weak from loss of blood and delirious. He is mumbling about twinkling stars.

The two dicks load Roscoe into their car and speed away.

Musgrove, behind the wheel, shoots up Jefferson into St. Clair Shores. They can't chance bringing Roscoe to a hospital, so they take him to the home of a doctor who's a Black Legion sympathizer.

The doc answers the doorbell in his bathrobe and steps aside as Musgrove and Pistole carry Roscoe inside.

"What happened?" the doc asks.

"Don't waste time asking questions," Musgrove says. "He got shot. Just find out where and patch him up."

"Bring him into the bathroom," the doc says. Musgrove and Pistole carry Roscoe through the tiny bungalow into the bathroom.

"Lay him in the tub," the doc says. "I don't want him bleeding all over the place."

They lay Roscoe in the empty bathtub. The doc wrestles Roscoe's coat off of him. Musgrove and Pistole huddle in the front hall.

"All the confusion, I don't know if he did it or not," Musgrove says.

"Did he have the gun when we picked him up?"

Musgrove shakes his head and Pistole goes back to the bathroom to search through Roscoe's coat.

Nothing there.

Pistole returns to the front of the house. "Dumb shit must have dropped it."

"We better go back for it," Musgrove says. "First I'll call in, see what happened."

Before calling, he goes back to check on Roscoe, now lying in the bathtub with his shirt off. His skin is pearly gray, like the belly of a dead fish. Musgrove can see a small neat hole in the side of his belly. The doc gently washes it with what smells like alcohol. Roscoe is too out of it to feel anything.

"How's he doing?" Musgrove says.

"He'll live," the doc says. "He'll have a long recuperation. Gut shots are no picnic."

"Okay if I use your phone?"

Concentrating on Roscoe, the doc gives Musgrove a crisp nod. "On the little table in the dining room."

Musgrove goes back to the dining room and dials a number on the candlestick phone. Says, "Yeah, it's me. We got him. He's hurt. Doc says he'll live. What happened?"

Musgrove listens for few moments. Grunts his acknowledgement, and hangs up.

"Well?" Pistole asks.

"Murphy's still alive. Not a scratch on him."

"I knew this was the wrong mug for the job. What now?"

"We can't do nothing until the word comes down."

Pistole nods in agreement. "And we know what it's going to be."

"Yeah. But we still got to wait."

When Roscoe is stable enough, Musgrove and Pistole lift him out of the doctor's bathtub and carry him into one of the doctor's bedrooms.

He gets feverish during the night. In his delirium, he imagines he is caught in a bright spotlight and shot full of buckshot over and over.

57

CLARENCE BROWN

The Detective Bureau at the Hunt Street Station is empty by the time Clarence brings in Ben Rubin. The night watch is thinner than the day watch, and most of the officers would be out at the mayor's house.

Ben isn't happy to be here. Clarence himself isn't happy, either. He only brought Ben in because the commissioner told him to. He wants to be able to write in his incident report that Ben actually set foot in the station per the commissioner's order. Clarence has no intention of holding him.

"Have a seat," he tells Ben. Points to the chair beside his desk in the bullpen.

"Seriously?"

"Got to."

Ben sits.

"Why does the commissioner think you're involved with this?" Clarence asks.

"That scumbag standing behind him at the mayor's house?"

"The one who asked about you?"

"Yeah. Horace Howcroft. He's got it in for me."

"Who is he?"

"He's with the police department. He's the head lawyer for the red squad. He told Elizabeth I was going to kill the mayor tonight. So I would be shot."

"Why?"

Ben shrugs. "Wants Elizabeth for himself. Holds it against me we're friends."

"He must have known there was going to be an attempt made on the mayor's life."

"And he wanted to frame me for it."

So did Ben know who was really going to do it? Clarence puzzles.

"Why did he shoot Elizabeth?"

"What?!"

"Yeah. He was the guy who shot your girlfriend."

"Howcroft shot Elizabeth?"

"Yeah. And the guy who shot at you? The leader of the Detective Bureau here."

"Are you serious?"

"As a heart attack."

"You took him down."

"I had to. He was going to kill me."

"What's going to happen to you now?"

"Let me worry about that." Clarence rubs his hand over his face. He wishes he could rub away the exhaustion. Erase this city itself.

"This city, man," he says. Remembers what Robinhood Rowe said. "It's savage."

"That's a fact."

"Look, I just need to do one thing and I'll drive you home."

"Can you drop me back at the mayor's house? I need to pick up the car. It belongs to Elizabeth's neighbor."

"Sure thing. Be a couple minutes."

Clarence searches through his drawers for a clean copy of an incident report. Can't find one.

Goes over to the desk of Carmen Brierly, the Bureau secretary, who keeps stacks of empty forms on a shelf beside her desk.

He passes the duty board.

Happens to see Ray Lindenauer is signed out at 5:30 tonight.

5:30?

On Carmen's desk is Lindenauer's schedule book. Albert Norquist said he got his information about Lindenauer's whereabouts from her.

The book is open to the page for tomorrow. He flips back to tonight's page.

In Carmen's book, too, Lindenauer is signed out as *Home, 5:30*.

Clarence stares at Carmen's precise block printing. This is not what Albert Norquist told him. He said Carmen's schedule called for Lindenauer to be at the mayor's house tonight.

He hears laughter coming from one of the interrogation rooms down a hall off the bullpen. Goes to see what's going on.

The closer he gets, the more he hears hoots and men's raucous voices, along with the whirring of a projector. The door to the interrogation room stands ajar.

From the hall, Clarence sees the Bureau's 16mm projector on the table in the middle of the room. A screen is set up against one wall. Sitting around the table are a half-dozen men, two detectives and the rest uniformed coppers. Smoke from their cigarettes swirls in the cone of light from the projector. On the screen appear grainy black and white images of an epic blow job in extreme close-up. A white woman's lips and sinuous tongue slaver up and down a Negro's monster hard-on glistening with stringy spit.

For a moment, the animal rawness of it stuns Clarence. When another Negro man comes into the frame and begins to take his clothes off, first anger grips his heart, then a great sadness washes over him.

It's no use being angry. This is how it is. This is how they are, these white men he works with. This is how the city is. Clarence lacks enough imagination to conjure up a different kind of city, a different kind of life for himself and all the Negroes in this country.

He turns away from the movie and returns to his desk in the bullpen.

Stows the clean form in his top drawer.

"Come on," he says to Ben. "Let's get out of here."

"Don't you have to—?"

"I don't have to do shit. You said you want to go back and pick up the car?"

"Yeah," Ben says. Surprised. Relieved.

"Let's go."

The mayor's street has cleared out by the time they get back. The police barricade is gone. The coroner's wagon has left. Only one squad car remains in front of the mayor's house.

A copper with a shotgun stands on the mayor's front stoop.

Clarence pulls up next to Elizabeth's borrowed car.

Ben holds his hand out and Clarence enfolds it in his own big mitt.

"Okay then," Clarence says.

"Where are you off to now?" Ben asks.

"I'm going to pick up my wife and take her home."

"I don't know how to thank you."

"Don't worry about it," Clarence says. "We're good. Just stay out of trouble."

"Easier said than done."

Clarence snorts. "I hear that."

58

Ben Rubin

Ben gets to Elizabeth's apartment building after midnight. Taps on Gladys Hart's door. No response.

He goes down to Elizabeth's. He gets the key in the lock in Elizabeth's door and Gladys's door swings open. A man in an undershirt with suspenders looks out. Big bruiser. Heavy five o'clock shadow. Hairy shoulders. "Yeah?"

"Oh," Ben says, "I was looking for Gladys."

Gladys peeks around the guy. "Ben!"

"You're up," Ben says.

"Is everything all right? When you didn't come back, I got worried."

"Everything's fine."

She peers at his injuries. Ben can only imagine what he looks like. "Everything doesn't look fine," she says.

He walks up to her door. Hands her the keys to her car. "Sorry it's so late."

"Don't worry about it. How's Elizabeth?"

Ben sighs. "Long story short, she's fine."

"Where is she?"

"She's staying overnight in the hospital. We had a slight . . . incident. Your car's fine."

He gave her car a good once-over at the gas station. Fortunately, none of the bullets flying around the mayor's house hit it.

"All right," Gladys says, "you look beat. We'll talk in the morning."

Inside Elizabeth's, Ben takes a close look at his reflection in the bathroom mirror. His nose is twice its normal size. Partly it's the packing, which the nurse said he can remove in the morning. He has even more bruises emerging on his face than before, thanks to the pistol-whipping the would-be assassin gave him.

In Clarence's car on the way back to Palmer Park, Ben asked Clarence if the detective wanted him to make a statement, or give a description of the shooter.

Clarence was quiet for a long time. Then he shook his head. "Not necessary."

Fine by Ben. He wanted to get away from this whole thing, anyway.

Would he be able to walk away, with the Purples after him? And Horace Howcroft still on his ass? And the cops, for his role in the Madison Theatre job, along with whatever they might blame him for in the other detective's death?

Too much tonight. He gets a towel and goes out to the living room. Flops on Elizabeth's couch with the towel under his head. Would rather not sleep in her bed in case his nose starts to bleed during the night.

He just begins to doze off when the telephone rings.

Rushes to it.

Tom Glover.

"Hey. Just want to find out how you're doing," the reporter says. "And to thank you for the tip."

"I'm tired. And sore. Getting sorer."

"Yeah, you will be. And your friend?"

"She's going to be okay. They're keeping her overnight at Receiving for observation."

"Watch the *Times* tomorrow. Going to be a front-page story about this. And it's all thanks to you."

Ben says he will look for it. They agree to talk again soon and disconnect.

He returns to the couch. Lies there staring at Elizabeth's blank ceiling. Unable to fall asleep despite his exhaustion, he gets up and stands by the big window overlooking the park. He can't see anything except his own reflection in the glass and, beyond, the black emptiness of the Detroit night.

What's going to be the result of tonight?

He remembers with an ache that earlier in the day he found out about Moe's death. What problems will this cause going forward?

Are his troubles with the Purple Gang over? Or will the animosity between them continue until they finally get Ben, too?

Which shouldn't be hard, now Moe isn't there to protect him. Maybe it's one of the reasons they iced his uncle . . . to clear the way for clipping Ben.

What kind of problems will Ben now face with Howcroft? And with the police?

And what kind of problems will Elizabeth face with Howcroft? Why did he shoot her? Was he trying to kill her, or just punish her for spending time with Ben? Or anger because she had already been released and it spoiled his plan for Ben?

Or did he go crazy in the loud moment and shoot at anything moving? Did he even know it was Elizabeth he was shooting at?

The cops, the Purple Gang, the Black Legion . . .

All the events of the day weren't enough to make him sleepy. The thought of the awful things still in store for him and Elizabeth make him want to shut his eyes and lock out the world.

So he lies back down on the couch and waits for sleep to release him from his heavy thoughts.

FRIDAY, MARCH 11, 1932

59

ELIZABETH WATERS

In the morning, Elizabeth sits on the edge of her bed, waiting to be cleared for discharge from the hospital. She sees Horace Howcroft enter her ward.

In his pinstripe three-piece suit and snappy fedora.

Shit.

He spots her among the women who were brought in overnight.

He comes over, smiling broadly.

"Morning," he says. "How are you?"

"How did you know I was here?"

"I told you. It's my job to know things. How's the shoulder?"

"Painful."

"They giving you anything for the pain?"

"Oh yes."

He stands there with a frozen smile.

"How much do you remember from last night?" he asks.

The events of the night before are still hazy in her mind. She remembers seeing Ben Rubin tackle the guy shooting at the mayor. Then it's a blur.

"Not much," she admits.

He takes a deep breath, lets it out slowly. Says, "It's under investigation so I can't tell you much about it. Fortunately, the mayor wasn't hurt. I just wanted to swing by and see how you were doing."

"Doing okay. I just wish I knew how I got shot."

He rocks on his heels. "Stray bullet, I'm guessing. Part of all the confusion. Also, I confess, I came because I thought you might need a ride home."

"It's covered." She doesn't mention Ben sent word through the nurse that he's going to pick her up.

"Maybe once you're back on your feet, we can have dinner? Maybe a return match?" His smile turns into a leer.

"No."

He must take it as a yes, because he leans in to hug her, big oily smile back on his face.

His bug spray cologne lingers in her nose.

She holds up her good hand to push him away.

Ben is in the lobby when the nurse brings her in a wheelchair.

"How did you get here?" she asks.

"Streetcars. I didn't want to ask Mrs. Hart to borrow her car again. We'll take a taxi home."

Her left arm is immobilized in a sling and a bandage covers a large patch on her forehead.

"Sure you're going to be okay, hon?" the nurse asks.

"I'll be fine. Thanks."

"Remember, nothing strenuous for a few days. And change the dressing on your forehead every day. You got a nasty knock there when you fell."

"I will."

"Take good care of her," the nurse says to Ben.

"I intend to."

A taxi waits. The driver helps Ben maneuver Elizabeth into the back seat and Ben gives him her address.

"How's the wing?" Ben asks.

"Hurts. They said it should heal fine. The bullet missed the bones. What happened last night? I don't remember much after I got out of the car."

"I don't remember much myself. Most of what I know comes from Detective Brown. He told me the guy who was shooting at me was a Detroit police detective."

"Looked like he was trying to kill you."

"He surely was."

"Why?"

"I suspect Howcroft told him the same lie he told you about my plot to kill Murphy."

"Speak of the devil. He came to see me this morning."

"Howcroft?"

She nods.

"For what?"

"To see how I was."

"What did he say?"

"Nothing much. Why?"

Ben looks at her for a long moment. "Elizabeth, Horace Howcroft is the guy who shot you."

She is silent for several seconds. "I don't believe it."

"It's true. Clarence told me. He saw it happen."

Why on earth would he do that? And come the next morning and ask her out to dinner?

"Why would he want us both dead?" she wonders.

"If he can't have you, nobody can? Especially me."

"Is he that crazy?"

"You tell me. I don't know the guy."

"I haven't had anything to do with him for years, so . . . who knows?"

"Clarence told me he's been looking for the killer of a Negro who was found dead on Belle Isle. This policeman, guy named Lindenauer, is the one who killed him. He's a member of the Black Legion. Apparently, Lindenauer was seeing a prostitute at one of the whorehouses in town and Darius was giving the woman drugs. The madame fired her and Lindenauer felt Darius needed to be punished for ruining his good thing."

"What's the Black Legion?"

He explains it to her as Glover the reporter told him.

"What happened to the man who was trying to shoot the mayor?" she asks.

"He got away. Clarence told the police commissioner they'd find him. I doubt they will. According to our reporter friend, the police and a lot of the local politicians are in the Black Legion. This guy could easily get away with their help."

She sits back in the taxi. Lays her head against the back seat and closes her eyes. "What a week," she murmurs.

Ben takes her hand. "You said it."

Ben helps her into her building. Mr. Fox, the elevator operator, greets her with a tip of his cap. Again he ignores Ben. Fox sees her sling and says, "Miss Elizabeth, what happened?"

"Slight accident," she says.

"Sorry to hear it, miss. I'll pray for your recovery."

Ben helps her off the elevator and into her apartment. She is happy to be here. They are awkward with each other, as if they haven't made the transition from the events of the past week to the sudden enforced intimacy of being alone together in the confines of her apartment. Sitting on the couch, she feels the need for time alone to process everything that's happened. She's glad Ben is with her— she knows she's developing genuine feelings for him—but at the same time she wants to be alone.

He must feel it, too, because he says, "How about I go out and get us a bite to eat?"

"Lovely."

"What would you like?"

"There a luncheonette on Six Mile, down the street from the Chinese restaurant. I'd love a grilled cheese sandwich. I'll make coffee for us here."

"Fries?"

"Read my mind."

"You got it."

He leaves. The easy friendliness of the exchange makes her feel a little better about his being here. Still, she feels as if she needs to withdraw into herself to come to terms with it all . . . losing her job, being shot, being shot by Horace Howcroft, being at the center of so much violence.

Even now, she feels like it's pushed her onto the verge of something but she can't figure out what, exactly.

She makes a pot of coffee for them. Runs a bath. She can be in and out by the time Ben gets back. She didn't mention it, but the luncheonette is notoriously slow. Maybe when he gets back and she gets some food in her, she'll feel more balanced.

She is out of the bath and drying off as she hears him come in. As though shutting the front door closed a circuit, the phone immediately rings.

"Can you get it?" she calls.

While he talks, she gets dressed. Comes back into the living room to hear him say, "Okay. Thanks for letting me know." He hangs up.

"Who was it?" she asks.

"Tom Glover. His article's going to be in the afternoon edition of the *Times*."

"Can't wait to see it."

"Not so fast. He said he wrote a long piece about what happened last night, including the plot against the mayor. He just told me his editor rewrote it."

She can't speak.

"He said they took out everything about what happened," Ben continues. "Said we're going to be very disappointed. It's just a little bit of a thing now, way back in the paper. He was just calling to let me know."

"Did he say why they rewrote it?"

"Well, you know, William Randolph Hearst owns the paper. He's a rabid anticommunist. Evidently Horace Howcroft got to the local editor and convinced him a full exposé of what happened would make it seem like they didn't have the Communist threat under control in Detroit. Hearst wouldn't like it, and it would make Howcroft look bad. That was enough for the editor."

"But this had nothing to do with Communists."

"You and I know that. But Howcroft wanted to play it all down. So the article's just a two-liner."

"Fucking Howcroft."

"I'm sure he'll squash any investigation, too. And he'll continue to blame me, I suppose."

"Well, there you have it." She sighs. "At least you got the food. We should eat before it gets cold."

He sets the dishes out on the dining room table. Once again, the domestic intimacy moves her.

And scares her, too. After the bath, clarity: she knows she's growing closer to him. And she's certain she's on the verge of a change in the direction of her life. But she's equally certain the change can't simply be another involvement with another man.

It has to be more.

Ben goes out to get the *Times*.

Tom was right. The events of the previous evening were reduced to a minor street disruption in a tiny notice on page 15.

Exchange of Gunfire Disturbs Mayor's Neighbors

Late last night, gunfire erupted on Parker Street in Detroit, briefly disturbing the peace of the quiet West Village neighborhood.

Detroit police responded immediately and no injuries were reported.

Later Elizabeth gets a call from Erroll Lembeck of the Young Communist League.

"You're free," Lembeck says.

"I am. You are, too?"

"They never got me. I kept on the move."

"Lucky. It was awful."

"That's what I hear. Look, I'm calling to let you know the funeral march is going forward tomorrow in support of the four members of the Young Communist League who were slaughtered. Tonight there's going to be a protest meeting at Arena Gardens. Afterwards we're going to the Workers Hall on Ferry, where the bodies are laying in state. Then tomorrow the procession starts at 2:30 at the hall. We'll march down Woodward to Grand Circus Park. From there, we'll process to Woodmere Cemetery. That's where the four men will be buried in a mass grave. The theme of the procession's going to be, 'Smash Ford-Murphy Terror.' Will we see you there?"

Elizabeth closes her eyes. Fights back a wave of nausea.

Says, "Sure. Count me in."

60

ROSCOE GRISSOM

When he awakes in the morning, Roscoe's fever has broken. The doctor's wife sits by his bedside and feeds him toast and a cup of sweet tea. Roscoe can't remember when he has been treated with this much kindness.

Afterward, he sleeps.

Later in the afternoon, Derrick Musgrove and Hollis Pistole come to pick him up. The doctor and his wife help dress him in clean clothes. He is still weak and drowsy, so he leans on Derrick going out to the squad car.

No one mentions anything about the mayor, or what happened the night before.

They drive Roscoe home.

Where Roscoe's wife Melanie watches stonily as the two Highland Park detectives bring him inside.

"Where do you want him?" Derrick asks her.

"Who said I want him anywhere?"

"Ma'am, we got to put him someplace."

"Take him down the cellar. What happened to him?"

Derrick explains there was a little trouble the night before, and Roscoe got caught in an exchange of gunfire.

Which is true. They leave out his failed attempt on the life of the mayor of the City of Detroit.

They lay him out on the cot in the cellar. They leave a bottle of tablets beside the cot. "Doc gave you these for pain," Derrick tells him.

Melanie walks them out. The two coppers tip their hat to her and take their leave.

When they're gone, she goes into the basement. Roscoe lies flat on his back on the cot, watching her as she stands at the bottom of the stairway.

"Gonna tell me what happened?" she asks.

"Didn't they say?"

"They gave me some cock and bull story." She comes the rest of the way down and stands beside the bed. "Now I want to know what really went on."

He shifts his position. His belly aches where the bullet was and the stitches are now.

Why can't she just leave him alone? He can't even keep two thoughts in his head right now and she's asking him these fucking questions.

"What do you have to say for yourself?" she asks.

"Can I get a drink of water?"

She keeps looking at him.

"You don't come home all day or all night, and when you do get here, two policemen bring you in the house and drop you off and run. And all you got to say for yourself is, 'Can I have water?'" Her imitation of his accent is harsh and mocking.

He just stares daggers back at her. Easy to be so tough when he's here flat on his back.

"Please," he gets out.

She goes up to the kitchen to retrieve a glass of water. Comes back and places it on the floor beside his cot.

"You turned me in to the coppers," he says.

"I did," she admits. "And I'll do it again, if I have to."

"You wait'll I'm back on my feet again. Give you a thrashing you'll never forget."

"You're not in any condition to do anything more than beat your own gums."

Goes back upstairs.

"Melanie!" he croaks.

That woman's going to be sorry.

She's going to be the sorriest bitch in Detroit, once Roscoe gets on his feet again.

He reaches for the bottle of pills the coppers left. Shakes two tablets out and takes them with the water she brought.

Closes his eyes.

He is thinking about how he will punish his wife for her disrespect when his pain pills kick in and the world goes mercifully black.

SIX WEEKS LATER

61

ROSCOE GRISSOM

His gunshot wound never properly heals. First the site where the doc stitched him up becomes infected. Instead of going to the hospital (which Musgrove and Pistole told him not to do), Roscoe visits a free clinic on Mack near his house. The nurse gives him a powder to sprinkle on the wound. The pus and inflammation finally go away. It burns like crazy, but he still has those pain pills left from that night and they help.

That night . . .

He tries not to dwell on that night. It's hard because it haunts his dreams. Every time he closes his eyes and tries to sleep, he's back on that street, with bullets whizzing around him and a deep, paralyzing fear gripping him.

He can't sleep without the pills the doc from St. Clair Shores left with him. They not only knock the pain, they put him out completely. But he's running out. He's going to have to get back in touch with Musgrove or Pistole, and he don't know how to. He hasn't heard from either of them since . . . that night.

The other problem is, Roscoe's afraid the bullet he took messed up his insides somehow, because he can't keep any food down and he spends most of his days on the cot in the cellar, exhausted. He's basically moved down there.

At least it's an excuse for not eating with Melanie and the brats. She brings his meals down to the cellar. These days she spends as little time in his company as possible.

Small mercies.

Now he takes two more tablets from the diminishing supply of pills. Soon the world goes black again.

He wakes up again in darkness. The clock on his nightstand tells him it's 8:30.

How can it still be dark at 8:30? He must have slept through the day and it's night again.

He hears a knock at the front door upstairs.

Hears Melanie's footsteps creak across the floor. Hears the front door opening.

Hears the murmur of men's voices. Melanie's voice. The men again and the thump of heavy boots tramping across the living room.

Coming down the stairs to him.

He smells them before he sees them. The odors of tobacco and male sweat push ahead of them.

Two men come into the cellar.

Bleary-eyed, cotton-brained, he thinks it's Musgrove and Pistole.

"Hey, guys," he says.

They each get on one side of his cot. He takes a closer look. These are not Musgrove and Pistole. Two other guys. He can't remember if he's ever seen them before.

"Roscoe," one of them says.

He recognizes Enoch Jones's voice.

"Oh, hey, Enoch."

Enoch pulls the covers back and helps Roscoe out of bed. "Come on, old son. You need to go with us," Enoch says.

"Why? Where?"

"We's having us a little party."

"I ain't in no shape for a goddamn party. What the hell?"

Roscoe flaps his arms but Enoch pins one. Says, "Duke, grab that other arm there," to the other guy.

They get Roscoe to his feet.

Roscoe is dressed; at least he gets his clothes on every day, even if it does take all his energy and he's back to bed immediately after.

"Can I get my shoes on?" Roscoe asks. They let him get his shoes on and walk him up the stairs and through the living room. Melanie's there, sitting on the sofa with her arms around the three girls. They watch him in silence. Enoch gives them a nod.

In the driveway is a Chrysler coupe. Enoch and Duke wrestle Roscoe into the back seat. Duke sits next to him. Enoch drives.

"Where we going?" Roscoe asks.

"Okemos," Enoch says.

"Where the hell's Okemos?"

"You'll find out when we get there."

They drive for over an hour through the rural Michigan darkness. Through the fog of pain medication, Roscoe grows more and more anxious about where they are taking him. No one speaks on the ride.

They pass the Village of Okemos near Lansing and continue on until they reach a lake, dark and silent in the pitch-black night. A sign says it's Lake Lansing.

Enoch pulls up on an easement by the side of the water. He and Duke help Roscoe out of the car. They navigate along a sandy path until they come to a wooden pier. It stretches into the lake for around fifty yards. Roscoe hears peepers in the darkness

Enoch and Duke walk him onto the pier.

"Where we going?" Roscoe asks.

"Almost there," Enoch says.

Roscoe's woozy. Has trouble focusing. Trouble getting one foot in front of the other.

At the end of the pier is a rickety wooden railing. Another man stands there in Black Legion hood and robe.

When he sees the man, Roscoe's head clears. He backpedals furiously. His strength to get away fails him. Enoch and Duke hold him tight.

"No," Roscoe says. "No!"

Enoch says, "Don't make this no harder than it has to be."

"No!"

Together, Enoch and Duke drag Roscoe to the end of the pier. He struggles as much as his weakened condition will let him. He can't shake out of the two men's grasp.

"Roscoe Grissom," says the hooded man, "you have been found guilty of betraying your solemn black oath."

"No," Roscoe says. "That's not right. I never did!"

"You were given the mission of eliminating an enemy of the Legion," the hooded man continues, "and you failed."

"No!" Roscoe says. "I've been a good soldier! I can explain! It wasn't my fault!" He struggles against Enoch and Duke's grips. He remembers the whipping he gave to a man on his first night in the group. Shouldn't that come first?

He can't form the words with his thick tongue.

"The time for excuses is past," says the man in the robe. He hands Enoch a .38. "Carry out the sentence."

"Enoch, wait," Roscoe gets out. He starts to whimper. "Please. Don't do this. Please."

These are his last words.

"Sorry, man," Enoch says. He double-taps Roscoe, head and chest.

Duke lets Roscoe's limp body crash through the pier railing into the water below.

On his back, Roscoe drifts away toward the center of the foul lake. He leaves a trail that runs black with his blood.

62

ELIZABETH WATERS

D oors slamming in her face. All day long.

At times with regret, at times with apologies, usually with nothing except a sneer and a shout of Italian. She does not understand the language, though she can pretty much guess what they're saying.

She tries to tell them she's not from the police, she's on their side. These poor people don't believe *anyone* is on their side, especially a skinny redhead who looks like she'd be more at home in Grosse Pointe than on the east side of Detroit.

Maurice told her it would be difficult. "These people don't trust anyone," he had said. "With good reason."

Still, she continues up and down the street, knocking on doors and trying to get her spiel out before the door shuts.

"Hello, I'm Elizabeth Waters. I work for a labor attorney and I'd like to ask you about your recent unfortunate experiences at Ford."

She usually can't get any further. Once they hear the magic word—"Ford"—they don't need to hear anything else. They don't even need to understand anything else. Often they don't.

When she moves to another street, she picks up a follower. A little girl with serious dark eyes and a tattered coat begins to trail after her.

After one particularly nasty man bawls Elizabeth out in mile-a-minute Italian, the little girl comes up to her on the sidewalk and opens her hand.

She holds a little stone, egg-shaped, pitted, with faint veining.

"Wow," Elizabeth says, "it's beautiful. *Molto bello.*"

The girl gives her a snaggle-toothed smile. She holds up the rock for Elizabeth to take.

"For me?" Elizabeth asks.

The girl nods silently.

"Thank you!"

Elizabeth takes the stone. "I'll treasure this the same way you do."

An even wider smile.

"What's your name?"

"Gina."

Elizabeth holds her hand out. "Gina, my name's Elizabeth."

Gina takes her hand and Elizabeth gives it an exaggerated shake.

"Pleased to meet you," Elizabeth says. "Where do you live, Gina?"

Gina points to a house across the street.

"Well, you know what? It's a little too cold today for a rock-collector like you to be out by yourself. How about I walk you back across the street?"

Gina shrugs under her threadbare woolen coat.

Watching Gina, Elizabeth flashed on the girl's entire life—after a deprived childhood, a difficult marriage to an alcoholic and abusive man, children, endless money struggles until the day she dies an early death.

Elizabeth reaches out a hand, cups the child's cheek. "*Mi hermana,*" she says.

"What's that mean?" Gina asks.

"My sister."

A snaggle-toothed giggle. "You're not my sister."

"Let's go," Elizabeth says. She takes Gina by the hand and walks her to the house Gina has pointed out. The front door swings open and a woman around Elizabeth's age appears in the doorway. She could be a grown-up version of Gina—same dark eyes, same serious frown, same disheveled black hair. A rehearsal for Gina's own life.

"*Eccoti!*" the woman says. "*Te ragazza impertinente!*"

"*Mi dispiace, mamma,*" Gina says.

Mamma pulls Gina inside. Looks at Elizabeth. "Can I help?" Mamma says in a heavy accent.

"Gina was following me and I thought it would be best if she came home."

"Yes," Mamma says, "thank you."

"My name's Elizabeth Waters," Elizabeth says.

"Maria Cataldo," the woman says, and extends her hand.

When Maria doesn't slam the door in her face, Elizabeth says, "I'm working for a labor attorney and I'd like to ask about your experience working at Ford."

"*Mio marito*—my husband—worked at Ford, not me. Until fired," she adds angrily.

"Do you have a minute to talk about it?"

"You from Ford?"

"Not at all. Like I said, I work for a labor lawyer. We want to know about unfair labor practices at Ford."

Maria stands back from the door. "*Per favore*. Come in."

Maria serves her thick Italian coffee. Coffee turns into late lunch. She heats up left-over spaghetti from the night before and throws together a salad from brown, wilted leaves she says her husband scavenges at Eastern Market.

And she talks.

Elizabeth spends another few hours walking the neighborhood. She finds nobody as helpful as Maria.

Inez is on her way out the door by the time Elizabeth gets back to Maurice Sugar's office. "Couple of messages for you," she sings.

Elizabeth falls into the chair at the desk Maurice has set up for her in the corner of Inez's area. Her desk's already piled high with folders and stacks of briefs. That's fine. She loves her desk. She has a vase with daffodils on the corner of it.

From back in the suite of offices comes Maurice's voice. "Elizabeth?"

"It's me. I just got back."

"Come tell me what you found."

She goes into his office. "Sit," he says. "You look beat."

"I am," she admits. "It's been a long day of getting doors slammed in my face."

"I bet you persisted."

"I did."

"I knew you would. Find anything?"

She tells him what she learned from Maria Cataldo.

"One of the Italian workers in his unit was suspected of taking part on March 7th," she says. "He wasn't there, but the bosses thought he was. He lived on Maria's block. So all the Italian workers who live on her block were fired. No reason, just because they live on the same block as a worker who was 'suspected' of being in the march."

"Including this woman's husband?"

"Yes," she says. "The family's destitute."

Maurice takes notes. He knows she will write all this up in a report. His habit, as she now knows, is to take notes of every conversation.

"Ford Service Department workers perform random and unjustified searches of workers' lunchboxes and clothes," she says.

"What are they looking for?"

"Anything connecting them to the Communist party or the Auto Workers Union."

"The two organizations that can most help these poor schnooks."

"It's all I could get today. I'm planning on going out tomorrow in another neighborhood."

"Good deal. You'll write it all up for me?"

"Of course."

He tosses his pen on the pad he was taking notes on. Rubs his forehead. "Any progress finding the detective who beat you while you were in custody?"

"Not much," she says. "Nobody wants to say anything."

"Of course. The preservation of the capitalist state depends on the use of force. And the closest this comes for most people is the policeman. Well, keep trying, eh?"

"I will."

"We have to bring these bastards to justice," says Maurice Sugar. "It's a never-ending battle."

Back at her desk, she sorts through her phone messages. One is from her friend Mary Tatum. She's finally out of the hospital and back at her job with the Urban League. She wanted to know if Elizabeth was free for lunch earlier. Elizabeth will have to call her tonight and make plans for meeting her.

Another message is from Ben.

She's sorry she missed his call. He calls her once a week and they chat if he catches her in. Usually she's out. Since Maurice hired her as his investigator, she's been busier than ever. And happier. She loves the work. Feels like she's contributing to the larger battle for workers' rights in a way she never did before.

And learning so much from Maurice . . . it's like being back in college. Except this is enjoyable and important.

She has also started weaning herself off of Miss Em. She needs to be as sharp as she can for this job, and it just gets in the way. She hopes she can outgrow the need for it to dull her pain.

To dull all her pains.

One of which is Ben. There's nothing to be done about that. At least for the time being. He sounds good when she talks with him— engaged, satisfied, getting used to teaching and to northern Michigan. They had talked about meeting up there when the weather warms up. Only she can't say when she'll be able to get away.

If ever . . .

Another message is from Horace Howcroft. Just checking in, he told Inez. He wanted to know if she was interested in dinner.

And no doubt still hoping to tell her his side of the story.

Not interested.

She tears his message up into little pieces and goes over to the window. She opens it and tosses the pieces outside, where the wind scatters them in a hundred directions over Griswold Street in downtown Detroit.

Leans on the sill. Several of the offices in the buildings around Maurice's are still lit up at this hour. Capitalism never stops.

Until it will.

And I, she tells herself, am going to do everything I can to make sure that happens.

She closes the window and returns to her desk. She begins writing up her notes from the interview with Maria Cataldo.

63

BEN RUBIN

He wakes in the dark. These mornings are iron cold. Last night the temperature was close to zero. Even the locals say it's unusual for this time of year.

The first thing Ben does is start the fire in the pot belly stove in the corner of the great room in his apartment. The building has no central heating. The stove provides the only heat he'll have until he gets to school.

He makes a mental note to remind himself to bring more wood up when he gets home later. He has taken to letting the fire go out during the night to save on fuel. With the cold snap, he's been going through a ton of it.

He washes his face in the basin in his bedroom and shaves. The water is hard and—what else?—ice cold. Still, he manages. His injuries are mostly healed, though he still gets headaches every day.

He's thought about growing a beard, but he's too much in the habit of shaving every day. Maybe next winter, if he's still here, he will grow one.

The thought of being here the following winter saddens him.

Still, he reminds himself, you have it better than a lot of people. Uncle Moe, for example. Or Eddie Millman. Or his brother Allen, the war hero.

For one thing, you're still above ground.

He fills the coffee pot with water and a spoonful of coffee, puts it on the burner, and gets dressed. He's stiff in the cold. He usually eats nothing before going in to school. They will have food there—rolls or bread or if he's lucky even a hot breakfast.

He does need his coffee, though.

By the time he's dressed, the stove is pumping out heat nicely and the coffee's ready. He pours a cup, throws a teaspoon of sugar in it, and sits at the table to drink it while he gets his mind ready for his students.

Never in his life did he consider the prospect of being a teacher. If not for Maurice Sugar, he wouldn't be here . . . indeed, if not for Maurice, Ben might not be anywhere.

A few days after things calmed down following the attempt on Frank Murphy's life, Maurice sat down with him.

"We need to talk," Maurice said.

Ben thought it was going to be about Elizabeth—leave her alone, maybe, or speed it up with her. The subject turned out to be entirely different.

"Ben," Maurice said, "you're not safe here anymore."

"Where?" Ben asked. They were sitting in Maurice's office.

"Detroit."

Ben was silent.

"As long as Harry Millman is around, he's going to be a problem for you. And everything else is still on, and dangerous as ever."

"Like what?"

"Horace Howcroft, for one," Maurice said. "His vendetta's going to be a continuing problem. He'll blame you for the attempt on Murphy's life. Or he'll frame you for something else you didn't do."

"So what can I do? I can't go to the police with it. They're the ones who tried to kill me."

"No police," Maurice agrees. "It would be best if you left town for a while."

"How long is a while?"

"A few months. Maybe as long as six months. Possibly a year."

"A year! Where am I supposed to go for a year?"

"I come from a little town in the Upper Peninsula," Maurice said, "name of Brimley. My family's all gone, though I still have contacts up there. Friendships with the Jewish community. It's small but cohesive. As it happens, a high school in Sault Ste. Marie is looking for a teacher right now. Where the locks are. It's near Brimley. I took the liberty of putting in a call about it on your behalf."

"A high school teacher? To teach what?"

"Tenth grade."

"I don't know anything about teaching the tenth grade. Or any grade."

"Do you have any college?"

"Two years."

"Perfect."

"You're saying I should just run away to the Upper Peninsula?"

"It's not running away. You'll be lying low. No one will find you. Let all this blow over and come back to fight the good fight for the unions. Think about it for a day, all right? We'll talk again tomorrow. You can be up there by tomorrow night."

"But I want to work with you on the unions."

"I understand. And I appreciate it. And it would be my honor to keep working with you. But right now, I have to tell you, it's too dangerous for you. You've got too many people angry with you."

"I agree," Elizabeth said later that night. "It's the best thing for you right now."

"I don't want to be away from you."

"Maurice is right. Too many people are after you."

"What about you?"

"I don't have as many people after me as you do. And I'll come up and visit."

"What are you going to do?"

"That has yet to be determined."

So Ben wound up in Sault Ste. Marie, Michigan—the Soo, as the locals called it—350 miles and a world away from Detroit. It was a difficult adjustment. He missed the comforts of his previous life, and missed Elizabeth. They have been writing to each other, and she has promised to make a trip up here at some point. So far there are no definite plans.

Though he's still learning to manage the change, he has to admit he doesn't miss the pressures of Detroit . . . the constant presence of anti-Semitism, the race hatred, the desperation of life during a global economic crisis. People don't have much up here, either, but they never did. They always had to make do with little, and they help each other out more than downstate. People of different creeds and colors live in more harmony than they do downstate.

It's not Eden, of course. But it's better than Detroit.

And nobody's trying to kill him.

Always a plus.

He finishes his coffee, rinses the cup out, shrugs on his heaviest coat, and puts a fur hat on his head. He starts out for the school.

The high school is only four blocks away, so he walks. The zero temperature and strong headwind make it seem much further.

He is frozen when he gets to school despite his winter clothing. As he had hoped, Cecile Nadeau, the school secretary, has brought in a hot meal of boiled oats sweetened with honey for all the teachers. He wolfs down a bowl in the teachers' room and goes into the office to thank her.

She is full-blooded Chippewa, like roughly half of the students and about a third of the other teachers. The cheerful, heavy-set older woman has taken him under her wing.

"Thank you, Cecile," he tells her.

"Oh, my pleasure, *Beshkno*," she says. She has told him *Beshkno* means *Bald Eagle* in Potawatomi. It's her name for Ben. He loves it.

He goes into his first period class, tenth grade English. The building has central heating. The stuffy heat warms his cold, cold bones.

The students' faces, bright and dark, turn toward him when he walks in the room. They are quiet, respectful. When he first moved up here, he knew nothing about teaching. He's getting better. The other teachers are helping him, and fortunately the previous teacher left a course plan before she died. Cecille has told him the students in his class start dropping out of school around this age. He has already convinced a few to stay longer before giving up on education.

Maybe he could learn to live up here after all, he tells himself, looking around at the students. They are beautiful young people, different shades of brown and tan, different abilities, all having come from harsher backgrounds than he comes from. It's cold in the winter, true. But it's peaceful.

Anyway, the future is too nebulous to plan for.

For now all he has to do is start talking about Alfred Tennyson's "Charge of the Light Brigade" with his students.

Half a league, half a league,
Half a league onward,
All in the valley of death
Rode the six hundred.

"Good morning, everyone," he says.

"Good morning, Mr. Rubin," some of the brighter students say in unison.

His school day begins.

64

CLARENCE BROWN

Tipton's Luncheonette. Raining outside, as it always seems to be these days. They're having a soggy spring.

It's a late hour for lunch, so the place is mostly empty when Clarence fills the doorway. Just a few stragglers over coffee at the counter. A handful of people sit by themselves at tables.

One of them is Albert Norquist. He sits at a table in the center of the restaurant with nothing in front of him, no water or silverware or menu.

Clarence has to laugh. Tipton really knows how to make a white man feel unwelcome.

Clarence approaches. They shake hands and he eases his bulk into the chair on the other side of the table from Albert. Shrugs out of his raincoat and adjusts his two guns and the metal plates.

At once the waitress appears with a Coca-Cola and menus under her arm.

"Hey, Mr. Clarence," Etta says. She puts the menus in front of them. "Would your friend like coffee?"

Albert says, "Yes, please." Etta gets the pot and fills up a cup and brings it to the table.

"Special today is fried catfish, greens, and candied sweets," Etta says.

"Sounds good to me, Miss Etta," says Clarence.

"Make it two," Albert says.

Etta sweeps the menus away and goes to put their order in.

"Best food in town," says Clarence.

"Good," says Albert. "I'm hungry. Good thing you showed up, I might have starved."

"They're not used to seeing people with your complexion in here."

Albert heaps three spoons of sugar into his cup. Albert looks bad . . . broken veins in his nose, deep circles under his eyes. Clarence smells the alcohol seeping from Albert's pores.

"Been a while since we sat down together," Albert says. "You doing okay?"

"Keeping busy. You?"

"Likewise. Bessie good?"

"Never better."

"Good."

After a few moments of awkward silence, Albert says, "I'm glad you called. I was starting to feel like you were avoiding me."

Clarences looks at him, keeping his face impassive.

"Feels like you've been dogging me," Albert goes on, "ever since we met at the cemetery. Never see you at the precinct house anymore. Never hear from you."

Clarence takes a sip of his drink, smacks his lips. "Best Coca-Cola in town."

Albert says nothing.

"I have been," Clarence admits at last. "Avoiding you."

"Thought so. Mind telling me why?"

"You're right. It was that day at the graveyard."

"That's what you've been stewing about for over a month? What for?"

"You told me Lindenauer was signed out for the mayor's house that night."

"So?"

"Problem is, he wasn't. I checked his schedule on the roster board and Carmen's appointment book, both. Neither one said he was going to the mayor's."

Albert keeps looking at him. "No. I'm sure Carmen told me he was going to be at the mayor's house."

"Wasn't anything about any meeting. He was just supposed to clock off duty at home."

Etta comes with their meal. She sets the plates in front of them, says, "Careful, these hot."

"Thank you, Miss Etta," Clarence says.

"Enjoy your lunch, now," Etta says, and leaves them to eat.

Clarence digs in immediately. Albert just looks at the food on his plate.

"Something wrong with your meal?" Clarence asks, though he knows the food isn't the problem.

Now Albert can't meet his eyes. "How long have you known?"

"Since that night."

"Can I explain?"

"You can try."

"It was Lindenauer. He threatened me, Clarence. He said if I didn't tell you he was going to be at Murphy's, he'd make sure my drinking and taking bribes from the Purples caught up with me. I'd be cashiered. I didn't know he was going to try to kill you, Clarence. Please. It's the God's honest truth."

Albert sounding a lot like Clarence's snitch Junior, who also didn't know Clarence was supposed to be killed. Lot of deliberately ignorant people around this town.

"What did you expect he was going to do?" Clarence asks. "Give me a medal?"

"I thought he was just going to talk to you, tell you to drop the whole thing. I swear on my child's life—I didn't know he was going to whack you."

"That's what you tell yourself? I thought we were friends."

"We are."

"Funny way of showing it."

Albert stares down at his fingers entwined on the table. "It's the truth," he says. "I couldn't lose this job, Clarence. If I did, my son—"

He hesitates. Clarence says, "What son? You never said you had a son."

Albert swallows hard. "I have a son," he admits. "He lives in a private asylum down in Athens, Ohio."

"What's wrong with him?"

"He's a mental defective. He's . . . not right in the head."

"The hell does that mean?"

"There was a problem with his birth. The doctors said he was deprived of oxygen for too long. Said he'd never live a normal life. They told me and Edith not to even take him home from the hospital. Just put him right in an asylum where he'd get taken care of. So we did."

Clarence can't think of what to say. Finally, he gets out, "Why Athens, Ohio?"

"It's where my wife comes from. Her parents still live there. And the rest of her family. They visit with Richie whenever they can. He don't even know they're there," he adds glumly.

Albert is silent for a few moments. "It's private, like I say. I have to pay for his care myself. If I lost my job, I'd never be able to find another one. Not now, not at my age. And they'd throw him out, Clarence. Richie would have to leave the only home he knows. He'd have no place else to live. And—"

He chokes back the rest of whatever he was going to say.

This is the first Clarence has ever heard Albert speak about a son.

"That's why when Lindenauer told me what to say to you," Albert says, "I had to do it."

Albert looks him in the eye. "I'm sorry, Clarence."

When Clarence doesn't reply, Albert lays his napkin on the table beside his untouched lunch. He stands. Looks like he's going to say something else, but he just shakes his head and walks out of the restaurant.

Etta comes right over. "Something wrong with the food?"

"No, Miss Etta. Something was the matter. But it wasn't the food."

Outside, Clarence buttons his raincoat. Settles his fedora. Raises his head, inhales through his nose, closes his eyes. The rain has stopped, but there's more coming. Going to be a big storm, too. Probably hit just as Clarence goes home.

He lowers his head and opens his eyes.

He looks directly into the face of Andre Young standing across St. Antoine Street from him.

The two men stare at each other for several moments.

Andre takes off in the opposite direction.

Clarence bellows, "Stop!"

Andre starts to run. Goes a few steps. Halts, shoulders slumped in resignation. Waits for Clarence to cross the street.

"I got you now," Clarence says. Grabs Andre by the arm.

"What you going to do to me, Mr. Clarence?"

"I'm going to arrest your sorry ass, what else?"

"You do what you have to."

"I need to handcuff you, Andre?"

"No, sir. I'll come quietly."

Holding him nonetheless, Clarence walks him up to where he parked the Ford. Gets him in the front seat. Comes around to the driver's side. Settles himself behind the wheel.

Says, "Your thieving days are over, Andre."

"Yessir. I know they are."

Clarence looks at him. Andre sits in total submission.

No, he's more than submitting. He's in despair.

"Andre," Clarence says, "what's the matter? You know you could have outrun me. Why'd you stop? And why so sad, man? This isn't the first time you been pinched. It's not like you're going to the electric chair for stealing cough syrup."

Andre looks at him with sad eyes.

"Mr. Clarence, do you know why I been stealing cough syrup?"

"I assume so you can sell it to the hopheads and make a little bread."

"But you don't know why?"

Clarence huffs in exasperation. "What are you trying to tell me, Andre?"

"I've been stealing cough syrup for my son. He been sick."

"I saw your son last week. Seemed fine to me."

"No, you saw Andre Junior. Burrell, he's my other son. He had the consumption, you know."

"I didn't know. Cough syrup won't cure consumption. "

"No. But it helped him sleep at night. And you're right, I sold what was left over."

"Why didn't you take him to the doctor? Plenty of doctors around here let you pay over time."

"I did. They're why I needed the extra money. I had to pay the doctor I took him to."

"So?"

"Don't need to pay no doctor no more, Mr. Clarence. My little boy passed yesterday morning."

Clarence examines his face for signs he's lying. Andre's the unhappiest man Clarence has ever seen. Nobody's that good an actor.

Now Andre covers his face and sobs into his hands.

Clarence lets him cry. Reaches out and puts a hand on Andre's shoulder. "Sorry to hear it," he says. "I know how you feel. I lost my boy, too."

He waits until Andre pulls himself together.

Asks, "Are you taking up a donation for the funeral?"

Andre shakes his head. "I was just on my way to see Henry Chenault, over to the funeral parlor. He's my wife's cousin. He said he'd bury my boy for nothing. We were going to talk about the arrangements."

Andre's pain reminds him of his own when DeMarco died. All we have is pain. Regardless who we are, or how much money we have, in the end, there's only the pain of loss.

"But now it'll have to wait," Andre says.

Clarence considers for a moment.

Says, "Andre, get out of the car, man."

"What?"

"Go on. Get out the car and go about your business. We'll pretend I never saw you. Do what you have to do for Burrell. Next time I hear you're stealing anything, though, you and me are going to have a problem."

"Won't be no next time, Mr. Clarence. My word on it." He reaches out to shake Clarence's hand. His hand is damp from his tears.

"You're a good man," Andre says.

"Go on, now. Go make plans to bury your boy."

After dinner, Clarence and Bessie sit in the living room. They agreed they don't want the radio or music on tonight; they just want to sit, grateful for being home and together, the silence broken only by the pounding of rain outside and the occasional crash of thunder.

Clarence was right. This is a big storm.

Bessie reads. She will doze off with the book open in front of her. After a day of work, she finds it hard to keep her eyes open at night.

Clarence watches her, his heart filled with love for the woman who he's been through so much with.

Who he's put through so much, too.

He pulls his baseball notebook out from the drawer in the table beside his chair. He is almost ready to schedule tryouts. The schedule of games is done. The warm weather will be here before you know it.

He stares at the cover for a full minute.

He opens it and looks over the list of boys who have told him they want to play this year. There are good prospects, some new, most returning from last year. Good boys. They deserve so much more than this world will ever let them have. He will have trouble finding another player as naturally gifted as Darius Turner. Still, you never know who will turn up to the tryouts.

What gangly, underfed kid in tattered, too-small, hand-me-down clothes is out there, waiting for Clarence to find him and show him what he's capable of.

EXTRAS

CAST OF CHARACTERS

AUTHOR'S NOTE

READING GROUP QUESTIONS AND TOPICS FOR
DISCUSSION

ACKNOWLEDGEMENTS

ABOUT THE AUTHOR

THE MARTIN PREUSS MYSTERY SERIES

CAST OF CHARACTERS

MISTRESS ANITA. A dominatrix.

ALDEN BAKER. Member of the Black Legion.

SIDNEY BALLENGER. Creative director at WXYZ Radio and Elizabeth Waters's boss.

HARRY BENNETT. Real-life director of Ford Motor Company's Service Department, the security service for the automobile company.

BESSIE BROWN. Clarence Brown's wife.

CLARENCE BROWN. Detective with the Detroit Police Department.

ISAAC BUCHALTER. Miriam's husband and brother-in-law of Ben Rubin.

MIRIAM BUCHALTER. Isaac's wife and sister of Ben Rubin.

JERRY BUCKLEY. Real-life radio commentator.

DANNY CANAVAN. A young Detroit Police Department detective.

HARLEY CLARKE. Highly-placed member of the Black Legion.

FATHER CHARLES COUGHLIN. Real-life "radio priest" from Detroit.

MOE FEIGENBAUM. Member of the Purple Gang and uncle of Ben Rubin.

HENRY FORD. Real-life industrialist.

TOM GLOVER. Fictional reporter for the real-life *Detroit Times*.

MELANIE GRISSOM. Roscoe Grissom's wife.

ROSCOE GRISSOM. Unemployed, unhappily married Black Legion recruit.

BOOKER HARRIS. Injured participant in the Ford Hunger March.

GLADYS HART. A neighbor of Elizabeth Waters.

HORACE HOWCROFT. The brother of an old friend of Elizabeth Waters and legal counsel for the Detroit Police Department's Special Investigation Bureau.

MARGARET HOWCROFT. Mother of Horace Howcroft.

ENOCH JONES. Friend of Roscoe Grissom and member of the Black Legion.

FRIDA KAHLO. Real-life Mexican artist.

IRV KAMINSKY. Friend of Moe Feigenbaum and a low-level influence- and information-peddler.

SARAH KIRSCHNER. Elizabeth Waters' college lover.

ERROLL LEMBECK. The district organizer of the Young Communist League of Detroit.

BERNICE LERNER. Ben Rubin's former girlfriend.

RAY LINDENAUER. Detroit Police Department chief of detectives and Clarence Brown's superior.

FRANCES MCKENNEY. A maid at Madame Savoyard's brothel.

EDDIE MILLMAN. Ben Rubin's friend and nephew to Harry Millman.

HARRY MILLMAN. Real-life psycho enforcer for the Purple Gang.

YOLANDA MONTGOMERY. A former prostitute at Madame Savoyard's brothel.

PHIL MULCAHY. Alcoholic script writer for WXYZ Radio.

FRANK MURPHY. Real-life mayor of Detroit.

DERRICK MUSGROVE. Detective with the Highland Park Police Department and member of the Black Legion.

ALBERT NORQUIST. Detroit Police detective and friend of Clarence Brown.

LAVERNE PENNEY. Head of a Black Legion regiment.

HOLLIS PISTOLE. Highland Park detective and member of the Black Legion.

TONY JACK POLIZZI. Associate of Black Bill Tocco in the Detroit Sicilian mob.

HAROLD PRATT. Chairman of the Michigan Communist Party.

DIEGO RIVERA. Real-life Mexican muralist.

MADAME ROSITA. A brothelkeeper and old flame of Clarence Brown.

QUINCY "ROBINHOOD" ROWE. Head of the Paradise Valley and Black Bottom numbers operations.

BEN RUBIN. Wannabe Purple Gangster.

RUTH RUBIN. Ben Rubin's mother.

MADAME SAVOYARD. A brothel keeper.

MAURICE SUGAR. Real-life labor lawyer.

LEONARD "JUNIOR" SYKES. Clarence Brown's informant.

MARY TATUM. Friend of Elizabeth Waters.

BLACK BILL TOCCO. Real-life head of the Sicilian mob in Detroit.

DARIUS TURNER. Small-time dope peddler in Black Bottom.

ELLA TURNER. Mother of Darius Turner.

VINCE VITALE. Elizabeth Waters's supplier.

ELIZABETH WATERS. Assistant to the creative staff at WXYZ Radio.

JAMES K. WATKINS. Real-life commissioner of the Detroit Police Department.

ANDRE YOUNG. Petty thief.

Author's Note

This book is a work of fiction. With certain exceptions, the events of this novel are fictitious. I don't claim to be writing a historical account, but I have tried to remain true to those incidents that actually took place, most especially the Ford Hunger March on March 7, 1932, and its aftermath.

Likewise, the Black Legion was a real group terrorizing Michigan and the Midwest for a short period of time during the 1930s. Though no character named Roscoe Grissom existed, he might have, and his experiences with the Black Legion might have gone as described in this book.

One of the central characters of the book is the City of Detroit itself. I have tried to remain true to the city's historical, political, and economic setting, as well as to the great social movements—including the Great Migration north, the tense racial climate, the crime landscape, the growth of the automotive industry and concomitant labor battles—that helped to define the city during the first third of the Twentieth Century.

I am indebted to the following authors, works, and scholars for information and ideas on the Black Legion, the Purple Gang, the Hunger March, and the City of Detroit:

Alex Baskin, "The Ford Hunger March—1932," *Labor History*, 13:3, 331-360 (1972).
Ernest H. Borden, *Detroit's Paradise Valley*. Arcadia Publishing, 2003.

Scott M. Burnstein, *The Detroit True Crime Chronicles: Tales of Murder and Mahem in the Motor City*. Camino, 2013.

Frank Donner. *Protectors of Privilege: Red Squads and Police Repression in Urban American*. University of California Press, 1990.

Sidney Fine, *Frank Murphy: The Detroit Years*. University of Michigan Press, 1975.

Christopher Johnson, *Maurice Sugar: Law, Labor, and the Left in Detroit, 1912-1950*. Wayne State University Press, 2018.

Paul R. Kavieff, *The Purple Gang: Organized Crime in Detroit 1910-1945*. Barricade, 2005.

Tom Stanton, *Terror in the City of Champions: Murder, Baseball, and the Secret Society that Shocked Depression-Era Detroit*. Lyons Press, 2016.

Maurice Sugar, *The Ford Hunger March*. Meiklejohn Civil Liberties Institute, 1980.

Jeremy Williams, *Detroit: The Black Bottom Community*. Arcadia Publishing, 2009.

All errors are my own.

Reading Group Questions and Topics for Discussion

1. The metropolitan Detroit area plays an important role in this book. How are the city and suburbs portrayed in the book? What effect does the setting have on each of the main characters?

2. How does the time period—the Great Depression—impact each of the main characters and the action? How did your own settings—that is, the geographical locations and the time periods you live in—affect you?

3. Why is the book titled *Savage City*? What expectations did the title raise in you? Were those expectations met?

4. Each of the four main characters struggles with different kinds of challenges in the book. What are they for each character? How well does each meet those challenges?

5. Share reactions and thoughts about each of the main characters. What, if anything, does each of the four main characters learn by the end of the book? Are they different at the end than they are at the beginning? If so, how?

6. Did you identify more strongly with one or more of the main characters? If so, which ones? Why do you think you felt that identification? If not, why do you think you couldn't identify with them?

7. On the surface, the four main characters seem very different. Yet each of them deals with the aftermath of traumatic loss. They have

all experienced events that could have destroyed them. Identify what these are for each character and compare how they each handled those events. In what ways did they succeed in overcoming the traumas of their past? In what ways do they still carry the traumas with them?

8. Are there other similarities between the four main characters that you could find?

9. How would you characterize Elizabeth? Did she have qualities that put her out of step with her time? Which qualities?

10. Only two of the main characters, Clarence and Roscoe, have wives. Compare and contrast the state of each one's marriage and relationship with his wife.

11. Each of the four main characters experiences feelings of isolation. What are the causes of each character's sense of isolation? Are they different from each other? How does each character deal with his/her isolation?

12. Discuss the relationship between Ben and Elizabeth. What draws them to each other? Why do you think their relationship turns out the way it does at the end of the book? Were you surprised?

13. The novel takes place a long time ago, in 1932, seemingly in a different world than today's. What connections can you make between the events of the novel and events that are happening in the present day? What conclusions can you draw from those connections?

14. Betrayal seems to be a recurring element in the book. How or by whom is each character betrayed? How do they deal with the betrayals? How did their strategies work for them?

15. The world that is portrayed in the book is corrupt in a number of ways. What are some kinds of corruption that you found? Did each of the main characters come to any insights about how to live in a corrupt world, or not? Did you take any insights away about that from your experience with the book?

ACKNOWLEDGEMENTS

Authorship seems solitary, but is really multiple. I am happy to acknowledge the following people whose assistance made this book a reality:

Immense gratitude goes to historian Thomas Klug, Ph.D., for his help with Detroit history, and for reading an early draft of the book. Thanks, too, to Thomas Galasso, author of *When the Swan Sings on Hastings* (Aquarius Press, 2017) for his help and support.

Warm thanks to Jerry van Rossum for his support, and to Andrew Lark, Virginia Moyer, Harlan Moyer, and Lisa Allen for their support and editorial expertise.

My great thanks go to Joe Montgomery for his design of the cover.

As always, my deepest appreciation goes to my wife, Suzanne Allen, my first and best reader, whose love and support continue to sustain me.

ABOUT THE AUTHOR

Donald Levin is an award-winning fiction writer and poet. Besides the seven Martin Preuss mystery novels, he is the author of *The House of Grins* (Sewickley Press, 1992), a novel; two books of poetry, *In Praise of Old Photographs* (Little Poem Press, 2005) and *New Year's Tangerine* (Pudding House Press, 2007); *The Exile* (Poison Toe Press, 2020), a dystopian novella; and co-author of *Postcards from the Future: A Triptych on Humanity's End* (Whistlebox Press and Quitt and Quinn Publishers, 2019). He lives in Ferndale, Michigan.

To learn more about him, visit his website, www.donaldlevin.com, and follow him on Twitter @donald_levin and Instagram at donald_levin_author.

If you enjoyed this book, please post a review on Goodreads, Amazon, or your favorite book review site.

ALSO BY DONALD LEVIN

The Martin Preuss Mystery Series

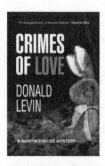

One cold November night, police detective Martin Preuss joins a frantic search for a seven-year-old girl with epilepsy who has disappeared from the streets of his suburban Detroit community. Probing deep into the anguished lives of all those who came into contact with the missing girl, Preuss must summon all his skills and resources to solve the many crimes of love he uncovers.

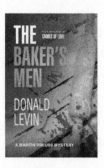

Easter, 2009. Ferndale Police detective Martin Preuss is spending a quiet evening with his son Toby when he's called out to investigate a savage after-hours shooting at a bakery in his suburban Detroit community. Struggling with the dizzying uncertainties of the case and hindered by the treachery of his own colleagues who scheme against him, Preuss is drawn into a whirlwind of greed, violence, and revenge that spans generations.

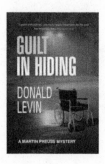

Preuss is called out to search for a van that has disappeared along with the woman who was driving and her passenger, a handicapped young man. Working through layer upon layer of secrets, Preuss exposes a multitude of contemporary crimes with roots in the twentieth century's darkest period.

When a friend asks newly retired detective Martin Preuss to look for a boy who disappeared forty years ago, the former investigator gradually becomes consumed with finding the forgotten child. Preuss revisits the countercultural fervor of Detroit in the 1970s—and plunges into hidden worlds of guilty secrets and dark crimes that won't stay buried.

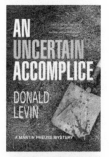

Twenty years have passed since Raymond Douglas went to prison for the kidnapping and murder of a local businessman's wife. Now Douglas's daughter has hired private investigator Martin Preuss to track down a previously-unknown accomplice to the crime—who may or may not even exist.

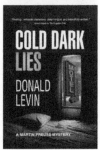

A young man takes a walk on the wild side and ends up clinging to life in a suburban Detroit motel. When private investigator Martin Preuss searches for the reason, he plunges into the young man's dark world of secrets and lies.

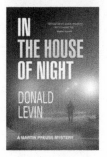

When the police investigation in the murder of a retired professor stalls, friends of the dead man plead with PI Martin Preuss to learn what happened. The twisting tale leads him across Detroit into a treacherous world of long-buried family secrets . . . where the painful relations between parents and children meet the deadly gathering storm of domestic terrorism.